THE LANTERN OATH

THE LANTERN OATH

Some oaths were never meant to be broken.

Don Massenzio

First Edition

Published by DSM Publications

For those who know the dark doesn't always stay buried.

"What light cannot reach, shadow must cleanse."

PROLOGUE

They kept the chamber at a temperature that curdled the skin, high as a butcher's locker and two degrees colder than any holding cell in Ironwood. Calvin Bass's first thought, as they walked him in—left, right, left, like he was learning to march all over again—was that this place was for meat, not men. The antiseptic smell burrowed up his nose and nested there, burning behind the eyes, masking anything human.

The guards brought him to the gurney in the middle of the room, not much wider than a hospital bed, with padded vinyl and steel rails. Everything was pale blue or bone white, except the webbing of black straps coiled and waiting. Bass studied the straps with a slow, predatory interest. The guards—four of them, faces blurred by practiced vacancy—maneuvered him onto the slab without roughness, but also without mercy. His arms splayed open, wrists cinched down first, then ankles, then the wide band across his chest that stole any illusion of breath. Each closure clicked with finality.

He kept his eyes open, cataloging everything. There was no clock in the chamber. There were no windows, only the rectangular glass of the viewing panel opposite the gurney. Beyond it, a small amphitheater of seats. The lights above were so bright that they erased all color from the faces on the other side of the glass—ghosts blinking down at him, close enough to study his death in high definition.

Directly ahead, the woman in the tailored suit. She stood with her arms folded and feet planted wide, as if the whole ordeal might tip over if she let her posture slip. The hard edge of her jaw, the vertical slit of her mouth—these he recognized from every stage of his trial. She had hunted him for years, assembling each scrap of evidence like a bead on a string. Now she watched with a stillness that was almost clinical. If she felt satisfaction, she buried it deep.

To her right, a knot of people whose faces Bass remembered only from crime-scene and tabloid photos. The man in the tan jacket—father of the first girl. His hands gripped the seat in front of him, every tendon a white wire. Next to him, a mother, her lips moving in a silent loop of prayer or curse. Most kept their eyes on the gurney, but one man never looked up from his lap, as if refusing to give Bass the dignity of a last glance. There was a rhythm to their hatred, a pulse that pressed in from the other side of the glass.

He rolled his head slightly. The ceiling tiles were speckled with mildew, lines of green and brown. The hum of the fluorescent fixtures was relentless, a mosquito whine that made every nerve in his skull tremble. He followed the sound down to the floor, where the doctor's and the nurse's feet shuffled in methodical tandem. The doctor wore scrubs and a surgical mask; the nurse did not. Their hands were already gloved, their faces set with an anesthetized calm. They adjusted the IV stand, checked the tubing, and bled the air from syringes. Bass watched the clear liquid drip, then coil along the plastic like a ribbon of molten glass.

He noticed, with a kind of bitter humor, that nobody asked him if he was comfortable. Nobody spoke to him at all. Not the guards, not the medical staff, not the woman at the window. He supposed he should be grateful. Any kindness at this point would have been obscene.

He turned his gaze to the steel tray where the syringes waited, labeled in slanted block letters he could read upside down: 1. PENTOBARBITAL, 2. PAVULON, 3. POTASSIUM. The order mattered. It was a ceremony. He wondered if anyone had ever gotten the order wrong, or what would happen if they skipped a step.

The doctor leaned over him, fiddling with the vein in his right arm. The needle slid in with a clean, practiced pop. A strip of tape locked it in place, followed by a loop of tubing. There was no warning, no small talk, only a nod to the nurse who began adjusting the plunger of the first syringe.

Bass stretched his fingers, feeling the bite of the restraint at his wrist. He watched the fluid leap into the line and head for his heart. The cold flooded up his arm, so sharp it hurt. He felt his lips twist in a smile.

The ghosts behind the glass leaned forward as if drawn by magnetism. The woman in the suit blinked once, slowly, like she was trying to capture every microsecond. The mother's face was fractured, wet with something between joy and agony.

Bass closed his eyes for a moment. He waited for fear to come. Instead, all he felt was curiosity—a scientist in the body of his own lab rat, hungry to see what came next.

When he opened his eyes, the room had flattened. Bass felt a curious distance, as if he were watching himself from somewhere above the steel tray. He angled his gaze to the gallery.

The first row of witnesses pressed close to the glass, eager for a final proof of his mortality. The man with the tan jacket—whose daughter had provided Bass with the only real challenge—was white-knuckled on the railing. His jaw moved in a locked rhythm, as if chewing through every word he'd rehearsed and never delivered in court. Bass pictured him running a mental tally, waiting for the scales to finally tip.

To his left, the mother with the looped prayer. She rocked gently, hands clutching a cross at her throat, not looking at Bass but at some invisible point halfway between herself and the slab. Tears ran, unchecked, pooling at her chin. Bass thought it odd that she would waste water on him, but perhaps that was what the glass was for: to keep his death clean, their grief contained.

A few faces were anonymous, placeholders for the state. The man with the downcast stare—lawyer, cop, maybe a sibling—would not meet his eye. Bass recognized the type: the sort who believed justice was a story told to comfort children. There was, too, a woman with an acid smile, her hair helmeted tight against her skull. She radiated a chemical delight, a need to see him suffer, but even her eyes looked hollow, like a puppet's buttons sewn on at the last second.

Some watched with fascination, others with dread, one with something close to pity. They were here for a spectacle, but not for him—never for him. Bass was merely the reagent, the catalyst for their secret experiment: Would his ending fix what had been broken? Would it fill the invisible hole left by absence?

He scanned the faces for satisfaction, for any glimmer that his death would be enough. There was nothing. Even in their hate, they seemed diminished by the ritual, as if the act of watching had drained them of the last reserves of hope.

Bass let the thought roll around his skull: this was not punishment, not even retribution. It was a wake, a vigil for the living more than the dead. They had come not to see him die, but to see if anything happened after. If the lights dimmed, the pain softened, the world moved forward. He found himself perversely amused by the possibility that it wouldn't.

The hum in the ceiling climbed a register. The woman in the suit remained perfectly still, but her fingers had started to twitch, tapping out a pattern only she understood. The mother's prayer had slowed, voice gone to a raw whisper.

Bass closed his eyes again, willing the rest of him to do the same.

***

The next phase began not with a drumroll, but a clipboard. One of the guards—a thin man with teeth too white for the rest of him—read a checklist into the stale air. "Inmate secured. Intravenous lines established. Witnesses present and observing." Each phrase was an old bone, picked clean of meaning.

The doctor and nurse hovered over Bass, their movements synchronized but joyless. The nurse pinched a strip of his forearm, smacked the vein for a little showmanship, and nodded to the doctor, who slid the needle home without a word. Bass studied the doctor's hands: smooth, hairless, surgical-glove tight. He wondered if the man knew he looked like a mannequin, or if the scrubs did that to everyone.

The tubing ran from Bass's arm to a port on the wall, where the syringes were lined up in a neat, color-coded array. The names and dosages were taped on, as if this were a hospital medication round and not a one-way ticket to whatever came next.

A voice—Bass thought it belonged to the warden, but he'd only ever seen the man once, in a courtroom—spoke from somewhere behind his head. "Proceed on my mark. Begin with protocol one."

The doctor murmured, "Ready," and the nurse echoed, "Ready." There was a crackle of radios, a series of distant clicks, as if the prison itself was ticking through a list of errands. The finality of it was almost comic.

Bass realized, with a throb of amusement, that nobody in the room even looked at him anymore. Not the guards, not the medical staff, not the faces behind the glass. He was an object, a point in a process, no more or less important than the needle or the tray.

He savored the ordinariness of it. The routine. The cold, bureaucratic grace of a machine doing what it was built to do. No speeches, no eye contact, no last rites. Only the hush before ignition.

The warden's voice again: "Administer protocol one."

A plunger was depressed. The world held its breath.

The cold hit instantly, like liquid mercury poured into his arm. Bass tracked the sensation as it rushed upward, a silver thread snaking toward his heart, his brain. For a fraction of a second, everything else receded: the humming lights, the glass wall, the air thick with bleach and breath. There was only the chill, expanding to fill him, then settling into a slow, deliberate weight.

He flexed his fingers, or tried to. They responded sluggishly, the skin already numb. It was as if he'd been submerged—every limb suspended, his torso pressed to the gurney by a force stronger than gravity. The world at the edges of his vision began to soften, then sway, like a room glimpsed through water.

Bass opened his eyes wide, forcing the blur into focus. The faces behind the glass had grown even more rapt. The father in the tan jacket leaned so close his nose nearly touched the panel. The praying mother had stopped rocking; her mouth hung open, an O of shock or anticipation. The woman with the helmeted hair had her phone out, discreetly filming or taking photos, hungry for a souvenir.

Bass found this funny—he wanted to laugh, but the only sound he made was a wet rasp. The laugh vibrated inside his chest, a private joke he would take with him.

The first chemical slowed his mind, but it did not dull his senses. If anything, everything became more vivid, the colors oversaturated, the voices behind the glass amplified into a chorus of shallow breathing and mumbled curses. The ceiling tiles undulated, the mildew stains spreading like bruises on diseased skin.

He watched as the nurse bled the second syringe, the liquid inside tinted faintly yellow. She glanced at the doctor, who nodded once, a priest granting permission for the next step.

Bass fixed his gaze on the viewing glass, drinking in the scene: the animals in the zoo, craning for a better look at the beast. The corners of his mouth twitched, then failed to rise. The heaviness spread from his fingers to his toes, then curled up his spine, enfolding him in an invisible blanket.

He was still there—still aware, still himself—when the world finally began to darken at the edges. He welcomed the blur. He wanted to see how far it went.

***

The next chemical was a killer of motion. Bass felt it enter, not as a burn or a sting, but as a shutting off—click, click, click—of every circuit that once belonged to him. His arms and legs went slack. He tried to turn his head, to spit at the glass, but nothing obeyed. Even his eyelids, slow and heavy, refused to close.

The panic arrived on schedule. His mind screamed at the muscles to move, but they lay dead under the skin. He tried to shout, to gurgle, even to blink a message—no one could have missed the terror in his eyes—but the only sound was the faint hiss of the oxygen line near his face.

The world beyond the glass receded. The father's face, once red with rage, now looked sickly yellow, as if all the hate had drained out and left only nausea. The mother's prayers had dried up; she sat limp in her seat, wrung out by the show. The DA woman didn't move, not even a tremor. Maybe she was waiting for confirmation that he felt every last second.

Bass tried to remember the order of symptoms, the sequence of failure. He'd once read, in a hospital pamphlet, about "locked-in syndrome." This was that, but on a cosmic scale. He couldn't even twitch a muscle. Every sense narrowed to the thin beam of vision, the cold tightening around his chest. His breaths grew shallow, mechanical, as if a hand was squeezing his ribs with increasing pressure.

A static hush replaced the hum of the lights. He heard his own pulse, the weak flutter of blood in his temples. The room—his world—had collapsed to the length of the IV line and the glass wall beyond.

Bass fought to keep his mind above water. He tried to count, to measure the seconds, to inventory each fleeting sensation. But the panic chewed through his thoughts, gnawed them to ribbons.

When the next syringe was raised, his eyes followed it. He was still there, still awake, still ready for whatever finale they had scripted for him.

Let's see how far it goes, he thought. Let's see if it ever ends.

***

The third syringe gleamed in the tray, a bullet of amber fluid. The nurse drew it up, purged the line with a practiced flick, and pushed it into the port.

Bass felt nothing at first, then everything at once. The liquid burned as it hit his veins, a blossom of acid that raced to his heart and detonated there. His chest seized, every cell shrieking in silent protest. He wanted to gasp, to arch his back, to claw at the pain, but he was pinned in place by the drugs and the straps.

The burn spread outward, a ring of fire crawling through his ribs, up his neck, behind his eyes. The only movement left was in his vision: the world narrowing to a tunnel, the faces beyond the glass warping into grotesque masks. The mother's face—eyes wild, mouth open in a howl—froze in his memory like a photograph. The DA woman's head was bowed, in shadow. He tried to find her eyes, to see if there was any victory in them, but she refused to look up.

Bass felt his heart stumble. One beat, then a long pause, then another, weaker. His brain flooded with panic, but the oxygen wasn't coming. Each pulse grew softer, more distant, until it was only a rumor in the blood.

The darkness closed in at the edges, a velvet curtain pulled tight. Bass's mind, still fighting, tried to memorize every detail, but even that betrayed him. The faces receded, became shapes, then shades, then nothing.

He was still waiting for the end when the lights finally went out.

***

There was no tunnel, no light, no last roll of greatest hits—just a rapid, almost comic, subtraction. One moment, Bass was a body: the next, a memory of a body. Even pain abandoned him; the fire in his chest flickered and was snuffed out, replaced by perfect, formless dark.

He waited. For what, he wasn't sure. There were no clocks here, no breath, no heartbeat, not even the phantom pain amputees complained about. Only a void so complete it erased the idea of waiting itself.

If there were thoughts, they were slow, floaty, more a suggestion than a sentence. Did he exist? Was this existence? Was this some kind of holding pen for defective souls? If so, where was the next step—the judgment, the gavel, the cosmic laugh track?

Bass tried to muster outrage, but even that was an old recording, hissing and thin. Everything he'd been—rage, wit, curiosity—had been smothered by the darkness, each trait dimming and drifting away.

He was almost content with the nothing. It felt clean. Uncluttered. Pure in a way life had never been.

But then—against all sense or mercy—there was a sensation. Not a sound, but the memory of a sound. Not a light, but the shadow of one, a pinprick bleeding into his field of void.

And just like that, the world started up again, with a violence that made death seem gentle by comparison.

***

The return to living was a punch in the mouth. Bass jerked awake, lungs clawing at the air, throat raw with a scream that died before it left his lips. For a moment, he thought he'd dreamed the execution, but the pain that greeted him was more convincing than any nightmare.

His wrists were lashed behind a tree trunk—something rough and splintered, bark biting deep into the skin. His legs, slick with cold mud, were pinned at an unnatural angle. Every joint screamed, every muscle in his back seized. He was upright, arms stretched, feet barely brushing the ground.

Above and to his right, a light source dangled from a branch. Its glow was sickly orange, more shadow than light, but enough to carve the world into shapes: the gnarled arms of trees, the shifting bodies of those who'd brought him here.

For a while, all he could do was gasp and drool. His mouth was so dry it felt caked shut. He twisted, but the ropes cut deeper. The shock of being alive—being alive—was so total that it crowded out any hope of explanation. The last thing he remembered was the dark, then this: cold, wet, noise, pain.

The air stank of swamp and something coppery, maybe blood. He craned his neck, trying to spot the IV, the hospital, the guards—anything to put him back in the script—but there were no white walls, no glass, no audience: just the woods, the mud, and the ghostly lantern.

Bass tried to speak, but only managed a wheeze. He blinked, blinked again, hoping to reset the world to normal, but the only thing that changed was the number of shadows moving at the edge of the clearing.

It occurred to him, dimly, that this was not a rescue. Not a miracle. He had been transferred from one holding pen to another, traded up from a gurney to a crucifix.

The pain was convincing, but the terror was better.

***

The first to emerge from the black was a figure in a hooded rain poncho, steps slow and squelching. Bass blinked, fighting to focus, but the figure stayed blurred—no face, no voice, only the gloved hands cupped around something small.

It was a child's shoe, impossibly bright pink, the kind with cartoon eyes sewn onto the toe. The figure knelt and placed it at the base of the tree, not two feet from Bass's own bare, mud-splattered foot. The shoe was wrong here. It pulsed with color, obscene in its innocence.

A second figure followed, slightly taller, carrying a limp backpack. The kind kids wore to first grade: blue nylon, straps frayed, zipper half-broken. There was a patch on it—Bass recognized the cartoon, remembered peeling it off a different bag in a different basement. The backpack joined the shoe at the foot of the tree.

A third figure laid down a stack of photographs. Bass squinted, but he knew what he would see: faces of the missing, grainy and creased, their eyes caught between suspicion and hope. Some faces he recalled in detail, others only as gestures or stains. The photos fanned out on the ground like a police lineup.

More items followed. A plastic tiara. A charm bracelet. A bundle of colored pencils, snapped and taped. Each thing was placed with ceremony, as if the objects themselves held the power to convict. Bass's chest filled with an electric nausea. The pain in his wrists and legs faded; the terror took over, rooting him deeper into the bark.

The figures never spoke. They moved with methodical care, as if handling relics rather than evidence. Each time they returned to the woods, they reappeared with a new offering. The ritual had a rhythm, a logic, a weight.

Bass tried to scream, to beg, to laugh it off. But the world had no room for noise, not in this shrine. His eyes rolled, searching for faces, for any sign of mercy or even malice. There was none. The figures might as well have been mannequins, animated only for this task.

He wanted to close his eyes, but the light found him every time.

By the end, the pile at his feet looked like the end of a lost-and-found bin, but he knew it for what it was: a tally, an accusation, a verdict already rendered.

This wasn't about him. This was about what he'd left behind, and who was left to clean it up.

One figure broke ranks, stepped into the lantern's heart. Its mask was blank—plastic, molded to a child's smile, but painted black. The figure grabbed Bass's jaw, forcing his head down, grinding his teeth against the bone.

"Look," said the voice. It was not a voice at all, but the echo of one, processed through a box or a speaker or a throat ruined by years of silence. The hand released, but the gaze held Bass's eyes to the pile of things below.

"Do you know these?" said the mask.

Bass tried to shake his head, to lie, to vanish into the pain. But the words stuck to the inside of his skull. He remembered each piece, each child, each time he'd thought himself a god in the darkness. Now, the relics glared up at him, proof that the past never stays buried.

The masked figure knelt, picked up a photograph, and pressed it to Bass's lips.

"What light cannot reach," said the voice, "shadow must cleanse."

A chorus of whispers repeated the phrase, the words stacking and folding into one another, louder each time.

The figure produced a folded sheet of paper, read a name from it, and repeated it out loud. The group at the edge of the woods echoed the name, in unison, as if calling attendance in a classroom. The names came slowly at first, then faster. Each one stabbed a nerve, detonated a memory.

Bass whimpered. His mouth was dry as sawdust, but the mask forced him to nod, to face each name, each charge.

The light source seemed to flare with each repetition. The light burned through his closed eyelids, branding him from within.

It was a litany, a tally, a final accounting. When the last name was spoken, the clearing went silent except for Bass's raw, keening breath.

The masked figure replaced the photo. The rest stepped forward, closer now, forming a circle around the tree.

Bass knew, in the root of his spine, that he would never leave this place. Not as the man he'd been, not even as a memory.

He was a name on a list now, a footnote, a thing to be wiped clean.

***

The first strike was not a strike at all, but a caress. Gloved hands traced Bass's forearm, finding the old needle tracks, the soft patches of skin, then dug in with a blade so fine it might have been a paper cut. He gasped. Blood ran, slow and sticky, pooling with the rain on the bark. The pain was clean, surgical. He thrashed, but the bindings ate into him, refusing to give.

Another figure took a turn. This one carried a length of copper wire, which it threaded around Bass's thumb, then twisted tight, tighter, until the blood stopped and the flesh swelled purple. Bass howled, spit flying, but the figure only watched, eyes blank behind the mask. There was a cold logic in the way they worked—a checklist, a job to be done.

Next came a baton, rubber-tipped, aimed at Bass's knees. The blow cracked bone, dropped him onto the ropes, and tore a scream from his gut. Memory folded in on itself: a boy in a hallway, a girl in a ditch, the pleasure of making someone helpless. Now it was his turn to beg, but the circle of figures paid no mind.

A woman's voice—a real one, unfiltered—crooned a lullaby as she scraped Bass's cheek with a knife, peeling the skin in ribbons. The song burrowed into his ear, clung to him like a fever. He tried to block it out, but the words chased him around the inside of his skull.

Hands held him upright as the next figure forced something into his mouth—a sock, soaked in gasoline or bleach. Bass gagged, coughed, choked. His vision blurred; the light became a pulsing halo. Somewhere, the list of names was recited again, but now as a whisper, a background noise to his agony.

Every act had a purpose, a symmetry, as if the pain had to be measured and matched to his crimes. Each cut, each break, each humiliation. They used their tools with restraint, never rushing, never letting him fade too soon.

He tried to dissociate, to float above it, but the pain kept dragging him down. The memories they'd exhumed, the bodies he'd buried—they all came back, ugly and insistent. He tasted iron, dirt, and urine. He smelled hair burning, skin splitting.

Time lost meaning. He wept. He begged. He promised anything, but his voice was shredded, useless.

The figures finished their work with a precision that felt holy. By the end, Bass was nothing but a vessel for pain, a raw nerve lashed to a tree, waiting for the final mercy.

The leader retrieved the light source from the tree above Bass. It was a lantern; he could see it more clearly now. The leader brought it close and looked into Bass's eyes. There was no hatred there. No satisfaction. Only the confirmation that the world could be put right, if only for a moment.

Bass sobbed, or tried to. He was ready for it to end.

The lantern flickered, shadows crowded in, and the knife came last.

***

Bass's world shrank to the size of the lantern flame. He saw it through a curtain of tears and blood, its orange heart trembling in the night air. The leader stood before him, knife in hand, mask unreadable.

There was no speech, no final confession. The leader pressed the blade against Bass's throat, just above the collarbone. The pain was white-hot, a single flash, and then nothing—no air, no sound, not even the rustle of the trees. The world folded up, neat and black, with only the afterimage of the light floating behind his eyes.

He slid out of himself. The hands that had held him upright released their grip. He slumped, chin to chest, the ropes doing the rest. Blood pattered down, darkening the ground at the base of the tree.

The figures moved quickly, efficiently. They gathered the artifacts, bundled the photos, and packed away the tiara, the shoe, and the backpack. Each item was brushed clean of mud and blood, sealed in plastic, and returned to a duffel bag.

The leader lingered, holding the lantern high. The flame guttered, dipped, then steadied. For a moment, the clearing was a stage, everything illuminated—Bass's body, the spattered bark, the footprints in the wet soil.

Then the leader exhaled, snuffed the flame, and closed the lantern.

One by one, the figures slipped away, dissolving into the woods, the dark swallowing them in sequence. The clearing was empty. The tree stood silent, its cargo stilled and cooling.

The hush that followed was absolute. Not even the insects dared to break it.

By morning, the only evidence left was the circle of flattened grass and the stain where shadow met earth. The rest was memory, or myth, or perhaps nothing at all.

The woods took the secret back. The night kept it.

CHAPTER 1

Savannah's sky in November was a bruised, indigo dome. On nights like this, the light from the riverfront and the spires downtown couldn't push past the mist rolling in from the marsh, so the only illumination worth anything came from the stadium lights at Thurmond Memorial Field. Four banks of halogens hung in the air like the eyes of God, burning down on the field and the aluminum bleachers, bleaching the blue and gold paint along the railings. The glow spilled into the haze, tinting it sickly yellow and making every breath taste faintly of electricity and wet tin.

The homecoming crowd was restless, jostling along the rows, parents in windbreakers and old letterman jackets, children sniffling in oversized sweatshirts, teenage girls huddled in little tribes, boys flicking popcorn kernels at each other's heads. Someone had brought a portable radio, and the static of the play-by-play drifted through the stands, layered with the metallic rattle of cowbells and the dry snare of the marching band warming up on the track. The air was cooler than usual for a Georgia fall, and every exhale hung visible, little ghosts sent up by every mouth in the stadium.

Below, the field was a patchwork of torn sod and mud. Home team in white, visitors in crimson—both stained and indistinct under the glare. The game had ground itself down to the final minutes, clock ticking away toward a close that had everyone pressed forward in their seats, knuckles white on the rails. The scoreboard showed a home deficit: 21-17, three minutes and change left. A row of cheerleaders bounced and shouted on the far sideline, the "H" on their uniforms shining slick as oil.

On the visitors' side, fans banged on the bleachers with their boots, chanting the quarterback's name. On the home side, the tension was brittle. Fathers muttered to sons about fourth downs and blown coverages. Mothers clutched coffee in styrofoam cups, not drinking but drawing warmth through their gloves. Above it all, the drumming of the band rattled like a mechanical heartbeat.

The final drive started at the twenty-seven. The offense jogged out, white jerseys huddled under the vapor, the quarterback—number eleven, WALTON—wiping his palms on his thighs as he scanned the defense. The crowd noise crested, then thinned, anticipation straining against the humid dark.

Every eye in the stadium watched, hoping for a miracle but bracing for the slow grind of inevitability. Everybody leaned forward, as if will alone could push the ball another yard. In Savannah, hope and dread always mixed in the air, heavier than the fog, impossible to separate.

The band reached the end of its fight song and let the last drumbeat echo across the metal rows, waiting for what would come next.

***

The huddle was a closed circle, helmet-to-helmet, every voice a whisper amplified by the hush in the stands. Mathew Walton crouched low, hands pressed to the back of the center's muddy jersey, and spat the play call through his mouthguard. The sound was guttural, consonants chewed by the rubber, and the tightness in his chest.

He felt the cold air settle on the sweat clinging to his jaw, the condensation of his own breath curling inside the face mask. The world narrowed to the glint of the helmet decals and the tight cluster of shoulders hunched together, every man locked in a private countdown. It was the last two minutes of his last high school game, and Mathew was acutely aware of it—the ticking clock, the pounding in his ears, the knowledge that he'd never feel this particular combination of adrenaline and dread again.

"Hawk Right, 82 Waggle, on one," he barked. The wideout—Rooney—nodded, eyes wide and unblinking. The backs exchanged a quick fist bump. Only Mark Hughes, the right guard, didn't move at all. Mark was the only senior on the line who hadn't missed a snap all season; his knuckles were already split and bleeding from the last series, blood soaking through the tape like red paint on canvas.

Mark kept his eyes on Mathew, but not with hero worship or fear. There was something else there—calculation, maybe. He was already reading the defense, picking apart the three-point stances on the other side of the ball, watching for the twitch of the nose tackle or the delayed blitz from the linebacker.

"Clock," Mathew said, jerking his chin toward the scoreboard. "One-nineteen. Don't look at it again."

A ripple of nervous laughter ran through the group. They all knew the score, the stakes, the ritual of what had to happen next. Mark grunted, flexed his fingers in their too-small gloves, then brought the huddle in closer. His voice was softer than you'd expect for a kid his size. "We pick him up," Mark said, nodding at Mathew. "Nothing gets through."

The huddle broke. The world outside the helmet was a roar of white noise—band, crowd, the public address system blaring someone's last name in three sharp syllables. Mathew jogged to the line, wiping one gloved hand across his facemask to clear the condensation, the other pressed to the black stripe along his thigh pad. Every muscle in his legs felt like it had been lit up with jumper cables. He was lightheaded, nauseated, invincible.

The line set. Mark hunched over, hands anchored, eyes forward. The defense shifted, crowding the interior, daring Mathew to throw. Sweat stung the cut on Mathew's cheek, the one he'd gotten two series ago when the blitzing linebacker got too close. He remembered the sound of his helmet slamming into the turf—submerged, metallic—then shook it off.

He drew a breath so deep it felt like it might rip something open inside him. He waited for the sound, the snap count, the raw physics of bodies colliding, and the thin hope of a play no one would ever forget.

In the final huddle of the final drive, there were no speeches. Just the communion of breath, the shared heartbeat, the knowledge that nobody gets out of the moment alive.

***

From the stands, everything looked smaller and more exposed. The white uniforms huddled around the ball, glowing, spectral, and alone, surrounded by a red perimeter that seemed to tighten with every down. Samantha Walton leaned on the cold rail, biting at the inside of her cheek, while beside her, Josephine Hamilton alternated between squinting at the field and jotting notes on a creased program with a ballpoint pen.

"They're crowding the box again," Josephine muttered, not to Samantha so much as to the universe. She circled a formation diagram with deliberate precision, then tapped the pen against the margin. "That's the third time in four plays. You'd think they'd adjust by now."

Samantha bounced on the heels of her sneakers, breath puffing in little clouds. Her brother's number—eleven—was half-obscured by mud and grass stains, but she picked him out instantly, even with the helmet on. "They will," she said, voice shaky with cold or nerves. "Matty always figures it out."

Josephine snorted. "He's got a stacked front and zero help in the backfield. If he doesn't audible, he'll get flattened."

Samantha elbowed her. "You can't just say things like that. It's his last game."

"That's exactly why he needs to be smart about it," Josephine said. She ran a finger down the column of player stats, then folded the program and tucked it into her coat sleeve. She sounded like she was prepping for cross-examination in a courtroom rather than calling a football game. "You can see it, can't you? The left end is dragging his leg. Probably a high-ankle sprain, and he's still starting every snap. If I were a coach, I'd run a sweep to that side and take my chances on the edge."

"You're so sure of yourself," Samantha said, but she smiled, the tension breaking just a little.

"I'm right," Josephine replied, her mouth thinning into a line of concentration. "There's a weakness, and if Mathew misses it, they lose. Simple as that."

A band parent in the row behind them coughed loudly, blanketing the back of their heads in the sweet, greasy perfume of concession-stand kettle corn. The noise around them was deafening—the shrieks of little kids, the slap of foam fingers against the rail, the echo of the P.A. system. But Josephine tuned it all out, eyes fixed on the field, waiting to be proven right or wrong.

On the sideline, the offense broke its huddle. Samantha gripped the bar and held her breath. Josephine leaned so far over the rail that she had to be yanked back by the hood of her jacket when the people behind them tried to squeeze through. She barely noticed.

"They're shifting," Josephine said, voice low, as if she were speaking into a wire. "Left side, just like I said. He's going for it."

Samantha let out her breath in a hiss. "Please, Matty," she whispered, "just don't get hurt."

Josephine grinned, all teeth and mischief, but underneath there was something else—anticipation, a hunger for proof. "He won't," she said. "He's about to make them all look stupid."

Below them, the line set. The crowd went silent, waiting.

***

Robert Dean watched the field analytically, taking in every potential scenario. While the rest of the crowd rose and fell in tides of hope and dread, Robert filtered out everything but the raw data: the stagger in the safety's backpedal, the fresh blood on the quarterback's mouth, the odd angle of a taped finger on the right tackle. He perched on the edge of the bench, knees pointed together, one thumb methodically massaging the knuckle of his opposite hand.

He'd been friends with Mathew since Little League and knew the warning signs—knew, for example, that when Mathew started wiping sweat from his brow with the back of his glove, he was bleeding somewhere. Knew, too, that if the helmet stayed on between possessions, it meant he was hiding something from the coach. Robert cataloged each clue, as if the outcome of the game hinged less on the scoreboard and more on how well he could diagnose the wounds as they happened.

Samantha glanced back at him. "He's fine, right?" she asked, the concern knotted in her words.

Robert grinned. "He'll be fine as long as he keeps his head attached," he said, deadpan. "That's more than I can say for that kid." He pointed at the linebacker, who was limping so badly he seemed to be dragging his entire left side.

"Looks like a partial tear," Robert continued, almost to himself. "They'll ice him at halftime, maybe shoot him up, but by the third quarter, he's done. Watch the way he plants—see how he favors the outside of the foot?"

Josephine rolled her eyes. "Robert, can you go one whole game without pretending you're on some sports-injury CSI show?"

He shrugged, unbothered. "It's not pretending if it's correct. And, uh, you were right about the left end," he added, tipping an imaginary hat to Josephine.

She smiled, but refused to look at him.

The play clock was winding down. The noise level in the stadium swelled, but Robert stayed detached, measuring every movement. He watched Mathew lick blood from his lip and reset his feet in the pocket. Robert could almost feel the synapses firing in his friend's head, the decision tree branching, the thousand possible futures splintering out from this one snap.

Robert wondered if the people around him even saw the same game. For most, it was just a way to feel something bright and communal, to stave off the creeping dark for another Friday night. For Robert, it was about pattern and prediction, bodies in motion, the relentless arithmetic of flesh.

On the field, the ref's whistle cut through the noise. Everything went still.

"Here it comes," Robert said, and let himself hope, just a little, that his friend might escape without breaking anything too important.

***

From his spot three rows above the rest of the group, William Lee watched the world unfold like a series of silent arguments. The field itself was easy to parse—plays and counterplays, the geometry of motion—but William's real fascination was with the people around him: the way a fight nearly started over a spilled drink, the nervous laughter of a freshman couple sneaking their first beer, the cluster of old men who dissected every call as if the universe depended on it.

Beside him, Jimmy Lee vibrated with kinetic energy. At fifteen, he was already taller than most of the adults in the stadium, his voice a battering ram that could cut through any din. Jimmy wasn't so much a fan as a force of nature, and his commitment to supporting the home team was absolute, even if it meant nearly breaking the bones of everyone in his immediate radius.

"Let's go!" Jimmy bellowed, launching two fingers into his mouth and letting loose with a whistle so sharp the entire row in front of him flinched. A little girl in a cheer uniform shot him a dirty look; Jimmy grinned and flashed her a double thumbs-up, undeterred. He turned and, for a second, locked eyes with Samantha at the rail. He gave her a nod that said, I'm watching, nothing will get past me.

William scanned the scene. He caught sight of the security guard wandering toward the section with the rowdy band kids, the way a single mom kept tugging her son's hood over his ears against the cold, the gentle collapse of an inflatable tunnel on the far sideline as the air pump failed. It was all so predictable, and yet William never got bored with it. He liked the way the night gathered everyone in—how, for two hours, all the weird edges and old grudges got sanded down by the shared obsession of watching people run into each other at top speed.

"Watch the shift," William said, tilting his head toward the field. The defense was sneaking a safety up, hiding the move behind the noise and confusion. Jimmy didn't miss a beat.

"That's cheating," Jimmy said, loud enough that a nearby grandmother jerked in her seat. "Somebody call the ref, they're loading the damn box!"

A few adults looked up, some with irritation, but most with appreciation. Jimmy had a gift for bluster that made his disruptions almost charming.

"You think Mathew sees it?" William asked, watching as the home offense took their stance.

"He better," Jimmy replied, "or that linebacker's gonna pop him like a balloon." He rolled his shoulders, almost as if preparing to take the hit himself.

William noted the way Jimmy's fist clenched the back of the seat in front of them, the white under his fingernails. Jimmy might have been a loudmouth, but he paid attention—especially when it came to their friends on the field.

Down below, the teams froze in perfect symmetry, the calm before the collision.

Jimmy leaned in, breath hot with anticipation. "C'mon, Matty. Make 'em eat it."

William smiled, a slow, knowing thing. "He will," he said, and let the noise of the stadium roll over them both.

***

Fourteen seconds on the clock. The line of scrimmage was a shallow trench gouged into grass and mud, and Mark Hughes crouched at its edge, staring down the nose of the biggest defensive tackle he'd ever seen. The kid across from him looked like he'd been grown in a lab to ruin dreams: six-four, three hundred easy, neckless and breathing like a pit bull in summer. Mark tasted adrenaline at the back of his throat and wondered if he'd have teeth left by the end of the play.

Mathew was behind him, feet shuffling in the dirt, eyes flickering from sideline to defense and back again. Mark could feel the tension in the quarterback's voice as he shouted out the cadence, and could hear the subtle waver even through the plastic and metal of his helmet. They'd been together since peewee, knew each other's habits the way twins might, and Mark recognized the panic—but also the iron underneath.

"Watch zero, watch zero!" Mathew barked, and the snap count adjusted. Mark reset his grip, clenching his fingers around the laces of his gloves until the bones in his hand creaked.

The crowd was a living thing now, surging with every shift in the backfield. Mark felt the rumble of feet against the stands vibrate through his ribs. The world contracted to the three-foot gap between him and his opposite number. On the edge of his vision, the referees paced the sideline like crows on a wire, black-and-white stripes flickering in the haze.

The tackle snorted, spat a rope of saliva onto Mark's shoe, and grinned widely. "Last ride, Hughes," he said, the words syrup-slow and mean. "Hope you packed a lunch."

Mark smiled back, all gums and defiance. "Your mom packed it for me when I left this morning."

He drew in a lungful of cold air and let his body settle. He had one job: keep the mountain away from Mathew for exactly two seconds. After that, the rest of the world could fall apart. He could live with that.

Mathew called an audible, the code words flying fast. Mark repeated them under his breath, a litany he'd rehearsed all season. He saw the linebacker slide over, saw the corner drop into man, and knew what was coming. He braced himself, loaded every ounce of anger and pride into his legs.

Somewhere far above, the press box announcer tried to work the crowd into a frenzy, but all Mark heard was the sucking sound of the center's hand on the football, and the click of the tackle's teeth as he set his jaw.

The stadium stilled for a heartbeat.

"Set—"

The world exploded forward.

***

Josephine shot up from her seat, nearly knocking Samantha sideways. She jabbed a finger toward the field, hair escaping from under her beanie. "Did you see that? The nose shifted—early. They're overcommitted on the strong side," she said, voice slicing through the chaos.

Samantha tried to follow her gaze but mostly caught a blur of white and red, the glare of the lights flattening every movement. "Are you sure?" she whispered, clinging to the hope that this was all under control.

"I'm positive," Josephine replied, eyes never leaving the line of scrimmage. "They're leaving the left flat wide open. If Mathew rolls out, he's gone." She said it with the finality of a judge delivering a verdict. "I bet they didn't even notice. He can walk it in."

Behind them, Robert cackled, then covered his mouth with his hand to muffle the sound. "Maybe you should go down there and run the offense yourself," he said. "You sound like my dad with a remote."

Josephine snapped her head back, shot him a glare, then turned to Samantha. "You believe me, right?"

Samantha shrugged, a smile trembling on her lips. "I don't think he can hear you, Jo."

Josephine snorted, the beginnings of a laugh, and then shouted at the top of her lungs: "LEFT SIDE, MATT! RUN LEFT!" The words dissolved into the crowd, drowned out by the wail of air horns and a collective exhale from the bleachers.

On the field, the offensive line tensed, then snapped into motion. Josephine leaned out so far that she nearly toppled over the guardrail.

"He's got it," she muttered. "He's really got it."

Robert craned forward, squinting with clinical interest. "Or he's about to get pasted by three hundred pounds of regret," he deadpanned, but there was hope buried in it.

Samantha's knuckles blanched on the bar. She closed her eyes and wished for once that Josephine would be wrong.

The ball was in play.

***

As soon as the snap hit, William Lee tracked the chaos with surgical calm. The defensive front collapsed inward, every jersey converging on the ball like sharks on a bleeding swimmer. William noted the overcommit instantly—the red helmets bunching, the linebackers pinching so tight they left a seam at the edge. He saw the telltale twitch of the safety, late on the coverage.

"Watch outside," William muttered, almost too soft for Jimmy to hear.

Jimmy heard. He was halfway over the railing, hands drumming a tribal rhythm on the cold steel, voice bellowing above the surge of the crowd. "Go, go, go!" he screamed, as if the force of will alone could punch a hole through the defense.

William didn't move, but his eyes flicked side-to-side, analyzing the possibilities. He could sense the pattern emerging even before the play fully developed—the way the offensive line strained left, Mark Hughes acting as the wedge, and Mathew ghosting in the pocket, eyes scanning for daylight. William wondered, absently, whether Mathew had noticed the same opening, or if he was about to trust his arm and take the risk.

Jimmy's whole body vibrated with anticipation. "He's got room! He's got it!" he shouted, voice breaking on the last word. The people around them echoed the sentiment, a sudden wave of hope rolling through the section

Below, the line buckled. The red mountain tried to crash through the middle, but Mark held his ground just long enough, and then Mathew was running—legs churning, jersey flapping, a comet's tail of mud spraying behind him.

Jimmy slammed a fist against the rail so hard it rattled the whole row. "YES!"

William smiled, small and secret. "Told you," he said, and for the first time all night, he let himself believe in the possibility of victory.

The play was not over, not yet, but momentum had shifted, and everyone in the stadium could feel it.

***

Mark Hughes felt the moment before it happened, a tightening of the air, the promise of violence about to break. He could smell the inside of his own helmet—blood and plastic and old sweat—and hear the quarterback's cadence reverberate through the turf. Every cell in his body screamed at him to survive the next two seconds.

The defensive tackle across from him was already lunging, eyes wide with predatory joy. Mark's world narrowed to the man's face, the way the lips curled in a snarl, the flecks of spit arcing through the air. When the ball snapped, it was less a movement than an explosion. Mark absorbed the first hit, shock running up his arms and into his chest. His feet dug into the mud, cleats fighting for purchase.

The two of them locked together, a slow-motion car crash. The tackle tried to bull rush, but Mark anticipated, dropped his hips, and redirected the force just enough to deflect the uniformed behemoth. Every muscle screamed in protest, but Mark refused to yield.

He caught a glimpse of Mathew behind him, jersey streaked with grime, eyes locked on the chaos ahead. If Mark lost this fight, the play was dead. If he won, there was a chance at glory.

The tackle growled, tried to twist him sideways, but Mark countered with a desperate shove, using every ounce of his weight to redirect the charge. He felt something pop in his shoulder, pain radiating down his arm, but he clung to the block with grim satisfaction. All he needed was a heartbeat, one window of daylight.

He got it. The tackle stumbled, momentum spent, and Mark drove forward, opening the seam. He felt the air rush behind him as Mathew slipped through the gap.

For an instant, Mark allowed himself a breathless smile, the taste of blood and triumph mixing in his mouth.

Then he heard the roar from the stands, and he knew the play had worked.

He didn't see the finish—didn't need to. His job was done. The collision had been won, and everything else was just an aftermath.

***

For Samantha Walton, the world shrank to a single heartbeat.

She clung to the metal railing, palms sweating in the cold, and watched as her brother sprinted toward the left sideline. Everything else—the shrieking fans, the pounding of the band, the slapstick chaos of the stands—dropped away until only Mathew was left. He was all motion and grit, legs pumping, arms tucking the football close like it was the last fragile thing on earth.

Time stretched, then folded. She saw the defenders closing in, red jerseys closing ranks, Mathew's white uniform the lone spot of clarity in a blurring storm. Her mouth tasted like cotton. She didn't breathe.

He dipped past one tackler, then another, shoulders twisting to slip the grasping hands. Every time he staggered, Samantha felt her own chest clench, the pain of imagined impact rippling up her spine. The end zone looked impossibly far, but Mathew kept running, head down, refusing to be caught.

Samantha found herself shouting—didn't remember deciding to—but her voice joined the tidal wave of noise without a trace. She squeezed the rail so hard her knuckles went bone white.

He was so close now—two yards, then one. A final defender dove, arms outstretched, and Mathew launched himself into the air, stretching for the pylon.

In that instant, time stopped.

All Samantha could see was her brother, airborne, the field falling away beneath him.

Everything hinged on what happened next.

***

Mathew hit the grass with such violence that his breath flew from his lungs. The world tilted, the taste of dirt filling his mouth, a half-second of blindness before his vision snapped back into place. He kept his arms locked around the ball, even as a tangle of legs and arms landed on top of him.

He couldn't hear anything at first—just the drumming of his own pulse and the hiss of air trying to get back into his chest. He wanted to look up, to see the end zone marker, but all he could do was lie there, gathering the pieces of himself, while the stadium sound slowly filtered back: at first a single note of hope, then a rising, ecstatic scream.

Hands pulled at his shoulders, rolled him over. His helmet was askew, chinstrap digging into his throat. Above him, for one perfect instant, was the sky, deep blue and endless, shot through with the stadium lights. He blinked, and then Mark Hughes was there, looming, face covered in mud and blood and pure joy.

"You did it!" Mark shouted, yanking him upright.

Mathew wobbled to his knees, the ball still clutched in a death grip, and looked behind him. The line judge was running in, arms up, signal clear: touchdown.

All around, the world was noise and color and electricity. The home sideline erupted, players pouring onto the field, coaches hugging, water bottles flying. Mathew felt the pain in his ribs, the scrape of turf burn down his arm, the dizzying relief that they'd actually pulled it off.

He wanted to laugh. He wanted to puke. He wanted to live in this moment forever.

He'd done it. Somehow, he'd done it.

***

The celebration was immediate and violent.

Mathew barely had time to stand before Mark crashed into him, arms wrapped tight, both of them screaming at the top of their lungs. The rest of the offense poured in, a pile of bodies crushing Mathew at the bottom, helmets thudding against pads, breath steaming into the cold night.

Mark was laughing, ugly tears streaking down his cheeks, blood from a split lip mixing with snot and sweat. "You crazy bastard!" he howled, pounding Mathew on the back. "You actually did it!"

Mathew couldn't find words, just choked out a laugh and let the others drag him upright. They circled him, every player wanting a piece of the miracle, the sideline surging in to sweep them off their feet.

The scoreboard still flashed the final score, unreal and perfect. Above the din, Mathew could hear the marching band blare the fight song, its rhythm echoing in his ears.

He looked over at Mark, saw the same wonder and disbelief reflected there.

For the first time all season, Mark looked like a kid again—no fear, no anger, just raw joy.

They stood together in the middle of the field, the noise of the crowd rolling over them, and for a little while, the world was nothing but light and sound.

***

After the field cleared and the lights began to cool, the friends found each other under the aluminum overhang by the concession stands. The air still buzzed with leftover adrenaline and the sweet, sticky smell of spilled soda. They clustered around a battered picnic table, Mathew slumped at one end with a bag of ice pressed to his ribs, everyone else talking at once.

"I told you," Josephine said, brandishing her program like a legal brief. "I called it. The left side was wide open. All they had to do was listen to me."

Jimmy laughed so hard he nearly choked on his hot dog. "You screamed like a banshee, Jo. Mathew would've had to be deaf not to hear you."

"She's got a point, though," William added, sipping from a bottle of orange Gatorade. "It's the only time all night they left the edge uncovered."

Robert grinned, eyes still lit up from the game. "I can't believe you survived, man. That hit at the end—" He shook his head in admiration. "Do you even have bones left, or did they all turn to jello?"

"Shut up," Mathew groaned, but he was smiling, even as the bruise bloomed dark along his jaw.

Samantha perched beside him, bumping his shoulder with her own. "He's fine. He's basically a cockroach. Indestructible." She beamed, then turned to the group. "You were all amazing. Even you, Jimmy."

Jimmy flexed his biceps and tried to mimic Mathew's last-second leap, almost knocking over a row of empty cups. "Next time, just give me the ball," he crowed, "and I'll run it in myself."

The group dissolved into laughter, easy and familiar. They recounted every detail of the play—who had seen what, who had missed what, who had already forgotten the rest of the season in the glow of a single, perfect moment.

Josephine leaned over and ruffled Samantha's hair. "Told you not to worry," she said, softer now. "With all of us around, you're untouchable."

Samantha rolled her eyes, but let the words sit there, warm and comforting.

For a while, they just sat, letting the night deepen and the stadium empty around them. The only sounds were the hum of the distant streetlamps and the soft murmur of their own voices.

Eventually, Mathew stood, wincing. "Same time next week?" he said, the old joke, even though they all knew the season was over.

"Always," said William, and the others nodded.

They walked off together, heads bowed against the chill, steps in sync. For the first time in a long time, nothing felt fragile or temporary. They were simply there, together, untouchable.

None of them knew it, but it was one of the last easy nights they'd ever share.

***

The five of them made their way across the gravel lot, sneakers crunching in rhythm, the stadium now a distant glow behind them. Overhead, the sky was cloudless, stars sharp and white, the moon hanging low enough to touch. The air was cool, but none of them seemed to feel it.

They walked in a loose formation, laughter trailing behind them in fading echoes. Every few steps, one would nudge another, sling an arm over a shoulder, or share a look that said, "We did it, and nothing can take that away."

For a while, they talked about nothing at all—what movie to see tomorrow, who was bringing snacks to study hall, and whether the bakery near the square would be open for breakfast. Their voices were soft and aimless, unhurried, like the world would wait as long as they wanted.

Near the end of the block, they stopped beneath a streetlight. The yellow glow painted their faces with shadows, and for a moment, it was as if they stood at the center of the universe.

Samantha looked at her brother and her friends and said, "Let's never change, okay?"

Mathew laughed, but didn't say anything. No one did. They didn't need to.

They walked on, deeper into the heart of Savannah, the night folding gently around them.

Behind them, the empty stadium hummed with the memory of victory.

Ahead, the city waited—full of promise, and danger, and things that could never be undone.

But for now, they belonged to each other, and to the bright, perfect moment they'd made.

CHAPTER 2

The final bell at Habersham Middle School was not so much a sound as a full-body event—a dull, pneumatic hiss followed by the slamming of a hundred steel lockers and a thousand sneakers stampeding down the waxed linoleum. It was May of 1991, and the air outside was thick enough to taste. The grounds around the main entrance became a churning soup of children in oversized T-shirts, girls with high ponytails, boys in mesh shorts, all scrambling for the buses or the freedom of the soccer fields beyond.

Robert Dean, age twelve and running slightly behind schedule, shouldered his backpack more tightly as he threaded through the crowd. He kept his head low, hair wet with sweat, conscious of the redness still burning at the tips of his ears. The others—Mathew, William, Jimmy, and even Josephine—tracked his progress with practiced orbit, drifting closer or further according to the invisible tides of middle school social danger.

None of them spoke for the first minute. Jimmy walked with fists jammed so deep in his pockets the denim was liable to tear, face locked in a scowl that dared anyone to meet his eye. William trailed at the rear, eyes darting along the perimeter for threats—jocks, teachers, his own brother, whatever. Mathew moved like a shadow just over Robert's left shoulder, silent but coiled. Josephine flanked Robert on the other side, expression tight as wire.

They reached the bike racks before anyone broke the silence. Jimmy kicked a crushed Fanta can into the gutter and spat. "Stupid assholes," he muttered.

William shot him a look. "You want to get grounded again? Keep saying that word."

"I'm not talking about you, genius," Jimmy said. "I'm talking about Kessler and his goon squad."

"I know who you're talking about," William replied, but his voice was lower now.

Robert knelt to unlock his battered Huffy, the padlock combination fighting him the whole way. He felt the group close ranks around him, blocking the view from the gym exit where Kessler and his friends liked to make a show of 'disciplining' sixth graders with basketballs and the occasional handful of mulch.

Mathew finally spoke, soft but insistent. "Let's just get out of here. If we take the alley behind the gym, we can skip the main drag."

Josephine glared at the building, then back at Robert. "That was bullshit," she said. "You didn't even do anything."

"I know," Robert replied, yanking the lock open with a wet snap.

"You should have told Principal Raines the truth," she pressed, voice rising. "That Kessler swapped the slides, that it was all a setup. It wasn't even your microscope. It's not fair."

Mathew shot her a look, half warning, half sympathy. "Like Raines would have listened. He never listens to us."

Robert shrugged. "It doesn't matter. I got in school suspension for one period, that's it. I don't care."

"You're full of shit," Jimmy said, but not unkindly. He thumped the handlebars with his palm. "You care. Everybody cares."

They turned as one, moving as a single, lopsided organism down the cracked sidewalk. The after-school sun turned the pavement into a griddle; the air hummed with the cicadas that lived in the live oaks lining the street. They passed the line of buses, their diesel engines chuffing clouds of gray, then cut across the old tennis courts, avoiding the bottleneck where teachers herded the last stragglers.

Mathew's voice was barely audible over the din. "We should have done something," he said.

Jimmy bristled. "Like what, Matt? Go punch out a bunch of eighth graders? Great plan."

"They stole your notebook, Robert. Then they got you blamed for cheating. And nobody said shit." Josephine's words hit with the precision of a dart. "We all just stood there."

William kept his eyes down. "It's not like it matters. Once you're labeled a narc, you're screwed. Just makes you a bigger target."

Robert wanted to argue, to insist he didn't care, but the flush on his neck said otherwise. He remembered the laughter in the science room when the teacher found the doctored slides—how the older boys smiled at each other, already immune from consequence. He'd never even touched the microscope. But the look on Mrs. Cross's face, the slow disappointment, had hurt more than any punch could.

He pedaled harder, trying to outpace the shame.

Josephine jogged ahead and spun, blocking the narrow trail. She grabbed Mathew's sleeve. "You're the leader. You should have said something. They would have listened to you."

Mathew's jaw flexed. He looked at Robert, then back at the ground. "It's not about being a leader. It's about not making things worse."

"Well, you failed at both," Josephine snapped.

Jimmy snorted and stepped between them. "I don't know what's dumber: thinking Matt could fix it, or thinking Kessler would ever let us off the hook." He jabbed a finger at Josephine. "You don't even get it. You're barely with us half the time."

She recoiled, stung.

William, voice even and calm, tried to cut through. "Nobody could have done anything. It's just how school is."

"That's such bullshit," Josephine said, quiet now. "If you don't fight back, they just keep pushing."

"Yeah," Jimmy said, "and then you get your head shoved in a toilet, and they push harder. It's called escalation."

Robert slowed his bike, wheels hissing on the loose gravel. "Can we just drop it?" he asked.

No one did. They walked in silence another block, the heat and resentment curdling between them.

At the end of the street, Mathew stopped, hand raised like a crossing guard. "Wait," he said, scanning the intersection. There was no traffic, just a dog barking somewhere out of sight and the distant, brittle sound of a screen door slamming.

"We can cut through the field," he said. "If we stay low, nobody'll see us."

Nobody argued. They slipped behind a chain-link fence, past the clotted runoff ditch, and into the unkempt baseball diamond that separated the school from the tract housing beyond. The grass was knee-high in places, and gnats swarmed their faces as they walked. Robert dismounted and pushed his bike through the thicket, chain ticking quietly.

No one spoke. The anger was spent, replaced by a slow-burning helplessness that felt like swallowing a mouthful of cold oil. Robert was glad for the silence; it let him hide the way his hands trembled, the way his heart kicked at the thought of facing his father with a "disciplinary notice" for cheating. He thought about the teacher's frown, the snicker of Kessler and the others, and the empty helplessness of being outnumbered, outgunned, and always one mistake from disaster.

Mark broke the silence first. "You know, my brother says that if you hit a guy hard enough with a bike lock, he'll never mess with you again."

William made a face. "Yeah, until you get arrested. Great advice, genius."

"It worked for him," Mark said.

Josephine rolled her eyes. "How many times has your brother been expelled?"

Mark shrugged. "Four, but that's not the point."

"The point is," Mathew said, "nobody's fighting anyone. Not unless there's no other choice."

William looked at Mathew, thoughtful. "So what do we do next time?"

Mathew considered, then glanced at Robert. "We watch each other's backs. That's it."

They reached the far side of the field, a break in the fence opening onto an overgrown path. For the first time since the bell, Robert felt the tension ease. There were no teachers or bullies out here, just the smell of cut grass and the low hum of insects.

"Fine," Mark said, "but if I catch Kessler alone, I'm breaking his nose."

"Just make sure he doesn't break yours first," William replied.

They laughed, sharp and quick, the sound peeling away the last of the day's dread.

Josephine turned to Robert, her expression gentle. "Sorry for yelling. I just hate it when bad things happen to good people."

Robert managed a smile. "Thanks. Next time I'll try not to be so good."

They walked on, the group slowly untangling, the wound already scabbing over. Behind them, the shouts and slamming lockers faded, replaced by the wind threading through the grass and the distant, constant promise of summer.

***

The shortcut through the fields spat the group onto Atlantic Avenue, an uneven run of cracked sidewalk lined by battered mailboxes and the skeletal remains of hurricane-bent azaleas. Jimmy led the pack, every stride telegraphing aggression, shoulders hunched up to his ears. Robert wheeled his bike beside him, silent, and trailed by Josephine, whose arms windmilled as she talked, arguing points with the ferocity of a trial attorney. William and Mathew lagged a few steps behind, lost in the perimeter.

The air was sweet with the sick rot of magnolia blossoms, the humidity welding their shirts to their skin. Midges swarmed around the storm drains, and the steady drone of lawnmowers rose from the depths of the neighborhood, cutting through the late-afternoon haze. The group moved as a loose flotilla, drawn together by momentum and the gravitational pull of shared outrage.

"I'm just saying," Mark said, pitching his voice above the slap of his sneakers on the pavement, "if we let guys like Kessler get away with it, they're gonna do it again. And next time it's not gonna be a science prank, it'll be something worse."

Josephine pointed a finger at him. "So your answer is to beat him up? That's your big plan?"

Mark stopped walking and spun to face her. "It worked for my brother. Nobody messes with him anymore. Ever. Sometimes violence is the only language people understand."

William, who'd been cataloging the houses as they passed (every one a subtle variation of beige, with the same low-pitched roof and the same sun-faded shutters), piped up. "That's not how it works, Mark. If you hit someone, you just get hit back. Or worse, you get caught. And then your life is over."

Mark scoffed. "Better than being a punching bag for the rest of your life."

Mathew said nothing, just watched the debate ping-pong back and forth, lips pressed into a straight line. He always listened first, as if he were taking notes for a future cross-examination.

Robert walked a half-step behind, head down, hands white-knuckled on the handlebars. He looked up long enough to say, "You guys remember how, when that kid last year got suspended for fighting, nobody even talked to him after? Like, he was invisible."

"I remember," William said. "He ate lunch by the dumpsters for three weeks."

Josephine jabbed at the air. "See? The system is rigged. Doesn't matter if you're right or wrong, you lose either way." She kicked at a rock, watched it skip into a puddle. "But at least if you do something, you don't have to sit around and take it. I'm sick of taking it."

"I'm not scared of Kessler," Mark said, flexing his hands like he was already wrapping them around the other kid's neck.

"You're scared of his friends," William countered. "And you should be. There are six of them."

"Yeah, well, there's six of us, too," Jimmy snapped. "If you count Samantha and Jo."

Josephine's nostrils flared. "Don't lump us in with your cowardly revenge fantasies. Matt is right."

Mark shrugged. "Maybe, but I bet he'd want somebody to stand up for him if it happened."

The argument built and built, each line sharper than the last, until Mathew finally broke in. He didn't raise his voice, just spoke with a calm that quieted the rest. "We can talk about what to do next time, but right now we need to get Robert home before his dad finds out."

Josephine turned on him, hands on her hips. "So you're just going to let it go?"

Mathew met her gaze, unblinking. "What else do you want me to do? I'm not the principal. I'm not his dad. I'm just trying to make sure we don't all end up in the office tomorrow."

Robert was grateful for the change of subject, but the words stung anyway. He wanted to tell them all that it didn't matter, that nothing they did ever changed anything. That the world was just a series of humiliations you learned to swallow, one after another, until you graduated and maybe got to be the one doing the humiliating. But he couldn't make his mouth work, not with everyone watching.

They turned down a side street, the houses thinning out, yards growing shaggier, until the road ended at a chain-link fence and a tangle of pine woods beyond. The air was cooler here, shaded by the long-needled canopy, and the only sound was the distant caw of a crow and the slap of Mathew's hand against the metal fence.

He stopped, turned to the others. "You want to fight about it all day, or do you want to actually do something?" He gestured at the woods. "We can go to the clearing. Figure it out there."

Jimmy and William exchanged a glance. Josephine rolled her eyes but climbed the fence first, quick and practiced. Robert hesitated, but then Mathew was there, steadying the bike as he handed it over, offering a boost. No words, just the simple mechanics of teamwork.

They dropped into the woods together, the neighborhood and its codes of conduct fading behind them. The argument lingered, raw and unfinished, hanging over their heads like the Spanish moss strung from the branches. For a moment, nobody knew what to say.

Then Jimmy found a stick and started hacking at the underbrush, carving a path. William followed, ducking under a low bough. Josephine muttered something about "idiots" but kept pace, and Mathew brought up the rear, glancing back at Robert just once, as if to say: Are you okay?

Robert nodded. He wasn't, not really. But it was better out here, among the needles and the dirt and the absence of authority, than anywhere else in the world.

***

The path into the woods started as a deer trail and then vanished under the soft crush of pine needles. Each step was muffled, the air already cooler and shaded, the sun diced into fragments by the tall pines overhead. The group followed Mathew single file, the order less a matter of decision than gravity, each person falling into their assigned place like marbles in a groove.

They'd only been in the trees for a minute before the sounds of the neighborhood—the grind of lawnmowers, the drone of mosquitoes, even the distant thud of basketballs on driveway hoops—evaporated, replaced by the layered hush of the woods. A breeze carried the faint sour-sweet of marsh, and the only constant was the dry hiss of cicadas and the crackle of cones underfoot.

Mark walked point behind Mathew, every few steps turning to see if the others were keeping up, now carrying a stick as a makeshift sword. He occasionally whacked it against a trunk just to watch the bark flake off in chunks. Josephine and William, with William keeping an eye on Jimmy, as he felt responsible for his younger brother. They moved together, less as friends and more as adversaries locked in a temporary truce, both still simmering from the sidewalk argument but, for now, content to focus on the path. Robert drifted at the rear, bike left at the fence, arms crossed over his chest, and eyes darting everywhere but at his friends.

Mathew never looked back, just pressed forward with the patient, dogged confidence of someone who'd grown up in these woods. When the trail forked, he picked the left, always left, and the others followed.

The silence was companionable, not awkward, the type that only existed among people who'd spent entire summers together inventing games and rules that changed by the hour. Occasionally, a low branch would slap someone in the face, and the person behind would stifle a laugh, but nobody said much.

After five minutes, the path gave way to a strip of hard-packed dirt hemmed in by palmettos and Spanish moss, which hung so low in places you had to duck. At one such spot, William stopped and pressed a moss curtain aside, holding it for the others. "It's like walking through a haunted house," he said.

Mark snorted. "Haunted houses don't have real ghosts. These woods do."

Josephine rolled her eyes, but there was a faint smile tucked at the corner of her mouth. "Ghosts are just stories parents tell, so you don't wander too far," she said.

Mark brandished the stick at her. "Says the girl who cries at Friday the 13th."

She batted it away. "That's different. Those are movies. This is real life."

Robert said nothing, but watched them with the detached interest of a scientist observing test animals.

The world under the trees felt older, more complicated. Roots crossed the trail like veins, and fat banana spiders hung at eye-level, their webs shimmering in the angled light. Every now and then, a lizard would dart across their path and vanish into the leaves.

They reached the midpoint, a stretch where the pines grew in perfect ranks, forming a kind of cathedral. Here, Mathew slowed, and the others fell into a loose semi-circle around him. The argument from before was gone, replaced by a different energy—a quiet mutual recognition that out here, the rules shifted.

Mathew bent down and scooped up a smooth, oval rock, then lobbed it at a stump. "You ever think about how nobody can touch us out here?" he said, not looking at anyone.

Josephine considered, then nodded. "Yeah. It's like being invisible."

Mark added, "Or untouchable."

Robert finally spoke, voice soft. "We're never really untouchable."

William shot him a glance, but didn't contradict him.

For a long minute, the group just stood there, breathing in the woody air, letting the heat of the day slip away. The feeling of being followed, of being hunted by older kids, teachers, or whatever, faded with each step deeper into the woods. They belonged here, in this patch of wildness.

After a while, Mathew picked up the pace again, and the others followed, the mood lighter now. They even talked a little, the earlier wounds scabbed over by the ritual of the walk.

The clearing was close. They all felt it, the unspoken anticipation of reaching their spot. For a moment, even the burdens of the day felt lighter.

***

The clearing was exactly as they'd left it the week before: a rough oval gouged out of the bramble, ringed by scrubby palmetto and one ancient live oak that looked like it had been struck by lightning at least once in every decade. The floor was pounded flat from years of foot traffic, the dirt scuffed and streaked with the ghosts of stick fights and aborted bonfires.

In the center, a log served as a bench, mottled with lichen and chewed at the ends by insects. Someone—Mark, probably—had wedged a two-by-four into the fork of a tree and declared it a "sniper's perch," though none of them had ever managed to balance on it for more than a minute without tumbling off. A circle of flat rocks, blackened by past attempts at campfire-building, marked the unofficial council chamber.

The group emerged from the green tunnel and dropped their burdens: Mathew first, setting his backpack gently on the log, followed by Josephine, who unslung her battered canvas book bag and flopped onto the dirt with a sigh. Jimmy let his load fall, then grabbed a half-rotten branch and started whittling at it with his pocketknife. William found a seat on the edge of the log, picking at a splinter in his thumb. Robert stood for a second on the periphery before perching on the lowest limb of the oak, sneakers swinging.

For a while, nobody spoke. They just took up positions; the choreography of arrival so practiced it needed no discussion.

Josephine opened a can of Coke, the snap of the tab cutting the hush. "Okay," she said, "here's what I don't get. If everyone knows Kessler's a liar, how come he never gets in trouble?" She didn't wait for an answer. "It's like the teachers want him to get away with it. Or they're just scared."

William snorted. "Teachers aren't scared. They're lazy. It's easier to blame us than figure out who really did it."

Mark jabbed the knife into the wood for emphasis. "They're scared of his dad. You know he's on the school board, right? That's how you get away with anything—be the rich kid."

Mathew picked at the seam of his backpack, eyes on the ground. "Doesn't matter who's on the board. Nobody listens to us anyway. We're just kids."

Robert, from his branch, said, "It's like being invisible until you mess up. Then everyone sees you." He said it quietly, almost to himself, but the words hung in the air.

Mark made a show of ignoring the heaviness, turning to William. "You ever think about what would happen if we just beat the crap out of him? Like, actually did it? Not for fun, but to make it stop?"

William looked at him, skeptical. "We'd get expelled. Our parents would kill us. Yours would probably throw you a parade, but the rest of us would be screwed."

Josephine picked up a pinecone and rolled it in her palm. "Maybe that's what it takes. Maybe if someone fought back, people would stop letting him do whatever he wants."

"Or maybe," Mathew said, "he'd just find new ways to make our lives hell. Bullies always have backup plans."

Mark grinned, showing a row of teeth. "I could take him. You give me one shot, and I'd lay him out. He cries when he gets hit. You can see it in his face."

William rolled his eyes. "Congratulations. You want a trophy for imaginary fights?"

Mark hurled the stick into the underbrush, where it landed with a dry snap. "I just want it to stop."

Mathew finally looked up. "It doesn't stop. Not really. But maybe we can figure out how to make it less bad."

Josephine tossed the pinecone into the fire ring. "How?"

Mathew shrugged. "We stick together. They can't get all of us at once."

Robert dropped from the branch and landed with a soft thud. "What if they do? What if they come after our families?"

"Then we make sure we're there for each other," Mathew said, voice steady. "That's the only thing we control."

They all fell silent, considering this.

William, who'd been quietest, cleared his throat. "My dad says people always make promises they can't keep. Like, they mean it, but then when stuff actually happens, they bail." He said it with the matter-of-factness of someone who'd watched it play out too many times.

Josephine looked at him, something like sympathy flickering in her eyes. "We're not like that."

William shrugged, but didn't push it.

For a few minutes, the group sat in the sun-dappled hush, picking at the log or tracing shapes in the dirt. The space around them felt like a fortress, the outside world unable to penetrate its walls.

Mark found another stick and started stripping it of bark. "We could make a rule," he said. "Like, if you mess with one of us, you mess with all of us. No matter what."

Josephine nodded, brightening. "Like a pact. Or a contract."

Robert sat cross-legged, thinking. "What happens if someone breaks it?"

Mark didn't hesitate. "You get exiled. No more games, no more secret paths, nothing."

William grinned. "That's harsh."

Mark grinned back. "So's getting blamed for stuff you didn't do."

They all laughed, the sound bouncing off the ring of trees and out into the wider woods.

The debate was not over, not really. But for now, the rules of engagement were suspended. They sat together in the clearing, as they always had, the log, the dirt, and the sun their only witnesses.

***

The idea of a pact took shape as soon as it was spoken. Mark was first to seize it, eyes narrowed, voice taking on the husky cadence of a preacher or a drill sergeant. "No more going solo. We see something happen, we act. Doesn't matter if it's in the halls, the lunchroom, or out here. If you mess with one, you mess with all."

He slammed a fist into his open palm, splattering sap and dirt. The others watched, expressions flickering between skepticism and curiosity.

William was the first to challenge. "What if someone does something stupid?" he said, rubbing at the splinter in his thumb. "Like, what if you're the one who starts the fight and the rest of us just get dragged in? It's not fair."

Mark looked at him with genuine incredulity. "Why would I start a fight unless it was for a reason?"

William gave him a flat stare. "You started three last week, and one was because someone called your sneakers fake."

"They were calling me fake," Mark shot back. "There's a difference."

Josephine stretched her legs, dusting pine needles from her jeans. "The point is, what happens if it's not fair? If one of us screws up and expects everyone else to bail them out?"

Mark rolled his eyes. "So what, we just sit around and let people walk all over us? What's the point of being friends, then?"

Robert, still picking at the bark of a stick, said, "You ever notice how people promise to have your back, but then when it gets bad, nobody shows? Like, my neighbor's parents used to be best friends, but when they lost their house, nobody even brought food. They just stopped talking."

Josephine nodded. "People are scared. Or lazy. Or maybe they just don't know what to say."

William snorted. "Or they just don't care."

Mathew had been listening the whole time, gaze drifting over the arc of the clearing. "It's not about caring or not. It's about what you're willing to risk. Sometimes, sticking up for someone means you take the hit, too."

Mark thumped his stick on the ground. "Exactly! That's what I'm saying. If you're in, you're in."

William looked at Mathew. "Would you get suspended for Mark? Even if it wasn't your fault?"

Mathew didn't answer right away. He stared at the dirt, then at the sky, as if calculating the odds. "I don't know," he said. "Maybe. If it was for something that mattered."

Mark grinned. "See? Loyalty."

Josephine wasn't buying it. "That's not loyalty. That's gambling."

Mark rolled his eyes. "Whatever. I'd rather take a risk than be a coward."

Josephine flushed. "You're not a coward if you don't want to get expelled. You're just not an idiot."

Robert shrugged, voice barely above a whisper. "Sometimes it's easier just to let things happen and hope it's not you next time."

There was a long silence. Even the cicadas seemed to have paused, waiting to see how the debate would shake out.

William spoke again, softer this time. "My dad always says, 'People only care as much as it costs them.' Like, everyone has a line they won't cross."

Mark frowned. "So we're just supposed to accept it? Just let people walk all over us?"

Mathew finally sat up straight, pulling his knees to his chest. "We're not saying that. We're just saying—maybe think before you drag everyone else into your mess."

Mark kicked at the dirt, sending a spray of needles into the air. "You sound like my mom. 'Think before you act.' You know what happens to people who think too much? They never do anything."

Josephine said, "At least they don't get everyone else expelled."

Mark glared at her, then at William, then at the rest of the group. "Whatever. I'm still in."

Robert looked at Mathew. "What about you?"

Mathew hesitated, then nodded. "I'm in, too. But only if it's for something real. Not shoes. Not stupid pranks. Real stuff."

Josephine let out a slow breath. "That's fair. I'm in, too. But if anyone tries to start a fight over something dumb, I'm out."

They all looked at William.

He shrugged. "Fine. But if we all end up dead in a ditch because Jimmy can't keep his mouth shut, I'm haunting you."

Mark barked a laugh, the tension breaking for a moment.

For a while, they just sat, the pact unspoken but settled. The sun was lower now, the shadows longer, the air sweet and a little less oppressive.

Mathew picked up a pinecone and tossed it at the fire ring. "So what do we call it?"

Nobody had an answer.

***

For a while, the question hung between them, tugging at the loose ends of their earlier arguments. Jimmy was content to poke at the dirt and hum something tuneless. Josephine chewed the edge of a fingernail, eyes distant. William traced circles with his sneaker in the pine needles, careful never to look anyone in the eye. Robert, stick in hand, drew and redrew the same pattern in the dust, as if rehearsing for a spelling bee he'd never attend.

Mathew let the silence settle, the way his father did when he wanted a point to really land. He looked up at the branches overhead, sunlight leaking through in cold white slivers, then back at his friends.

"I don't care what we call it," he said finally, "but it needs to mean something." The words were even, not dramatic. "Not just some joke. Not 'til we forget about it next week."

Mark grinned, ready to crack wise, but Mathew's face stopped him.

"I just…" Mathew started, then stopped, searching for the right words. "What happened today sucked. And it's probably gonna happen again, to one of us. Or maybe all of us. Maybe worse next time."

He looked at each of them in turn.

"I don't want to go through that alone," he said. "And I don't want any of you to, either."

Nobody spoke. Even Mark was quiet.

"So," Mathew continued, "the rule is: nobody faces real trouble by themselves. Doesn't matter if it's teachers, bullies, whatever. If it's serious, we show up. No excuses."

William frowned. "What's 'serious'?"

Mathew shrugged. "We'll know. If it feels like you need backup, you get it."

Josephine blinked, then nodded, a small smile breaking through. "That's fair."

Mark's voice was low, but steady. "Even if it's not our fight?"

Mathew looked at him. "If it's yours, it's ours."

The idea seemed to thrum in the air, charged and real. Robert stopped drawing in the dirt and wiped his hands on his shorts, eyes locked on the ground. He didn't say anything, but he was listening.

For a few minutes, the only sound was the cicadas, building to a fever pitch. Then William said, "Okay. But we still need a name."

Mark laughed, tension gone. "What, like 'The Justice League'?"

Josephine rolled her eyes. "That's lame. We're not superheroes."

Mathew smiled, just a little. "Doesn't matter what it's called. It just matters that we do it."

They all nodded, the decision made.

And just like that, the pact was real.

***

It wasn't until the pact was spoken, and the group sat marinating in the weight of their new rule, that Mathew reached for his backpack. He unzipped the largest pocket and pulled out something wrapped in a faded hand towel. Jimmy craned his neck to see, ready with a joke about secret weapons or smuggled lunch, but what Mathew placed on the log was even weirder: a squat, battered lantern, metal frame rusted in places, the glass sooty and warped by age.

William squinted. "Is that your dad's?"

Mathew nodded, wiping at the smudged glass with the towel. "He never uses it. Says it's too heavy for real camping."

Josephine grinned, the seriousness of the last few minutes dissolving. "You lugged that all the way here just in case we needed to build a lighthouse?"

Mathew shrugged. "Thought it looked cool. Like something you'd use for a secret meeting." He set it carefully on the stump at the center of the clearing, adjusting it until it stood straight and true.

Mark poked at it. "Does it even work?"

Mathew ignored the bait, twisted the knob, and produced a book of matches. He struck one with practiced efficiency, shielding the tiny flame from the wind with his cupped hand. The matchhead flared, sulfur sharp in the air. He touched it to the lantern's wick, and for a moment nothing happened, then the flame caught and grew, filling the lantern with a muted orange glow.

The effect was immediate and dramatic. The late sun was dropping fast, shadows flooding the clearing, but the lantern threw a circle of warmth over the log and the fire ring, painting the group's faces in shifting amber and shadow.

For a few seconds, nobody said a word.

Then Josephine spoke, softer than before. "It looks… official."

Mark nodded, voice uncharacteristically subdued. "Like a campfire, but way better."

Robert leaned in, the light flickering over his glasses. "We should make it the centerpiece. Every time we meet."

William, unable to resist, quipped, "Every club needs a relic."

Mathew just smiled, setting the matches beside the lantern. "From now on, it's our signal. When it's lit, the rule is in effect. Nobody stands alone."

The others nodded, understanding that the game had changed, even if they couldn't quite articulate how.

As dusk pressed in, the lantern's light drew them close, until the woods outside the clearing seemed a million miles away.

***

The lantern's orange heart flickered against the coming dark, drawing the boys in like moths. At first, they sat scattered around the clearing, but little by little they inched closer to the stump, drawn by the heat and the novelty of a real, working flame.

Mark was first to slide off the log and kneel by the lantern, elbows on knees, face lit up like he was warming himself by a campfire. Josephine edged in next, cross-legged, hair haloed in gold. William and Robert took spots opposite each other, feet nearly touching the base of the stump. Mathew hung back for a moment, then joined, forming the last link in a ring that felt accidental and inevitable all at once.

It was only then, with all of them circled tight around the light, that they noticed what they'd done. No one laughed. No one called it cheesy. The woods pressed in around them, their voices stilled by the weight of the new rule and the glow at its center.

For a long minute, they just sat. The air smelled of old oil and burnt wick and something sharp—maybe a pine bough dropped onto the hot metal. Shadows fluttered across their faces, carving out cheekbones and brows, turning them from kids into something older, harder.

When Mathew finally spoke, it was barely more than a whisper. "If we're going to do this, we do it right. We don't quit. We don't bail."

Mark nodded, his jaw set. "Swear on it."

The circle tightened, the lantern's glow reflected in every eye.

They were ready.

***

Mathew reached out first, his palm hovering over the lantern's steel frame. He paused, feeling the radiant heat, then set his hand down, careful not to flinch. The warm metal bit at his skin, grounding him in the moment.

"I promise," he said, voice clear and firm. "If any of us needs help—real help, not just dumb stuff—I'll be there. Even if it's scary, or it sucks, or we get in trouble. I won't bail."

The others watched, expressions unreadable in the shifting glow.

Mark, never one for ceremony, went next. He slapped his palm on the lantern with a clank. "Me too. Even if we gotta fight someone, or run from the cops, or whatever. No backing down." He tried to sound tough, but his hand trembled slightly on the metal.

William followed, more cautious, fingertips barely grazing the frame. "I'll do it. I mean, I'll try. I'm not a fighter, but I'll show up even if I'm scared. That's the rule, right?"

Robert hesitated, then pressed his hand down, knuckles white. "I swear. I won't disappear. Not if it's important." The last two words came out cracked, but nobody mocked him.

Jimmy, just thrilled to be included with the older kids, hesitantly put his hand on the lantern and simply said, "I promise".

Josephine went last, wrapping both hands around the lantern's handle, as if willing its heat into her bones. "I swear too. No matter what. Even if everyone else turns on you, I'll stand up."

They sat like that for a moment, all hands on the lantern, the heat and the glow fusing them together in ways they didn't have words for.

When they let go, the metal frame was left smudged by fingerprints, marked by the promise of five kids who, for one brief second, believed in something more than themselves.

The woods were nearly black now, and the lantern's flame burned with renewed life, haloing the circle in a shield of light.

***

After the last hand left the lantern, the group fell back into their seats, a hush settling over the clearing. The ritual was over, but the feeling it left behind clung like sweat on a humid night.

Mathew, face half in shadow, was the first to speak. "From now on, the lantern stays in the middle. Doesn't matter who's here or what we're doing—it stays lit until we all leave. That way, nobody has to be alone."

Nobody argued. Even Mark, who would have usually called it dumb, just nodded and picked at the dirt.

William broke the silence, trying to undercut the seriousness with a grin. "What, so if we come back and it's out, that means the world's ending?"

Mathew shrugged. "Or that someone broke the pact."

That got a low whistle from Robert, who wiped his palms on his shorts, as if to scrub off the gravity of what they'd just done.

Josephine hugged her knees to her chest, watching the lantern. "It should have a name," she said. "Like a code. Or a password."

Mark snorted. "How about 'the fire that never goes out'? Sounds dramatic enough."

William groaned. "Way too long. Call it 'The Light' and be done with it."

They argued for a few minutes, the way kids do—no winner, just noise. But the lantern remained, undimmed, the rule now a living thing at the center of their world.

As they started to gather their things, Josephine reached over and nudged the lantern, watching the light wobble. "You think we'll really keep the promise?" she asked, voice low.

Mathew looked at her, then at the others, then back at the heart of the flame. "I do," he said. "We have to."

And for the first time that day, it felt possible.

***

It was nearly full dark when Mathew reached out and, with a slow breath, snuffed the lantern's flame. The clearing collapsed instantly into shadows, the heat and glow replaced by the chill of oncoming night.

Nobody moved at first, eyes adjusting, nerves jangling from the sudden drop in brightness.

Then, one by one, they grabbed their bags, brushed the needles off their clothes, and shuffled back onto the path. The circle was broken, but the line of friends that filed out of the clearing felt tighter, more solid, each step echoing the promise they'd just made.

Mathew led the way, lantern tucked under one arm, the others falling in behind, careful not to let the person ahead slip too far into the dark.

The woods closed over their heads, alive with the sounds of frogs and distant cars and things that didn't care about pacts or promises. But somewhere behind them, in the black heart of the clearing, the scent of burnt wick and melted oil lingered, a ghost of the light that, for one afternoon, made them more than just scared kids with nowhere else to go.

***

They emerged from the woods into the yellow wash of a streetlight, the sudden illumination flattening the wildness out of their faces and painting them as just five tired, hungry kids on the edge of curfew. The hush of the pines gave way to the drone of sprinklers and the barking of a distant dog. Somewhere down the block, a porch TV flickered through a window, broadcasting the tail end of the Braves game. The world outside the clearing was the same as it had ever been, but the group walked with new gravity, the silence between them less awkward and more earned.

They didn't talk much on the way home. Mark cut off at the first cross street, muttering something about leftovers and a promise to see everyone tomorrow. William and Jimmy split next, veering toward the row of duplexes with a casual wave. Robert peeled away without a word, hands shoved in his pockets, head full of calculations. Only Mathew and Josephine walked the last block together, the lantern dangling from Mathew's hand, glass still warm.

At her corner, Josephine stopped and looked at the ground, scuffing a toe against the curb. "You think the others will keep it?" she asked.

Mathew thought about it. About the way Mark's hand shook when he made the promise, or the way William's voice cracked, or how Robert couldn't quite look anyone in the eye.

"They'll try," he said.

She smiled, not quite convinced. "You always think you can fix everything, Matt."

Mathew shrugged. "Doesn't hurt to try."

She lingered for a second, then hurried up her driveway, porch light blinking on as she reached the steps. Mathew stood in the street until she went inside, then started his own slow trek home, the lantern swinging at his side like a secret only he knew.

Behind him, the woods faded into silhouette. Tomorrow, the clearing would be just another patch of dirt and weeds. The pact might be forgotten, or it might not. But for now, the circle had held, and that was enough.

None of them realized how much it would matter someday, or how far the promise would travel before finally breaking.

Once lit, the light was not so easy to put out.

CHAPTER 3

The lobby of the auditorium was dense with winter coats, the air a stew of perfume, wet wool, and that uniquely Southern after-rain chill that crept up from the bricks and settled on your ankles. Parents and siblings stood in clusters near the posters, sloshing coffee in foam cups, trading nervous glances as the doors to the theater proper refused to open. The lobby itself was as Mathew remembered it—whitewashed cinderblock, bulletin boards crammed with band fundraisers and PTA bake sale flyers, the glass trophy cases smeared with the fingerprints of generations. But tonight, everything seemed downsized. He could see over most heads. Even the principal, holding court by the ticket booth, looked somehow smaller, like someone had put him through the dryer by mistake.

Mathew adjusted the collar of his suit jacket, fighting the urge to rip it off and stuff it in the coat check. His mother had insisted he wear it—"You're a Walton, you never know who might notice"—but it itched and pinched at his armpits and made him stand out among the parade of holiday sweaters and track jackets. He could already feel sweat prickling behind his ears. Two old teachers strolled by, pausing just long enough to scan the name tag pinned to his lapel (left over from his father's law firm Christmas party the night before, still sticky with residue).

He'd only been gone from Savannah for four months, but the effect was total. He felt like a ghost in a museum exhibit of his own adolescence, doomed to pace these linoleum floors forever while the rest of the world queued up for Christmas pageantry. Mathew moved toward the concession table, where a pair of band moms were unpacking Rice Krispies treats in festive cellophane. The sweets looked industrial, untouched by human hands. He considered nabbing one, but the thought of sugar and marshmallow churning in his stomach was almost enough to make him gag.

Someone called his name. He turned, scanning the lobby, and after a moment spotted Josephine Hamilton on the far side, perched on a bench beneath a spray of fake poinsettias. She wore a black peacoat over jeans, her hair shorter than he remembered—cut in a severe, almost disciplinary style that did nothing to blunt her presence. She had a book open on her lap and was reading intently, as if she'd rather miss the entire play than the next paragraph. He grinned. Some things survived even the culling power of college.

Mathew raised a hand, tried to look casual, but the gesture made him look like he was bidding on an item at an auction. Josephine glanced up, her gaze clicking to him with surgical precision, and for a second, she just blinked as if recalibrating to his existence. Then she smirked, dog-eared her page, and shouldered her way through the crowd.

A dad in a Santa hat bumped Mathew's elbow, nearly causing him to dump the entire tray of Rice Krispies onto the floor. "Sorry, chief," the man said, then disappeared into the throng. Mathew watched the crowd shuffle and knot, then slowly part as Josephine approached.

She stopped a foot away, cocked her head. "You look like you're about to be indicted," she said. "And I don't mean that as a compliment."

"Nice to see you too, Jo." He tried for breezy but landed somewhere closer to strangled. "How's Athens?"

She rolled her eyes, smiled despite herself. "Cold. Weird. There's a kid in my dorm who only eats spinach and talks to his sock puppet. I thought college would be better, but apparently it's just high school with more debt."

He nodded. "That sounds about right. The guy across the hall from me stole my razor. I'm pretty sure he uses it to shave his back."

They stood in a brief, contented silence. The energy in the lobby surged and ebbed, bits of tinny Christmas music leaking from a malfunctioning speaker in the ceiling. Josephine arched an eyebrow at Mathew's suit. "You got lost on the way to prom?"

He looked down, colored, and tugged at his sleeve. "Mom's idea."

She laughed, the sound unguarded and rich. "Moms never change."

"Neither do you," he shot back, then regretted it, fearing it sounded like an insult.

She shrugged, nonplussed. "Good. Somebody has to keep the idiots in line."

He was about to reply when a shriek of feedback silenced the crowd. A woman with a laminated badge and a headset announced that the auditorium doors would open in five minutes and asked that you please find your tickets and take your seats as soon as possible. A fresh wave of bodies surged toward the entry, parents dragging children, couples clinging together against the tide.

Josephine looked back at her bench, seemed to mourn the temporary loss of solitude, then fixed her attention on Mathew. "We should probably claim seats before the church crowd shows up."

He grinned, relieved by her decisiveness. "After you."

They fell in with the current, shoulder to shoulder, braced against the cold bite of the doors as the next phase of the evening pulled them forward.

***

Atlanta's winter had no Southern charm, only the relentless, predatory damp that slid down your neck and made you wish for the swampy heat of home. Mathew learned to keep his hands in his pockets, to walk fast between the bone-colored buildings of Emory's campus, to carry himself with a kind of loose-limbed confidence even when he was dying inside. It was a trick he picked up in his first semester, watching the upperclassmen barrel across the quad as if they owned every inch of the stone and grass.

Pre-law at Emory was not a curriculum; it was a series of controlled detonations, each one designed to destroy your faith in anything that couldn't be cited in bluebook format. The professors were ruthless, the lectures equal parts Socratic duel and blood sport. In the big, echoing classrooms, the first question of the day always had a body count. You learned to keep your answers short, your opinions armored, and your notebook open at all times.

Mathew found himself drawn less to the classes and more to the debate team, a ragged clique of insomniacs who lived on bagels, Red Bull, and the narcotic thrill of rhetorical combat. They met in the basement of the student center, a room that smelled of whiteboard dust and desperation. The walls were lined with printouts, newspaper clippings, and tattered legal pads covered in maps of argument chains. The only light came from a cluster of flickering fluorescents and the dim blue glow of laptop screens.

The first time Mathew spoke at a debate team practice, he froze. It wasn't the public speaking—he'd led more than enough group projects, read in church, even given a speech or two at rotary club dinners—but the intensity of the room was like nothing he'd felt. Every eye tracked him, hunting for the word he'd trip over. His hands shook as he shuffled his notes. He finished the round barely above water, every point scored against him burning like a slap.

But the second time, he noticed something. The best debaters didn't just recite facts or quote case law; they told stories. They wove the raw data into a narrative, laced it with just enough emotion to get under the other team's skin. They built arguments not as fortresses but as traps, luring opponents into a false sense of certainty, then springing the hinge at the perfect moment. The technical term was "rhetorical juxtaposition," but in practice it felt more like a magic trick.

Mathew started to win. First in scrimmage rounds, then in the actual competitions, where the stakes were measured in trophies and invitations to regionals. He got a reputation for being ruthless in cross-examination, not by bulldozing opponents but by letting them hang themselves—offering just enough rope and then pulling, slow and careful, until the whole structure toppled.

After the first big tournament win, his debate partner—an engineering major from Decatur—slapped him on the back so hard his teeth clicked. "You've got a killer instinct," she said, grinning. "Like a shark that realizes it's in a swimming pool."

Mathew was proud, but also embarrassed. He wondered if it was healthy to enjoy the fight this much. Sometimes he lay in bed after midnight, the walls humming with the noise of other people's lives, and tried to explain it to himself. The world ran on rules—explicit and implied—and he liked being able to see them, to find the pressure points and test the limits.

He liked the way a perfect argument could silence a room, or shift an entire panel of judges with a single phrase.

He also liked the camaraderie. The post-practice ritual was to gather at a diner just off campus, the kind where the tables stuck to your elbows and the coffee came black and endless. They'd sit for hours, dissecting the day, trading horror stories of disastrous rounds and miracle comebacks. It was here that Mathew felt most at home, the old fear of being alone replaced by a different, sharper anxiety: that if he ever let up, even for a second, the whole thing would come apart.

He never talked much about Savannah. When his friends asked, he'd give them a practiced line about coastal life and high school football, but he kept the Lantern Oath and the shadow of his own ambition buried. Still, sometimes a smell or a sound—salt air, the slow peal of a distant train—would draw him back, and he'd remember the promise made in the woods, and how much it had cost to keep it.

On the last night before winter break, the debate team war room was empty except for Mathew and the team president, a senior named Leslie who seemed to run on pure caffeine and contempt for the slow-witted. They stood at opposite ends of the long conference table, prepping for the big invitational.

Leslie leaned over a stack of printouts, voice flat. "You ever wonder if this is all just a rehearsal for the real thing?"

Mathew shrugged. "Isn't that the point? Get the arguments perfect, then go out and fix the world."

She laughed, sharp as broken glass. "Nobody fixes anything. You just learn to win faster."

Mathew thought about that as he packed up his notes, as he crossed the empty quad back to his dorm, as he lay awake listening to the rain batter the window. He wondered if that was what he wanted: to win, no matter the cost. Or if, somewhere along the line, he was supposed to find a higher purpose.

He rolled over, staring at the ceiling, and thought of the others—Jimmy, William, Robert, Josephine—and whether they felt this same pressure at the edges of their new lives.

Mathew drifted off to sleep, the ghost of an argument forming in his mind, ready to be sharpened and deployed when the time came.

***

Josephine led the way through the crush, ignoring the velvet rope and pushing past a volunteer dad who looked as though he'd been drafted at gunpoint to hand out programs. Inside the doors, the auditorium opened up—a three-tiered slope of red velour seats, the smell of fresh paint still lingering where the janitorial staff had attempted a last-minute cover-up of something that was likely unspeakable. The crowd shuffled in, guided to their seats by the nervous energy of holiday tradition.

Mathew hesitated at the threshold, but Josephine plowed ahead, picking a spot dead center and dropping her bag onto the seat with territorial aggression. She motioned for Mathew to join her, then flopped into the next chair with a practiced slouch, arms folded across her chest. She studied the stage with a faint, surgical smile, as if she'd already solved the mystery of the night.

"You ever notice," she said, voice pitched low so only Mathew could hear, "how everyone who leaves this place comes back pretending they're from somewhere else? Like two months in Atlanta makes you cosmopolitan, or Athens turns you into a poet."

Mathew grinned, settling beside her. "And two months in Athens turns you into a judgmental old lady?"

She bared her teeth. "No, that's genetics." Her gaze flicked up the aisle, then back to Mathew. "So what's the verdict? Is law school as soul-crushing as everyone says, or do you secretly love it?"

He considered. "I like the arguments. Not so much the paperwork. There's a kind of… purity in debate. Nobody can hit you except with words."

She snorted. "Only you would call that purity."

A ripple of noise came from the back, and Josephine jerked her chin, indicating a new arrival: Robert Dean, wearing a windbreaker that still had creases from the package, arms loaded with a precarious pyramid of candy canes. He navigated the steps with the caution of someone who had been burned by this very scenario in a previous life. Reaching their row, he dumped half the candy canes in Josephine's lap and nearly brained Mathew with the rest.

"Hey, hey," Robert said, breathing hard. "You know these are free, right? Nobody even checks. I could have filled a suitcase." He slid into the seat next to Mathew, brushing at a sticky red-and-white stripe on his sleeve. "Good to see you, man. You get taller?"

Mathew shook his head. "No, I think pre-med has made you shrink."

Josephine pocketed a candy cane, deadpan. "You look like you robbed a corpse at a funeral."

Robert ignored her, popping a candy into his mouth with a snap. "This is weird, right? Like, did anyone else forget half these people existed?"

Mathew scanned the crowd. It was true: almost everyone present was some version of a ghost from his past—former teachers, old teammates, the parents of kids he barely remembered. Some of them smiled and waved; others pretended not to see him; still others stared as if trying to place him in a decade-old class photo.

"Where are the others?" he asked.

Before Josephine could answer, another commotion in the aisle caught Mathew's attention. Jimmy Lee barreled in, wearing a Savannah High wrestling sweatshirt that looked like it had been slept in for a week, trailing the scent of menthol and sweat. William followed, moving with a nervous, liquid grace, hair parted so neatly it might have been glued in place. He wore a collared shirt that seemed to be fighting against his own body, the sleeves too short and the top button fastened under protest.

Jimmy spotted the group and waved, nearly decapitating a toddler with the force of his swing. "Sorry, sorry," he boomed, squeezing into the row. He dropped into the seat next to Robert, legs spread wide, owning his territory.

"Dude, you're late," Robert said. "All the good snacks are gone."

Jimmy snorted. "Not true. I stole half a tray of cookies from the green room. There's a back door if you bribe the janitor with a pack of smokes." He grinned at Mathew, then at Josephine. "Wow, Jo. I thought you'd go to college and mellow out. Turns out, nope."

She flicked a candy cane at him and hit him square in the chest. "You're one to talk."

William sat quietly, hands folded in his lap. He glanced at Mathew, offered a small, awkward smile, then focused on the program in his hands as if it held the secret to the universe.

Mathew leaned across Robert. "Hey, man. How's Kennesaw?"

William shrugged, almost apologetic. "It's okay. Not as bad as I thought." He looked up, eyes bright. "I joined the forensics club."

Jimmy whistled, loud enough to draw glares from nearby parents. "Look out. He's going to CSI your ass."

William blushed, but Mathew could see the pride lurking under the embarrassment. "I like it," William said. "It's... ordered. Everything makes sense if you know where to look."

Josephine gave a theatrical groan. "If this keeps up, we're going to start talking about our 401(k)s."

"Not me," Jimmy said. "I plan to die before thirty."

"Of embarrassment?" Robert said.

Jimmy considered, then nodded. "That tracks."

The noise of the auditorium swelled as the house lights dimmed. A hush swept the seats, broken only by the muffled clinks of candy against teeth and the nervous shuffling of programs. The stage curtains fluttered, hinting at the chaos behind them. Mathew felt the old, familiar tingle of anticipation, now shot through with the knowledge that, for the first time, he was an outsider looking in.

He stole a glance at the others, saw the same mixture of nostalgia and unease reflected in every face. They didn't fit here anymore—not really—but for tonight, they could pretend.

The curtain rippled. Mathew leaned forward, the pull of the past and the promise of the night tightening around him, waiting for the show to begin.

***

In Athens, the campus was less a place than a current: red brick and wet leaves, the constant ebb and flow of students pulsing along the broad walks between classroom clusters. Josephine navigated it like a predator in a river, always upstream, always half a step faster than the flow around her. She liked the way her boots sounded on the concrete, liked the way professors remembered her name even after just one class, and liked that she could cut through the noise with a word.

Participating in a mock trial had not been the plan. Her parents, both educators, expected she'd become a teacher herself—maybe English, maybe history, something safe and familiar. But after a single intro session in the law school's moot court, Josephine was hooked. It wasn't just the adrenaline of public speaking (though she'd always loved a spotlight), but the thrill of making someone else admit they were wrong. She lived for the moment when an opponent faltered, the way their eyes flicked down to the table, or their voice stuttered, or they tried to cover a mistake with a joke.

She was good at it. So good, in fact, that the team captain recruited her after her first solo round, pulling her aside in the hallway. At the same time, the other competitors decompressed over Gatorade and vending machine crackers.

"You're brutal," he said, with admiration and mild fear in his tone. "We could use that. Are you free on Thursday nights?"

Josephine shrugged. "Depends. Do you provide snacks?"

He grinned. "You just have to win. The rest is taken care of."

Mock trial practice was held in a windowless classroom in the depths of the old law building, a space that reeked of dry-erase fumes and anxiety sweat. The team was an odd bunch: econ majors, theater kids, poli-sci wonks. Josephine fit in by virtue of not fitting in; she had a knack for breaking up groupthink and calling out flaws, and the others quickly learned to respect her even when they hated her guts.

The first real test was the regional invitational in Macon, a Friday night affair in the courthouse annex. Josephine wore a thrift-store blazer and a skirt that made her knees itch, her hair pulled back so tight she worried it might never recover. Her parents made the drive from Savannah, sat in the back row, and watched as their daughter took apart the opposing team's "expert witness" with surgical glee.

"Would you say your credentials are… theoretical, then?" Josephine asked, eyes fixed on the trembling junior who'd drawn the short straw.

The witness hesitated. "I—well, I mean, technically—"

Josephine pounced. "So your entire analysis is based on assumptions, rather than, say, real-world data?"

The judge arched a brow, almost smiling.

By the end of the round, Josephine's team had swept the panel. The drive back was electric, the car humming with recaps and inside jokes, fast-food wrappers piling in the footwells. She leaned her head against the window, letting the conversation swirl around her, and felt a satisfaction that was raw and simple.

Her focus sharpened in the following months. She devoured books on criminal law, then moved to psychology and victimology. She didn't talk about her interest with the other students—not directly—but she liked the precision of the field, the way it made sense of chaos and horror. There was a kind of grim elegance in the language: proximate cause, mens rea, premeditation.

In class, she was fearless. She argued with professors, disagreed with casebooks, and challenged the study groups to dig deeper. One afternoon, her Constitutional Law professor called on her for a cold read. She nailed the answer, then pressed her point further, dissecting the hypothetical with a surgeon's care.

"Do you want to be a lawyer, Ms. Hamilton?" the professor asked, not sarcastic but truly curious.

She thought for a second, then answered honestly. "No. I want to be a prosecutor."

The professor nodded, as if this confirmed a private suspicion.

"You've got the temperament for it," he said.

Josephine wondered, later that night, whether that was a compliment. She was aware of her own edge—her capacity for anger, her impatience with weakness—but she also remembered what it felt like to be powerless, to watch bad things happen and do nothing. She'd promised herself, after that one terrible week sophomore year, that she'd never be the bystander again.

Sometimes, when she found herself alone in the law library at midnight, the words from the Lantern Oath circled her mind: What light cannot reach, shadow must cleanse. She tried not to think about the woods, or the secrets they'd left behind, but they were there, always, at the edges.

The second semester was even more intense. Regionals bled into state finals. Josephine led a cross-examination so merciless that the other team filed a complaint—not about rule-breaking, but about "excessive force in questioning." The coach bought her dinner that night and said it was the best performance he'd ever seen.

The campus bloomed into spring. Josephine watched the world change from behind stacks of case law, but sometimes she'd look up and see the light cut through the library windows, painting the table in gold, and, for a moment, feel like she was exactly where she was meant to be.

She texted Mathew sometimes, not often, but always after a win or a particularly thorny debate. He usually replied in one word, or not at all, but that was fine. She figured he understood. They'd always been more about action than talk, anyway.

On the night before winter break, Josephine was the last to leave the moot court, locking up behind her. The halls were empty and cold, but she felt an odd, defiant warmth in her chest, a certainty that she'd made the right choice.

She walked home alone, boots echoing, the words from the oath threading through her thoughts—not as a burden, but as fuel.

Back in Savannah, the old world waited, but she was ready.

***

As the last of the audience found their seats, the theater settled into a restless hush. The house lights glowed at half-mast, just enough to reveal every face, every fidget, every hastily re-tucked shirt tail. The red velvet curtains looked obscene under the glare, their folds too plush and too loud for the auditorium's faded grandeur.

Mark hobbled in just before the curtain rose, stowing his crutches at the end of the aisle and settling into the seat that Josephine had saved for him. He was uncharacteristically quiet, and his friends knew better than to prod him for answers.

The group had commandeered a row near the center, a power move that had nothing to do with acoustics and everything to do with being seen by everyone who mattered. Mathew sat between Josephine and Robert, with William and Jimmy flanking the ends like bookends too heavy for their shelves.

They talked in low voices, their words muffled by the carpet and the chatter of the crowd.

"Does anyone else feel like they're sitting in a time machine?" Robert asked, cracking his knuckles one at a time. "I keep expecting Mrs. Whitaker to pop up and yell at me for chewing gum."

"She's dead," Jimmy said, not unkindly, just stating the facts. "Heart attack last year. Remember? They named a bench for her."

Mathew nodded. "I saw it outside the science building. It's in the shade, she would've hated that."

Josephine was scanning the program, red pen in hand, circling names and scribbling little notes in the margins. "They cast the new drama teacher as Marley? That's almost cute. He's like, five-two and built like a Lego brick."

William leaned over, pointing at the program. "They let Samantha play Scrooge? Isn't she a sophomore?"

"Not just a sophomore," Jimmy said, grinning. "She's Mathew's sister, which means she gets whatever she wants."

Mathew shrugged, but he couldn't suppress the smile. "She's better than anyone else in the class. Trust me, I've run lines with her over the phone a few times. She had them all memorized before Halloween."

Robert rolled his eyes. "You say that like it's a good thing."

"I do," Mathew said, deadpan. "I really do."

Their words dissolved into laughter, sharp and nervous, the kind that thrums under your skin when you know everyone's watching.

Behind them, a cluster of parents traded gossip and tried to shush their younger kids. Up front, a row of teachers—some retired, some only recently promoted—sat with hands folded, the posture of people who'd learned to endure something required and unpleasant.

"I heard they re-did the gym," William said, as if the thought just occurred to him. "It's supposed to be state-of-the-art now. LED scoreboard, air conditioning, the works."

"Bet they still use the same moldy towels in the locker room," Jimmy shot back.

"Tradition," said Josephine, not looking up.

Mathew felt a ripple of nostalgia, sharp and a little painful. He remembered the first time he'd sat in these seats, nervous about his part in the Homecoming pep rally, afraid to speak in front of so many faces. He'd never admitted it to anyone, not even to Samantha, but the memory was so close he could taste it.

"Do you guys ever wish you could go back?" he asked, surprising himself.

Josephine snorted. "To what? Pop quizzes and puberty?"

Robert shrugged. "It wasn't all bad. Some of it was just... easier."

William stared at the stage, hands folded. "I think I like the view from here better. It's safer in the dark."

Jimmy stretched, arms over his head. "That's because you never got hit in the face with a dodgeball from the back row."

The laughter came again, this time looser, less jagged. The tension in the row eased a notch. For a minute, it almost felt like the old days.

The lights dipped lower, the pre-show mutter dropping to a hush. On stage, a thin line of illumination crept across the footlights, gold and harsh against the deepening gloom.

"Here we go," said Josephine, and the rest of them leaned forward, waiting.

The curtain twitched, then rose.

***

Valdosta in late October was a lesson in contradictions: the heat stubbornly clung to the air, but every patch of grass was slick with the warning of winter. On game day, the town buzzed with a low-level mania, parking lots spilling over with trucks and flags and the yeasty reek of tailgate beer. The campus itself was unremarkable—modular buildings, flat fields, a grid of sidewalks baked into the landscape like scars—but for Mark, none of that mattered. All that counted was the rectangle of grass at the stadium, the blunt geometry of the field, the snap and crackle of bodies colliding at full speed.

On the team, he was not Mark or Hughes. He was "Hurricane," a nickname bestowed by the defensive coach after his first week. It fit him the way a helmet did: awkward at first, then so tight it hurt. He liked the way the syllables sounded in the air, how they echoed down the line of scrimmage, how they stuck in the mouths of announcers and opposing fans.

Hurricane was a force. He took the line as a personal insult, every snap a challenge, every assignment a matter of honor. The violence of football was not a metaphor but a physical need, the only time he felt truly alive. He played through bruises, through concussions, through the quiet, persistent pain that followed him from the locker room to the cafeteria and back.

The locker room was a weird mixture of intimacy and menace. The guys alternately hyped each other up and tore each other down, everything louder and meaner than it had ever been in high school. Mark learned quickly that there was no real trust here—only alliances of convenience, shaped by the shifting politics of playing time and scholarships. He kept his distance, focusing on the tape, the weights, the playbook. When he spoke, it was only to correct a scheme or to shut down a trash-talker. But the coaches loved him, mostly because he did his job and never asked for more.

On the field, everything else disappeared. There was only the sound—the grunting, the pop of pads, the helmet's internal echo as he delivered a hit. Mark played both ways, O-line and D-line, a rare double-duty that made him a legend on campus. In the cafeteria, people he didn't know called his name, offered high-fives, and slid their trays over to make room.

He acted like it was nothing, but he liked it. He liked being the storm everyone else prepared for.

The season was nearly perfect. Mark led the team to an 8-1 record, the best start in school history. Scouts showed up to practice, whispered to his coach, and shook hands with his parents in the stands. He ignored the attention, kept his head down, and focused on the game ahead.

It was the week before Thanksgiving. The team was ahead by three touchdowns, the outcome so inevitable that the stands had started to empty by the fourth quarter. The sun was dropping fast, and the field glowed orange under the stadium lights.

Mark set for the snap, knuckles white against the grass. The play was routine: a simple trap, nothing fancy, just brute force and angles. He lunged forward, driving the defender back, but something felt off. The runner cut inside too early, and Mark twisted to adjust, his knee locked at the wrong angle.

He heard the pop—louder than the crowd, louder than anything. For a second, there was no pain, just a sensation of falling, the world tilting away from him. Then the pain hit, a pure white spike that erased everything else.

He tried to get up, but his leg buckled. Teammates loomed over him, their faces twisted in horror and awe.

"Jesus, Hurricane. You okay?"

He tried to answer, but the words stuck. The trainer ran out, started poking and prodding. Mark wanted to shove him away, to stand on his own, but the knee just flopped, unresponsive.

They helped him to the sideline. The crowd clapped—some out of sympathy, some just following the script. Mark sat, helmet off, sweat running down his face, and watched the rest of the game from the bench.

The hospital was a blur: x-rays, ice packs, and a doctor explaining the intricacies of ligaments and recovery timelines. Mark tuned most of it out, staring at the ceiling, counting the ceiling tiles until the painkillers did their work.

When he got back to the dorm, the whole team was waiting. They cheered, called him a hero, handed him a slice of pizza, and a cold beer. Mark smiled, ate, drank, but inside he was doing the math—how long before he could run, before he could practice, before he could play again.

He didn't sleep that night. The pain kept him awake, but it wasn't just the pain—it was the absence, the sense that something essential had been stolen. He stared at the wall, mind racing.

By morning, he'd made a decision: he wouldn't quit. He'd rehab harder than anyone else, come back stronger. It didn't matter what the doctors said. He was a hurricane. That was the point of the name.

For the rest of the year, he limped through campus, refusing to use crutches, ignoring the stares. He went to every practice, every film session. He made sure nobody forgot him.

But sometimes, late at night, he'd catch himself wondering what would happen if he never played again—if, for the first time in his life, there was no game to prepare for.

He pushed the thought away. There was always another season. There had to be.

***

The curtain's ascent drew the auditorium into darkness, but not before a brief, pointed silence from the group—one of those collective holds where everyone knew they'd just skirted something important. Jimmy, never one for subtlety, broke it first.

"So, Mark," he said, leaning in so close that Robert had to slide sideways in his seat, "you gonna be back in pads by spring?"

Mark stretched, arms overhead, as if his body wasn't mostly steel and tape underneath. "Not sure," he said, voice even. "The doctor says I'll walk before I run, but he doesn't know how bad their strength program is."

Josephine snorted. "You need me to write a nasty letter? I'll cite case law."

"Tempting," Mark said. He grinned, but it didn't reach his eyes.

William spoke up, softer. "Are you doing PT?"

Mark nodded. "Every morning. I'm their favorite lab rat." He caught Mathew's gaze, held it for a second, then looked away. "It's not as bad as it sounds. Gives me time to catch up on classes. Or whatever."

There was an edge to his "whatever," a weight that Mathew recognized but chose not to touch.

The lights dimmed further, signaling the start in earnest. The stage lit up: cheap painted backdrops, a fog machine working overtime, the sound of creaking boards as the cast shuffled into position. From somewhere offstage came the shrill, unmistakable voice of the drama teacher doubling as stage manager, hissing cues with military efficiency.

The first scene was rough—high schoolers in ill-fitting Victorian garb, lines delivered in the stop-start cadence of people who didn't fully understand the words. But after a few minutes, the rhythm caught. The cast settled. Samantha, as Scrooge, made her entrance with a stomp and a glare that bordered on homicidal. The audience laughed, the tension broke, and everyone—on stage and off—relaxed into the story.

Samantha's first entrance was not written to be a moment, but she made it one. She stalked onto the stage in a battered bathrobe and slippers, her hair slicked back and dusted with cornstarch, every inch of her posture screaming "old bastard." The audience giggled—at first because it was funny, then because it wasn't, not really. There was a chill in her voice that cut through the fake Victorian trimmings and landed somewhere deep in the auditorium.

Mathew barely breathed. He'd seen her rehearse, knew every beat of the script, but watching her perform was a different animal. She moved with a purpose that defied the play's thrift-store production values, her voice rising and falling in careful arcs. The other actors orbited her, sometimes thrown off course, but Samantha never lost the thread.

The friends in the center row leaned forward in unison, as if pulled by a wire.

"Jesus," Robert muttered, low enough that only Mathew heard. "She's terrifying."

"She's method," Jimmy whispered. "She called me 'worm' for a week just to prep."

Josephine scribbled a note in her program: S steals every scene, all-caps.

William stared, transfixed. "She's... really good."

Mathew swallowed, throat tight. He remembered Samantha as a kid—endlessly performing for the family, reading her lines to the mirror, demanding that Mathew play the other parts. She'd been a pain, but now it was obvious: she'd been rehearsing for this her whole life.

The script called for Scrooge to deliver a line—something about "the cold outside being preferable to the company within"—but Samantha improvised, pausing for an extra second, letting the silence curl around the room.

The audience waited, breathless. Then she exhaled: "There are worse things than winter."

It wasn't in the script. But it worked. The house shivered, a perfect little aftershock.

Mathew felt a flush of pride, mixed with something close to envy. He'd never been able to command a room like that. Not with football, not with debate, not with anything. He wondered if their parents noticed, if they understood that the spotlight had moved on for good.

Act I powered forward, the ghostly visitations rendered in bedsheets and Christmas lights. Samantha nailed every turn—her fear, her regret, her eventual, half-mocking joy. Even the mistakes looked intentional. When one of the "spirits" tripped and sent a prop candlestick skittering across the floor, Samantha rolled with it, cursing under her breath and sending the crowd into a fit of laughter.

Mathew watched Mark from the corner of his eye. The big man leaned back, arms folded, but his jaw was clenched. Every time a line landed, Mark tapped his thumb against his thigh, a nervous tell he'd never had before.

Robert nudged him at one point, whispered, "You okay?"

Mark shrugged. "Fine. Just tired."

It was a lie, but nobody called him on it.

The play moved fast. At intermission, the group stretched and swapped whispered reviews, most of them favorable.

"She's killing it," Jimmy said, pride clear in his voice.

"Runs in the family," William added, and for a moment, all the old loyalty returned.

Josephine sidled up to Mark. "Seriously. You're gonna be all right, yeah?"

He smiled, tired but real this time. "Yeah, Jo. I'm not made of glass."

She punched his shoulder, gently. "Good."

***

Mercer's science hall never really slept. The building was always at half-power, every corridor aglow in the cold blue of safety lighting, the hum of the HVAC system louder than any conversation. Robert liked it this way. He could slip into the biochemistry lab after midnight, let himself in with the ID badge he'd finessed from a forgetful TA, and work for hours without the distraction of other people's breathing.

The air in the lab was a cocktail of acetone, ethanol, and faintly rotten agar. The benches were scarred from decades of Bunsen burnings and corrosive spills. Robert loved the feeling of control: every beaker exactly measured, every pipette click calibrated to a tenth of a milliliter. He was a mess in the rest of his life, but in the lab, he could control every variable.

He'd gone pre-med by default, knowing from the Lantern Oath years that if he didn't make himself useful, he'd end up invisible. But where most classmates saw a grind—endless memorization, the slow death march toward the MCAT—Robert saw a puzzle. Every molecule, every cell, every reaction was a logic game he could win if he just stared at it hard enough.

In his first semester, he won the department's "freshman challenge," an unofficial competition to see who could sequence a protein chain with the fewest errors. The winner got a handshake from the department chair and a battered lab coat that smelled of old onions. Robert wore it anyway.

Lab partners came and went, most of them friendly but distant, not wanting to invest in a relationship with the weird kid who never left campus. Robert didn't mind. He liked the silence, the way his thoughts got louder in the absence of other voices.

He picked up a job in the campus morgue—not the real one, but the teaching annex where med students practiced autopsies on synthetic torsos and, sometimes, the unclaimed dead from the city. The first time he watched a real cadaver dissection, he nearly threw up, but by the second week, he was numb to the sights and smells. The human body was less miraculous than everyone thought. It broke down in predictable ways, each organ failing according to a schedule written in DNA and poor decision-making.

His favorite professor was Dr. Park, a pathologist who looked like he'd been carved from a single block of wax. Park never smiled, but he respected focus. One day after class, he asked Robert to stay behind.

"You're thorough," Park said, voice like sandpaper. "But you need to develop a tolerance for mess. Medicine isn't as neat as the textbooks."

Robert bristled. "I'm not afraid of blood. Or anything else."

Park nodded. "I believe you. But it's not the blood that gets you. It's the questions with no answer."

The next week, Park handed him an actual case file: a woman, 47, found dead at home. No sign of trauma, all the tests were negative. "Explain it," Park said. "If you can."

Robert spent the weekend combing through the data, constructing timelines, and sketching out possible causes. In the end, he couldn't solve it. The official report was "idiopathic cardiomyopathy," which meant nothing except that the heart had failed for reasons nobody could explain.

He hated that. He hated not knowing. But he also found it fascinating, the way some mysteries refused to yield.

Sometimes, when Robert left the lab in the early morning, he'd walk across the empty campus, letting the cold wake him up. He thought of the others—Mathew, probably already in a suit by now; Josephine, verbally assassinating her professors; Mark, pounding out squats in a weight room; William, doing God knows what. He missed them, but not the way normal people missed old friends. It was more like he missed a part of himself that had been cut off, a phantom limb he could still feel in the dark.

One night, after a marathon study session, he stood in the center of the quad and looked up at the stars, the same sky he'd grown up under, the same patterns of light. He wondered how many of his cells had been replaced since then—how much of the old him still existed, and how much was just memory, or myth.

He turned up his collar and walked home. The next morning, he would log the results of his experiment and start another. There was always another.

Back in Savannah, someone else would take the stage. But here, in the lab, Robert was the whole show.

***

At intermission, the auditorium buzzed. People who'd come only for their own kids leaned over the aisle to ask, "Who is that Scrooge?" The teachers near the front row shared a nod, as if confirming a rumor.

Mathew turned to the others. "She's going to do this for real," he said.

Jimmy nodded. "Yeah. She's got it."

Josephine smiled, soft around the eyes. "Just like her brother," she said, and Mathew caught the sarcasm but also the warmth beneath it.

Mark, who'd been unusually quiet, clapped his hands once, hard. "Best in show."

The house lights flickered, a warning. People shuffled back to their seats, conversations dying down as the promise of Act II drew them back in.

They laughed, the tension broken. But as the lights dipped for Act II, Mathew felt the old sensation of being on the outside, watching as the world reconfigured itself around new stars.

Mathew felt the shift—the way the group, for all its scattered trauma, still closed ranks when it mattered. Even if nothing was ever said outright, the connection remained, held together by the inertia of shared history.

The curtain rose again. On stage, the ghost of Christmas Yet to Come waited in the wings, shrouded and patient.

Samantha took the stage again, and this time, the audience listened with the respect usually reserved for grown-ups. She commanded it. She owned it.

For a moment, everything was exactly as it should be.

***

William spent the first three weeks at Kennesaw State convinced he'd made a colossal mistake. The business building was a maze of glass walls and ugly carpet, every corridor lined with motivational posters about teamwork and leadership. The classes were filled with people who'd already picked out their first BMW, kids who wore polo shirts like uniforms and never looked up from their laptops.

He went through the motions: microeconomics, spreadsheets, the occasional group project that ended with everyone hating each other. William drifted through it all, never quite failing but never really awake, either.

His roommate was a finance major who worked part-time selling timeshares. The guy had a girlfriend in every building and a running tab at the local bar. William learned to tune him out, but sometimes, late at night, he'd hear the roommate on the phone, plotting out the next big thing, and wonder what the hell he was doing with his own life.

It was by accident that William found the criminal justice elective. He'd misread the course number and ended up in a windowless room with a dozen other students, most of them wearing hoodies or sweatpants. The professor was a retired homicide detective named Harlan, a guy who looked like he'd been stitched together from leftover cop shows: big mustache, nose broken at least twice, and a voice that could fill a stadium without a mic.

The first day, Harlan walked to the front of the class and wrote two words on the board: EVERYBODY LIES. Then he turned and told a story about his first murder case—a love triangle gone wrong, a confession that made no sense, and the six months it took to untangle the truth from the pile of bullshit the suspects kept feeding him.

William was hooked.

He stayed after class and asked questions. Harlan seemed to appreciate it, even if he never said so. The lectures turned into conversations, the syllabus into something more like a scavenger hunt for the truth.

The detective brought in guest speakers—crime scene techs, former inmates, even a forensic psychologist. William listened to every word, taking notes in tiny, perfect print. The jargon made sense to him. The systems and patterns, the way every crime was just another kind of puzzle. It was messy, but if you dug deep enough, the mess started to resolve into lines and logic.

One week, Harlan assigned them to analyze a cold case pulled from the state archives. William dove into the file, spreading the paperwork out in his dorm room, cross-referencing times and phone records, drawing lines on the back of his notebook. He built a timeline, flagged inconsistencies, and pieced together a theory nobody else in class considered.

When he presented, the detective just listened, hands folded, not giving anything away. But after everyone else left, Harlan called him over.

"Have you ever thought about going into the field?" he asked.

William shrugged. "Didn't think I'd be any good at it."

"Hell of a lot better than half the idiots I've trained," Harlan said, with a rare smile. "You see through the bullshit. Don't lose that."

That night, William looked at himself in the mirror—really looked—and saw something new: someone who could impose order, not just be ruled by it. He thought about the pact with the others, about the promise to watch each other's backs, and wondered if this was what he'd been looking for all along. Not the badge, or the gun, but the sense that he could make sense out of chaos.

He changed his major the next day. Told his parents on the phone, bracing for a letdown, but they just sounded relieved he'd found something he liked. His mom joked that she always knew he'd end up "policing" the family. His dad said he hoped William would use his powers for good.

By the end of the semester, William was interning at the local sheriff's office, shadowing deputies and logging evidence. He was still quiet, still prone to overthinking, but now he felt less like a ghost and more like a lens—a way for the world to come into focus.

He missed the others. Missed their noise and their flaws, their way of being unafraid even when everything was falling apart. But he also felt, for the first time, that he could keep his own promise. That the next time someone needed backup, he wouldn't freeze or run. He'd know what to do.

On the last day of class, Harlan handed him a business card with the detective's private number on it. "Keep in touch," he said. "Somebody's gotta keep the rest of us honest."

William tucked the card into his wallet, next to his driver's license, and left the building with his head up. The campus looked different now—not smaller, but sharper, the lines cleaner and the shadows less frightening.

He walked home in the cold, already planning the next step.

Back in the present, Samantha's voice echoed from the stage, and William found himself sitting straighter, as if every word was another clue to a case he'd been waiting to solve.

***

Jimmy's first match was over in eleven seconds. He spent eight of those on his back, staring at the ceiling tiles, fighting to remember which way was up. The whistle sounded, and for a moment, he was so disoriented that he didn't realize he'd lost. His coach squatted down next to him, expression unreadable.

"Good effort," the coach said. "But next time, try not to lead with your face."

Jimmy sat up, wiping sweat from his eyes. The world was loud—parents cheering, teammates howling from the sidelines, the other kid's hand already raised in victory. He hated it, but he hated giving up even more.

Wrestling was nothing like football or baseball. It was solitary and raw, with no pads or helmets to blame when you lost—just you, your opponent, and the mat. Jimmy joined on a dare from his older brother, who claimed he'd never last a month. By the second week of practice, he was too stubborn to quit, even after puking on the coach's shoes and tearing up both knees.

The other guys on the team treated him like a mascot at first. He was the smallest in his weight class, the only one who hadn't wrestled since childhood. They called him "Bones," partly because he looked like a skeleton, mostly because he was always one step away from snapping. Jimmy took it. He took the beatings, the running, the endless drills, because underneath it all, he liked the clarity. Every match was a problem with a right and wrong answer. You either solved it or you got pinned.

He lost his next two matches, but lasted longer each time. He started to see patterns—how certain kids led with their right, how others faked a weakness to draw you in. He watched tapes, memorized the way state champions moved, and tried to mimic their footwork during solo drills.

Coach noticed. "You're a sponge, Lee," he said during one late practice. "You soak it all up. You just need to wring it out on the mat."

The breakthrough came in January, at a tournament in a cinderblock gym on the edge of town. Jimmy was matched against a kid from a rival school, a compact ball of muscle with a reputation for aggression. The first period went the way they all did: Jimmy scrambling to stay upright, barely avoiding a quick takedown. But in the second, he started to notice the other kid's tell—a hitch in his stance before every shot, a fraction of a second where he telegraphed the move.

Jimmy waited. Then, as the kid lunged, Jimmy sidestepped and rolled, using the other's momentum to flip him. The crowd went wild. Jimmy didn't hear it. He just focused on holding the pin until the ref slapped the mat.

He'd won.

Afterward, the team lifted him up, yelling his name, pounding his back. The coach clapped him on the shoulder. "That's how you do it, Bones. Read and react. Always be a step ahead."

Jimmy grinned, blood trickling from a split lip. For the first time in his life, he felt like he was good at something nobody else wanted. Not the glory stuff, but the hard, invisible work. He started winning more, not because he was stronger, but because he out-thought the other guys. He became the go-to for scouting opponents, for remembering weird tics and strategies.

Sometimes, in the quiet before a match, Jimmy would scan the gym, watching the other teams warm up. He'd notice the smallest things—a limping walk, a taped finger, a nervous tic—and file them away for later. Watching the perimeter, like William used to say.

By spring, he was no longer the team's mascot. He was their ace in the hole, the one who never quit, the one who could pull off a win even when the odds sucked.

He didn't brag about it. He didn't need to. The feeling of the win, the moment when the other guy gave up, was enough.

In the auditorium, Jimmy shifted in his seat, the memory buzzing under his skin. He glanced down the row at the others—Mathew, still tense; Josephine, biting her lip; William, calm but watchful; Mark, arms folded and resolute.

Jimmy leaned back, feeling the old confidence. Whatever happened next, he'd be ready for it.

***

The scene was set in Scrooge's cold, candle-lit bedroom: a single bed, a battered nightstand, a fog of dry ice inching across the stage. Samantha sat on the edge, shoulders hunched, the heavy chain of her own making coiled at her feet. The entire auditorium leaned in as she spoke.

"I have seen ghosts," she began, voice soft but impossible to ignore. "Not the ones you read about in books, or scare children with on cold nights. No—my ghosts are smaller, meaner. They live in the cracks of your house, in the bite of the wind, in the things you never said because you were too proud or too frightened."

She let the words hang, eyes searching the darkness where the audience sat.

"I used to think I was the only one haunted. That if I closed my eyes, if I worked hard enough, I could sweat the past out of me. But that's a lie. The past is a root, and it grows while you sleep, winding around your bones until you can't stand up straight anymore."

Her hand shook as she picked up the chain. "So I built myself an armor. I wore it every day. But armor is heavy, and sometimes, when you sit very still, you wonder if you can ever take it off, or if it will be the only thing left of you when they bury you in the ground."

For a long moment, nothing. No coughs, no whispers, not even the rustle of programs.

Samantha looked up, breaking character for just a second—a flicker of herself, the girl from the kitchen table, the mirror, the backyard stage.

"I don't want to be a ghost," she said. "I want to be real, even if it hurts."

Then the light faded to black.

On stage, she was motionless, the rest of the cast frozen in place behind her. It took several seconds for the audience to react, as if everyone was waiting for permission to breathe again. Then, slowly, a single clap from the back row, then another, until the whole auditorium filled with thunder. It was more than polite applause; it was the sound of people stunned by something they hadn't expected to matter.

In the center row, the friends said nothing at first. Mathew found himself blinking fast, willing the tears away. Josephine sat with her hands over her mouth, notebook forgotten. Mark just smiled, pride written in every line of his face. Jimmy thumped his fist once against his knee, eyes shining. Even William, who never cried at anything, let out a soft, shaky breath.

When the lights came back on, the audience was on its feet, teachers and parents, and siblings all standing. Samantha bowed, and for a brief, wild moment, she looked straight at Mathew, then at each of his friends, as if she'd performed the whole thing just for them.

The applause went on and on.

***

The whole cast packed the stage for the curtain call: Marley in a judge's wig that slipped over his ears, the Cratchits in sweaters a decade out of date, two dozen extras in mismatched bonnets and hats. Samantha stood dead center, arms linked with the "Tiny Tim" to her left and the Ghost of Christmas Past to her right.

The lights hit her full on. Mathew saw her blink, as if even now she couldn't believe the applause was real. The director stepped out from behind the curtain, pointed at Samantha, and mouthed something—probably "take your bow." She did, slow and careful, then broke into a wide, crooked grin.

From the crowd, a thousand hands clapped. Mathew cupped his hands and bellowed, "Way to go, Sam!" Jimmy let out a wolf whistle that three different teachers shushed, but it only made the noise louder. Josephine yelled, "Encore!" and Robert pounded on the seat until the row shook.

Samantha beamed, her eyes glistening in the stage lights. She looked down at her friends, found them instantly, and gave a tiny wave, just for them.

The applause kept rolling. Parents snapped pictures, teachers dabbed at their eyes. Someone in the front row threw a bouquet of fake poinsettias on the stage, and Samantha picked it up, holding it like a trophy.

For a second, Mathew imagined her years from now—on a bigger stage, a bigger crowd, the same defiant spark in her smile. He felt a twinge, not regret exactly, but something close to hope. Whatever came next for her, she was ready.

The rest of the cast took their bows in sequence, the crowd still on its feet. Even after the curtains closed, the clapping didn't stop right away. People kept talking, buzzing, replaying the best lines or the funniest slips.

When the house lights came up, everyone was flushed and alive, like they'd just survived a storm together.

In the aisle, the friends regrouped, high-fiving, shaking their heads in disbelief.

"Damn," Jimmy said, "she really did it."

"She's unstoppable," said Robert.

Josephine leaned on Mathew's shoulder, voice soft. "Are you proud?"

Mathew nodded, the lump in his throat making it hard to say anything else.

They watched as the crowd filed out, parents and siblings and old teachers threading toward the lobby, everyone eager to find Samantha and get in on the first round of congratulations.

Outside the auditorium, the night waited, cold and bright, ready for whatever came next.

***

The lobby after the show was a madhouse, the tile floors sticky with spilled punch and the air so humid you could chew it. Parents queued up near the stage door, programs in hand and phones primed for the big reunion. Teachers milled around, grabbing students for photos, barking last-minute reminders about set teardown and costume returns.

Mathew and the others wedged themselves between a makeshift coat rack and the "Congratulations, Cast!" banner strung over the stairwell. They waited, craning their necks, eyes peeled for a glimpse of Samantha.

She appeared in the center of the crowd, still in her old-man slippers and bathrobe, face half-wiped free of the ghostly makeup. Her hair was wild, cheeks flushed, arms packed with flowers and gift bags. As soon as she spotted the group, she launched herself at them, nearly knocking Robert into the coat rack.

"You saw it?" she said, voice bright and sharp.

"We saw everything," Mathew said, pulling her in for a hug that almost lifted her off the floor.

Jimmy grabbed her next, squeezing so hard she yelped. "You're famous now," he said. "You have to sign my program."

Samantha laughed, and for a second, she was just his little sister again, not the force of nature who'd taken over the stage.

Josephine handed her a half-melted chocolate bar, which Samantha accepted with the reverence of a holy relic. William offered a card, shy and plain, with "You were amazing" written in his neatest print.

"Best night ever," Samantha declared, clutching the loot to her chest.

Their parents wove through the crowd, faces flushed with pride and relief. Mathew's mom pinched Samantha's cheek, whispering something in her ear. His dad clapped him on the back, hard enough to make him wince. Other parents hovered, some with genuine congratulations, others with that competitive glint of parents who measure self-worth by their kid's applause.

Samantha made the rounds, giving hugs and posing for photos, but she kept circling back to her friends. Every time, she'd stand a little taller, the grin never slipping.

Teachers, both past and present, stopped by to say their piece. Mrs. Lawton, the old AP English teacher, told Samantha she was "the next Meryl." The math coach joked about finally understanding Dickens. Even the janitor who ran the green room gave her a thumbs-up.

When the crowd thinned, the group carved out a patch of floor near the window. They sat on the radiator, passing around leftover candy and dissecting the performance, trading favorite lines and the best audience reactions.

"You killed it," Josephine said, nudging Samantha with her knee. "Seriously. I've never seen anything like that here."

Samantha shrugged, but her eyes shone. "I just wanted to make you guys proud."

"You did," said William, soft and certain.

Mathew looked around at the faces—older now, tired in some ways, but more themselves than ever. The old pact, the Lantern Oath, felt closer than it had in years. He wondered if any of them realized how rare it was to have this, to hold onto a group of friends this long.

Outside, the night pressed against the glass, the streetlights casting halos in the damp Savannah air.

"Let's get out of here," said Mark, who'd been quiet, smiling the whole time. "I'm buying Waffle House."

Jimmy stood first, pumping a fist. "Hell yeah. Scrooge deserves an Oscar."

They gathered their stuff, Samantha wrapping the bathrobe tighter around her, and pushed through the doors into the dark.

The air outside was cold and clean, and for a minute, the whole group just stood there, letting their breath cloud the air, not saying anything at all.

It was enough.

***

They lingered in the parking lot, the sodium lamps overhead flickering halos onto the wet asphalt. Someone had left a pile of folding chairs stacked by the side door, and the group used them like thrones, circling up just beyond the reach of the crowd.

The cold was sharper here. Breath came out in clouds, and Mathew noticed how Jimmy's exhalations formed perfect rings before dissolving. They passed around a single sleeve of Oreos that Samantha had smuggled from the dressing room.

For a while, nobody wanted to break the spell. They talked about nothing—who'd gotten fat, who'd started smoking, who still lived with their parents. The old patterns reasserted themselves: Jimmy telling stories too loudly, Josephine cutting in with corrections, Robert quietly keeping track of the facts.

Eventually, the talk drifted to college and what awaited in the new year.

"Pre-med is a scam," Robert said. "They tell you it's about helping people, but really it's about surviving."

Jimmy nodded. "Same with wrestling. I figured out real quick that nobody cared about you unless you won."

"You always win, though," Samantha said, nudging him.

"Not always," Jimmy admitted, softer than usual.

Josephine chewed on a cookie. "Law's even worse. It's like being in a room full of people who all think they're the smartest, and you're supposed to prove them wrong."

"You're the smartest," Samantha said, not as a joke.

Josephine smiled, letting it land.

Mark, picking at the wrapper, said, "Coach says I'll be back by spring, but I don't know. Maybe I don't even want it anymore."

The silence that followed wasn't awkward. It was a space for the truth.

William broke it. "I changed my major," he said. "Didn't tell anybody yet. Criminal justice."

"Hell yes," Jimmy said. "The world needs more good guys."

"I'm not a good guy," William replied. "But I want to figure out how to do it right. I want to make it make sense."

Mathew listened, trying to absorb it all, the way the others had changed and the ways they hadn't. He thought about the promise they'd made as kids, the lantern in the woods, the idea that they'd always have each other's backs.

He wondered if it was possible to keep a promise like that, after all this time.

A breeze picked up, rattling the last brown leaves in the parking lot. Samantha huddled into her bathrobe, arms wrapped tight.

"What about you, Matt?" she asked.

He looked at the ground, then at the faces around him.

"I just want to do the right thing," he said. "Whatever that means."

Nobody argued. Nobody laughed.

For a long minute, they just sat there, silent and breathing, watching their ghosts drift up into the Savannah night.

Then Jimmy stood, shaking off the cold, and the rest followed.

They walked to their cars, splitting off one by one, calling out promises to text, meet up, or crash at Waffle House. But as Mathew turned back for a last look, he saw that none of them had really left. They were still there, clustered under the streetlight, as solid and as stubborn as ever.

He got in his car, started the engine, and watched the group shrink in his rearview mirror. The parking lot faded into darkness, but the memory of the moment stuck, bright and persistent.

Some things, he thought, really do last.

***

After the last car door slammed and the engines faded into the distance, the parking lot was silent except for the buzz of the overhead lights and the echo of far-off traffic. Mathew lingered by the hood of his car, watching as the other five straggled toward their vehicles, trading one last set of gestures and jokes, unwilling to leave the night behind.

A memory floated up, unbidden: the clearing in the woods behind the old neighborhood, five kids circling a battered lantern, each of them with a hand stretched out, swearing never to let the world get between them. The details were fuzzy—who said what, who flinched, who laughed—but the feeling was clear, indelible, even now.

He wondered if they all remembered it the same way. Maybe not the words, but the heat from the lantern, the thrill of breaking rules together, the certainty that nothing would ever change.

Out in the lot, Jimmy and Mark stood by the bed of Jimmy's pickup, talking low and seriously. Josephine and Robert argued playfully over who was more likely to get into grad school, their voices drifting on the wind. William hovered at the edge, already thinking about tomorrow, but every so often, he glanced back at the group, as if making sure the headcount still matched the old roster.

And Samantha, a few yards away, turned in a slow circle, arms out like she was spinning on a stage, head tilted to the stars. Mathew felt a rush of something like pride, but also a pang—knowing that the best of her was meant for the world, not just for him.

He walked over, hands jammed in his pockets, and stood next to her. For a minute, they just looked up together, the city lights drowning out the stars but not completely.

"Think it'll ever be like that again?" she asked, not specifying what "that" meant.

He considered it. "Maybe. Or maybe it'll be something better."

Samantha smiled, all the makeup and bravado gone, just his little sister again. "Promise?"

He reached out and ruffled her hair. "Promise."

The others joined them one by one, falling into place out of old habit: no ceremony, no speeches, just six friends huddled together in the Savannah night.

They didn't light a lantern or swear a new oath. But the circle held, and in that moment, it was enough.

Far off, a car horn sounded. The group scattered, peeling away in pairs, laughing, shoving, each step a little lighter than before.

Mathew stayed behind, watching as the last of them turned the corner and disappeared.

He started his engine, headlights sweeping across the empty lot, and drove home. The world outside was cold and uncertain, but he felt it—somewhere beneath the skin—a pilot light, steady, waiting for the next time they'd need to find each other in the dark.

CHAPTER 4

If you woke early enough, before the humidity came off the river and the streets filled with the day's regrets, the Sunrise Diner still felt like the only honest place left in Savannah. It was the kind of spot that changed nothing: same chipped mugs, same ancient register, same hand-painted "Cash Only" sign propped above the case of congealed pies. The regulars hunched over their eggs at the counter, muttering to the TV that hung crooked over the pass window, its static hum a permanent feature.

Mathew found the group at their usual booth, the one by the window with the blind always stuck at half-mast. The light cut diagonally across the table, picking out the dust on the ketchup bottle and the water rings on the Formica. Jimmy was already there, tearing into a short stack with enough syrup to pickle an elephant. William sat next to him, reading the sports section like it owed him money. Robert nursed a glass of orange juice, squinting at something on his phone.

Josephine and Samantha took the far side, knees bumping. Samantha wore the afterglow of the previous night's performance—her hair still gummed with leftover stage makeup, lips raw from scrubbing at the ghostly foundation. She looked tired, but in the proud, humming way that comes after a victory.

Josephine, for her part, was in the midst of an impassioned retelling. "—I'm serious, Sam, the entire back row was sniffling. You could have started a cult right there. And you—" she pointed her fork at Samantha, nearly impaling a passing fly, "—don't even act like you didn't know what you were doing. That monologue was a war crime."

Samantha ducked her head, grinning. "You're just soft, Jo."

"Soft? I was emotionally waterboarded. Ask Mathew, he saw me."

The table turned to Mathew. He shrugged, smothering a smile. "You did kind of lose it."

"I did not lose it." Josephine stabbed a triangle of toast, her cheeks pink. "It was an involuntary physiological response."

"That's what people say when they ugly-cry in public," Jimmy said, mouth full.

Samantha raised her mug in a faux-toast. "To involuntary physiological responses."

Jimmy clinked his glass against hers, sloshing milk onto the table. "You're a psycho," he said, affection in every syllable.

William glanced up from the paper. "There's an article in here about your play, you know. Says you stole the show."

Samantha blinked. "Seriously?"

"Front page of the local section. They call you 'ferocious and tender in equal measure.'"

"Yeah, that sounds about right," said Robert, setting down his phone. "You get that from your brother."

Samantha shot Mathew a look, then gave an exaggerated eye roll. "I get it from the women in the family, thank you very much."

Josephine grinned, savoring the tease. "Maybe next time you'll let someone else have a moment. I was emotionally spent for hours."

"You called your mom at midnight," said Jimmy.

"Because she would understand! She's a woman of culture."

Samantha took a long, theatrical sip of her coffee. "I'm glad someone finally gets me."

Mathew let the conversation swell and crest, enjoying the way the group orbited each other—old chemistry, never out of practice. Even the insults had a kind of weightless affection, a comfort that made the diner feel less like a waiting room and more like home.

A waitress with a rattail and a nose ring topped off their coffees. She looked at the cluster of empty plates and shook her head. "Y'all having the reunion or the last supper?"

"Depends on how long you let Jimmy keep eating," said William.

"Nothing wrong with a healthy appetite," Jimmy replied, spearing another sausage.

The clink of utensils, the heat of the sun on the glass, the steady drone of the TV—it all layered over the group's laughter until the world outside felt impossibly far away.

After the worst of the hunger faded, Mathew looked around the table, the faces more grown than he expected. He saw the faint outline of who they'd been—scraped knees, muddy shoes, the pulse of possibility—and the sharper edges of who they were now, all of it fusing in the slanted morning light.

He wondered how many more times they'd get to do this, and if he'd ever find words good enough for what the moment meant.

But for now, the world was small and bright and full of promise, and that was enough.

***

It didn't take long for the post-breakfast haze to break, and for the table's energy to turn outward, toward the lives they'd been building out in the world. Josephine started it, naturally, with her typical blend of self-deprecation and barely concealed pride.

"So, did I mention my roommate's rat staged an insurrection?" She wiped her mouth with a napkin, eyes wide. "I swear to God, the thing figured out the latch on its cage and started terrorizing the whole hall. Our RA found it under someone's mini fridge, staring them down like a mob boss. Campus police got involved. They sent an actual incident report to my parents."

"Your parents must be thrilled you're finally learning responsibility," said William, who wore his own brand of amusement like a tie.

"Honestly, my mom's just happy it isn't me starting the riots for once." Josephine sat back, arms folded. "Besides, it's not all rodents and anarchy. My mock trial team made regionals. We took out this Ivy League powerhouse in the semis. I think the other captain cried afterward."

"I bet you made them cry," Mark said, popping a grape into his mouth. "I'll bet Jo is savage in the courtroom. Remember how she got Mrs. Tanner to apologize for giving us homework?"

"I have never seen a grown woman so scared of a high schooler," Mathew said, smiling. "You were always going to be a shark."

Josephine accepted the compliment with a magnanimous bow of her head.

William finished his orange juice and cleared his throat. "I'm not as exciting. Accounting is just… numbers. So many numbers. My biggest victory was not failing Stats. But, uh, I took this elective in criminal justice, and it was weirdly awesome." He looked down, like he hadn't meant to say that last part. "The prof was an ex-cop. He had stories. Made everything sound less like math and more like—" He gestured at the table, searching for the right metaphor.

"Like an episode of COPS?" Robert supplied.

"Yeah. Less depressing, though."

"You'd be a good detective," said Samantha, prodding him with her fork. "You notice stuff nobody else does."

William flushed, but there was a quiet pride in the way he nodded. "I might change majors. I haven't told my parents yet. My mom will probably die."

"Mine will die when I don't get into med school," said Robert. "But at this point, I'll be happy if I make it through Biochem alive."

Jimmy grinned. "That bad?"

"Worse. My TA once spilled formaldehyde all over the bench and just wiped it up with a hoodie. I watched a grad student pass out during a fetal pig dissection. There was a fire in the chem lab—small, but real. We were told to evacuate, but the professor just closed the door and kept lecturing."

"Science waits for no man," Josephine said, raising her mug.

"I feel like I'm going to wake up one morning and discover I have superpowers or extra appendages," Robert replied.

"Extra appendages?" Jimmy said, nearly choking on his coffee.

"Extra appendages could be useful," Josephine said, nodding sagely. "Depending on which appendage it is, you could be really popular with the girls."

"That's the dream, really." Robert shrugged, grinning.

They laughed, the sound bright and open, filling the small room like sunlight.

Jimmy, who'd been content to listen, piped up with his own update. "Wrestling is hell, but I haven't died yet. Coach says I'm the 'grittiest' on the team. Which I think is code for smallest and loudest, but whatever. We made it to State, which is a first for the school."

"That's incredible," said Mathew. "Congratulations."

Jimmy flexed a bicep. "Thanks, but mostly I just try not to get pinned in under a minute. Keeps the bar low."

"And you, Matt?" Samantha's voice was gentle, but curious. "Any courtroom showdowns, or just more debate?"

"The debate team is intense," Mathew admitted. "But it's good. I like the pressure." He hesitated, feeling the group's gaze. "Sometimes I think I only feel normal when I'm arguing."

"Some things never change," Josephine said, with a warmth that took out any sting.

Samantha beamed at her brother. "You're the best arguer I know. If you ever run for President, I'll make your posters."

"President of what?" said Jimmy.

"Of America, idiot."

"Oh, right." Jimmy looked thoughtful. "I'd vote for you, Matt, unless I ran against you. Then I'd vote for me."

Samantha shook her head. "You'd lose in a landslide."

Mathew sat back and let the wave of laughter hit. There was an ache in it—a sense of time passing, of things slipping away even as they happened—but it felt clean, like the start of something instead of the end.

"I missed this," said William, soft but audible. "All of us together."

"Me too," said Josephine. "Even if some people can't handle their breakfast meats." She gestured at Jimmy's carnage.

Jimmy raised both hands, sticky with syrup. "No regrets."

The waitress arrived with the check, and the group made a show of fighting over who would pay. It was a ritual: every time, Mathew won by stealth, sneaking his card to the register while the others were distracted.

"Next time, it's on me," Josephine said, as they shuffled into the chilly sunlight outside.

"Yeah, right," Mathew replied. "You still owe me five bucks from middle school."

She didn't deny it, just hooked her arm through his and led the group down the sidewalk.

They walked in loose formation, not needing to decide where to go next. That was the thing about old friends: the world was smaller, the possibilities fewer, but each step still felt like a homecoming.

And that morning, in the quiet lull before adulthood started up again, it was enough to be moving together, for however long it lasted.

***

They didn't plan the next stop, but the group migrated naturally toward Forsyth Park, following the line of trees and the hush of the side streets. The air was brittle, the ground sodden from the last rain, and every so often, a city bus would rumble by, adding a note of vibrato to the morning's quiet.

Mark trailed the group by a half-step, hands deep in his jacket pockets, hood pulled up against the wind. He didn't limp, not exactly, but there was a stiffness in his walk—a careful economy, like every movement was rationed. At first, no one said anything. They let him set his own pace, letting the conversation flow around him instead of at him.

Jimmy was the first to breach the subject. "You ever miss two-a-days?" He grinned, elbowing Mark as they passed a tangle of playground swings.

Mark shrugged. "I miss the free food. And hitting people without getting arrested."

"That's the best part," Jimmy agreed, voice bright. "I heard Valdosta State put your jersey up in the weight room. You're basically a legend."

"Yeah, well, legends don't have to run suicides. That's the upside."

The others laughed, and the conversation veered away, but Mark's smile faded quickly. He stared at the frost-shined grass, shoulders hunched. When the path narrowed, Mathew fell back beside him.

"You holding up?" Mathew asked, softly, just for him.

Mark glanced at him, then back ahead. "I'm good. Doc says the knee will be fine if I don't try to play god anymore." He flexed his leg and grimaced. "So I just do what I can. Rehab and school. They're pushing me into coaching, which is basically yelling at freshmen for money."

"You'd be great at that," Mathew said, genuinely.

Mark made a face, skeptical. "I'd rather play, but you don't always get to pick." He watched Jimmy and Robert arguing up ahead, then nodded at the rest of the group. "They don't ask about it, you notice that? Nobody brings it up unless I do."

"They care," said Mathew. "They just don't want to make it worse."

"Yeah. I know. It's weird, though. Sometimes I wish someone would just say it: 'Hey, it sucks to lose the one thing you were best at.' Just get it out."

Mathew didn't respond right away. He thought about all the times he'd wanted someone to name what he was feeling, instead of dancing around it. He decided to try.

"It does suck," Mathew said, meeting his friend's eye. "You were the best. And it's shitty and unfair. But you're still you. And we're still us. I don't know if that helps."

Mark let out a long, slow breath. "Yeah," he said. "It does, actually."

They walked a few more paces, letting the quiet settle between them.

Up ahead, Josephine had climbed onto the edge of a dry fountain, arms spread for balance. "You know, I always thought Mark would be the first one of us to get famous," she called. "Or arrested. Or both."

"He's still got time," William replied.

"Don't bet on it," Mark said, but this time the smile stuck.

Samantha jogged back to join them, her hair blowing wild in the wind. "We're going to the woods, right? I want to see if the lantern's still there."

Samantha had been brought into the lantern group when she started 6th grade.

Mathew looked at Mark. "You up for it?"

Mark shrugged, the motion more loose this time. "I go where the herd goes. Just don't make me race anyone."

They laughed, and the knot of tension unwound. For a moment, they were just six kids in a park, the world's old rules bent in their favor.

The path bent away from the city, toward the stand of pines that marked the edge of their old territory. Mark took the lead for the first time, his stride confident, the others falling in behind him like always.

Nobody needed to say anything more. The group understood that sometimes, the best way to carry someone's pain was just to keep moving alongside them.

And in that, at least, nothing had changed.

***

The shortcut to the woods ran behind a strip of abandoned row houses, the windows all plywood and the yards overrun with dog fennel and pokeweed. The group cut across a patch of gravel and into the stand of pines, the ground springy underfoot and the air suddenly alive with the electric hush of needles in winter.

Samantha took the lead, her stride buoyant, even as the others slouched or shivered in the cold. She pulled at Mathew's sleeve, dragging him a few steps ahead.

"Wait 'til you see this idea I had for a set design," she said, breathless. "It's for a new play—sort of like A Christmas Carol, but, you know, set in a mall. Scrooge is a security guard who hates Christmas music, and the ghosts are just weird mall employees. I've got sketches."

She rummaged in her backpack and produced a spiral notebook, the pages scrawled with frenetic charcoal outlines and sticky-note dialogue. The group gathered around, peering over her shoulder.

"I want to build these out of old mannequins and foam core. But, like, make it look intentionally cheap. So people get that it's all theater, right? Meta, but also funny."

Jimmy squinted at the sketch. "Are those… sunglasses on the ghost?"

"Yeah! The Ghost of Christmas Yet To Come is a girl at a sunglasses kiosk. She only speaks in cryptic brand slogans."

Josephine started giggling. "I'd pay money to see this. You could get the whole drama department involved. Or the art kids."

"That's the plan. I want to direct it, too. Ms. Carlton said she'll fight the principal if he tries to censor us again."

Mathew thumbed through the notebook, admiring the lines. "You've always been good at this," he said, softly.

Samantha rolled her eyes, but she was glowing. "Thanks. I just think if you're going to spend four months obsessing over something, you might as well make it weird as hell."

Robert took the notebook, flipping to a page filled with wild, looping signatures. "Are you collecting autographs already?" he asked.

"No, that's for a mural," Samantha replied. "I want everyone in the cast to sign a wall backstage. So they feel like a part of it, even when it's over."

William nodded. "That's a cool idea. It's like you're building a memory before it even happens."

Samantha grinned, then shrugged off the compliment. "It's just fun. Way better than being home alone watching Nick at Nite reruns."

"You're going to be famous," said Jimmy, mock-serious. "And when you are, just remember: I want free tickets. Plus a guest spot on your reality show."

Samantha punched his arm. "No reality shows. If I'm ever on TV, it's because I committed an art heist."

"Or political sabotage," Josephine added, winking.

Samantha grinned wider, looking at her brother. "Matt, what would you do if I got arrested for performance art?"

Mathew pretended to ponder. "I'd argue it was entrapment, then run for District Attorney."

The group cackled, the sound carried off by the wind through the pines.

They reached the start of the old deer trail, the ground muddy from yesterday's thaw. Samantha darted ahead, vaulting a fallen log and landing in a spray of needles.

"Come on," she called. "I want to see if the clearing is still there."

Mathew watched her go, a mix of pride and protectiveness stirring in his chest. He felt the others at his shoulder, sharing the moment, understanding it without words.

"You ever think," Robert said, "she'll actually pull all this off?"

"She's a Walton," Josephine replied. "They always do."

They picked their way down the trail, shoes wet and cold, but the pace lighter now, the mood lifted by Samantha's exuberance.

At the far end of the path, the world opened up into the clearing, ringed by palmetto and moss. The group paused at the edge, just for a second, taking it in.

Samantha turned, hair wild in the wind, eyes bright as the sunrise. "Let's go!" she said, and ran ahead, her laugh echoing behind her.

The others followed, drawn forward by the energy and the promise of the next thing.

It was impossible not to believe in her, even if only for that moment.

***

The path back to their old haunt traced the memory of a neighborhood more than its reality. The houses leaned in on themselves, their paint sun-faded or curling at the corners. Where once there'd been clusters of kids and dogs and the summer's shriek of lawnmowers, there was now only the drone of far-off traffic and the slow tick of the wind moving through empty yards.

"Remember when the Jenkinses used to leave a sprinkler running, and we'd all cut through their yard?" said William, gesturing at the blue-plastic dinosaur still tipped sideways in the grass.

Jimmy shook his head, grinning. "You mean remember when you tripped on that and broke your front teeth? I still have the Polaroid."

"That was years ago," William protested, but he couldn't help laughing.

Mathew fell in beside Josephine, who was scanning the row of mailboxes, reading the names out loud. "There are so many new people. All the old families are gone."

Josephine shrugged. "Gentrification, baby. Now it's all realtors and people who own Teslas."

Samantha, never able to walk a straight line, zigzagged from yard to yard, touching every fencepost, kicking at the rocks, breathing the neighborhood in like she could taste the difference.

"They painted the church yellow," she called, pointing down the block. "I kind of like it."

Robert glanced up from his phone, squinting at the glare. "It used to be white. Now it looks like a banana."

"I like bananas," Samantha said, not missing a beat.

They walked past the spot where the city had finally paved the old drainage ditch, the scars of sidewalk patches still visible. For a second, the group fell into silence, each lost in their own recollections.

"I remember thinking these streets were endless," said Mathew. "Like you could ride your bike forever and never hit the edge."

"Now it's all so—" William tried to find the word.

"Compressed," said Josephine, supplying it. "Like somebody ran the neighborhood through a dryer and shrunk it down to size."

"I still feel like a giant here," Jimmy said, reaching out to palm the top of a battered mailbox.

They meandered, pausing at every house that meant something: the one where they'd gotten chased off for stealing figs, the yard where Mark had broken his arm doing a daredevil jump, the porch where Josephine first kissed a boy and then spent the rest of the summer pretending it never happened.

It was all familiar, but also new—strange in its sameness.

The group reached the edge of the woods, the trees darker and taller than they remembered. The clearing was up ahead, shielded from the street by a thicket of palmetto.

"I wonder if the fort is still there," said Jimmy.

Samantha grinned, showing a flash of the kid she used to be. "Only one way to find out."

They plunged into the trees, the air suddenly sharp with the scent of pine and wet leaves.

For a few seconds, they were children again, running from nothing, chasing the shadow of who they'd been.

At the end of the trail, the world opened up, and the old clearing waited, unchanged.

***

The trail had shifted, like the woods had rearranged themselves while no one was looking. The path that used to be a dirt rut was now cluttered with fallen branches, and the palmettos had crept in, their saw-edged fans brushing at knees and ankles. Jimmy led the way, using a broken stick to hack at the worst of the overgrowth, pretending he was forging a path through virgin jungle.

Samantha kept pace, hopping from rock to root, narrating their progress like a TV nature host. "Notice how the native species of suburban teens use environmental camouflage," she said, flicking a leaf at Josephine's face. "Observe their pack behavior and innate love of processed carbohydrates."

"Shut up," Josephine laughed, but she liked it.

Robert was more tentative, picking his steps, ever the scientist cataloging bugs and lichens, but he made up the rear without complaint. William and Mark hung in the middle, keeping a running commentary about which trees they'd once tried to climb and which ones had secret initials carved somewhere up the trunk.

"It's smaller than I remember," said William, as the trees thinned and the clearing came into view.

"It's us that got bigger," Jimmy said. "Or maybe just Mark."

Mark snorted, but the joke didn't sting. He ducked his head and stepped into the sunlight, the others fanning out behind him.

The clearing was more or less as they'd left it: a wide bowl of packed dirt, ringed by brush and palmetto, with the battered stump standing sentry at the center. Around the stump, the faint outline of their old "fire pit"—just a circle of blackened rocks—still showed through the leaf litter. Somebody's plastic action figure, sun-bleached and missing an arm, peeked out from under a root.

"Holy shit, it's the same," said Robert, wonder in his voice. "I can't believe nobody trashed it."

Samantha made a beeline for the stump, running her hands over the top. "The Lantern Throne," she intoned, putting on her best movie trailer voice. "Seat of power. Site of the legendary oath."

She jumped up and perched on it, arms spread. "Swear your loyalty, peasants!"

Josephine bowed with mock solemnity. "Queen of the clearing."

Jimmy knelt, which looked ridiculous, and recited, "What light cannot reach—"

"—shadow must cleanse," finished William, deadpan.

They all laughed, but the sound was half-nostalgic, half real.

Mathew stood at the edge, taking it in. He remembered how the clearing had felt enormous, a world apart. Now it was just a patch of dirt and a rotten stump, but he could see the old magic layered over it—the place where secrets were shared, where stupid dares had left scars, where they'd once promised not to let the world mess them up.

Mark sat on the edge of the fire pit, picking up a chunk of charcoal and tossing it from hand to hand. "I thought this was indestructible," he said. "Like it would always be here."

"It is, kind of," said Josephine. "Nobody else even knows about it."

"Maybe some future weirdos found it and made their own club," said Robert. "Like we started a tradition."

Samantha hopped off the stump, landing with a crunch. She dug in her backpack and pulled out a tiny, battery-powered lantern—the kind sold in camping stores. She twisted it on, and a harsh white beam cut through the afternoon shadows.

"For old time's sake," she said, setting it on the stump.

The group circled up, not holding hands or making a ceremony out of it, but close enough that their shadows all pointed in.

For a second, no one said anything.

The light flickered in the breeze, and the sounds of the city faded until all that was left was the creak of trees and the distant drone of cars on Victory Drive.

"I don't remember what we actually promised," said William, quietly.

Jimmy shrugged. "It didn't matter. Just that we did it."

"Let's not get sappy," said Mark, but his voice was softer than before.

Samantha grinned, hair lit up by the fake lantern. "I think we should promise to always come back here. No matter what."

Josephine rolled her eyes. "You're such a theater kid."

"Promise?" Samantha said, sticking out her hand.

One by one, the others touched her hand, a chain of palms and fingertips, half mocking and half real.

"Promise," they said, almost together.

Mathew hung back for a second, then joined, feeling the weight and the lightness of the moment.

After, they scattered around the clearing, each finding their own place, watching the trees and the light as the day wound down.

It wasn't magic, not really. But it was something.

And in the woods, away from everything else, that was enough.

***

After a few minutes of just sitting with the trees and the chill, the conversation drifted back toward the stump, the lantern glowing like a misplaced UFO on its mossy pedestal. It was Robert who broke the silence, tossing a pinecone at the circle of rocks.

"You guys remember how we took the oath super seriously? Like we thought it actually meant something cosmic?"

"We were eleven," said Jimmy, "we also believed Mountain Dew could give you X-ray vision."

"Speak for yourself," said Josephine, swinging her legs over the stump. "Some of us have always understood the importance of a sacred trust."

Mark snorted. "We were basically junior Illuminati. Do you know how many secret passwords we invented?"

"At least four," Samantha said, counting off on her fingers. "But we forgot them all by seventh grade."

"That's how you keep a secret," said William, deadpan.

Mathew watched the interplay, nostalgia tinged with a strange pride. Even now, the old dynamics reasserted themselves—Mark as the cynic, Josephine as the defender of lost causes, Robert as the quiet observer, William as the straight man, Jimmy and Samantha forever the wildcards.

"I'm just saying," Mark continued, "we thought we were founding fathers, but we were really just bored kids with a lantern and a surplus of melodrama."

"But that's the whole point," said Josephine, warming to her argument. "Even if it was all pretend, the feeling was real. You can't fake that."

"Yeah," said Jimmy, "but you can fake the blood pact part. I definitely used ketchup."

The group lost it for a second, the laughter bouncing off the trees and rolling into the underbrush.

When it died down, Samantha hugged her knees to her chest. "Maybe we were melodramatic," she said, "but I liked that we cared enough to make a big deal out of nothing. Adults never do that."

"Adults make a big deal out of everything except the stuff that matters," said Josephine.

William nodded. "It's like the world only wants you to believe in important things if there's a profit in it."

Robert, who'd been quiet, finally spoke. "I think it's nice we remember. Even if it's all different now."

They sat with that for a moment, letting it sink in.

Mark picked up the lantern, flicked it off, then set it back down. "Promise me we will never start a pyramid scheme, okay? That's where secret societies go to die."

"Agreed," said Mathew.

"Agreed," echoed the others, almost in unison.

The mood was loose and easy, but underneath it ran a strong current of something more—gratitude, maybe, for the dumb luck that had brought them all back together, even for a day.

Samantha glanced at the sky, which was already taking on the color of dusk. "We should probably head back before it gets dark. I don't want to get eaten by possums."

Jimmy grinned. "You could take a possum. You'd be their queen in a week."

"Stop," she said, but she was laughing.

They packed up, leaving the lantern on the stump, a tiny beacon for whatever kids might find it next.

As they picked their way back through the trees, the old oath hung in the air—less a spell now, and more like a promise to never forget how much the small things had mattered.

And for the first time in a long while, it felt good to believe in something, even if it was just the memory of who they'd been.

***

On the way back through the woods, the mood shifted. The light turned blue and flat, and the voices dropped, each step sinking into a hush that felt both heavy and holy. They didn't have to say it, but everyone knew: this was the last time, maybe, that the day would stretch so long and so empty, with nothing pulling them in six directions.

Jimmy and William talked quietly, sometimes lapsing into silence that was easy, not awkward. Josephine and Robert argued about the best route back to the main street, but only half-heartedly, like they needed to keep up the performance.

Mathew and Samantha walked at the rear, her arm looped through his. She was quieter now, not subdued, but softer around the edges.

"You think it'll be different next year?" she asked. "When you all come back?"

Mathew considered it. "I think it'll be different every time."

She nodded. "I just hope we don't lose it. The group, I mean."

"We won't," said Mathew, with more certainty than he felt. "We always find each other."

Up ahead, Mark stopped and waited, letting the rest catch up. When they reached him, he looked at each face in turn, as if committing them to memory.

"Best day I've had all year," he said, and no one disagreed.

They emerged from the trees just as the sun dropped behind the rooftops, the houses casting long, deep shadows across the yards. The streets were even quieter now, the only movement a single porch cat stalking something invisible.

The group drifted to a stop at the edge of the park, the unspoken question hanging between them: what now?

Nobody wanted to be the first to break away.

"We could get pizza," said Jimmy, as if proposing a state funeral.

"We should," agreed Josephine. "One last time before everybody scatters."

They walked together, tighter now, as the night crept in. The air was cold and sharp, but it didn't matter.

The thing that held them together wasn't the past, not really. It was the belief—however fragile—that somewhere ahead, they'd find each other again.

And for tonight, that was enough.

***

The football field felt abandoned in the dark. The stands were empty, the bleachers slick with dew, and the only light came from the sodium glow of the streetlamps lining the parking lot. Mathew kicked at the frozen grass, hands shoved in his pockets, the steam of his breath fogging up in front of him.

The group gravitated toward the fifty-yard line, drawn by the memory of Friday nights and the thump of marching bands. Even Mark, who should have hated the place now, looked almost peaceful as he lay back on the cold turf, arms folded behind his head.

Jimmy jogged the length of the field, then ran a victory lap, arms out like an airplane. Samantha followed, laughing, her voice ringing out in the open space.

"Last one to the end zone owes me a Coke!" she yelled.

They sprinted, the others cheering them on, until both collapsed in a heap near the goal post.

In the stands, the rest of the group huddled together, knees pulled up against the cold.

"Can you believe we used to think this was the center of the universe?" Josephine said.

William shrugged. "For a while, it was."

"It's weird how fast everything moves," Robert said. "One minute you're a kid, and the next it's like… what now?"

"College," said Mathew, "then grad school, then real life. It's like a conveyor belt."

"I don't want to get on the conveyor belt yet," Samantha called from the field. "It looks boring."

"It sure does," said Jimmy, coming back to join them. "But sometimes it's funny. Like when you realize you have no idea what you're doing and nobody else does either."

Mark rolled over, sitting up. "I think that's the secret. Everyone's just faking it. Even the professors."

Samantha dusted grass off her jeans and climbed up to join the others in the bleachers. "Let's just promise to meet here again. Next winter break."

"You and your promises," said Josephine, mock-exasperated, but she didn't say no.

"I like that idea," said William.

Robert nodded. "We could even bring the lantern next time. Do it right."

They sat for a while, trading stories and talking about classes, professors, and the things they missed about home. The air got colder, the night pressing in, but nobody seemed eager to leave.

Eventually, the conversation slowed, turning to plans for tomorrow: drives, schedules, all the things pulling them away.

"I don't want to go back yet," said Samantha, her voice small.

Mathew put an arm around her. "We've still got tonight."

For a few minutes, nobody spoke. They just watched the empty field, letting the memories pile up.

When it was finally time to leave, they did it together, climbing down the metal steps in a clattering mess, shoving and joking and lingering at the edge of the parking lot.

For all its emptiness, the football field felt full again, if only for a little while.

And that was enough.

***

They reached the edge of the parking lot, the air colder now, every breath a sharp reminder that the day was ending. The group lingered under the yellow streetlights, hands jammed in pockets or arms wrapped tight against the wind.

Jimmy was the first to go, peeling off toward his truck with a lazy wave. William left next, backpack slung over one shoulder, promising to text when he got in. Robert and Mark lived in opposite directions but walked off together, still talking about something from the field.

That left Mathew, Josephine, and Samantha, the parking lot quiet but for the hum of far-off traffic.

"I'm just a few blocks away," said Samantha, smiling at both of them. "You don't have to walk me. I'm not a kid anymore."

Mathew hesitated, the old urge to protect flickering up. "You sure?"

Samantha grinned. "Positive. Besides, if anybody tries to kidnap me, I'll stage a dramatic monologue and bore them to death."

Josephine laughed. "They wouldn't stand a chance."

Samantha hugged them both, quick and fierce, then stepped back. "I'll see you next time," she said, and meant it.

They watched her walk away, her hair lit gold in the streetlight, until she turned the corner and disappeared.

For a few seconds, Mathew just stared after her.

"She's gonna be okay," said Josephine, reading his mind.

He nodded, even if he didn't quite believe it. "I know."

They stood there, not ready to let go of the day, not just yet.

Eventually, they drifted apart, heading for their own homes and their own routines.

But for a little while longer, the memory of the group lingered, warm against the chill.

In the ordinary hush of a Savannah night, it was easy to believe that nothing bad could happen.

Which is how, for a time, it stayed.

***

The walk home was short, familiar: two turns past the rec center, a straight shot down Magnolia, then left at the candy-cane striped mailbox. The night was as still as it ever got in Savannah, just the hush of tires on wet pavement and the slow, distant chime of a grandfather clock from somewhere behind drawn curtains.

Samantha walked fast, more out of habit than fear. Her boots thumped a rhythm on the concrete, and sometimes she sang snatches of show tunes under her breath, the sound pulled apart by the cold. At each intersection, she glanced both ways—never paranoid, just trained—and then kept going, arms folded against the wind.

She thought about the clearing, about the group, about how weird and wonderful it was that they all still fit together even after being flung across the state. She thought about her next play, about the mural she'd paint in the drama room, about what it would feel like to be old enough to leave this place and never look back.

The porch lights changed from yellow to blue to nothing, block by block, as she went. At one point, she looked up and saw the pale half-moon tangled in the branches of the live oaks, and for a second, the world felt bigger and smaller all at once.

She was almost home.

Elsewhere, the others had already peeled away—Jimmy gunning his engine, William waving from his front step, Josephine disappearing into the glow of her parents' living room. Mathew walked the longest, alone, the afterimage of the night stretched out in his mind like a shadow.

In the dark, nobody thought about what might go wrong. Not tonight, not here.

Samantha rounded the last corner, her house in sight, porch light blinking like a heartbeat.

She smiled.

On the street, the night folded quietly around her, holding its breath.

And for a moment, everything was exactly as it should be.

CHAPTER 5

Night in the Walton house was never truly silent, not in the old sense of the word. There was always the drip of the kitchen sink, the low groan of the furnace kicking on, the skittering of raccoons gnawing at the trash bins outside. But this night, every sound was both amplified and dulled by the absence at its center—a silence that throbbed, like a toothache, with the shape of Samantha's missing laughter.

Mathew prowled the circuit between the living room window and the indentation where Samantha's armchair pressed into the rug. He tracked invisible routes: up the hall, across the front entry, a detour through the kitchen where her sneakers still waited by the fridge, then back to the window. The street beyond was empty, a faint glaze of frost on the lawns, the only movement the slow oscillation of the neighbor's inflatable Santa, knocked askew by last night's wind. He stood in the dark, cold air leaking through the glass, and tried to conjure the sight of her—a flash of her red jacket, a smear of untamed hair, a stomp of boots up the stoop.

He saw only himself, reflected faintly in the glass, gaunt and sleepless, a boy stretched too thin over an expectation that Samantha would appear, that she had to.

The living room still wore its Christmas best, but the ornaments were gaudy in the dimness. The tree's lights, once cozy, now hissed and flickered, each colored bulb a tiny surveillance camera trained on his failure. Samantha's stocking hung limp by the gas fireplace, never filled. The cookie plate she'd set out for the UPS driver—a family tradition since third grade—remained untouched, two mummified snickerdoodles fossilized to the ceramic.

His mother was a fixture on the couch, cocooned in a tangle of blankets, the mug of tea cooling between her hands. The tea, Mathew noticed, never grew smaller, only denser, as if she intended to will the caffeine back into the bag by sheer persistence. She didn't blink, didn't seem to breathe. Only her thumb traced circles on the stoneware, again and again, as the hours bled from one to the next.

Once, at three in the morning, she'd tried to call Samantha's cell, and the sound of her own voice in the voicemail box had broken something—Mathew had watched the tremor move through her shoulders, a ripple and then a hardening, as if the loss could be calcified in place. Now she only watched the window, like him, waiting for a miracle or at least a reprieve from the parade of silence.

His father had not left the study in hours, not even for coffee. The door was shut, but sound leaked out in bursts: the dial tone, the click and clatter of the Rolodex, the testy bark of his "This is Michael Walton, you will call me back at once" voice. Occasionally, the old man would hiss a string of curses, then fall silent, then resume the cycle. At dinner, which nobody touched, he'd said, "If she's not home by midnight, we call the sheriff," and then retreated to his den with the look of someone about to face a firing squad.

Mathew could hear the tempo of his father's calls change—first slow, then faster, then frantic and overlapping, as if repetition alone could summon his daughter home.

It had been six hours since Samantha was supposed to come in. She'd said goodnight to her friends, walked the three blocks home, and vanished somewhere in the elastic darkness between sidewalk and porch.

Mathew tried to reconstruct the route in his mind, block by block, each patch of streetlight a frame in a stop-motion film. She would have cut behind the rec center, maybe stopped to swing on the monkey bars, maybe detoured past the corner store for a soda or a scratch-off ticket. There were a thousand safe choices, and only one that led to this.

At midnight, the house felt airless, the windows fogged by the breath of three people who could not admit the worst was possible. Even the Christmas tree seemed to stoop, exhausted by the effort of pretending nothing was wrong.

A car rolled past, headlights flaring through the blinds, and Mathew's mother straightened in her seat. She stood, tea sloshing over her hand, and hovered by the door, not touching the knob, just listening to the engine fade.

Mathew turned from the window. His mother met his gaze, and for a moment, neither of them said anything. Then she whispered, "You think she's just—" but the rest of the sentence vanished, as if the effort of hope had erased it.

He wanted to tell her yes. He wanted to believe it.

Instead, he went to his room, pulled on his jacket, and slipped out the back door, the old hinges silent for once in their lives. He grabbed the heavy flashlight from the garage, found the battered gloves Samantha used for theater paint projects, and started down the driveway, the cold so sharp it felt like punishment.

He would retrace every step. He would not let the silence win.

***

The first thing the cold did was numb his hands, even through the gloves. The second was to sharpen every sound—a branch scraping window glass, the distant scrape of a cat in the gutter, the hollow echo of his own boots on the sidewalk. Mathew kept the flashlight aimed low, the beam crawling along the curb and grass, hesitant to betray his presence to the blank windows of the street.

He started with the tennis courts behind the rec center. The chain-link was rimmed with ice, the gate padlocked, but he hopped it anyway, landing heavy in the cinders on the other side. Samantha had a habit of detouring here when she needed to burn off steam, sometimes hurling a rock at the fence or practicing pirouettes on the painted service lines. He swept the beam along the perimeter, looking for anything—a scarf, a shoe print, the red jacket. But the court was sterile, the surface undisturbed except for a few animal tracks.

Mathew checked the playground next, swinging the light under every slide, into the hollow of the spinning drum, beneath the low benches where kids hid from the wind. He called her name, first tentative, then louder, the syllables brittle in the empty night. "Sam," he tried, then "Samantha!" The echo returned alone.

He opened the notebook and jotted a quick map: rec center, check; tennis courts, check; playground, check. The ink ran thin in the cold, but he pressed harder, making the letters thick and black.

Next, he followed the shortcut Samantha used behind the decommissioned firehouse, the path worn from years of neighborhood kids cutting across to avoid the long way round. There was a muddy patch by the fence line, frozen solid now, but even so, he scanned for marks—treads, imprints, a dropped glove. Nothing.

The babysitting house was just past the intersection, a ranch with yellow shutters and a gnome by the mailbox. The lights were out, but Mathew saw the TV glow moving in the den. He considered knocking, but what would he ask? Had anyone seen a ghost pass by, trailing worry in her wake? He moved on, faster, the anxiety starting to bubble up under his ribs.

Every block was a storyboard of Samantha's old habits. There was the front stoop where she'd once left a bag of gummy worms in the summer heat, the mailbox she'd dented with a stolen baseball bat, the alley where she and her friends hid to smoke menthols and dare each other to eat whole packets of wasabi. With each spot, he imagined her standing there, illuminated by the cone of his flashlight, ready with a smirk or an insult or the pure, unfiltered scorn she reserved for her big brother's overreactions.

He checked the shortcut by Moonrise Lane, the only place in the neighborhood that felt remotely dangerous. Mathew kicked through the brittle brush, pausing every few feet to listen. There were no voices, only the wind and a far-off, thumping bass from some closed-window party. He scrawled another note in the book: "Moonrise path—clear."

After an hour, Mathew's legs were humming with fatigue and a deeper, knotted exhaustion. The only thing left was the canal—an old storm drain behind the utility lot, where the drainage cut a shallow trench parallel to the backyards. He hated the place, even as a kid, but if Samantha had been chased or just wanted to vanish, this would be the hiding place.

The canal smelled of rot and something chemical, the black water sluggish under a crust of ice. He ran the flashlight along the edge, looking for a splash of red or a sign of struggle. The banks were littered with the usual debris—beer cans, a torn plastic bag, the warped skeleton of a shopping cart. The mud had hardened overnight, so if anyone had been there since the last thaw, they'd left no mark.

Mathew crouched by the culvert, pressing his hand to the frozen concrete, feeling the cold radiate up his arm. He called her name once more, voice catching. It sounded stupid and hollow, the cry of someone who already knew he wouldn't be answered.

He closed the notebook, shoved it in his pocket, and retraced his steps toward home. The wind had picked up, lashing his face with raw chill. Every porch light he passed was a rebuke—a reminder of families intact, of kids safe in bed, of normal nights.

He didn't want to go back, didn't want to face his mother's ruined hope or his father's silent war with the phone. But he had nowhere else to search. As he turned onto his street, the house looked smaller, as if Samantha's absence had shrunken it from the inside.

When he opened the door, the silence was absolute. His mother was still on the couch, eyes rimmed red, her thumb running slow laps around the rim of her mug. His father stood in the entry to the study, phone pressed to his ear, jaw clenched tight enough to splinter teeth.

And then the phone on the wall rang, a sound so unexpected that Mathew jumped. His father lunged for it, nearly wrenching it from the cradle.

"This is Walton," he snapped. Then a pause, as the voice on the other end spoke.

Mathew watched his father's face—at first blank, then flickering with a desperate kind of hope, then set into a mask. "Thank you," he said, but his eyes went nowhere.

He hung up, met Mathew's gaze, and said, "They think someone saw her. She was headed toward Moonrise Lane around nine."

Mathew felt the news like a shot of adrenaline—enough to keep going, not enough to bring relief.

He pulled the notebook from his pocket, thumbed to the page, and circled the words "Moonrise path—clear."

He would start again at first light.

***

The phone call changed the atmosphere in the house instantly. Where before there had been only the heavy drag of despair, now everything bristled with a new, erratic energy—still desperate, but no longer numb.

Mathew's father sprang into motion, marching back and forth across the entryway, barking orders into the phone. He called the sheriff's office again, then the emergency dispatch, then the head of neighborhood watch, as if sheer volume could shake more facts loose. The old man's voice, usually controlled to the point of artifice, now cracked and wavered with each retelling: "My daughter, red jacket, last seen nine PM, Moonrise Lane—yes, I know it's late, yes, I know the odds, but we're not waiting until daylight." The repetition was almost a ritual, an incantation against the void.

Mathew's mother held the receiver after each call, hands white-knuckled, staring at the wall as if the act of listening hard enough could bridge the distance to her missing child. She cycled through states: pacing, shivering, hugging herself, retreating to the couch, then back to the phone. At one point, she even attempted to pour a fresh cup of tea, but when the hot water splashed her hand, she barely flinched.

Mathew watched it all from the base of the stairs, notebook open on his knee, the pen digging gouges in the paper. The lead was good, but it was old. If Samantha had been on Moonrise Lane at nine, that left six hours unaccounted for. Six hours for something to happen, or for someone to make her disappear completely.

He replayed the tip in his mind, working the timeline like a puzzle he was supposed to solve. Nine PM—walking home, alone. Did she make it past the firehouse? Past the canal? Did someone spot her and follow, or did she go willingly, always craving some new thrill, some way to prove she couldn't be managed? There were too many variables, and none of them fit the Samantha he'd last seen at the diner, hair wild and eyes shining, the queen of her own goddamn world.

He drew a circle around Moonrise Lane in his notes and wrote, "start here." He didn't allow himself to consider what he might find.

The phone rang again at four, this time with an officer from the sheriff's department. They would assemble a search team at dawn. In the meantime, Mathew and his parents were advised to get some sleep, in case the morning brought news.

None of them slept, not really. Mathew retreated to his room, but instead of lying down, he sorted through Samantha's things—her old debate medals, the shoeboxes of playbills, the tangle of scarves and costume jewelry at the bottom of her closet. He fingered the edge of her favorite scarf, red and soft, the one she wore even in Savannah's muggy springs. It was still there, which meant she hadn't planned to run.

He wrote a list of names in the notebook: friends, ex-friends, teachers, the last boy she'd dated, the girl from the theater department she sometimes fought with. He would ask every one of them if he had to.

By the time the sky faded from black to a watery blue, the house had transformed from tomb to command center. His father's voice was already in the driveway, greeting the first patrol car, waving in volunteers. His mother was in the kitchen, sleeves rolled, taping together stacks of Samantha's best photos—baby pictures, middle school yearbook shots, the awkward eighth-grade headshot Mathew had always teased her about. The photos looked raw in the cold morning light, every smile now a kind of rebuke.

Mathew pulled on a clean sweatshirt, laced his boots, and wrote one last thing in the notebook: "No one vanishes into thin air." He clung to it, the way you clung to a life raft after a shipwreck.

When he stepped outside, his breath fogged in the air, and the street was full of strangers determined to find his sister.

Hope, he realized, was just another name for dread in motion.

***

By seven, the house was swarmed. The first wave was the police—two officers, a civilian in a reflective vest, and the patrol captain, who brought a folder thick with protocol. They spoke in low voices, careful to direct all questions to Mathew's father. The next was the neighbors: the English teacher from three doors down, the kid with the curly hair who'd once borrowed Samantha's bike and never returned it, the parade of concerned women bearing casseroles and boxes of donuts, as if calories could be deployed as a weapon against bad news.

But it was the arrival of his own friends that made the scene real for Mathew. They came in a staggered file—first Josie, in black windbreaker and battered Chucks, holding a stack of flyers with Samantha's face on every page; then Robert, who wore a clean white lab coat over his hoodie, as if he'd come straight from the hospital basement; then William and Jimmy, together as always, lugging a backpack loaded with first aid supplies and an industrial staple gun. Mark was last, trailing the group by half a block, hands in the pockets of a varsity jacket he hadn't worn since the surgery.

They clustered in the driveway, avoiding the front porch where Mathew's mother had set up a makeshift war room of coffee urns and notepads. Josie took immediate charge, corralling the others onto the hood of the old station wagon, arranging the flyers in neat piles. She had a set of six walkie-talkies that she distributed to the group as well.

She handed one to Mathew, the photo centered in the rectangle: Samantha, chin up, half-smirk, hair a tangle. The headline read, in bold: "MISSING – Last Seen 12/22, Moonrise Lane." The text was tight, factual, with no room for speculation. Josie's handwriting scrawled the sheriff's number in fat marker at the bottom.

"They're good," Mathew said, voice hoarse. "She'd hate the picture."

"She can yell at us when we find her," said Josie, not looking up. She wore her decisiveness like armor, slicing through doubt with a tone that brooked no argument. "We divide into two groups. Matt, Robert, and I cover the east streets. Jimmy, William, and Mark go west, then circle back by the canal and the woods. We meet at the old church at ten sharp and coordinate with the deputies. Got it?"

Jimmy nodded, zipping the backpack with a loud rip. "What if we find something before the cops do?"

"That's what the walkie-talkies are for," said Josie. "And don't touch anything."

William checked his watch, already mapping the route in his mind. "We'll get started now. The sooner we move, the better."

Mark was restless, shoulders tight, the old power of his presence dampened by injury and something else—maybe fear. He eyed the patrol car parked across the street, then looked at Mathew. "You sure the cops are up for this?"

Mathew shrugged, trying not to let the doubt show. "They're following the rules. Doesn't mean we can't do better."

Josie grinned, and for a second, the old warmth returned. "See? It's just like a group project. Only this time, nobody gets to flake."

They fanned out across the sidewalk, taping flyers to every available surface—lampposts, telephone poles, bus stop benches. Mathew felt the ghost of Samantha beside him with every stapled page, her voice in his ear: "Don't let them use that photo. I look like a Muppet." He stapled it anyway, harder, as if force could conjure her from the ether.

By eight, the sun was barely above the rooftops, but the neighborhood pulsed with motion. The joggers slowed to read the flyers; the dog walkers offered cautious, sympathetic glances. At the intersection by the elementary school, a crossing guard flagged down Josie and asked if she'd seen the "strange van" parked outside the day before.

Mathew didn't linger for the small talk. He moved methodically, one pole to the next, his hands stiff with cold and the ache of repetition. He marked each location in the notebook—every possible sightline, every possible witness. When he stopped to catch his breath, Robert was already waiting at the corner, peering through binoculars borrowed from the science department.

"What are you looking for?" Mathew asked.

Robert didn't answer right away. He adjusted the focus, tracking a hawk overhead, then shifted to the next house. "Patterns," he said. "Anything that doesn't belong."

Josie called them over. She'd set up a base by the gas station, using the pay phone as a message board. She'd written a schedule on a legal pad, listing every hour between now and sunset.

Mathew took a deep breath. For the first time, he felt the smallest flicker of possibility. Not hope, exactly, but the knowledge that there were people who would not give up. It was enough to keep him moving.

He flipped open the notebook, scanned the map, and started toward Moonrise Lane.

The day was just beginning, but already he felt the exhaustion clinging to his bones.

***

The city in the morning looked nothing like the city at night. Now, under the glare of day, every imperfection stood out—cigarette butts pooled in the gutters, puddles of oil catching the sun, the frost receding in streaks across the lawns. But it wasn't the weather that made the day feel off. It was the way people moved through the streets, eyes darting to the flyers, then away, as if acknowledging the problem meant to take some responsibility for it.

Mathew and Josie started with the playground by the middle school, blanketing the fence and jungle gym with Samantha's picture. A teacher on early-morning yard duty came over, hands stuffed deep in his coat. "Is she your sister?" he asked, voice full of rough sympathy. Mathew nodded. The man offered nothing but a long look and a promise to "keep eyes open." It felt both genuine and completely powerless.

At the convenience store, the cashier remembered seeing "a girl, maybe in red, with a couple of boys, but that was yesterday." Josie pressed him: "Did you see where they went?" The clerk shrugged, already back to scanning lottery tickets.

Robert combed the apartment complex on the corner, methodical as always, ticking off units from his map. He rang doorbells, made notes, and even checked the trash bins for any clues that might have been missed in the night. Most doors stayed closed. The few who opened answered with the same formula: "Sorry, haven't seen her," then a gentle closing, as if unwilling to let the bad luck inside.

The pattern repeated everywhere. At the donut shop, the regulars shook their heads and muttered about the "state of the world." The school crossing guard recalled nothing out of the ordinary. A neighbor swore she saw Samantha's shadow on the edge of the church parking lot, but the timestamp was all wrong.

By ten, Mathew's hands ached from the staple gun, his voice was hoarse from explaining the story, and his heart was calcifying into a lump behind his ribs. He stopped on the steps of the old church, letting the sun heat his face, and tried to remember when he'd last felt something other than this.

Josie arrived next, dusting off her hands, scanning the horizon for the others. "Any luck?" she asked.

Mathew shook his head. "Nothing solid."

Robert appeared from the side, notebook clutched tight. "I'm tracking every non-sighting. If she's not here, she had to go somewhere."

Josie clicked the button on her walkie-talkie, and unintelligible voices answered her as she put the unit to her ear. "Jimmy and William are on the other side of the neighborhood. Mark's with them."

Robert raised an eyebrow. "Did they find anything?"

"Just rumors. The lady at the deli said she saw a kid with a red jacket near the canal, but it could have been anybody. Half the town owns a red jacket."

Mathew took a flyer from the stack, crumpled it in his fist, and let it drop to the steps. "She wouldn't run," he said, more to himself than anyone else.

Josie's gaze softened. "I know."

They sat in the silence, broken only by the distant squeal of a city bus and the hum of a lawnmower. Mathew looked at the faces on the flyers, Samantha's smile frozen mid-insult, and wondered if they'd ever find out what really happened.

He looked up at the cross on top of the church, trying to draw something—courage, hope, anything—from the empty sky.

When the others arrived, they looked as battered as Mathew felt. William's hair was flattened with sweat, Jimmy's hands stained from poster ink, Mark moving stiffly, as if fighting both the cold and his own bad thoughts.

Josie stood, squared her shoulders, and said, "We regroup. We check the canal. We keep moving."

Mathew nodded, feeling the resolve flicker and catch in his chest. He opened the notebook, drew a line under the morning's efforts, and wrote: "Nothing is ever as lost as it seems."

They pushed off the church steps, the six of them moving together, each step erasing a little bit of the darkness that had settled over the night before.

***

The canal in daylight was uglier than Mathew remembered—banks scabbed with trash, the water gray and sluggish, a film of ice on the edges that fractured under the sun. The group fanned out along the path, boots crunching on the hard dirt, each step an accusation: you should have been here sooner.

Robert led the way, hunched and intense, as if physically willing the world to reveal its secrets. He paused at a patch of mud sheltered by the overpass, knelt down, and waved the others over.

"Look," he said, voice tight.

Mathew squatted beside him, squinting at the disturbance: two sets of prints, side by side, the smaller one splaying out near the heel, the larger one pressed deeper at the toe.

Josie whistled softly. "That could be her," she said, not quite daring to believe it.

Robert nodded, following the line of tracks along the bank. "They go north, toward the woods."

Mark's face sharpened, jaw set. "Then what are we waiting for?"

They followed the prints as far as they could, the group silent except for the brittle crack of ice underfoot. For a few minutes, hope propelled them—maybe this was the moment, maybe she was just around the bend, crouched in hiding, waiting to be rescued or at least found.

But the further they went, the fainter the trail became. The mud gave way to a tangled mat of dead leaves and frozen grass. The tracks dissolved into nothing, swallowed by the indifference of winter.

Mathew scanned the horizon, searching for a splash of color, a scrap of red, any sign that his sister had left a marker for him. He saw only trees, shivering in the wind.

Jimmy kicked at a chunk of concrete, frustrated. "We were so close."

Josie knelt at the last visible print, tracing it with a gloved finger. "It doesn't make sense. She wouldn't just disappear."

William, quietly practical, said, "Maybe she got in a car. Or someone helped her."

Robert stood, dusted off his hands, and looked to Mathew for direction.

Mathew swallowed, the taste of failure bitter. "We keep looking," he said. "We don't stop."

They spread out along the canal, calling Samantha's name, voices bouncing off the water and back at them. After twenty minutes, they regrouped at the footbridge, winded and empty.

The footprints had given them a purpose, but now, standing in the flat winter sunlight, all they had was a vanished trail and more questions.

Mathew stared at the water, watching the current slip past, and felt time itself sliding away from him.

***

They worked their way from the canal to the park, then across the wide, ugly stretch of abandoned lots behind the bowling alley, each new terrain sucking a little more energy from their bones. The air never warmed, even as the sun climbed, and by noon, Mathew felt like the world had shrunk to just the next patch of ground, the next possibility.

Josie grew short-tempered, snapping at anyone who moved too slowly or strayed from the plan. "We're not just wandering," she barked at Mark after he chased a hunch down a side path. "We stick to the grid." Mark rolled his eyes but didn't argue. He'd stopped arguing hours ago, instead resorting to muttered curses and bursts of speed that left him winded and hunched, rubbing his knee.

Jimmy and William took turns, sometimes working ahead, sometimes lagging behind, their conversation growing sparser as the day wore on. Even Robert, usually a fountain of theories, grew silent, keeping his eyes down, scanning for prints or any scrap of color against the frozen mud.

They ended up at the edge of the old mill property, a patch of woods that had been off-limits when they were kids but irresistible for every game of truth-or-dare. The factory itself was now a gutted shell, the windows broken out, the brickwork tagged in a dozen layers of graffiti.

Mathew stared at the building, memory overlaying the present: he saw the ghost of his younger self, daring Samantha to race to the loading dock, both of them laughing, their fear a game instead of a warning.

Now, the place just looked hungry.

They spread out under the trees, boots punching through the leaf litter. Mark called out, "Sam! Samantha!" his voice cracking on the second syllable.

No answer.

They trudged through the underbrush, scraping arms and catching pants on brambles, checking every outbuilding and ditch. Every time Mathew's heart lurched at a flash of red—plastic, a beer can, a dead leaf—but never the jacket he hoped for.

The hours bled together, hunger and exhaustion stacking like bricks. The search had lost all logic, all direction; they were just moving, filling the air with their calls, desperate to force the world to give her up.

Dread crept in sideways, worming its way through the cracks of hope. Josie called a halt at the edge of a dry creek bed. She looked at the group, face drawn, and said, "We need to regroup. If we don't—"

But before she finished, Robert's head snapped up. He'd heard something, or seen something, and he took off at a run, the others chasing after.

They caught up to him at the creek, where the bank had collapsed, leaving a muddy shelf above a drainage culvert. Robert pointed wordlessly.

At the edge of the mud was a scuffed print—deep, but blurred by another, heavier step.

Mathew's chest tightened. It could be her. It could be nothing.

He looked up and down the creek bed, hoping for movement, a voice, a sign.

Nothing.

They stood, listening to their own breathing, the quiet suddenly absolute.

Then, from farther down the creek, Josie's voice echoed: "Matt! You need to see this."

They ran.

***

Josie came crashing through the underbrush, sneakers skidding in the mud, her hair wild and matted against her face. She didn't slow, barely registering the others as she staggered up the slope toward them.

Mathew caught her at the edge of the creek, steadying her by the shoulders. Her breath was ragged, her eyes full of something that looked like terror. She tried to speak but choked on the words, chest heaving.

"What is it?" he asked, voice flat and foreign.

She shook her head, wiped her mouth with the back of her hand, and tried again. "In the woods," she managed, gesturing behind her, arm trembling. "Past the service road, near the—near the old drainage ditch."

Robert was already scribbling notes, his own hands shaking so hard the pen left jagged lines across the page.

Mark moved to her side, his anger gone, replaced by a frozen blankness. "Did you see—" he started, but couldn't finish.

Josie swallowed, blinking away tears. "There's—" She stopped, as if the thing itself was waiting in her throat. "You have to come. I can't—" She sagged against Mathew, her knees almost giving out.

Jimmy and William hovered behind, unsure whether to comfort or keep their distance.

Mathew looked at the others, then back to Josie. "Show us," he said, barely above a whisper.

She nodded and led the way, feet dragging, eyes fixed on the ground.

They moved in a loose, terrified line, the woods closing in around them. Every sound seemed to vanish, replaced by the pulse in Mathew's ears.

The group followed Josie across the service road, down a narrow path choked with weeds and broken glass. The ditch was half-filled with runoff, black and stagnant. She stopped a few yards short, pointing.

No one moved at first.

Mathew stepped ahead, feeling every heartbeat in his teeth. He heard someone behind him whisper, "Oh God," but he kept walking.

The dread was so thick it choked out thought. He was ready for anything—except the answer they'd spent all day denying.

***

The ditch stank of rot and antifreeze. The water was so dark it looked solid, a strip of black glass knifing through the winter mud. She was there—Mathew saw it immediately—a bloom of red caught on the lip of the bank, one boot still hooked to a root, her hair fanned in the current like a trailing flag.

For a moment, he didn't register the body as hers. The form was wrong, too still, the familiar jacket caked with filth, face turned away, half-submerged. But then the mind did what it always does: stitched the evidence together, forced a match, and left him with no doubt.

He heard himself say her name, but it came out as a whisper, the syllables chewed up by the wind.

No one moved. Then Josie crumpled, knees hitting the mud, arms over her head as if warding off a blow. Robert turned and doubled over, retching dry. William stared, eyes glassy, unmoving, hands clamped white to his sides. Jimmy went pale, his whole body locked, the noise in his chest a desperate, choked animal sound.

Mark stood rooted, head tipped back, staring at the pale sky through the trees. "No," he said, over and over, as if the right number of denials could reverse the flow of time.

Mathew crouched at the edge, hands buried in his hair, unable to look away. The world contracted to the stretch of mud, the water, the jacket. He kept expecting her to move—to cough, to flip over, to yell at him for making a scene. But she didn't, couldn't.

It was real.

He closed his eyes, but the image burned itself on his brain, every detail precise: the torn sleeve, the laces of her boot, the tangle of her hair against the water. He tried to catalog each thing, as if by counting them he could finish the task and make it less terrible.

He didn't know how long they stood like that, the six of them in the cold, the sky so clear it made his teeth hurt.

When the shock receded, pain rushed in to fill the void.

Josie sobbed, low and raw. Robert wiped his mouth with his sleeve, eyes refusing to meet anyone else's. William knelt by the water, not touching, just staring. Jimmy slumped to the ground, back against a tree, hands trembling so bad he could barely hold them still.

Mathew wanted to be angry, wanted to scream, but all he could do was breathe. In and out, each inhale another confirmation, each exhale letting go.

He thought about the night before—the booth at the diner, the way she'd promised to walk home, the memory of her smile fading into the dark.

He opened his eyes and let the reality in, every inch of it.

Samantha was gone.

***

The first car to arrive was the sheriff's unmarked sedan, its wheels sending up a rooster tail of mud as it fishtailed to a stop. Next came the ambulance, lights strobing uselessly in the daylight, then two more patrol cruisers and a battered minivan that could only be the Waltons' own.

Mathew heard his mother before he saw her. She shrieked his name, barreling down the slope toward the ditch, arms outstretched. The deputies tried to stop her, but she pushed through, landing in the mud next to Samantha, clawing at the water as if she could pull her daughter back into the world by force.

"Sammy, oh my God, oh my baby, please—" Madeline Walton's voice went up, then broke, dissolving into a wail that sent birds scattering from the trees. She rocked forward and back, hair in her face, nails scraping the dirt, heedless of the deputies' attempts to guide her away.

Mathew's father took it differently. He stood at the edge of the bank, fists knotted at his sides, jaw clenched, eyes narrowed to hard slits. He did not cry or yell, but when the sheriff approached with a gentle hand, Michael Walton batted it away, barely containing his rage. He had phone calls to make—first the lawyer, then the grandparents, then someone at the office. His face was cold and precise, no evidence of the carnage beneath.

The deputies worked the scene with grim efficiency. They put up tape, snapped photos, and measured everything with little yellow rulers. When they pulled Samantha's body from the ditch, they zipped it in a black bag and laid it on the grass, and the sight of it undid Madeline all over again. She clung to Mathew, digging her nails into his back, sobbing until she ran out of voice.

Neighbors clustered at the edge of the woods, drawn by the sirens and the crowd. A news van rolled up, crew spilling out with cameras and notepads, ready to turn tragedy into a headline.

Mathew felt himself split in two. Part of him was still kneeling in the mud, staring at the spot where his sister had been. The other part drifted above, watching the performance unfold: the police radios squawking, the camera crews, the buzz of a drone overhead. His private world had burst open, and all of Savannah was here to pick through the wreckage.

He tried to focus on his mother, on her shaking hands, her ruined voice. He tried to focus on his father, refusing to let anyone see him break. He tried to focus on anything except the bag on the grass.

But the worst thing was the moment when a deputy, not much older than Mathew himself, looked up from his notepad and met his gaze. For an instant, the man's face showed nothing but pity, and it was that—more than the grief, more than the noise—that made Mathew want to scream.

He didn't. He just stood there, letting the cold sink into his bones, and watched his family splinter under the weight of it all.

***

The hospital was a different kind of cold—sterile, humming, a chill manufactured by compressors and bad lighting. The morgue was in the basement, far from the life and noise of the emergency room. Still, Mathew could feel the machinery working even here, the hum of refrigeration under every footstep. He insisted on accompanying his parents to make the final identification of Samantha's body. He just had to be sure before he abandoned all hope.

Josie and Robert walked on either side of him. Neither said much. Josie's hands were jammed in her pockets, head down, hair in her face.

Robert had a blank look, but Mathew could see the panic flickering at the edges.

They were met by a man in blue scrubs, who introduced himself but whose name vanished instantly. He led them down a hall lined with cleaning carts and vending machines, then into a waiting area with cracked vinyl chairs and a dead plant in the corner.

"There's some paperwork," the man said, holding out a clipboard. Mathew's father took it and signed without reading.

Matthew didn't remember the rest of the walk to the viewing room. Only the sensation of moving, the sticky floors, the way Josie's elbow pressed into his side like she was keeping him from floating off.

The room itself was shockingly small. The lights were too bright. There was a window, the kind you saw in drive-thrus, but thick and set in steel. Behind it, a gurney. A sheet pulled up to the neck.

The man in scrubs pressed a button. The curtain rolled back.

Mathew hoped to see a stranger. Some version of someone who resembled Samantha, but not her; Someone abstract or out of focus. But there she was, her face both exactly right and entirely wrong. The skin was too pale, lips too blue, but her hair fell the same way, the earring in her left lobe still the one he'd given her for her birthday. There was a bruise on her cheek, and another mark on her neck.

For a second, he thought she might sit up, make a face, say something biting. Instead, she just stared through him, the eyes glassy and fixed.

He pressed his palm to the glass, needing to feel something solid.

Behind him, Josie made a soft sound, then covered her mouth. Robert looked away, hands trembling. He heard commotion as his mother collapsed in a wailing heap, her fall cushioned by his father.

The man asked, "Is this Samantha Walton?"

Mathew swallowed. "Yes," he said, and the word hung in the room, impossible to pull back.

They left the viewing room. Josie wiped her eyes on her sleeve, said, "I'm sorry," over and over, as if it mattered.

Mathew didn't reply. He walked until the hospital faded behind them, until they reached the parking lot, and the cold outside felt almost gentle compared to the cold inside.

He stood by the curb, looking up at the sky—gray, endless—and thought about what came next.

He would find out who did this. He would not stop.

That was all that mattered now.

***

The woods at night remembered everything. Mathew could smell it in the moldy bark, the broken branches, the sweet decay where the deer beds rotted every spring. He'd walked this path a hundred times as a kid, but now it felt alien—deeper, stranger, the trees crowding overhead in a way he'd never noticed before.

The clearing looked almost untouched, except the edges were pinched in, the palmetto grown thick, their fans edged with frost. The old stump was still there, pitted and mossy, the surface blackened from a dozen forgotten bonfires. Someone—maybe them, years ago, maybe kids since—had hammered a rusty nail into the top, and a strip of blue ribbon hung limp from it, fluttering in the faintest wind.

Mathew stood in the center, hands in his pockets, feeling the cold seep through his jeans. The moon was barely a suggestion behind the clouds, just enough light to cast the clearing in gradients of gray and black.

He'd come here to be alone, but after a few minutes, he heard movement—boots scraping on frozen leaves, the careful breath of someone trying not to cry.

Josie was first, hair pulled back, coat zipped to the chin. She carried nothing, but her posture was different: shoulders squared, chin tucked, as if holding herself upright required more effort than usual. She nodded at Mathew but didn't speak.

Jimmy and William came together, silent as shadows. Jimmy looked older, his frame hunched, hands jammed deep in sweatshirt sleeves. William's face was blotched red, eyes raw. They circled the edge of the clearing, then sat on the same downed log they'd used a hundred years ago.

Robert arrived next, a plastic grocery bag in one hand, the other clenched tight around his phone. He hesitated at the edge, then stepped inside, setting the bag beside the stump.

Mark was last, moving slower than the rest, his limp more pronounced on the uneven ground. He wore his letterman jacket, the sleeves stained and torn at one cuff. He didn't look at anyone, just collapsed onto a patch of frozen grass and stared at the ground.

The silence was total. Even the air seemed to hush.

Mathew felt the memory of the old oath vibrating in the dirt beneath his feet, a current running from the past to this moment. He waited, letting the cold settle in his chest, until everyone was present.

No one asked why they were here. No one needed to.

When he finally spoke, his voice was low, not much more than a rasp. "We should light the lantern," he said.

Josie nodded, her eyes bright in the dark.

Jimmy reached for the lantern in the bag, his hands shaking as he set it on the stump. It was the same one—dented, scuffed, glass fogged by time.

They formed a rough circle around it, the ritual as automatic as breathing.

Mathew took the matches, struck one, and held it to the wick. The flame caught, shivering, and then the clearing was alive again, the shadows circling the group in new, sharper shapes.

They stood there, six points of a broken star, the silence unbroken but for the hiss of the lamp and the slow, deliberate breathing of everyone present.

This was where it had started, and now it was where it would begin again.

***

The lantern's glow was sharper than Mathew remembered—no longer cozy, but edged with something raw. The light cut through the circle, sketching their faces in gold and shadow. For a long time, no one moved. They simply watched the fire burn, letting the hush settle over them.

Josie went first. She reached into her coat and pulled out a folded sheet of printer paper, corners softened from being crumpled and smoothed a hundred times. She knelt by the stump and slid it under the lantern, careful not to touch the flame. In the glow, the words "POLICE REPORT: OPEN CASE" were visible at the top, along with a Xeroxed photo of Samantha—her real smile, this time, not the one from the flyers.

Josie swallowed and sat back in the dirt, arms folded tight around her chest.

Next was William, who didn't bring an object. He just stood in the light, looking at the flame, and said, "I'll help. However, I can." His voice was soft, but the conviction in it made Mathew's throat tighten.

Jimmy stepped up with a battered spiral notebook, the cover smeared with ink. He tore out a page, wrote something quick in block capitals, and set it next to the lantern. Mathew leaned forward to read: "NO ONE GETS AWAY WITH THIS." The letters were uneven, the message ugly and beautiful at the same time.

Robert, ever the scientist, had brought a printout from his phone. A spreadsheet, maybe, or a map of the neighborhood, each location they'd searched marked in red. He didn't say anything, just placed it down and stepped away, his hands already trembling for the next task.

Mark limped to the stump and set down a strip of blue athletic tape. For a moment, it looked like he might say something, but he just stared at the lantern, jaw clenched, until he was ready to rejoin the circle.

Mathew was last. He pulled from his pocket a scrap of fabric, torn from the cuff of Samantha's jacket at the creek. He held it over the lantern's flame until the edge browned and curled, then set it gently atop the pile.

The group watched as the smoke rose, twisting and blue in the night air.

No one spoke. They didn't need to. The oath was there in every gesture, every promise, every ounce of pain and purpose that had brought them back to this place.

Mathew closed his eyes, and for the first time since the morning, he didn't see the ditch or the morgue or the cameras. He saw only the faces of his friends, each of them lit from within by something fierce and unbreakable.

He knew what they would do next.

They would keep the fire burning for as long as it took.

***

The lantern light turned their faces into masks—each one marked by fatigue, but also by something new. Mathew felt the air shift as Josie stepped forward, her shadow thrown wide.

"I swear," she said, "I'll make them pay. Every single person who let this happen, who failed her, who fails anyone—" Her voice caught, but she pushed on. "I'll take them apart, one case at a time."

No one laughed. No one doubted her.

William followed, posture rigid, almost military. "I'll find the truth," he said. "No matter how long it takes. No matter what it costs. If the police can't, then I will."

Jimmy was next, his hands curled into fists at his side. "If anyone ever hurts someone like this again," he said, "they'll answer to me. Even if I have to break the rules."

Robert, eyes rimmed with exhaustion, took a shaky breath. "I'll find out how. I'll learn everything I can. I'll use it, I promise, so no one has to feel helpless again."

Mark stood with effort, the pain in his leg ignored for the moment. "I protect what's mine," he said. "Always did, always will. She was family, and this—" he gestured at the circle, the fire, the clearing, "—so are you. Nobody messes with my family."

Josie gave a nod, as if sealing the deal.

When it was Mathew's turn, he didn't move closer to the light. He looked at his friends, one by one, and said, "I promise I won't stop. Not until we know what happened. Not until we fix it. We owe her that."

The lantern's flame sputtered, then settled. In the sudden quiet, the weight of what they'd said pressed down, not as a burden, but as something binding.

They were no longer just the kids who'd once played at secret oaths. They were witnesses, survivors, the last defense for someone who couldn't speak for herself.

They all knew it: this was the start of something that would define the rest of their lives.

For a long time, they stayed there, the lantern burning low, every promise hanging in the cold air, clear as the stars overhead.

***

For a while, nothing needed to be said. The six of them stood or sat in the lantern's circle, watching the fire burn down, the heat almost gone but the light still strong. Mathew felt the unity—more powerful, somehow, than even the blood-bond they'd sworn as kids.

Josie broke the silence first. "We're the Lantern Oath now," she said. She didn't say it as a question or as a proposal. She said it as if it had always been true, waiting for them to catch up.

William echoed her, voice steady. "The Lantern Oath."

The name took root, passed from one to the next. Even Mark, who had never much cared for words, gave a solemn nod. Jimmy rolled it around in his mouth, almost smiling, before repeating it under his breath.

Mathew heard his own voice join in, quieter than the rest, but with more conviction than he'd ever felt before. "The Lantern Oath."

He remembered the old rules: nobody faces real trouble alone. That was the heart of it, always. Now it was more than just a game—it was the only thing holding them together, the only shield they had.

Robert stared into the flame, then said, "We'll need to remember this. Every time we want to quit, or move on, or pretend it doesn't matter. This is who we are now."

They all nodded. They all understood.

Somewhere in the dark, an owl called. The woods pressed in, the clearing no longer a secret place, but a sanctum. They were not the same people who had entered. They never would be again.

When the lantern finally sputtered out, Mathew closed his eyes and felt the warmth linger long after the last spark was gone.

***

When the others finally drifted off, one by one, the clearing emptied in minutes. Only Mathew stayed, sitting on the cold stump with the lantern guttered in front of him, the ashes still warm. The woods, which had once seemed full of promise, now felt like a tomb.

He reached into his pocket and pulled out a length of black ribbon, the kind Samantha used to tie her hair for performances. He looped it around the lantern's handle, knotting it tight, the motion slow and precise. The ribbon caught the faintest breeze, snapping like a banner.

Mathew stood and looked at the lantern for a long time, memorizing its shape, the way the glass reflected the stars. He thought about all the nights they'd sat here, all the dumb promises and secrets, the things they'd sworn would matter forever.

Now, only this mattered.

He picked up the lantern, ribbon trailing, and walked to the edge of the clearing. He didn't look back.

As he pushed through the trees, the cold bit at his face, but he didn't feel it. Not really.

He knew, now, what he was meant to do. He would spend the rest of his life chasing justice—first for Samantha, then for everyone like her. He wouldn't stop. He couldn't.

Behind him, the woods closed over the clearing, erasing the last traces of their childhood.

Ahead, the dark was absolute, but Mathew walked on, the black ribbon a tether to everything he'd lost, and everything he had yet to find.

CHAPTER 6

The funeral home was built in the style of a roadside bank: all beige brick and false columns, a heavy front door that closed with the hush of insulation, like a vacuum seal over the world outside. Inside, the air throbbed with sweetness—buckets of lilies and chemical roses packed onto every flat surface, their scents clawing at the throat and sticking in the sinuses. Someone had tried to mask it with an industrial deodorizer, the kind used in hospitals and old folks' homes. The effect was a chemical war, the sweetness and sterility fighting for supremacy. Nobody won.

Mathew found himself gripping the sleeves of his borrowed jacket, the black polyester gone shiny at the elbows, the lining stiff and scratchy against his wrists. The collar didn't sit right; the pants pooled over his dress shoes, cuffs threatening to eat his ankles. Josie walked next to him, her own dress a size too big, hanging limp from the shoulders as if afraid to touch her. Behind them, the others drifted in a loose, uneven V: Jimmy in a clip-on tie patterned with cartoon bones, Robert in a suit that fit better than he did, William and Mark both tugging self-consciously at their collars, eyes sweeping the room and then skittering away from anything that might look back.

The parlor was packed beyond code, the overflow crowd standing two and three deep at the back, families with names Mathew recognized only from the honor roll or the sports pages, the odd patch of teachers in funereal pairs. There were classmates he hadn't seen in years, parents he barely remembered, everyone crowding together as if the sum of their presence might block out what they'd all come to see.

At the front, the casket: modern, contoured, a blue so dark it looked black until the light from the fake crystal chandeliers caught it. It sat on a dais under a spatter of spotlights, capped at both ends with flower sprays as thick as bridal veils. There was no viewing. No one had argued with the family's decision. The lid was shut and locked, the seam a thin, merciful scar. But above it, on a folding easel, was the school portrait: Samantha, her hair tamed and swept behind one ear, lips pinched at the edge in a smile that looked defiant, almost mean, a challenge to anyone who dared pity her.

Mathew stared at it until his vision blurred, until the color drained from her face, leaving only the negative: the eyes bright, the tilt of her chin stubborn, the whole of her alive in a way that made the rest of the room seem out of phase. He wanted to look away, but it kept drawing him back, a magnet to the bruise behind his ribs.

They found seats in the second row, flanked by a row of debate kids on one side and the high school theater director on the other. Mathew didn't know what to do with his hands, so he clasped them on his knees and watched the ceiling, pretending to count the tiles.

Somewhere in the crowd, his mother's voice pitched above the hush, a brittle giggle that cut the silence like a dropped glass. She sat with the family, surrounded by a thicket of distant aunts and a few of his father's work friends. The matriarch's posture was a warning—one hand clutching a handkerchief, the other digging trenches in the armrest of her chair, eyes locked on the casket as if expecting it to rise.

People kept trickling in, coats slung over arms, faces shining with effort. Mathew felt Josie's elbow bump his, the smallest of collisions, and glanced at her out of reflex. Her eyes were red, but dry; she blinked slowly, as if every movement cost double in this air.

"Can you breathe in here?" she whispered.

He shook his head.

She exhaled, and the conversation ended.

The hum of the crowd changed pitch as the priest made his entrance, flanked by a pair of altar boys in oversized surplices. He was a slim man with the practiced gait of someone used to navigating hospital beds and living rooms full of dying people. He wore his grief like a medal: visible, polished, but slightly apart from his own skin. He crossed himself at the foot of the casket and launched into the liturgy.

Mathew heard the words—"gone too soon," "mourned by all who knew her," "brightest light in any room"—but they didn't register as real. They were placeholders, code for the thing no one wanted to say: Samantha was gone, and none of the words could make the casket look less obscene.

In the row behind, Jimmy sniffled audibly, then tried to mask it with a throat-clearing that sounded like a muffled yelp. Robert produced a tissue from his pocket and passed it down the line, the gesture so ordinary and out of place that for a second, Mathew wanted to laugh. William kept his eyes down, tracing invisible lines on the back of the seat in front of him, while Mark sat rigid, arms folded, jaw set in a way that dared anyone to look at him for too long.

Mathew's father was a statue at the head of the family row, jaw clenched, hands folded in a knot. If he felt anything, it was compressed to a needle-point and locked behind his eyes.

They rose for the hymn. Josie's voice, always strong in choir, barely made a whisper. Mathew tried to sing, but the words tangled in his throat and died on the way out. He let the others carry the tune, letting the familiar strain of "Be Not Afraid" wrap around the room like a funeral shroud. The adults mouthed the words or looked straight ahead. The kids in the back row—too young to understand, too bored to pretend—fidgeted and passed notes, the sound of paper and denim as loud as any prayer.

After the hymn, the priest gave his address. He spoke of potential, of community, of the way a single life could touch so many others. He did not mention the circumstances; that was left to the edges, the negative space around every word. Instead, he talked about Samantha's "irrepressible spirit" and her "unwavering kindness," which made Mathew want to stand up and correct him, not for the sake of being right—though Samantha would have insisted on it—but because the lie felt bigger than the casket itself. She had been fierce, sometimes cruel, but always honest. She had hated platitudes. She would have hated this.

The priest offered a moment of silent reflection. The room fell so quiet that Mathew could hear the faintest rattle from the heating ducts. He looked at the floor, then at his hands, then finally at the portrait again. The eyes stared back: not softer, not gentle, but alive, as if daring anyone to forget her.

When the service ended, the family stood for the receiving line. Mathew dreaded the approach, the parade of faces contorted into the mask of perfect sympathy, the firm grip of a handshake, or the awkward hug from people who'd never so much as spoken to Samantha when she was alive. The crowd flowed forward in a slow tide, each mourner adding a layer to the story: "She was so bright," "She'll be missed," "Let us know if you need anything." The words ricocheted around the room, piling up until they meant nothing at all.

Mathew saw Becca—Samantha's best friend, the one she'd fought with every other week and made up with the next day—standing off to the side, clutching a wad of tissues in one fist. Her eyeliner had run in black streaks down her cheeks, but she didn't bother to fix it. She stared at the casket with a kind of rage, as if daring it to answer for what it had done. Mathew caught her gaze for a moment. She nodded, not in greeting, but as a signal of truce, a silent promise to keep fighting on some other front.

Outside, the winter light was flat and gray, the parking lot already filling with idling engines and clouds of exhaust. The crowd funneled into the lot in clusters, each group clinging to its own version of the story, each head bent against the wind.

Inside the funeral home, under the harsh fluorescents, Mathew and his friends lingered by the casket, the portrait of Samantha the only thing left unblurred by grief. For a minute, they stood together, six points on a broken star, unwilling to move, afraid to let the memory dissipate with the crowd.

Mathew looked at the portrait one last time, memorizing the angle of her chin, the challenge in her smile, and thought, "You win. You always do."

Then he followed the others into the cold, the world outside colder than he'd ever felt it, and the smell of the flowers trailing behind him all the way to the curb.

***

The ride to the cemetery was slow, the hearse creeping through traffic with its headlights on even though the sun hadn't set. The sky was a single sheet of cloud, the kind that made everything look colorless, as if the city had been draped in a sheet. The only sound in the car was the engine's drone and the hiss of Mathew's own breathing, each exhale fogging the window a little more.

At the cemetery, the wind cut through even the thickest coats, turning every hand into a raw, pink claw. The crowd clustered by the grave, a patch of black and gray flecked with the occasional navy or beige. Someone had spread a strip of green artificial turf over the lip of the hole, and the casket sat above it on a frame of steel bars, the blue finish deep and slick in the winter light.

Mathew felt the cold in his teeth, in the roots of his hair. He and his friends drifted to the side, then found themselves—without speaking, without even looking at each other—lining up in the same order they'd stood so many times before: Josie at the left, then Jimmy, Robert, William, Mark, and finally Mathew himself. He didn't know if the others noticed, but he could feel the shape of it, the way the formation held, the way it made the wind easier to stand.

The priest said a few words, quicker this time—something about dust and earth, about peace and reunion, about the "mystery of life's ending." He made the sign of the cross over the casket and stepped back, giving a tiny, almost imperceptible nod to the funeral director.

The mechanism started slowly, a grinding noise as the casket sank inch by inch. For a second, Mathew thought it might stop halfway, but then it settled into the earth, level and silent. There was a long pause before anyone moved.

Mathew's mother clutched the arm of his father, her face turned away from the grave. His father stood so rigid, Mathew wondered if he'd ever unbend. The rest of the family gathered in a knot, the little cousins fidgeting, the aunts and uncles wiping their eyes or blowing their noses in turns.

Beside him, Josie let out a long, shaky breath. "She'd hate this," she whispered. "All of it."

Jimmy nodded, arms crossed so tight his knuckles whitened. "She'd have wanted fireworks or something. Not—" he gestured at the hole, unable to finish.

Robert shifted, as if to say something, then just shrugged, the motion tiny but enough.

Mathew kept his eyes on the dirt, the exposed sides of the grave, the way the roots looked like veins in clay. He tried to feel something profound, but all he could think about was how cold his toes were, how the ground must be even colder down there.

After a while, the crowd started to peel off. Some dropped flowers, some just turned and walked back to their cars, their shoes crunching on the gravel. The adults gathered in small clusters, talking in low voices, as if the wind could carry their words straight to the dead.

The priest lingered by the grave, hands folded, waiting for the last of the mourners to leave. Mathew felt the group sway, the invisible thread that held them together pulling tighter as the rest of the world slipped away.

He looked at his friends, each of them locked in their own orbit of grief, and wondered if this was what it meant to be grown: to stand still in the cold and let the ground swallow your sister, your friend, your memory of what life was supposed to be.

They stayed like that, six in a row, until the only sound was the wind, and the only thing left above ground was the echo of her name.

***

After the casket had settled, the priest gave a gentle, practiced gesture, inviting those who wished to say goodbye. The crowd responded in slow, uneven waves—some drifting forward alone, some in pairs, each moving as if underwater.

The first in line was Becca, flanked by her mother. She placed a folded sheet of lined paper on the casket, smoothed it with her palm, then pressed her lips to the lacquered surface. The gesture was private, but the pain in her face was public, unguarded. She stepped away, shoulders shaking, her mother drawing her back into the anonymity of the crowd.

A few of the teachers approached next: Ms. Lawton set a purple pen on the lid, the same brand she'd used to grade Samantha's papers; the theater director laid a dog-eared script—A Christmas Carol, still smudged with Samantha's penciled stage notes. The soccer coach, awkward in a too-small suit, left a whistle, its lanyard looped around a clutch of flowers. He lingered a second, hand on the casket, before stepping back.

The rest came in trickles: a clutch of debate kids who left a stack of index cards, each scribbled with a different Samantha quote; two freshmen from the school paper who brought a clipping of her first feature story; a group from the rec center who tossed in a battered friendship bracelet, its beads spelling out "No Regrets." Every token was a story, every gesture a last attempt at contact.

When it was his friends' turn, Josie went first. She placed a worn theater mask—a piece of some long-ago costume—on the casket, then touched her fingers to her lips and brushed them against the blue shell. "See you, Scrooge," she whispered, the nickname sticking even after everything else had slid away.

Jimmy followed, fishing in his pocket for a strip of paper. He unfolded it, revealing a crude, blocky cartoon of a wrestling match, Samantha's stick-figure triumphing over his own. He taped it next to the script, nodding as if sealing a pact. "You win," he muttered. "Fair and square."

Robert, ever precise, left a tiny glass vial, sealed with wax. Mathew recognized it as part of a home chemistry set, the kind they'd once used to prank the science teacher. Inside the vial, a piece of paper was rolled so tight it was barely visible. Robert didn't look at the others, just set it down, wiped his nose, and walked off without a word.

William had nothing in his hands; instead, he placed both palms flat on the casket, closed his eyes, and stood still for a full count of ten. When he opened them, his cheeks were wet, but he left the tears there, unashamed.

Mark hesitated at the edge. His limp was pronounced on the cold turf, but he took the steps slowly, then reached into his jacket for a battered high school letter. He set it down, then traced the outline of the "S" with his thumb, pressing so hard the paper dented. He stood back, eyes locked on the casket as if daring it to resist.

Mathew was the last of the group. He waited, letting the others finish, then approached the casket, the world narrowing to the sound of his shoes on the mat and the taste of iron in the wind.

He took the black ribbon from his pocket—the one he'd knotted around the lantern just days before. It was stiff with cold, the ends frayed from too many retellings. He laid it lengthwise over the seam of the lid, flattening it with his palm until it matched the line of the casket, a thin, dark divide between what had been and what was left.

For a second, the crowd and the sky and the grave all blurred together, and he imagined the ribbon as a boundary: this side memory, that side nothing.

He stepped back, hands empty, and looked at the tokens piled on the casket. The collection was strange, ridiculous, perfect—a map of who

Samantha had been, mapped out in pens and papers and pieces of old life. For a moment, it looked like she might come back, just to sneer at the mess or correct the order or make some final, ruthless joke.

But the wind just lifted the edge of the script, flapping it like a flag, and the rest settled into place.

The priest gave a final prayer. The family retreated to the cars, the crowd thinned, and the funeral director made a discreet move to clear the space.

The last things anyone saw of Samantha Walton were the objects that wouldn't fit in any obituary: the black ribbon, the wrestling cartoon, the crumpled letter, the mask. The sum of a life, left on the cold lid, waiting for the earth to cover it.

Mathew stood with his friends, watching as the gravediggers moved in, careful but quick, their shovels biting into the winter dirt. He watched until the casket was gone from sight, until the tokens and the ribbon were memory only.

When he turned away, he felt the smallest lift—a breath, a beat, a pause in the ache. Not peace, not closure, but the beginning of something else.

***

They left in a slow, somber convoy, the heat of their vehicles slowly relieving the chill. The family had arranged a wake at the church hall, but none of them wanted to go, not really. There was nothing left to say to the adults, no comfort in the promise of sandwiches and sheet cake and old people trying to find the right words.

Instead, they gathered at Robert's battered Civic, the blue paint oxidized to a dull powder, the windshield already filmed with salt from the last cold snap. No one argued over seating: Robert took shotgun, Jimmy and William crammed into the back, and Josie pulled her coat tight and climbed in beside Mathew in the driver's seat. Mark, who still favored his bad leg, sprawled across the rest of the back row, one foot braced against the door.

Nobody spoke for the first few minutes. Mathew started the car, cranked the heater, and rolled down the windows anyway. The air inside was thick with the sweat of grief and the stink of lilies, as if the funeral had followed them home. He let the engine idle, not in any hurry to move.

After a while, Josie broke the silence. "Where to?"

Mathew shrugged. "Drive?"

"Drive," said Jimmy, voice flat, like he was testing out the word for the first time.

He pulled out of the cemetery lot and let the city drift by. The winter had scraped Savannah clean: the oaks hung bare over the streets, moss limp as rags, and the houses looked smaller than he remembered. Downtown was half boarded, the bakery windows already painted over with FOR RENT signs. The river glared in the distance, bright and hard as a knife.

They passed the school, and for a moment no one breathed. The parking lot was empty, the flag at half-mast, the banners from last week's winter concert still strung up in the front windows. Mathew thought about stopping, but just kept going, one hand locked at twelve o'clock on the wheel.

Josie leaned her forehead against the glass, breath fogging the window. "You ever think," she said, "that this is all we'll ever remember about here?"

William snorted. "We'll remember the science lab fire," he said. "And the time Jimmy locked himself in the weight room."

"Emergency," Jimmy muttered. "Nature called."

They almost laughed. It was a brittle, papery sound, but it was something.

Mark stretched in the back, grimacing as his knee popped. "I think about the woods," he said, voice distant. "And the old clearing."

They lapsed back into quiet. The city slid by: strip malls, gas stations, empty playgrounds. At every red light, Mathew caught glimpses of other cars, other families, faces pinched with cold or just life. He wondered if anyone looking back could see the grief in their car, the way it seeped out the seams and made every silence heavier.

He turned onto Victory Drive, the old east-west artery, and let the Civic eat up the miles. Nobody told him to stop. The road unspooled, and for a few minutes, the only thing that mattered was the sound of the tires and the warmth of bodies pressed together in a machine too small for secrets.

Finally, Josie reached over and nudged his arm. "You want to go to the woods?" she asked, her voice less a suggestion than a dare.

Mathew glanced at the rearview: Jimmy and William nodded in sync, Mark already pulling his jacket tighter, bracing for the walk.

He turned left at the next light, cutting toward the old neighborhood. The streets narrowed, the houses grew older and closer together, and the trees formed a tunnel overhead. He eased the car to a stop by the edge of the woods, the familiar path already trampled into the winter grass.

They piled out of the car, their breath misting in the air, and stood for a moment on the curb, looking at the line of trees.

No one said a word. They just started walking.

***

The path into the woods was unchanged: a seam of packed earth winding through the pines, palmetto fanning out on both sides like the teeth of a broken zipper. But the cold made everything sharper, the shadows deeper. The branches above clicked and whispered, and the air smelled less like sap and more like wet ash.

Mathew led, the others falling in behind him without question. They moved as a single animal, each step pressed into the exact footprint of the one before. Nobody joked or reminisced. They just walked, breath clouding ahead of them, shoes crunching the rime.

Josie was first to step in. She moved to the center, looked up at the canopy, and then down at her boots. The others joined, forming a rough pentagon, the geometry instinctive.

For a long time, nobody spoke. The silence pressed in, heavy as dirt.

Mark finally broke it. "Remember how Sam used to claim she was the only one who could talk to trees?" His voice was flat, almost a challenge.

Jimmy scratched the back of his neck. "She used to say the trees were just bored. That's why they creaked so much."

"She said we were supposed to listen," added Robert, staring at the ground.

William shuffled his feet. "Never got what we were supposed to hear," he said, almost to himself.

Mathew didn't answer. He felt the chill biting through his jacket, the memory of summer nights spent here, the way Samantha had always filled every silence with words or laughter or just pure motion. Now, her absence buzzed in the cold, a negative space you could trip over if you weren't careful.

Josie crouched by the stump, dragging her fingers through the moss. "She would've made a joke," she said. "Or tried to spook us."

"Yeah," said Mathew, the word catching in his throat.

They stayed there, ringed by trees, until their hands hurt from the cold and the ache had nowhere else to go. Eventually, Josie stood and dusted off her knees.

"I don't want to go home," she said.

"Nobody does," said Mathew.

He looked at the others, at the frost in their hair and the way they all leaned toward each other, not for warmth but for gravity. For the first time since the morning, he felt the smallest thread of connection—the sense that maybe, just maybe, they could carry each other through the worst of it.

He took a breath, filling his lungs with the icy air. "We should make a pact," he said, surprised to hear the old word come out of his mouth.

"A Lantern Oath?" said Jimmy, voice trembling just enough to notice.

Mathew nodded. "Yeah. Like before. Only this time, for her."

They circled the stump, the old way, arms out so their hands brushed at the wrists.

No one said the words out loud, but Mathew felt them all the same.

They would not let her be forgotten. Not by the woods, not by each other, not by the stupid, stubborn world that tried so hard to erase things that mattered.

The wind picked up, rattling the palmettos. For a moment, it almost sounded like laughter.

They turned and walked back the way they'd come, single file, the memory of the oath stitched into every footfall.

The clearing stayed behind, waiting, but it was different now—Emptier, but also a little less dark.

***

It was a Tuesday morning, too early for anything real to happen, the world still half-frozen from the night before. Mathew was hunched over the kitchen table, hands wrapped around a mug that had once belonged to Samantha, the handle chipped and the cartoon cat's face worn down from years in the dishwasher. He sipped cold coffee and watched his mother make slow, silent laps around the island, opening and closing cabinets without ever taking anything out.

His father was upstairs, already dressed for court, the scent of his aftershave leaking through the stairwell like solvent. The phone rang, shrill enough to make the mugs rattle on the shelf. His mother froze mid-step. Mathew set his own cup down, bracing for bad news.

"Walton residence," his father answered, the forced cheer of the phrase flattening every syllable.

Mathew listened, only half on purpose.

"Who's calling?" His father's voice sharpened. "You're certain?"

A silence, stretching.

"When was this?" Now his father was pacing. Mathew could picture him, phone cord stretched taut, one finger pressed so deep into his temple it would leave a bruise.

The conversation was quick. His father's voice never rose, but the timbre changed, gathering static. "No, thank you for letting us know," he said, then hung up so abruptly it sounded like a gunshot.

The next sound was the soft thump of a fist on the wall, then the heavy tread of feet coming down the stairs. His father didn't look at either of them as he entered the kitchen. He poured himself a glass of water with hands that shook just enough for Mathew to notice.

"It's over," he said, looking out the window at nothing. "They caught him. The man who did it."

His mother didn't react at first. Then she put both hands over her mouth and started to cry, the tears rolling down her wrists and soaking the sleeves of her robe. Mathew wanted to go to her, to hold her or say something, but his body wouldn't move.

His father just stood there, knuckles white on the glass.

"They said he confessed. To Sam's murder and—" he cleared his throat "—others. Three states. They're charging him federally, too. He… he gave details."

A dead, practical silence filled the kitchen.

Mathew's mother wiped her face on the back of her hand. "Does it help?" she whispered.

Her husband let out a sound that was almost a laugh, but bitter as old coffee grounds. "No," he said. "Not at all."

He turned to Mathew, his eyes red and unblinking. "I want you to remember this," he said. "Sometimes they do get caught. But it doesn't fix anything."

Mathew nodded, feeling the words burn a slow path down his spine.

The rest of the day passed in a blur of calls and casseroles, neighbors and friends, and even reporters wanting to know if the family "felt closure." The word rang hollow, as if closure were something you could fold up and fit into a Tupperware.

Mathew went up to his room and sat on the floor, back to the wall, eyes unfocused. He thought about the man—no, the monster—who'd stolen his sister, and how even knowing his name didn't make her any less gone.

He wondered how it would feel to look him in the eye.

He wondered if he'd recognize anything at all.

***

The conference room at the courthouse was windowless, a bunker lined with battered legal pads and cups of bad coffee. The walls were painted a color Mathew suspected had once been called "Cream" but had faded into the shade of old teeth. There was a flag in one corner, a set of mismatched office chairs, and a clock that ticked so loud it made conversation difficult.

Mathew sat at the end of the table, his father beside him, both facing a woman in a navy suit whose posture screamed that she'd been up all night. She introduced herself as Assistant District Attorney Wallace, but everyone just called her "ADA." She wore reading glasses on a chain and held a thick manila folder in her lap.

"We appreciate you coming in on short notice," she said, her voice practiced but not unkind. "I want to be as transparent as I can."

Mathew's father nodded, his jaw working a slow grind.

ADA Wallace opened the folder, flipping past several sheets. "First, the case against the suspect—Mr. Pearson is strong. Very strong. There's physical evidence, a confession, and witnesses. We have him dead to rights for Samantha's murder, as well as several other cases."

Mathew's throat tightened at the sound of her name. He counted the staples in the folder to keep from looking at her face.

"The complication," Wallace continued, "is that Mr. Pearson is offering to provide the locations of additional victims. Children who disappeared in other states. He's… willing to cooperate, but only if we agree to take the death penalty off the table."

There was a long silence.

Mathew's father spoke first, his voice a rasp. "So he wants to live. After what he did to my daughter, to those other families, he wants to spend the rest of his life breathing."

The ADA pursed her lips. "He's agreed to plead guilty. No trial, no appeals. He'll be locked up for life, with no possibility of parole. He's asking for protective custody, but that's likely a fantasy. The system is—" she hesitated "—not kind to men like him."

Michael Walton's hands curled on the table, the knuckles gone white. "Why are we talking about what's kind? You have his confession. You have evidence. What else do you need?"

"Closure for the other families," Wallace said, not backing down. "They don't know what happened to their children. They need a body, a place to mourn. Pearson is their only chance at answers."

Mathew listened, the words folding in on themselves. He could see his father's argument, could feel the rawness of the wound that never closed. But he could also hear the logic, the cold calculus of the ADA: more lives touched, more pain possibly eased.

"What happens if we say no?" his father demanded.

"We'll try him anyway," Wallace replied. "He recants, and we lose any hope of finding the others. He might get the death penalty, but it will take years. Decades, maybe. The process is long. And ugly."

Mathew's father exhaled, a sound between a snarl and a sigh. "He should burn."

Wallace nodded, her voice softening. "I don't disagree, sir. But this is the best chance we have of bringing peace to those other families. And, ultimately, to yours."

Mathew looked up at her. "Does he feel anything? Regret?"

She took off her glasses and folded them in her lap. "No. He's a monster. But monsters can still be useful."

The room went silent again. Mathew watched the second hand on the wall clock drag itself around the face.

Finally, his father stood. "I want to look him in the eye," he said. "He took everything from us. He shouldn't get to walk away clean."

"He won't," said Wallace, her gaze steady. "I promise."

They left the room, Mathew trailing behind, the chill of bureaucracy colder than the wind outside.

In the hallway, his father stopped and put a hand on Mathew's shoulder, the grip hard enough to bruise. "Don't let anyone tell you this is justice," he said. "It's just a deal. Never forget that."

Mathew nodded. He didn't think he ever would.

***

That night, after the meeting, Mathew sat in the dark of the living room, the only light coming from the blue wash of the television. The news was on, cycling through the day's horrors—traffic deaths, layoffs, a fire that gutted an old apartment block. Then, with a flick of static, the anchor shifted to the story everyone in Savannah was waiting for.

"Arrest in the Samantha Walton case," the anchor said, eyes wide with simulated empathy. "Local and federal authorities have confirmed the capture of suspect Peter Pearson, linked to multiple abductions across three states."

They showed his mugshot, full screen. Mathew stared.

Pearson's face was a bland slab of meat—pale, slack, hairline already retreating at the temples. His eyes looked straight into the camera, not mocking or cruel, just blank, as if the world was happening somewhere else. There was no sign of the monster, no hint of the evil his father described. If you passed him at a store, you wouldn't even remember.

Mathew memorized every inch: the close-set eyes, the ridged skin above his left eyebrow, the mouth set in a line so flat it looked like a surgical scar. He thought about Samantha, the force of her personality, the fact that this man had erased it with nothing more than a choice.

The anchor droned on, listing the other names, the other towns. The screen shifted to the sheriff's press conference. Mathew's father was there, just off to one side, his face harder than any stone in the city.

Mathew turned the TV off and sat in silence.

He tried to summon rage, or satisfaction, or anything at all. What he felt instead was a slow, sick emptiness, like a hunger that never went away. He pictured Pearson's face again, tried to imagine what it would be like to see him in a courtroom, to sit only a few feet away and know that nothing—no sentence, no verdict—could give back what had been stolen.

The urge to break something, to smash every dish in the house, rose and faded. He just sat, letting the darkness press in.

He knew, deep down, that the world would go on. That there would be more monsters, more tragedies, more headlines. The system would churn, Pearson would rot in a cell, and Samantha would become a story people told in soft voices for a year or two before moving on.

Mathew promised himself, right then, that he would never let himself forget. Not the face, not the feeling, not the way the world had revealed its teeth and left them to pick up the pieces.

He stayed up the rest of the night, staring at the ceiling, burning the mugshot into his brain.

Tomorrow would come, and he would be ready.

***

The courthouse was a circus. Photographers and camera crews clustered at the bottom of the steps, their gear bristling like the antlers of some predatory species. Mathew followed his father through the front doors, shoulder to shoulder with a dozen other families, each of them pressed into stiff suits and clutching folders thick with old newsprint.

Security scanned everyone twice, the guards ashen and businesslike. The waiting area was already packed with survivors—parents, siblings, people who'd driven all night just to see the man who'd devoured their worlds. The room smelled of sweat, fear, and the burned-metal tang of vending machine coffee.

Inside the courtroom, the air was heavy. The judge's bench looked like an altar, raised and distant, flanked by flags and the all-seeing gaze of the state seal. The prosecution filled one side, the defense two seats at the other, with Peter Pearson in the middle. He wore an orange jumpsuit and a paper-thin smile, as if the trial were just another day to get through. He slouched in his chair, hands cuffed in front, a dullness to his eyes that made Mathew itch to throw something, anything, just to see if it would make him flinch.

The judge read the charges: murder, kidnapping, assault, on and on, the list unrolling like a scroll of curses. Pearson said nothing, didn't look up, not even when the bailiff said, "Stand and face the court." When he did finally rise, Mathew felt a jolt—this was no monster. This was a man. An unremarkable, shuffling, flesh-and-blood man.

The sentencing hearing began, and each family called up to speak their loss into the record. Some read from sheets, some improvised, and a few broke down and had to be led away. Mathew recognized their pain, could feel it like a current, but also noticed how the judge kept looking at the clock, the lawyers shuffling papers, the system grinding forward no matter how raw or true the words.

The time for victim-impact statements came at last. The judge called the Waltons, and Michael stood, spine so straight it looked painful. He stepped to the podium and glanced once at Pearson, then fixed his gaze on the judge.

"My name is Michael Walton," he began, voice even but sharp enough to cut glass. "I am Samantha's father, and I am here not because I believe in closure, or forgiveness, or the redemptive power of law. I am here because I want the court to know exactly what was taken, and what cannot be repaired."

He paused. The room was silent, every face turned to him.

"Samantha was the reason our house was never quiet. She was stubborn, brilliant, and honest, even when it hurt. She once told me that when you lose someone, the world keeps going just to spite you. She was right. Every day I wake up and see her empty chair at breakfast. Every night, I hear her footsteps in the hallway, but it's just a memory, just air."

His hands gripped the podium, the knuckles gone bone-white. "I want the man who did this to rot. I want him to be so afraid of dying alone that he can't sleep for the rest of his miserable life. I want him to feel the darkness the way we feel it, every hour, every minute."

He turned then, looking not at Pearson but at the lawyers and the judge. "But what I want more than anything is for the court to admit that this is not justice. This is a performance. You will lock him away, and eventually, people will forget. But not us. Not ever. My daughter is in your file. For us, she is everything you failed to protect."

He stepped back, voice steady but eyes blazing. "That's all I have to say."

He returned to his seat, not looking at anyone. The judge cleared her throat, adjusted her glasses, and moved the hearing along as if the last three minutes had never happened.

When all statements were completed, the prosecution summarized the evidence, the defense offered nothing, and the judge set the sentencing date. Pearson never said a word, never even acknowledged the room.

As they left, Mathew looked back one last time. The killer's gaze was fixed on the ceiling, as if counting tiles, waiting for the show to end.

Outside, the sky was bright and cold, the sun doing its best to bleach the whole ugly business out of the city's memory. Reporters called after them, wanting quotes, reactions, anything that would fit into the day's story.

Mathew ignored them all, walking next to his father in silence.

He wondered what it was like to matter so little to the world that it just kept spinning, no matter how hard you screamed.

He wondered if Samantha would have laughed at its absurdity.

He decided, in that moment, to never stop remembering. Not the trial, not the face, not the way the system had failed them all.

He would find a way to make it right, even if it took his whole lifetime.

***

Sentencing day came on a Monday, as if the city wanted to get it over with before the week had a chance to get ugly. The courtroom was quieter this time, the rows full but subdued, everyone worn out from months of waiting and telling their stories over and over. The media presence had thinned; only the local paper sent a reporter, who typed with slow, deliberate stabs, the keys loud in the hush.

The judge—same one as before—called the court to order and asked the accused to stand. Pearson shuffled upright, wrists manacled, his face as blank as it had been on the first day. Mathew sat with his father in the front row, the two of them still as stone.

"This court finds the defendant, Peter Pearson, guilty on all counts," the judge intoned. "The sentence is life in prison, without the possibility of parole. May you use the remainder of your existence to reflect on the pain you have caused."

There was a beat, just long enough for the words to sink in. Then the gavel came down.

Pearson blinked once, then looked at the floor.

The court clerk started reading the paperwork, the words legalistic and heavy, a recitation meant for the record more than the room. The families in the gallery exhaled as one—some in relief, some in grief, some just in exhaustion. Mathew felt the noise but not the feeling; it was like listening to a thunderstorm through a pane of glass.

Afterward, the deputies led Pearson out, his shuffling steps almost comical, as if he'd forgotten how to walk in a straight line. No one in the gallery said a word to him. There were no threats, no outbursts, just the hollow sound of the door closing behind him.

The judge collected her papers, nodded at the ADA, and exited through the side door. The rest of the room emptied in slow motion, people hugging, crying, lingering in little knots as if afraid to leave and find the world unchanged.

Mathew's father shook hands and exchanged words with a few of the other parents, his face set in the tight, private smile he reserved for situations where words had already failed.

They made it to the courthouse steps before Mathew spoke.

"Is that it?" he asked, voice low. "It's over?"

His father let out a breath. "That's all there is. The rest is just the aftermath."

Mathew nodded, feeling the weight of it settle on his shoulders. He looked up at the sky, searching for something—a sign, a feeling, anything at all.

All he saw was the sun, bright and indifferent, shining on a world that didn't know or care that justice had been done.

They walked home in silence, the echo of the gavel trailing them like a shadow.

***

That night, the house felt smaller than ever. The furnace kicked on and off in bursts, the vents clattering like old bones. Mathew wandered into the kitchen, expecting to find it dark, but the light over the table was on, casting a soft yellow circle over the scarred Formica. His father sat at the far end, a glass of whiskey in front of him, the bottle half-empty and sweating on the vinyl placemat.

He looked up when Mathew entered, his face drawn and older than it had been even that morning. "You want one?" he asked, voice sandpaper-rough.

Mathew hesitated, then shrugged. "Yeah. Sure."

His father poured with the careful precision of a man used to being watched for mistakes. The liquid caught the light, amber and clean, and Mathew took the glass, cradling it in both hands. He'd tasted whiskey once before, on a dare, but tonight it felt less like a test and more like a rite.

They sat in silence for a while, each sip burning a line down Mathew's throat and settling in his stomach like a pilot light. The clock on the wall ticked, the minute hand jerking forward, the sound exaggerated in the hush.

"You did well today," his father said at last. "Better than I did, probably."

Mathew shook his head. "I just watched."

"That's what everyone does," his father replied. "You watch the world go sideways and hope someone else is keeping track." He stared at the glass, the reflection of the kitchen bulb warped by the curve. "I always thought the law would… I don't know. Fix things. Make them right. Your mother used to say that was my only religion."

"Is it still?" Mathew asked, voice barely above a whisper.

His father smiled, the corners of his mouth curling up without reaching his eyes. "Not really. Not after today."

Mathew drank again, slower this time, letting the taste linger. He thought about the judge, the ADA, the way the process had felt like a conveyor belt moving too fast for anyone to get off. He thought about the mugshot, the way the monster had blended into the background, unremarkable and immortal.

"I want to understand it," he said, surprising himself. "The law, I mean. I want to know how it actually works, and why it doesn't."

His father looked at him then, really looked, and Mathew saw the exhaustion and something else—maybe pride, maybe resignation, maybe just the relief of not having to carry the weight alone.

"You will," his father said, raising his glass. "You're already smarter than I ever was."

They drank in silence, the whiskey warming them both, the kitchen shrinking until it was just the two of them and the long night ahead.

Mathew watched the shadows creep across the table, the edges of the world getting fuzzier as the bottle emptied.

He made a promise to himself, right then, that he would never stop looking for the answers.

Even if he had to burn down every old truth to find a new one.

***

Time, when it finally moved, did so in fits and jumps. One moment, Mathew was standing in his high school graduation gown, the cheap fabric itching his skin and the tassel brushing his nose every time he turned to look for his father in the bleachers. Next, he was packing boxes in the sticky heat of late summer, loading the Civic for the drive to Atlanta, the trunk barely closing over the weight of textbooks and battered notebooks.

The group scattered the way seeds do in a strong wind. Josie won a scholarship to Tulane, her parting words a warning: "Don't let the Yankees turn you into a bastard." Jimmy stayed local, working construction with his uncle and taking night classes at the community college. Robert left for Duke, the acceptance letter taped to his bedroom door for months before he could say goodbye. William and Mark both ended up at UGA, roommates by default, their dorm room decorated with wrestling posters and a single, battered lantern on the desk.

They wrote letters—actual paper, with stamps and envelopes, and the taste of ink on your tongue when you licked the glue. Mathew kept a shoebox of them under his bed, the pages creased and smudged, each one a lifeline back to a version of himself he could barely recognize. When phones became affordable, they racked up collect calls and three-hour Sunday marathons, voices bouncing across state lines and static.

Every winter break, without fail, they met up. Sometimes at the diner, sometimes in the woods, once in a Waffle House at midnight with a line of truckers in Santa hats eavesdropping on their stories. The reunions were both smaller and sharper than memory allowed—no great revelations, just the comfort of old jokes and the reassurance that you hadn't vanished.

Samantha's name came up less, but her absence hung over every conversation, a missing puzzle piece no one was willing to replace. When they talked about her, it was in the form of what she would have said: the punchline to a joke, a scathing review of some new pop song, a monologue on why college mascots were all secretly perverts. It hurt, but the pain had softened, scar tissue forming over the rawest parts.

Mathew threw himself into classes, working at a coffee shop in the mornings and shadowing his father at the courthouse whenever he could. He kept a running tally of injustices, big and small: the kid caught with a dime bag who lost his scholarship; the woman in a wheelchair denied access to the jury box; the neighbor who had his house seized over an unpaid tax bill and died in a motel room three months later. The law was a game, but the deck was stacked, and every time Mathew lost a round, he filed it away for future revenge.

He kept in touch with Josie the most. Her letters were always too long, half gossip and half legal theory, each one littered with sarcastic asides and the occasional cartoon. She'd switched majors three times already and was planning to do it again. "I want to major in revenge," she wrote once, in pink highlighter. "But apparently it's not an accredited program."

Jimmy sent postcards, all in caps, usually from places like "FORT SUMTER" or "WORLD'S LARGEST CHICKEN FRIED STEAK." The messages were short but sincere. "MISS YOU GUYS," one said. "DON'T DO DRUGS." He still signed everything "JIMMY THE BONE," as if afraid someone would forget.

Robert wrote only when he had something important to say. His letters arrived every few months, single-spaced, typed, and annotated with footnotes. He was working in a lab, obsessed with pharmacology and the perfect efficiency of chemical reactions. "Biology is just chemistry at scale," he explained once, and Mathew could hear the excitement in every sentence.

William and Mark sent a letter together at Christmas. It was one page, written in two colors of ink, alternating lines. "COLLEGE IS HELL," it began. "TELL EVERYONE WE'RE NOT DEAD." The rest was sports scores, inside jokes, and a promise to meet up in Savannah for the New Year.

And every December, just before break, they made a point to call. No matter where they were—library, dorm, warehouse floor—they picked up, and for a few hours it was like nothing had changed, the years folding back on themselves and the world righting its axis.

Through it all, Mathew felt himself changing. Not better or worse, just different. The edges were harder, the optimism gone, replaced by a slow, patient anger that felt almost like hope.

He knew, deep down, that every letter, every phone call, every pilgrimage back to the woods was just another version of the oath: we are still here, we remember, we are not done yet.

The rest of the world moved on. But for them, the future was still something to fight for.

***

The law library at Emory was a palace of quiet: floor-to-ceiling stacks, the air always fifty degrees colder than necessary, every surface scrubbed so clean it squeaked under your sleeve. Mathew spent most nights here, a perimeter of casebooks barricading his desk, outlines scribbled in blue highlighter and Post-it notes blooming from every margin. He had a seat by the window, far from the study groups and the cliques, just close enough to see the campus quad lit up like a spaceship in the dark.

· He took to his studies the way a drowning man takes to the surface—hungry, desperate, each gasp a matter of survival. The first semester, he aced everything, but it wasn't the grades that mattered. It was the footnotes, the contradictions, the stories buried in the footers of Supreme Court opinions: men and women who'd lost everything because a cop forgot to read a warning, or a clerk mixed up two files, or a judge decided to teach a lesson about "personal responsibility." The failures were everywhere. Once you saw them, you couldn't stop.

He spent his weekends at the local courthouse, shadowing a public defender named Ms. Ritter who wore orthopedic shoes and a permanent scowl. She let Mathew tag along as long as he didn't ask questions during the trial, but afterward, she'd take him to the courthouse basement and run down every mistake she'd made that day, every time the law bent or snapped in her hands.

"You want to win, Walton?" she asked once, lighting a cigarette under the exhaust fan. "You'd better be willing to get dirty. The Constitution is a beautiful lie. The rest of us? We're just trying not to drown in the paperwork."

He wrote it down, word for word.

Mathew's classmates were mostly rich, mostly from families where the law was tradition rather than necessity. They wore monogrammed jackets, talked about summer clerkships in DC, and argued over which Supreme Court Justice they'd want to party with if forced at gunpoint. Mathew listened, smiled when it was required, then returned to his notes, cataloging every shortcut and every flaw in the system.

He started a file on case collapses—wrongful convictions, deals made in back hallways, the plea bargains that swapped time served for a lifetime of lost opportunities. It grew faster than his textbooks, eventually filling three boxes under his bed. His roommate called it the "Failure Archive."

On a rainy October night, he took the train downtown to observe a sentencing. The defendant was a sixteen-year-old kid who'd been in a fight at a high school football game and ended up with an aggravated assault charge. The victim's injuries were real, but the story had metastasized in the papers until the kid was the devil. The judge gave him six years, no chance for parole, and the public defender didn't even stand up to object.

Mathew watched the family—parents, a little sister clutching a teddy bear—crumple in on themselves as the bailiff led their boy away in handcuffs.

He left the courtroom sick to his stomach, walking in the cold until his shoes filled with water and his hands went numb. When he got back to campus, he wrote a letter to Josie describing everything, every detail, the smell of the courtroom, and the sound of the gavel. She wrote back: "I know. The law was never meant to heal."

He kept that line taped to his desk, under the lamp, a daily reminder that winning an argument wasn't the same as making things right.

His father visited once, in the spring. They went to a diner near campus, ordered bad coffee, and watched the traffic slide by in the rain.

"You look tired," his father said.

Mathew smiled. "I'm learning. That's the point, right?"

His father nodded. "Just don't let it eat you. That's the real trick."

After he left, Mathew stayed at the table, replaying every word, every silence. He wondered if his father regretted pushing him into the fight, or if he'd simply accepted that some wounds never closed.

In the dark of his room, Mathew read through the Failure Archive, page by page. He started making lists—ways to beat the system, ways to break it, ways to turn the rules upside down so nobody else ended up like Samantha.

The more he learned, the angrier he got. But the anger was different now: slow-burning, patient, a heat that never quite cooled off. He understood what it meant to be powerless, but he also saw, for the first time, that power was just another tool. You could steal it, borrow it, remake it in your own image if you were smart enough and ruthless enough to pay the price.

He decided then and there that he would be both.

No matter how long it took, no matter what it cost.

He wrote to Josie: "The law is a maze. I plan to get lost in it."

She called him at 2 a.m., laughing so hard he could barely make out the words. "Just don't forget which way is out," she said.

He promised her he wouldn't.

But even then, he knew the real answer.

***

Josie took to law school like a hurricane takes to open water. She tore through the syllabus, devouring every tort and statute, leaving study partners and would-be rivals in her wake. Her hair was shorter now, easier to maintain, and she favored thrift-shop blazers over the usual sorority uniforms. She kept a schedule so tight it left no room for anything but winning.

The mock trial program was her personal battlefield. She signed up for every round, volunteered for the toughest cases, and never hesitated to object, even when the judge's patience wore thin. Her voice—clear, unwavering—could slice a witness in half before they finished the oath. She once reduced a star athlete to tears during cross, then handed him a tissue on her way back to the table. "There's no rule against being kind," she explained later, deadpan, to a group of awestruck 1Ls.

But she wasn't just brutal in competition. She joined the Innocence Project and worked late nights reviewing old case files, flagging every instance where the system ate its own. She interned at the DA's office, the only first-year allowed in actual court, and developed a reputation for "scorched earth" legal briefs. Her supervisor, a career prosecutor with thirty years in, told her, "You're going to put us all out of business."

In her letters to Mathew, the jokes had a sharper edge. "It's all blood sport, Matt. The trick is making sure you're the one holding the knife." She sent him outlines of her trial strategies, critiques of famous Supreme Court dissents, and, once, a hand-drawn diagram titled "How to Dismantle an Expert Witness in Five Easy Steps." It ended with a cartoon bomb under the opposing counsel's chair.

Phone calls were briefer, more tactical. "I don't have time to date," she said once. "Not until I can out-litigate anyone who tries to ghost me." Her laughter was more bark than giggle, but Mathew heard the old warmth in it, a pilot light that never really went out.

The transformation wasn't just about the law. Josie started running—three, five, ten miles at a stretch—her sneakers pounding out the anger that books and arguments couldn't. She joined a boxing gym, sparred with men twice her size, and once split her lip on the glove of an ex-cop. "It felt good," she wrote to Mathew. "Like earning your pain the honest way."

She still kept the Lantern Oath alive, in her own way. "We should run the world," she said on a call one night, voice buzzing with fatigue and caffeine. "The whole thing is rigged, but that just means we have to be smarter than everyone else. It's what Sam would've wanted."

Mathew believed her.

At graduation, she made a speech about justice that had the Dean blinking back tears and half the faculty on their feet. She ended with a line from their woods: "What light cannot reach, shadow must cleanse." Only Mathew, in the audience, understood the secret punch of the phrase.

Afterward, she met him for drinks, her tie askew and her face flushed with victory. "You keeping up, Mat?" she teased, draining her beer in one go. "You better be. The good guys are never ahead at halftime."

He grinned, lifted his own glass. "I'm right behind you."

She clinked his drink, her eyes bright. "You better be," she said again.

He could tell she meant it.

Later that night, as they walked the empty streets, Josie confessed, "Sometimes I'm scared I won't be enough. That the system will break me before I can break it."

Mathew squeezed her shoulder, the gesture awkward but sincere. "Then we go down together."

She laughed, and for the first time in years, it was the same as it had been.

The rest of the world didn't know it yet, but they were building something. Something patient, something sharp. And if the law couldn't heal, then maybe it could be made to bleed for the right reasons.

They made a pact, over a basket of cold fries and one more beer: they'd never forget, never let up, never give in.

And they never did.

***

Robert liked the graveyard shift. The hospital at three in the morning was a city of ghosts, just the shuffle of nurses and the beep of monitors breaking the silence. He could walk the halls for hours without seeing another soul. In the lab, the lights stayed on all night, and the only sound was the slow, wet click of pipettes and the hum of the old refrigerator where they kept the samples.

He was an outlier among the med students: always first to arrive, last to leave, less interested in bedside manner than in what happened at the molecular level. His hands were steady, but his eyes darted everywhere, cataloging every instrument, every reaction, every minute change in the bodies he was learning to fix and, sometimes, to break.

Anesthesia fascinated him. The idea that you could erase consciousness, turn a person into a machine with the right mix of molecules, was both terrifying and beautiful. He read everything—old case studies, drug trials, the notes of doctors who'd invented new cocktails in wartime or under siege. His copy of Goodman and Gilman's was falling apart, its pages bristling with tabs.

He started running his own experiments, first with simulations on the hospital computers, then with samples he ordered online or scavenged from the supply closet. He recorded everything in a series of spiral-bound notebooks, each page written in a code only he could break. The symbols weren't much, just substitutions and cross-hatches, but they made him feel safe, as if the knowledge could only hurt him if he let it slip out into the world unfiltered.

Robert was careful—never reckless, never flashy. He tested new blends on tissue cultures, then on donated animal organs. He kept a freezer in his apartment, full of vials labeled only with numbers. He measured each variable twice and recorded the results in triplicate. If anyone asked, he was working on a grant proposal about pain management or prepping for his anesthesiology rotation.

But he was looking for something else. A way to turn off the human mind, to erase suffering without leaving a trace. He couldn't have explained why, not even to himself, except that the idea of control was like a drug, and he'd been addicted since the first time he saw the system fail.

His memories of Samantha were grainy and slow-motion, but he never forgot the way she'd insisted on knowing every detail about how her own body worked. "It's just chemistry," she'd said once, rolling her eyes at a school nurse who tried to bluff her about a vaccination. "Everything is chemistry."

He wrote that in the margin of his first notebook, and it became a kind of motto.

He didn't see his old friends much—too busy, too tired, too locked into the schedules of residencies and overnight on-call. But every time he got a letter from Mathew or a postcard from Jimmy, he read it twice, then tucked it into the back of his journal.

One night, after a particularly brutal shift, Robert found himself in the lounge, staring at a glass of water and thinking about how easily life could be altered. A nurse came in, nodded at him, and turned on the TV. The news was running a piece on another botched case, some kid given the wrong dose in a small town ER. The talking heads were already blaming the system.

Robert looked at the TV, then at his hands, then at the notebook in his pocket.

He wondered what it would take to make the system bulletproof.

He wondered if he could be the one to do it.

He closed his eyes, let the hum of the hospital lull him, and promised himself that if he ever figured it out, he'd use it to help.

Even if it meant breaking a few rules along the way.

***

William hated being late, but the grad seminar was already five minutes in when he found a seat at the back. The professor, a retired warden with a voice like a bass drum, was dissecting the latest state audit of Georgia's prison system. Every other line was a joke about how nobody read the reports, not even the people paid to fix them.

William flipped open his laptop, scrolled to the audit, and followed along in real time. He annotated every error, every cover-up, every line where accountability fell into a black hole. He highlighted the part where a medical contractor saved money by swapping generic meds for the real thing, and no one noticed for 6 months. He flagged the incident where three guards "accidentally" left a gate unlocked and an inmate disappeared for a week.

It wasn't just academic for him. William interned at the local detention center, running data analyses and shuffling paperwork for the deputy warden. He treated the place like a living organism, always watching for weak points: the shift change at three a.m., when everyone was asleep on their feet; the mailroom where nobody ever checked for contraband; the ancient HVAC system that tripped the alarms every time it rained.

He'd started mapping the entire operation, one spreadsheet at a time. He kept a whiteboard in his apartment covered with columns of names—guards, contractors, parole board members—along with colored lines showing who hated whom, who owed favors, who was just marking time until retirement. The board looked like a conspiracy nut's dream, but every connection was real, every angle double-checked.

The deeper William dug, the more he understood that prisons were never about safety or justice. They were machines built to run on as little fuel as possible, patched with duct tape and political promises. He kept a running list of how the system could be gamed: which forms to file, which statutes had loopholes, which county judges took bribes in cash, and which in campaign donations.

His professors loved his obsession. "You have a mind for this, Lee," one of them said after class, tapping the side of William's head with a sheaf of printouts. "But you're not going to fix anything from the back row."

William smiled politely, but inside he disagreed. Sometimes the best way to control a machine was to let everyone else think it was out of your hands.

He still kept in touch with the old group. His emails to Mathew were less about feelings and more about strategy: "Did you know they just privatized half the state's prison food service? Guess who's on the board." He sent links to news stories about botched executions, security failures, and the endless churn of the system devouring itself. Once, he mailed Josie a copy of a Supreme Court amicus brief, the margins filled with his own sarcastic commentary in red pen.

"Can't wait to see you wear the black robe," Josie wrote back. "Just don't forget to smile for the cameras."

He kept a file on the Walton case, too—every appeal, every motion, every time the killer tried to wiggle through a legal crack. Whenever a court hearing made the news, William watched the entire thing, even if it was just fifteen minutes of procedural wrangling.

But his real focus was the future: how the rules could be bent, how the gears could be jammed, how the machine could be set to work for people like him, not against them. He dreamed of a prison so efficient it could run itself. Or better yet, a justice system that didn't need prisons at all.

Some nights, he'd pull up his spreadsheets, lay them out across the screen, and stare at the pattern until it made sense.

William knew every machine had a breaking point.

He just wanted to be the one to find it first.

***

Mark started as a patrol rookie, Savannah PD, walking a beat through neighborhoods more familiar than his own front porch. His first uniform barely fit his frame, the shirt a size too tight across the chest, and the pants high-watered just above the boots. But he wore the badge as it belonged to him, because in a way, it did.

He spent his shifts learning the city: which alleys smelled like piss and old beer, which bodegas looked the other way, which street corners went silent when a cruiser rolled up. Mark wasn't a talker, but he listened, and people talked to him because he didn't flinch at the ugly parts. By the end of his first year, he could recognize half the city's repeat offenders by their walk alone.

His favorite part of the job was the notebooks—small, spiral-bound, carried in the breast pocket above his heart. He kept one for every six months, filling them with names, faces, stories, odd details. Some pages were nothing but descriptions: "short, tattoo under left eye, smokes menthols, limps on rainy days." Others were entire genealogies, tracing who owed money to whom, who was related by blood, by debt, or by time spent in the county lockup.

Mark learned to trust what the notebooks said over what his sergeant did. The system was always trying to fix problems on paper: a new program here, a crackdown there. But the people in the notebooks never really changed. The same names cycled through the jail, the same addresses showed up on every warrant. Sometimes, Mark thought, the only thing law enforcement did was give the city's ghosts a place to sleep for a night.

But he kept writing it down, every day, because it was the only way to make sense of it.

There was one section in the back of each notebook—a list he never showed anyone. He called it "The Unfinished," and it was for people who'd gotten away with something they shouldn't have—the drunk driver who killed a family and skated on a technicality. The street dealer kept popping up, no matter how many times he got locked up. The old man in the yellow house who never got caught, but everyone knew.

He checked the names regularly, watched the court dockets and the obituaries, and waited for karma or the law to catch up. If it didn't, he made a note: "Still out there."

Mark wasn't cynical, not really. He liked the work, liked seeing the city wake up every morning, even if nothing ever really changed. He went out for beers with his shift, played in the rec-league softball team, and laughed at the same dumb jokes about "perp walks" and "frequent flyers." But he never forgot why he started: not to wear the badge, but to see what the world looked like from the inside, to know how it could be bent without breaking.

He kept in touch with the group, more than most. Mathew was always calling to ask about court records or "patterns of criminal activity." Josie wrote him long, unfiltered emails about the latest Supreme Court outrage. Robert mailed him a bottle of homemade hot sauce once, no note, just a hand-drawn label: "Consume at your own risk."

Mark's loyalty was always to them, even more than the badge. When a name from "The Unfinished" showed up in Mathew's correspondence, Mark circled it three times, highlighted it, and made a separate file. It was a way of keeping score, even if the scoreboard never moved.

He wasn't sure what the group was building, not exactly, but he knew it was something real. When you're the only one who remembers, you get to write the ending yourself.

One night, off-duty, he parked in front of the old woods, engine idling, just watching the trees sway in the wind. He pulled a fresh notebook from the dash, scribbled a date and a single word—"Ready"—then tucked it in his pocket.

Sometimes, the world needed to know it was being watched.

And sometimes, it needed to remember who was really in charge of the story.

***

Jimmy flamed out of college by the end of sophomore year—too many skipped classes, too many half-assed assignments, too many nights spent working extra shifts instead of studying. It wasn't that he was dumb, just allergic to sitting still. He preferred jobs that made his arms ache and his head quiet: loading docks, demolition sites, the warehouse where he spent most of a year stacking boxes until his spine felt like rebar.

But it was in the private security gig that he found his niche. The company started him on overnights at a business park, where the only excitement was catching raccoons in the dumpsters. But Jimmy had a talent for spotting trouble before it started: a parked car with no plates, a shadow in a stairwell, the faintest whiff of gasoline near the loading bay. He logged every incident, no matter how minor, and earned a promotion to the company's real moneymaker—staffing the county jail.

Corrections was a meat grinder, and nobody lasted long unless they could stare down a cellblock riot without blinking. Jimmy could. He was the smallest guy on the shift, but he learned to carry himself loose and casual, like someone who didn't mind getting hit so long as he got to hit back. In the first month, he broke up a fight between two lifers by walking straight into the brawl and bellowing, "Save it for the judge!" His reward was a busted lip and a reputation as the only rookie who didn't scare easily.

He watched everything: who did favors for the guards, which inmates ran the canteen economy, and who was one bad day away from snapping. He kept notes in his head—never on paper, too risky—but could recite the entire roster of the cellblock at a moment's notice. The lifers called him Bones, partly for his build, mostly because he was always on the edge of breaking but never quite snapped.

The rules of jail were simple, but the exceptions were everything. Jimmy learned fast that the official policies mattered less than the unwritten ones: don't owe anyone, don't disrespect the kitchen, never turn your back on a janitor. When a guard got caught running contraband, Jimmy was the one who tipped the captain, careful to do it in a way that kept his own hands clean.

He sent stories to the old group, mostly to make them laugh. "The new guy thinks the stun baton is a toy," he wrote to Mathew once. "Guess how many stitches before he learns otherwise." He called Mark for advice, swapped gossip about Savannah's weirder repeat offenders, and sometimes even helped flag names on Mathew's growing case files.

But mostly, he kept his head down and built up scar tissue. He lifted weights after every shift, taught himself to break a chokehold using nothing but his forearm, and never once complained about overtime. He took up running again, pounding the pavement at dawn with a pack of ex-military types who respected silence over small talk.

Jimmy didn't mind the violence, or the noise, or even the long hours. What bothered him was how everyone assumed he'd never make it, that he was a burnout, a dead end. He made a game of proving them wrong, one shift at a time.

He still missed Samantha, even if he never said it out loud. Every time he had to lock a cell, he thought about her—how she would have roasted him for "playing cop," how she would have made a joke about his "hero complex." The memory stung, but it also made him sharper, more focused.

He never missed a reunion, never flaked on a phone call or a favor. The group was still the only family that mattered. He knew someday they'd need him for something big, something more than just breaking up a fight or running a background check.

Jimmy was ready.

And if the world wanted to keep underestimating him, that was fine.

He'd always been the last one standing, and he planned to keep it that way.

***

The Christmas break reunion was always supposed to be a joke—a way to keep the group from drifting so far apart that they couldn't recognize each other in a crowd. But this year, they all showed up. Even Josie, who arrived late and loud, dragging a battered duffel and a bottle of bourbon that had survived three connecting flights and a bus ride from the Atlanta airport.

The Waltons' backyard hadn't changed: the grass was still patchy, the patio lights half-burnt out, and the old swing set rusted into a permanent lean. Mathew shoveled the fire pit clear of wet leaves, lined it with bricks, and set up folding chairs scavenged from the garage. By the time the sun dipped, the air was cold enough that their breath hung in front of them, making every laugh look like a secret.

They ate pizza on paper plates and told the stories they'd each been hoarding—who'd gotten fat, who'd been arrested (twice), who was getting married in the spring. At first, it felt like a nostalgia act, everyone replaying the hits for old time's sake. But after a while, the edges softened, and they fell into the rhythm that only history could bring.

The lantern sat on the table, its dented brass shining dully in the light. No one mentioned it until the pizza was gone and the first round of bourbon had scorched a path through the chill. Then Josie stood up, picked it up in both hands, and gave a little theatrical bow.

"Let's get weird," she said, flipping the switch. The old LED bulb flickered to life, casting the same off-white glow they remembered from high school.

They all stood, forming a ragged circle around the fire pit. Mathew took the lead, holding the lantern high, and said, "Repeat after me."

He started the old words: "What light cannot reach—"

"—shadow must cleanse," they finished, almost in unison.

But this time, Josie cut in. "We're not kids anymore," she said. "Let's make it count."

One by one, they improvised their own vows.

"May we never forget what's been taken," said William.

"May we do better, every year, every time," said Robert, voice steady as always.

"May we watch the world so it can't sneak up on us," said Mark, gripping the lantern base with both hands.

"May we hold each other to the promise, no matter what," said Jimmy, surprising everyone.

Josie went last. "May we find justice, even if we have to steal it."

Mathew closed his eyes, felt the weight of all those words, all those years. He thought about Samantha—her grin, her stubbornness, her ability to set the rules just by walking into a room. He thought about the woods, and the oath, and all the nights he'd spent trying to figure out how to fix something that had never been whole to begin with.

When he opened his eyes, the group was watching him.

"I promise," he said, and meant it.

They each put a hand on the lantern, the metal warm from their touch. The light flickered, caught, and then burned a little brighter.

They stayed out until midnight, talking about the future in voices so low the neighbors couldn't overhear. When the fire burned down, they doused it, packed up the chairs, and went back inside, their faces red from the cold and the bourbon.

The lantern stayed on the table, casting shadows across the kitchen. Nobody turned it off.

Later, as Mathew lay awake in his old room, he heard Jimmy and Josie laughing in the living room, and Mark's voice rumbling in the hallway. The sound was different from what it used to be, but still familiar—a little rougher, a little older, but real.

He watched the lantern's glow seep through the crack under his door.

For the first time in a long while, he felt like something had been fixed, even if only for a night.

He promised himself they'd do this again, every year, until the world made sense or they did.

Whichever came first.

***

The years between reunions passed faster than anyone expected. They all got older, but the gap between them never widened; if anything, it tightened into something denser, more necessary. The reunions became annual, then twice a year, and eventually, Matthew realized they were as much a meeting as a memory, the conversations less about catching up and more about the world outside their circle.

The second Christmas, they met at William's apartment, which was mostly cinderblock and castoff furniture. Still, the kitchen table was a command center: case files, printouts, stacks of clippings, and legal pads. William ran the meeting, whiteboard in hand, breaking down a recent scandal in the county parole board. "They're rubber-stamping every case," he said. "Nobody's watching. Nobody cares."

Josie presented next, her laptop full of screenshots and annotated PDFs. "This DA's office is dirty. They've buried discovery in three cases in the last six months. I flagged them all, but nobody will do shit about it unless we make noise."

Robert had samples—actual vials, packed in cold packs—of his latest compound, a sedative that mimicked natural sleep without any trace on the standard toxicology screens. "Just a curiosity," he said, but everyone knew he meant it as proof of concept.

Mark arrived in uniform, but after a few beers, he pulled out a file folder thick with copies of "Unfinished" names. "Two of these are out on technicalities," he said. "I see them around town. They're not scared. I think they should be."

Jimmy brought a handwritten list of every code violation and safety hazard at the jail. "All the blind spots, all the overtime scams, every guard who'll look the other way. Just in case."

Mathew, for his part, kept the agenda moving, making sure every voice was heard, every idea logged. His own file grew thicker every year, stuffed with stories of families broken by bureaucracy, of laws twisted to protect the worst people. He mapped connections, looking for leverage, always wondering when the right moment would come to act.

After the meetings, they drank and laughed and remembered, but the Oath was different now: not a secret handshake or a childhood dare, but a living thing. It had rules, procedures, even a kind of mission statement. They joked about forming a nonprofit, calling themselves "The Lantern League," but deep down, they all knew this was about more than grants or meetings.

It was about control.

And for the first time, Mathew believed it might actually work.

He looked around the table—at the cop, the doctor, the lawyer, the systems guy, the enforcer, the strategist—and thought, not for the first time, that maybe the world was built to be bent by people who refused to give up.

The next year, they made it official: each person would bring one name to every reunion. Not just a headline or a sob story, but a real case. Someone who needed fixing. Someone who deserved better.

The Lantern Oath, version two.

They raised their glasses, swore to each other, and let the lantern burn all night. Outside, the city stayed the same. But inside, the rules were different. And this time, they would be the ones writing them.

***

By the fifth reunion, the ritual had a rhythm: someone always arrived late (usually Jimmy), someone always brought food nobody ate (Robert, with his "experimental" protein bars), and the lantern—now retrofitted with a hurricane lamp mantle—always held court in the middle of the table.

They met in different places now: sometimes a rented cabin on Tybee, sometimes a motel suite halfway to Atlanta, once in a borrowed church basement with folding chairs lined up like a support group. It was never about the venue. The draw was the gathering, the careful unpacking of the year, the chance to test their plans in the only court that mattered.

The ritual started with Mathew lighting the lantern, then saying, "For Sam," as if it were just a grace before dinner. But after that, the mood shifted. The room got quieter, more intentional. They went around the table, each person stating what they'd done, who they'd helped, and who they'd failed.

Mark spoke first: "Three from my Unfinished list are back in the system. The one who beat his wife is getting out next month, but I made sure the right people are watching him. He won't slip by."

Josie followed, flipping through a notebook. "Prosecutor in Chatham County—got him disbarred for hiding evidence. It's not enough, but it's a start. Next year, I'm going after the judge who keeps setting bail for violent repeaters."

William ran a hand over his hair, always neater than anyone else's. "I hacked the court database. We can track every new case in real time. I'll set alerts for the worst offenders. We won't be surprised again."

Robert shrugged, almost embarrassed. "My protocol for silent sedation passed the IRB. We're using it on terminal patients who want dignity, but I think it could have other uses. Humane ones."

Jimmy, mouth half-full of chips, grinned. "If you need something done, I know a guy. Or three. Had to bail a friend out after a bad night, and let's just say the paperwork disappeared."

Mathew took it in, nodding after each update. When it was his turn, he said, "I clerked for a judge who plays by the rules, but even he bends when the case matters. I watched him cut a break for a mother who stole groceries for her kids, and I made sure her record got wiped. It felt right."

They went around once more, each sharing a new plan for the coming year. The vows were less about revenge now, more about balancing the scales. Each promise was targeted, actionable, the language honed by years of watching the world's gears slip.

When the lantern's fuel ran low, Mathew refilled it, hands steady. He looked at the group, saw the old faces and the new lines in them, the way they still fit together even after all the change.

"For Sam," he said again.

"For everyone like her," Josie added, and the others nodded.

They sat for a while in the glow, the shadows flickering on the walls, each thinking about what came next. There was no speech, no grand gesture. Just the quiet certainty that they were building something bigger than themselves, something that might actually change the ending for someone else.

Outside, the world kept spinning, unknowingly. But inside, the light from the lantern held back the dark for one more night.

And in that space, they were not powerless.

They were just getting started.

***

The last of the group peeled away just after midnight, the parking lot crunchy with frost and the exhaust from Josie's rental already a smear of white against the dark. Mathew walked each friend to their car, sharing a hug or a joke, sometimes just a nod. He watched their taillights recede, one by one, until the street was empty and the only sound was the wind scraping dead leaves along the curb.

He returned to the house, locking the door behind him out of old habit. The kitchen table was still scattered with the detritus of the night—empty bottles, notepads, half-eaten chips. The lantern, now almost out of fuel, flickered stubbornly at the center. Its reflection doubled in the window, one image inside, the other hovering over the empty yard.

Mathew stood for a long time, hands in his pockets, the weight of the evening settling over him like a quilt. He listened for the old ache, the rawness that usually hit hardest after the laughter stopped. But it was different this time. There was a steadiness to it, a sense that something had shifted into place.

He gathered the bottles and lined them up in the recycling bin. Wiped the table with a towel, brushing aside the crumbs and the flakes of torn labels. Each movement was careful, deliberate, as if closing up a church after the last service of the year.

In the living room, the old family photos were still where his mother had left them a younger Samantha in the center, eyes daring the camera, the rest of them orbiting her like satellites. Mathew picked up the frame, traced the outline of her face with his finger, and set it back down.

He returned to the kitchen, sat at the table, and stared at the lantern.

It had started as a symbol, a way to keep their grief in check, to tell themselves they were still together even after everything else had fallen apart. But over time, it had become something else: a beacon, a warning, maybe even a threat to a world that had always underestimated what six broken kids could do.

They weren't just friends anymore. They were a team, a crew, a force with a name and a mission. The Lantern Oath had rules, protocols, and a playbook that was growing thicker with every year. The oath was no longer about remembering; it was about what came next.

Mathew thought about all the cases they'd tracked, the people they'd helped or haunted, the way their lives had braided together into something patient and implacable. He thought about the phone calls and coded emails, the midnight stakeouts and the slow, careful revenge on those who deserved it.

He thought about Samantha, the original spark, and wondered what she would think if she could see them now—if she would laugh, or roll her eyes, or just say "Finally" and push them onward.

The lantern sputtered, caught once more, then settled into a slow, even glow.

Mathew leaned forward, elbows on the table, and said, softly, "We're ready."

There was no audience, no need for ceremony. The words hung in the air anyway, binding the room to the promise.

He let the light burn until dawn, then doused it, cleaned the glass, and set it back on the shelf.

He knew the others would call, would regroup, and would bring more names to the table. He knew the time would come when the Oath would need to act—decisive, unstoppable, a shadow where light couldn't go.

Mathew poured himself a last glass of water, stood at the window, and watched the world turn silver as the sun rose over Savannah.

He smiled, just a little. They would wait as long as it took. But when the world needed fixing, they'd be ready. And this time, nothing would stop them.

CHAPTER 7

If you stood on Peachtree Street long enough in those years, you could watch the city change beneath your shoes. Atlanta shed its skin in layers: the six-lane highways widened and then doubled again, neighborhoods went down in the mud and came up with glass faces and fresh landscaping. Nothing stayed the same except the traffic and the heat, the wet river stench that lingered even after the old warehouses were scraped from the skyline. The city grew denser, meaner, harder. Its teeth were the parking meters and its bones the scaffolding that never left the edge of any view.

The friends—though none of them used the word anymore—moved through this city like a single nervous system. Their paths crossed less often, but never by accident. Mathew took a clerkship in a law firm with elevators that smelled of ozone and perfume. Josie lived in apartments that cycled every lease; she repainted every one on move-in, always the same shade of blue-gray. Mark switched precincts three times in five years, never telling anyone except the department's database. Robert drifted between hospitals like a rumor, collecting credentials and stories. William worked for the city itself, a consulting gig with an endless title and no actual office. Jimmy vanished for months at a time, then surfaced with a new job and a new badge number, always the same crooked grin.

Every December, the six made the same drive up Highway 75, past the shuttered rest stops and the new cut-rate outlets, into the teeth of the foothills. The cabin, once little more than a glorified toolshed, now had electricity, propane, and a router hidden in a coffee can nailed to the roof. They called the trip a reunion, but nobody brought spouses or significant others, not after the third year, when William's date left in the middle of the first night and hiked three miles to the next town before anyone noticed.

For the first hour, they always acted like their old selves: William making noise in the kitchen, Jimmy wrestling the logs into the fireplace, Josie mixing drinks and getting everyone to critique the playlist. Even Mark, who spent his days reading Miranda rights, let himself play the asshole just for sport.

But by the time the lantern came out—same battered metal, same soot-stained glass—something changed. They shut the music off. They set their phones to airplane mode. They poured new drinks and circled the table, the six of them radiating a tension that had nothing to do with nostalgia.

The first few years, the talk was about who'd gotten married, who'd flunked out, who was living with what disease or diagnosis. The next few years, it was about the city itself: how zoning laws could erase a street in one vote, how easy it was to get a warrant if you used the right words in the affidavit, how a single typo in a chain of custody could make a whole murder charge disappear.

Mathew, always at the end of the table, listened more than he spoke. He watched the others as they sharpened each other, the way old friends can. If they ever argued, it was over principle, never personality. Mark wanted the death penalty to hurt more. Josie wanted it gone entirely—except for the ones who "really deserved it." Robert kept proposing medical solutions to legal problems, then backed down at the first sign of real risk. William mapped out entire systems of reform, then circled back to the same cynical joke every time: "We're just cogs, but at least we know what the machine is for."

By midnight, the table was littered with bottles, legal pads, and half-drained coffee cups. The lantern's circle of light turned their faces into masks.

It was in that light, year by year, that the shape of the thing grew clearer.

No one ever said it out loud, not at first. They didn't need to. The city was a puzzle, and each held a different piece. Together, they could see the pattern. The flaws in the system weren't random—they were structural, predictable, exploitable.

One December, Mark brought a case file and tossed it onto the table, the cover spotted with coffee and something darker. "You want to see how the world really works?" he said, and made them read it cover to cover. The victim was nobody, the killer was nobody, but the way the case crumbled—bad evidence, bad luck, bad judge—made it unforgettable. Josie said, "This isn't just a failure. It's a prototype." Robert nodded, fingers tapping the glass, already writing the solution in his head.

Another year, Josie arrived late, her hair wet from the rain. "They moved the needle again," she said, dropping a folder thick with memos. "Told us to cut corners. Doesn't matter if we win or lose, just clear the case. Get it off the books." She sounded angry, but not surprised.

As the city built itself higher and tighter, the six friends burrowed deeper. They learned which court clerks drank at which bars, which assistant DAs hated each other, and which city contractors could be bribed with nothing more than a bottle and a promise. They charted every judge's bias, every defense attorney's weakness, every reporter's hunger for a story.

The annual meetings, once just a ritual, became something colder, sharper. Mathew started bringing spreadsheets instead of memories. William arrived with city blueprints, marked up in red ink. Mark and Jimmy showed up once in matching jackets, a joke that nobody understood until Josie pointed out the patch on the sleeve: a lantern, sewn in gold thread.

They built their own language for the city's flaws: "Blind corners" were the gaps in surveillance coverage; "ghost circuits" were the stretches of legal procedure nobody monitored. "Clean glass" meant a case without contamination; "dirty hands" meant someone owed a favor, or worse.

In the city, they saw their own faces everywhere: on the billboards, on the news, in the endless scroll of mugshots and obituaries. If there was grief, it was fossilized—compressed and hard, fueling the work but never softening it.

One year, as the last embers died in the fire, Robert said, "You realize we're building something here." Nobody laughed, not even William.

Mathew held the lantern in both hands, feeling its weight, the oil sloshing in the base. "We're just putting things in order," he said, but he saw the way the others looked at him.

They understood. They always had.

In the city, things broke down. But in the cabin, in the circle of the Lantern Oath, nothing ever slipped through the cracks. Every year, the machine ran smoother.

The system would be ready.

And when the world needed fixing, it would not be by accident.

***

On Matthew's first day at the firm, the partners took him to lunch at the kind of steakhouse that only existed in the glass-and-steel canyons of Midtown: twelve-dollar baked potatoes, walls papered with dead animals and Braves memorabilia. The managing partner did all the talking, rattling off the firm's lineage like a pedigree, but Mathew knew how to listen for the things that mattered. Who wore the cheapest suit? (The senior associate.) Who watched the door every five minutes? (The white-collar defense guy, ex-FBI.) Who got their steak well done and slathered it with ketchup? (The name on the letterhead.)

He spent the first week observing, letting the firm's rhythms sink into his bones. The early arrivals in the library, the mid-morning stampede for conference rooms, the 3 p.m. graveyard of legal pads abandoned in the copy room. He logged every detail, not just for future leverage but because, to him, every pattern was a kind of truth.

They started him on research—standard hazing, but Mathew finished every memo a day early and annotated the assignments with questions. The supervising attorneys pretended to be annoyed, but one by one they started passing him their oddest, most unwinnable cases. Mathew approached each problem like a puzzle box: not just "What is the answer?" but "What is the question behind the question, the flaw in the ask, the lever that opens the rest of the mechanism?"

He gravitated toward criminal appeals, even when the firm discouraged it ("Doesn't pay, too political, won't build your book"). He volunteered for every case that involved the death penalty procedure, sentencing challenges, and evidentiary loopholes. He pulled the old Southern Supreme Court cases. He memorized not just the holdings but also the concurrences and dissents, mapping the fault lines among judges and tracing how a single bad precedent could warp the state's entire legal superstructure.

In court, Mathew was unremarkable—soft voice, nervous hands, never a single memorable quote. But he made motions nobody had seen before, invoked rules nobody remembered. He'd file a habeas petition at the exact moment a judge's calendar cleared, or cite a year-old ethics memo from a rival firm to impeach their own star witness. Colleagues started calling him "the Machine" in the break room, at first as a joke and then as something else, a way of saying he was dangerous but not quite human.

He had few friends at the office. The happy hours bored him; the fantasy football leagues struck him as childish. If anyone invited him to a wedding, he sent a card and never attended. But when a new case hit the in-box—especially one with a body count or a technicality—he was the first to the file room, the last to leave the office.

He kept a personal database of every capital case in Georgia from the last fifty years. Not just names and verdicts, but the details: the prosecutor's win/loss record, which judges ruled on which pretrial motions, which expert witnesses showed up in which counties. He learned to anticipate every player, to know which arguments would land with which audience. When he lost, he dissected the loss like a post-mortem, recreating every step until he found the error.

The partners noticed. They started inviting him to closed-door meetings, using his memos to prepare for interviews with TV stations, even borrowing his research for statehouse lobbying efforts. But nobody promoted him, not at first. He didn't have the "fit," and he refused to flatter the right egos. Mathew didn't care; every win, every hack in the code, just made him more certain that the law wasn't about justice, but about the levers you could find if you looked hard enough.

He started visiting the state archives on weekends, digging for unpublished transcripts and yellowed court records. He took notes in the margins of his own case files, jotting down ideas for reforms that would never pass, loopholes that could only exist in a system run by exhausted, distracted humans.

Sometimes, after a particularly good day, he'd sit in his apartment and go over the Lantern Oath's group chat—the digital descendant of the old letters, now encrypted and full of jokes, code words, the occasional pointed "hey, look at this." William sent spreadsheets of prison construction budgets. Josie forwarded articles about DA misconduct. Mark sent mugshots, always with a comment about the suspect's posture or eyes. Mathew never replied in public, but he logged everything.

The more he learned, the more he saw the city itself as a kind of machine—a vast, creaking thing held together by paperwork, habit, and the fear of change. Every person in it was just a cog, or maybe a fuse, waiting to burn out.

Late one evening, after closing a case on a technicality nobody else had spotted, he ran into the managing partner in the elevator. The old man gave him a smile that didn't touch his eyes and said, "You're wasted in this place, Walton. You should have been an engineer."

Mathew smiled back. "I am," he said, and left it at that.

By the end of his third year, the nickname was official. "The Machine." Judges used it, sometimes with admiration, sometimes with open dislike. Opposing counsel treated his filings like unexploded ordnance. Nobody at the firm knew what to do with him, but everyone knew to send him the cases nobody else could close.

He was still young, but he'd already started rewriting the rules.

And he knew, with a kind of certainty that felt chemical, that it was only the beginning.

***

The appointment came on a Thursday, dropped in his lap like a warrant. No warning, no courtesy call—just a courier with a manila envelope and a handshake that left his palm smelling of latex. Superior Court, Atlanta Judicial Circuit, Division Five. The governor's signature glistened in wet ink, the words "effective immediately" underlined in blue.

He didn't celebrate, not even with his parents. He went straight to the courthouse and spent the next forty-eight hours walking every floor, every corridor, learning the feel of the building like he was mapping the veins beneath his own skin. He clocked the times when the clerk's office switched from coffee to diet soda, the hour when the cleaning staff swapped out, the precise moment when the metal detectors buzzed with the lunch crowd. He took notes on the hidden doors, the basement break rooms, the fire exits that could be dead-bolted in five seconds flat.

His first day on the bench, the staff expected a speech or at least a show of nerves. Instead, Mathew set his case calendar two weeks ahead and started calling dockets with the speed and authority of a man running a nuclear drill. He didn't allow late arrivals, or cell phones, or the word "um." His bailiff, a retired Army sergeant, took to saluting him as a joke, but the other courtrooms watched and followed suit. If you wanted to watch Mathew's courtroom, you had to be on time and prepared, or you got thrown out and blacklisted. By the end of the first week, the local defense bar had started calling his division "the Autoclave," because everything was sterilized before it left.

He didn't mind the nickname. He minded the inefficiency of the system itself—the way evidence was never filed right, how the DA's office used shock and spectacle over substance, the endless delays that turned justice into a slow-motion farce. He rewrote the standing orders, slashed the average hearing time by a third, and kept a running tally of every motion that came through his docket. The clerks started betting on how many times he'd overrule a lawyer before noon.

But it was the capital trials that marked his reputation. They never put him on a jury case first—too much risk, too much politics—but he watched the other judges from the gallery, scribbling notes on voir dire and opening statements. When his first murder trial came up, he cleared his calendar for a week. He memorized the case file, including the medical examiner's autopsy notes and the color of the lead investigator's necktie.

The trial ran for five days. On the second day, a juror fainted at the sight of a crime scene photo. Mathew didn't call a recess; he had the courtroom nurse revive the woman and let her decide whether to continue. She did. The defendant's mother wept through three straight cross-examinations of witnesses. Mathew didn't look at her. He focused on the evidence, the inconsistencies in the testimony, the gaps in the police work. He held the jury's attention like a surgeon clamping a vein. The verdict came in two hours.

When it was time to sign the order for a new execution warrant—his first—he did it with a gel pen, careful to keep his signature legible, as if daring the next judge to overturn it on a technicality. He triple-checked the documentation, stapled the addenda himself, and hand-delivered the file to the clerk's safe. The whole process took him forty-eight minutes, start to finish.

At home, the adjustment was harder. He'd gotten rid of his TV years ago, but now the silence felt heavier. He ate most of his meals from microwaved trays, standing in the kitchen, replaying transcripts in his head.

He slept less, reading case law until his eyes blurred. He started keeping a glass of water on the nightstand, the surface always flat, as if he could will the world into staying perfectly level.

He'd stopped answering personal calls, except from his mother, who left the same message every other week: "Proud of you, Matty, but don't let it eat you alive." Sometimes Josie texted after a big ruling, a one-word verdict ("Savage" or "Clean") that made him grin despite himself. William sent dry updates from the city government—"traffic cam contract is yours," "ADA audit went through"—the only hints that the Lantern Oath was still in operation.

The courthouse rumors grew. That he never smiled. That he remembered every word of every motion ever argued before him. That if you made a typo in a brief, he'd send it back with a note and a Post-It: "Do better." Even the most arrogant defense attorneys started prepping for his hearings as if they were preparing for war. Some tried to bait him into error, to trip him up on the little stuff. None succeeded.

He didn't mind the isolation. He welcomed it.

The only time he let himself think about Samantha was late at night, after the case files were stacked and the building's hum had faded. He'd run his finger along the edge of the bench, feeling the grain of the wood, and think about how she would have loved to argue in this courtroom—how she would have torn apart every piece of the process just to watch it twitch.

On a morning thick with fog, he got to his chambers early and found a letter waiting on his desk. No return address. Inside was a single page, a list of names. All were defense attorneys, all were notorious for getting murderers off on technicalities. At the bottom, in neat block print, a message: "You're not the only one watching."

He didn't have to wonder who sent it.

Mathew smiled for the first time in weeks. He fed the letter through the shredder, piece by piece, until nothing was left but a handful of dust.

He was the machine now. The rest would fall in line.

***

Josie hit the DA's office like a battery acid spill—corrosive, impossible to contain, with a taste that lingered long after she left the room. On her first day, she wore a tie just to see how many people would comment; when her supervisor said, "Trying to make partner already?" she grinned and said,

"Just trying to avoid the glass ceiling," and watched him die a little behind the eyes.

They put her in the Homicide Division's windowless annex, a room that smelled of old toner and lost appeals. Most of the other ADAs worked their cases like a treadmill: keep the numbers up, cut deals, push the files downstream before the news cycle caught up. Josie shredded that rhythm in a month. She cherry-picked the worst cases, the ones everyone else wrote off as hopeless or "media poison." Her first trial was a three-body gang killing in a housing project where the witnesses changed stories every interview. She called the star witness on the stand, knowing he'd lie, and let him torpedo the defense's whole case by contradicting himself eight times in an hour. When the verdict came in, the other ADAs took her out for drinks, but nobody invited her back for a second round.

Her prep was legendary, or maybe infamous. She'd stay in the office until midnight, pulling every case file, every jail call, every police report she could get her hands on. She mapped out the opposing counsel's prior cases, studied their body language in court, and even learned which paralegals were likely to leak privileged info over beers at the courthouse bar. She kept her notes on yellow legal pads, a code of arrows and slashes only she understood. When a file was ready for trial, she'd mark the cover in blue Sharpie: "Open Season."

The defense attorneys caught on. The public defenders called her "the Surgeon" because she cut so clean nobody saw the blade. She filed motions in clusters, overwhelming the court calendar and boxing her adversaries into procedural corners. In voir dire, she had a gift for making jurors confess things they didn't know they believed. "Do you think everyone deserves a second chance?" she'd ask, then use the answer to build her closing argument before opening statements had even started.

She didn't mind being hated. It meant she was doing something right.

Her first year, she lost only once, and it was a case where the body had never been found. The defense lawyer bought her a coffee the next day and asked if she'd ever thought about switching sides. "All the time," she said, "but only to see how fast I could ruin you." He didn't ask again.

The DA's office was a war of attrition, and the old guard hated her for making it look so easy. The women in the office either loved her or pretended to, depending on who was watching. The men alternated between condescension and genuine terror. After a televised trial in which she cross-examined a former police captain so brutally that the judge had to call a recess for the witness to regroup, her inbox flooded with both hate mail and job offers.

She saved the best insults, taping them inside her desk drawer. "Unprofessional," "cruel," "emotionally stunted." She added her own postscript to each: "Objective met."

Every month, she sent a short update to Mathew: "Trial won. Defense called in sick. Judge nearly cried." Sometimes he'd reply with a case citation or an inside joke—just enough to let her know he was still watching, still a part of the machine.

She didn't think about the Lantern Oath much during the workday, but it was always there, a low hum in her chest. When she read about another failed prosecution, or a killer set loose on a technicality, she felt it as a physical itch. The only thing that calmed it was the moment when the jury filed in, and she watched the defendant's eyes—hoping, doubting, finally realizing there was no way out.

She relished that moment. It was the closest thing to faith she had left.

By the end of her second year, the local news started featuring her in their courthouse roundups. They called her "the DA's Secret Weapon," which made her laugh—there was nothing secret about her. The only mystery was how she kept winning when the odds were stacked against her.

She started keeping a list of her own: not of cases, but of names. People who'd slipped through the cracks, who'd gotten away, or who'd hurt someone she couldn't reach. The list got longer every month.

One Friday, after a particularly rough week in trial, she stayed in the office late, reading old appellate decisions until the building was empty. At midnight, she logged into the Lantern Oath chat and found a new message waiting. It was a single word: "Ready?"

She stared at the screen, thought about everything she'd built, and typed back, "Always."

She shut the laptop, locked the file drawers, and left the office with a smile.

They'd taught her to hunt monsters. She was only just getting started.

***

Nobody ever expected Josie to play politics, least of all herself. But when the District Attorney collapsed in a bribery scandal, the mayor's office did what they always did: called for a committee, floated a few establishment names, and then threw up their hands when the public started howling for a real reformer. Josie had never run for office in her life, never even donated to a campaign. She just showed up to the press conference with her sleeves rolled, her hair in a knot, and a three-point plan she'd written on the back of a torn envelope the night before.

They gave her the "interim" job, figuring it would buy them time to find a permanent replacement. Within a month, she'd fired or transferred a third of the senior attorneys, moved another third to cold cases, and personally retried two murderers who'd skated on technicalities. The "interim" was quietly dropped. Nobody else wanted to run against her.

Her first year, she tripled the number of open capital cases. She didn't believe in death as a deterrent, not really, but she believed in the spectacle of consequences. When a defense attorney accused her of running a "chamber of horrors," she replied, "Not yet. But I'll let you know when we start one." The quote made the front page of the Journal-Constitution, and overnight, her email inbox tripled with requests from reporters and law students seeking to intern in her office.

She built a war room, not just for herself but for anyone who needed to track a case from arrest to verdict. A wall-sized whiteboard mapped every major felony in the city: color-coded for type, with pushpins for key players, and a red string connecting every witness, detective, and repeat offender. Staffers called it "the murder matrix," and she encouraged them to add to it, as long as they signed their names in the corner. "Accountability is a team sport," she said. Nobody laughed, but nobody quit, either.

She started a Friday night review session, ordering in cheap takeout and forcing the team to talk through the next week's dockets. If you missed a meeting, she called your personal number. If you showed up unprepared, she sent you home with twice the work. The turnover rate spiked, but so did the conviction rate. For the first time in city history, the homicide backlog shrank.

Josie took the hard cases herself: child killers, serial predators, the kinds of defendants that gave jurors nightmares. She'd sit with the files all weekend, line up the photos and transcripts in order, and memorize the medical examiner's diagrams until she could recite the wounds by angle and depth. In court, she moved like a chess engine: always three moves ahead, never taking the obvious attack if there was a more elegant way to corner the king.

Sometimes she'd stay late and run the city's crime stats just for fun, looking for new patterns. She liked to imagine she was playing against herself: could she find a gap in her own casework, could she spot a witness she'd missed or a detective who was sandbagging a report? Most nights, she found something, and the next morning, she'd assign someone to fix it. It was an endless loop, but it never bored her.

Other DAs in the state watched what she was doing, but few tried to copy it. When they did, they'd call her for advice, and she'd give it—straight, no bullshit—because she liked the idea of the whole system running at her level. She started getting invited to speak at national conferences, her inbox filling up with questions about management, discovery, and forensic labs. She replied to every message, even the ones that were mostly veiled insults.

She still made time for the Oath, though now it was mostly encrypted texts or the occasional late-night call. Mathew reached out after her first death penalty win, sending a link to the appellate ruling with a simple "Impressive." William sometimes pinged her with tips about jailhouse rumors or budget shifts in the prison system. Robert's updates were less frequent, but when he did write, it was always about a new medical angle in the execution protocols.

She started keeping a second wall, in a locked office behind her own. This one tracked only death penalty cases, past and present. Photos, transcripts, letters from families, sometimes even hand-written notes from the condemned. She updated it herself in neat, tiny script, almost as if she were memorializing each one.

If anyone asked why she worked so hard, she never answered the same way twice. "Because it's the right thing." "Because I want to win." "Because this city deserves better." All of them were true, but none captured the full edge of it.

She was the first to arrive every day and the last to leave. If a file went missing, she knew who took it. If a reporter leaked a story, she knew the source before the byline went live. Even the judges started to defer to her on questions of law—she'd once cited an obscure statute from 1896 in a bail hearing, and the judge not only granted the motion but cited her brief in his written opinion.

By her third year, people stopped referring to her as "the woman DA," or "the new one." She was just Josie, the last word on justice in the city.

One night, after a clean sweep in a triple-murder case, she stood in her office and looked at the two walls. The first is a chaotic map of crime. The second is a graveyard built in paper and ink. She thought about how much she'd changed, how far the Oath had brought her, and how much was left to do.

Her phone buzzed. A message from Mark: "Got a name for you. Call when ready."

She smiled. She already was.

She locked the door, turned out the lights, and left the office, her reflection sharp and cold in the glass. The city could rest for a few hours, at least.

She'd see to it personally.

***

Robert liked the precision of medicine, the click of a correct diagnosis, the beauty of a chemical equation balanced to the milligram. He'd always known he'd end up in a lab coat, but it wasn't until the third-year clinical rotation that he understood how much the system depended on people who never lost their nerve.

He did his time in the ER, the OR, even the psych wards, but what fascinated him most was the morgue. It was quiet there—no screaming, no phone calls, just the gentle hum of the refrigeration units and the methodical work of slicing, measuring, recording. The dead didn't lie, not the way the living did. Their secrets were always visible if you looked in the right places.

He finished med school at the top of his class and matched into a residency in forensic pathology residency at the state's flagship hospital. The work was monotonous at first, but Robert treated each autopsy like a riddle. He learned to spot the difference between a real suicide and a staged one, between a stabbing that was angry and one that was careful. He could estimate the time of death to within fifteen minutes on a cold day.

The Department of Corrections sent its worst cases to his lab. Deaths in custody, mostly: overdoses, shankings, the occasional "unexplained collapse." At first, the files arrived with half the paperwork missing, but Robert rebuilt the history from the tissue samples, the toxicology reports, and the little tells that made each case unique. He started flagging patterns: the same batch numbers for lethal injection drugs, the same medical examiner's signature on every third certificate, the same way corrections officers described the final moments.

One afternoon, the prison warden himself came to the hospital. He had the calm, deliberate manner of a man who'd spent decades in rooms without windows. He asked Robert to consult on a pending execution—not for the body, but for the process itself.

"The state wants this done clean," the warden said. "We don't want a scene like Texas last spring. Think you can make it go smoothly?"

Robert didn't hesitate. "Absolutely."

He read every protocol, every statute, every CDC advisory ever written on death by injection. He ran simulations in the lab, tested the effects of barbiturates on animal tissue, and even reverse-engineered the compounds used in other states. He noticed that the official protocols always left room for "judgment," a built-in margin for error that covered everyone's ass. Robert saw it as a design flaw.

He started writing his own guidelines, down to the timing of each dose and the gauge of every needle. He trained the nursing staff to double-check every step, to keep a log with no gaps, to treat the condemned with the same clinical dignity as a living patient. When an inmate's vein blew out during a dry run, Robert found a workaround: a pre-surgical cutdown, performed under local anesthetic, that made the rest of the process idiot-proof.

Word got around. Other states called him for advice. He got letters—some threatening, some grateful—from the families of both victims and perpetrators. At first, he kept his answers factual, but after a while, he started to enjoy the small ways he could nudge the system toward precision.

He didn't think much about the morality of it, not directly. He told himself that a system that killed by statute owed the condemned a perfect death. Anything less was a failure of the process.

On rare nights when the work didn't follow him home, he logged into the Oath's private message board. He read the updates from Josie, Mathew, William, and sometimes even Mark or Jimmy. He never replied unless he had something useful to add, but he archived every message, every case file, every thread that hinted at a new problem to solve.

His apartment was stacked with technical manuals, the kind nobody else bothered to read. On the wall above his desk, he kept a single page torn from a magazine: a schematic of the human circulatory system, overlaid with a flowchart titled "Final Administration." It was elegant, almost beautiful.

After his first "clean" execution, the warden shook his hand and said, "Nobody's ever done it better." Robert smiled, but the compliment didn't really register. He was already thinking of ways to improve the next one.

He started keeping a journal, tracking every variable, every success, every anomaly. If the system could be made flawless, he'd be the one to do it.

And when the Oath called, he'd be ready to deliver.

***

The execution chamber was cleaner than most operating rooms. Robert insisted on it. He'd trained the entire medical team himself, from the IV nurse down to the custodian who wiped down the gurney after each procedure. He wore hospital scrubs, a mask, and clear plastic goggles, not for the optics but because the powder from the latex gloves made his eyes sting for hours afterward.

On execution days, he arrived before dawn. The warden met him at the side entrance, with a quick handshake and a solemn exchange of "Ready?" / "Always." Robert reviewed the checklists, signed off on the chain of custody for the drugs, and double-checked the witness lists against the day's schedule.

He knew every step by heart, but he made himself walk through it anyway: prep room, holding cell, chamber. The air was cold, the lights a harsh blue-white. The hardware was manufactured by a company that also made dental chairs, and the adjustment mechanism tended to jam if not kept lubricated. Robert had fixed it himself more than once.

He greeted the inmate with the same calm, courteous tone he used for every patient. He explained the sequence: the first dose would make them sleepy, the second would stop their breathing, and the third would ensure the rest. He spoke softly, but not softly enough for the guards to miss a word.

The warden observed from behind bulletproof glass, flanked by state officials, lawyers, and, sometimes, the press. Robert never looked up during the procedure, not even to see if the witnesses were satisfied.

He monitored the inmate's vitals and adjusted the infusion rate with the lightest touch. He counted down the seconds between each injection, noting the muscle twitches and sighs that always accompanied the first drug. When the heart rate flatlined, he checked the pupils and called the time of death to the exact second. He recorded the numbers on a form he'd redesigned himself—clean columns, no ambiguity, no room for error.

The whole process took less than nine minutes, from start to finish.

Afterward, he escorted the body to the morgue, supervised the removal of the IV, and completed a brief post-mortem. He noted the absence of bruising, the scleral color, and the skin temperature. Sometimes, he dictated a summary for the file, but only if there was something out of the ordinary.

He was the last to leave. The corridor always seemed longer on the way out.

Back at his office, he logged the day's events, scanned the checklists, and archived the data on a secure drive. He updated his journal, not just the technical details but the human ones: which guards had trembled, which witnesses had looked away, which condemned man had said thank you, and which had spat on the glass.

He never spoke to the media, but the Oath always knew. Sometimes a message arrived in his inbox before he'd even changed clothes. A single word: "Perfect." Or, "Next."

Robert closed his laptop and looked at the wall, at the elegant diagram of the system he'd perfected.

There were no ghosts here—only the clean edge of a job well done.

When the time came for the real test, he would not fail.

He was the last word on death.

***

William never saw himself as a warden, not even a bureaucrat. He started at the Department of Corrections as an analyst, another cog in the chain of middle managers who shuffled paper from one inbox to another. But where others saw busywork, William saw architecture—a system of pipes and wires that, if mapped properly, could be bent to any purpose.

The first week, he memorized the org chart, not just the names but the feuds, the alliances, the off-the-record power brokers. He attended every meeting, even the ones that bored him senseless, just to see who spoke first and who got credit in the follow-up emails. He started a spreadsheet—color-coded, cross-referenced, updated daily—to track every disciplinary action, every transfer, every policy memo that came through HQ.

Within months, he'd written new templates for the incident reports, reducing them to six checkboxes and a signature. The guards loved it because it meant less paperwork. The warden loved it because the new system made it impossible for errors to pile up. The inmates, for a while, didn't notice anything at all.

But William noticed everything. He kept a second spreadsheet, this one encrypted and stored on a thumb drive he wore on a chain around his neck. Here, he tracked the unofficial system: which guard was sleeping with which nurse, which inmate had dirt on a supervisor, which "pilot programs" were actually smokescreens for something else. He learned how to read the language of the memos, the way a single word—"recommend," "urge," "immediate"—could move millions in budget, or get a whole block reassigned overnight.

His boss, a former Marine with a clipboard fetish, started relying on William to "scrub" the weekly reports before they went up the chain. William did it in half the time and with none of the mistakes. When the Commissioner asked who'd prepped the numbers for the legislative briefing, William got a handshake and a smile, and a seat at the next roundtable.

He rose fast, first to Director of Inmate Programs, then to a newly invented role: Chief of Process Improvement. The job was supposed to be a sinecure, a way to park a smart guy without threatening anyone higher up. But William used the title as a cover to root through every audit, every procurement file, every internal investigation that had been swept under a rug.

He found the inefficiencies, the cracks, the shadow budgets. He didn't blow the whistle; he just made notes. Sometimes he fixed a problem—reassigned a sadistic guard, closed a loophole in the commissary system, swapped out a corrupt vendor—but only if it advanced the bigger plan. Most of the time, he left the flaws intact, knowing that someday the Oath might need them.

His office was bare except for a whiteboard, which he updated every morning with the day's "levers"—three or four actions, small but cumulative, that could tilt the balance of the whole institution. He called it the "daily burn," and he never repeated a lever twice in a month.

The IT guys loved him because he never called unless something was really broken. The mailroom staff adored him for sneaking them donuts on payday. The warden respected him in the way a veteran respects the sniper who never misses.

Nobody knew about the Oath, but William kept them updated through secure channels. He sent Josie case numbers that would get lost in the shuffle, flagged new death penalty appeals for Mathew, and tipped Robert when a problematic inmate was headed for medical review.

His favorite trick was using the "urgent" line in the warden's inbox. It bypassed two levels of management and triggered a response within twenty-four hours, guaranteed. He used it sparingly—usually just to move a name from one list to another—but he loved its power, the clean feeling of setting a wheel in motion and knowing exactly how it would turn.

After work, he went home to a rented duplex in the suburbs, ate his dinner cold, and ran simulations on his laptop. He didn't watch TV, didn't bother with friends from college. He preferred the company of systems—things that made sense, that obeyed their own rules.

Late one night, he sat on his patio, smoking a cigar and watching the neighbor's dog dig in the trash. He checked his phone and saw a message from the Oath: "Ready for the next lever?"

He exhaled, smiled, and typed: "Already set. Pull the trigger anytime."

The machine was running exactly as he'd designed.

He just had to wait for the right moment to see what it could do.

***

The day William became Warden of Ironwood, the staff staged a betting pool on how long he'd last. The favorite was eight months—one full audit cycle and a riot, give or take. Ironwood was the kind of place that killed careers: a modern fortress dropped in the middle of nowhere, built to house the state's most dangerous, most political, and most forgotten inmates.

The drive up was a geometry lesson: turnpikes, razorwire, guard towers spaced so evenly you could chart them on a map. The front gate opened by appointment only, and the lobby was designed to make visitors feel like they were already halfway to the afterlife.

William spent his first week on the graveyard shift, shadowing the line supervisors and memorizing the routine: cell checks every hour, keys on a strict count, every inmate movement choreographed to the minute. He read the duty logs, the maintenance requests, and the disciplinary records. He even listened to the staff gossip, because that was where the real intelligence lived.

Ironwood had been through five wardens in seven years. Each had tried a different fix—militarize the guards, soften up the programs, privatize the kitchen, double the security in the yard. None of it stuck. The old hands kept their heads down, the new hires quit within a month, and the inmates ran their own society just under the surface.

William did things differently. He didn't try to out-tough the Alpha guards or charm the HR manager. Instead, he set about mapping the entire organism: who controlled the cell phones, who ran the commissary, which COs were on the take, and which ones just liked to look the other way.

He started with small changes, barely perceptible at first. He moved the shift change by ten minutes, which cut down on the fights in the showers. He rotated the food deliveries so the kitchen staff couldn't skim off the top. He had IT lock down the Wi-Fi so inmates couldn't bootleg their own networks. Every time he closed a loophole, he watched to see who flinched.

The riot didn't come in month one. It came in month five, just as he predicted, a coordinated surge in the South Block timed to the end of a televised football game. William was on-site within sixty seconds, used the "urgent" line to reroute every available staffer, and had the instigators locked down before the state police even arrived at the parking lot. When the local news tried to make a scandal of it, William met the reporters at the gate, handed out a timeline of events, and stood there until every last camera was packed away.

After that, even the skeptics on staff started to follow his lead.

He brought in Robert to audit the medical protocols, and together they overhauled the entire sick call system—cutting wait times, flagging at-risk inmates, and ensuring no one could game the system for contraband. Josie sent a prosecutor to observe disciplinary hearings, which kept the COs on their toes and the paperwork immaculate. Mark started feeding him unofficial "heads up" on problem transfers from the city jail. Jimmy, already a legend in the corrections world, joined as a shift supervisor and quickly earned a reputation for breaking up fights without ever raising his voice.

William ran staff meetings like a chess match: never yelling, always moving pieces, always keeping his endgame in sight. He used performance metrics to reward loyalty but also to spot those who were faking it. He instituted a rotating "red team" program in which guards simulated escapes or contraband runs to keep everyone sharp.

At night, he walked the yard, alone, letting the quiet settle around him. He liked the feel of the air—thin, a little metallic from the fence posts, carrying the hum of a thousand locked doors. He would think about the way a single decision could ripple through the whole system: a line in a staff memo, a change in the vending machines, a shuffled deck of keys.

He knew the inmates watched him, and he let them. He never played favorites, but he always remembered the names of the troublemakers and the peacemakers. He could tell within a week which cons were running a long game and which would burn out before the holidays.

Once, during a lockdown, an inmate passed him a note through the food slot: "You play it straight, boss." William didn't keep the note, but he remembered it. He was always listening.

The Oath stayed in touch, sometimes encrypted, sometimes through official channels. Josie let him know when a new high-value transfer was coming. Mathew flagged the legal cases that might end up in his facility. Robert visited every quarter, under the guise of reviewing the protocols, but William knew he was there to check the whole machine.

One evening, after a double shift, William sat in his office and reviewed the latest stats. Assaults down. Contraband was nearly eliminated. Staff turnover is half what it used to be. He didn't smile—he didn't have to.

He checked his phone and saw a message from Josie: "Ready for prime time?"

He replied, "Ironwood is. So am I."

The machine was his now. All he had to do was keep it running.

And wait for the day when it would matter most.

***

Mark was a cop, the way some people are born with their last names already tattooed on their arms. He transferred quickly from the Savannah PD as soon as an opening on the APD was available and started on patrol in South Atlanta, working the midnight shift in a part of the city where every porch light was a warning and every unlocked car was an invitation. His uniform never fit right—his shoulders too broad, the seams always threatening to split—but his eyes never missed anything. Not the glint of a knife, not the twitch of a liar, not the nervous shuffle of someone on the edge of running.

He learned the city block by block, rolling slowly through the alleys, remembering the faces that ducked when he drove by. He built a mental map of who controlled which corners, who owed who, who was ready to flip for a lighter charge, and who'd die before ratting. He was never chatty, but when he talked, people listened. Even the gangsters called him "Officer Mark," half-respectful, half-afraid.

The promotion to detective came sooner than he expected—two years in, after a string of robberies he solved with nothing but a busted shoelace and a hunch about a pawn shop on the edge of DeKalb. The detectives' bullpen was a chaos of mismatched desks and stale coffee, but Markfit fit right in. He ditched the uniform for a worn leather jacket, but kept the buzz cut, the boots, and the stare that made even the old-timers look away.

The first week, they gave him a stack of cold cases—mostly junk, the kind nobody really wanted to solve. He pulled two all-nighters, cross-checked addresses, and found a pattern in how the bodies were dumped. On the third morning, he had an answer: the killer was a plumber who did side jobs in abandoned homes. He knocked on the door before sunrise, read the guy his rights, and had a full confession before the ADA even finished her bagel.

Word got around. Mark didn't do politics, didn't play the ass-covering games. He just worked the case, made the arrest, and closed the file. He was surgical in interviews, never losing his temper in the box, but made sure the suspect knew exactly how close they were to being completely ruined. He could wait out anyone.

His boss, a three-decades-on-the-job ex-marine, started using Mark to handle "the uglies"—child murders, missing persons, anything that would make the news cycle. He didn't smile much, but when a reporter asked why the department's closure rate had doubled, he said, "We got a guy who hates losing more than he hates paperwork."

Mark kept his own list in a notebook with a cracked cover. Names of the ones that got away, the ones he was still watching, the ones that would slip up eventually. He went to every parole hearing he could, just to look the repeat offenders in the eye. Sometimes he'd follow them after, let them know he was always around. The word on the street was: "Don't mess with Officer Mark." The word in the department was: "Mark's got a nose for monsters."

His personal life was a rumor. Sometimes he showed up at Josie's parties, stayed twenty minutes, and left without a word. Sometimes he and Jimmy would drink in silence, never talking about work or the old days. He had a family once, but the hours and the nightmares killed that quickly.

He saw the system for what it was: a meat grinder, a slow machine that chewed up the desperate and the unlucky. But he never lost faith in his own methods. If you did the crime, you'd see Mark's face before the bars closed behind you. That was the rule.

He started feeding Josie tips about cases, flagged the ones where the DA's office could make a splash. Sometimes he'd pass a file to Mathew, knowing the judge could steer it the right way. He never said it out loud, but he liked knowing the Oath had its hooks in every stage of the process.

One winter, a string of disappearances made the news—girls from the same neighborhood, all found strangled, dumped in rivers or drainage ditches. Mark took the case, worked it for months, followed up every tip, every scrap of gossip. He was relentless. When he found the guy—an ex-con, a drifter with a long record and a bad attitude—he didn't bother with backup. He just knocked, waited for the door to open, and walked the suspect straight to the precinct in cuffs.

He didn't gloat, didn't high-five the team. He just filed the paperwork, sent a one-line email to Josie ("He's yours now"), and went home. He slept for two days straight.

When he woke up, there was a message from the Oath: "Perfect work. Next?"

Mark didn't reply. He didn't need to.

He had another case to close.

***

Jimmy started at Ironwood on the graveyard shift, the same way most rookies did: minimum wage, maximum danger, no hazard pay unless you got hurt bad enough to need a medevac. He was the youngest in his unit, but he learned fast—how to keep your mouth shut, how to spot a brewing fight from the way the hallways got quiet, how to file a use-of-force report so clean nobody questioned it.

He didn't swagger, didn't yell, didn't pick favorites. The lifers respected him because he didn't flinch when threatened, didn't gloat when he won a hand of poker in the breakroom, and didn't put up with the old-timers' war stories unless they had a point. He had a way of walking a tier that made the inmates chill out; if things got loud, Jimmy just waited, arms folded, until the noise drained out on its own.

His file was perfect, except for the part where he refused to write up coworkers for minor violations. "Handle it in-house," he'd say, and he did, usually with a talk in the locker room or a cold stare that left the problem fixed and nobody embarrassed. Supervisors took notice. He got promoted to sergeant in under two years, bypassing a couple of guys who'd been there since the place opened.

Jimmy's real skill was the way he never seemed to get surprised. During a full-blown riot in D-block, while everyone else was in body armor, Jimmy walked the perimeter with a first-aid kit, patching up both sides, ignoring the curses and the blood. When the SWAT team finally breached the barricade, Jimmy was already inside, helping a guard with a broken leg and talking down the leader of the inmate crew. The warden gave him a commendation; Jimmy stuck it in a drawer and never mentioned it.

He got tapped to run death row after the previous head guard had a meltdown and trashed his own office. The rumor was that Jimmy was too nice for the job, that he'd get eaten alive by the sharks up there. But on his first day, he called every CO and every inmate by name, shook their hands, and posted a new schedule on the wall: "We run this place on time, or we don't run it at all." Nobody laughed, but nobody tested him either.

He rewrote the shift protocols, cross-trained the staff, and set up a gym in the basement so the guards could burn off the stress instead of getting drunk or starting fights. He listened to the inmates' complaints, but he didn't promise more than he could deliver. When a condemned man tried to start a hunger strike, Jimmy sat with him for an hour, eating nothing, just talking. By morning, the guy was back on his tray, and Jimmy never said a word about it.

He ran the execution chamber with the same calm precision. He checked the restraints himself, verified every form, and made sure nobody—staff or witness—walked in with a cell phone or a grudge. On the day of an execution, he kept the guards steady, handled the condemned with respect, and stood by for the whole process. When Robert came in to supervise, Jimmy made sure the doc had everything he needed, and if there was an issue, Jimmy fixed it before it hit the warden's desk.

The team under him was loyal—not because he was the hardest, but because he was the most consistent. He never let anyone get blindsided by a surprise transfer, never let a guard take the fall for a warden's mistake. If someone screwed up, Jimmy owned it in the report and handled it behind closed doors.

He got a nickname: "the Icebox." The inmates meant it as a joke, but the staff picked it up for real. There was no drama in Jimmy's units, just the steady hum of everything running the way it was supposed to.

He never lost touch with the Oath. When William needed something moved or hidden, Jimmy handled it. When Mark needed a heads-up on a parolee or a visitor, Jimmy got the info. He kept Josie in the loop on anything that might make the news, and he checked in with Robert before every high-profile execution, just to make sure the process was perfect.

Once, after a particularly rough week—two executions back-to-back, plus an inmate suicide—Jimmy sat in the empty chapel and watched the dust float in the light from the high windows. He thought about Samantha, about how none of this would matter to her, and about how maybe, just maybe, all this was the only way to keep things from getting worse.

He checked his phone. There was a new message, a number he recognized but never saved: "We need a smooth hand on the next one. Can you do it?"

Jimmy typed back: "Easy."

He stood up, put on his cap, and went back to work.

He was the last link in the chain, and he never let it slip.

***

They never met in person in public. Not after college, not once the careers took off, and the risk of exposure became real. The Oath ran on signal and shadow, every message encrypted, every favor traded with a handshake no one else could see.

Mark's tips to Josie came as anonymous call logs, routed through three burner phones and disguised as routine crime updates. Josie's requests for records or inside dirt arrived in Mathew's in-box as footnotes in legal briefs, the relevant detail always buried in a block of boilerplate. William moved inmates, staff, or records by slipping a single word into an official memo—an adjective or typo that only the Oath would notice. Robert's supply requests for the execution chamber doubled as coded updates on the death row roster; if he needed to flag a problematic case, he'd cite a research paper on "unexpected outcomes" and leave it at that.

Even Jimmy got in on the act. His shift reports, submitted weekly to the warden, always contained a single out-of-place phrase: "All quiet on D-Block," or "Chapel attendance steady." In the right context, these meant more than any email ever could.

Sometimes, the messages crossed in transit—two requests for the same file, a memo that referenced a case not yet assigned. This never caused a problem. The Oath had learned, over years of practice, to read each other's intent like code. They were six brains in parallel, all working toward the same outcome, all patient enough to wait for the world to catch up.

The system worked because it was invisible. Even if the FBI had tapped every phone, even if the Inspector General sent in a mole, they would never see the pattern. The Oath didn't exist, not in any directory, not on any social, not even in the digital residue of their personal lives. To the outside world, they were professionals. Stars in their fields. If they ran into each other at a conference or a funeral, they didn't hug or even shake hands. At most, a nod, a glance, a shared joke about the weather.

But on execution night, the system hummed. Mark would walk the perimeter, just to make sure the press vans weren't camped in the wrong place. William would clear the admin building, so there were no last-minute "visitors" from the state. Josie would be at her desk, reviewing every last detail of the case file, making sure the witnesses were all in order. Jimmy would be on the cell block, keeping the staff calm, making sure the handoff to the chamber was seamless. Robert would scrub the IV lines himself, running the checklist twice, then waiting for the final signal.

Mathew's job was the quietest: he'd sit in his chambers, the phone muted, the warrant already signed, and just watch the clock. He never called. Never emailed. The others knew when the time had come.

When it was over, there was never a celebration. Sometimes, a message would arrive: "Clean," or "Closed," or just the case number with nothing else. Sometimes, days later, an envelope would appear in the mail—no return address, just a clipping from a newspaper, or a single page torn from a legal pad.

The Oath thrived in the spaces between. They kept the engine running with whispers and nudges, invisible as carbon monoxide. If anyone wondered how the system could run so smoothly, how all the gears stayed aligned, they never asked out loud.

No one ever saw them together. That was the rule.

And if the day ever came when they needed to act as one, the signal would go out, and the world would never know what hit it.

***

They called it the Lantern Meeting, though there was no fire, no woods, not even a table—just six windows on a secure video call, their faces lit by laptop glare and the odd glow of city lights outside.

Mathew started, as always. "Roll call?" he said, voice low enough that even in the empty room, it felt like a secret.

Josie was first to answer, her tie loosened but still on, a row of legal pads behind her like trophies. "DA's office, present. The city's a mess, but we're ahead on trial scheduling for the first time since I took over. We pushed four capital cases to the front this month, all on direct indictment. Not a single successful appeal so far."

Mark grunted from the dark corner of his home office, badge glinting on the shelf. "PD's as bad as you'd expect. Two homicides last week, but I got the shooters in custody. No leaks to the press, no grandstanding from the city council. I'm keeping the media off your back, Josie."

William looked half-asleep, but his spreadsheets filled the window behind him. "Corrections is running at ninety percent staffing—no major incidents since the last sweep. I can move anyone, anywhere, on forty-eight hours' notice. If you need a transfer, just mark the file."

Robert, white coat already off for the night, had a pile of journals in front of him. "Execution protocols are tight. The state board reviewed the last two; there were no complaints. I've implemented a triple-check on the compound mix—no more screw-ups, no more botched headlines. If they ask, it's by the book."

Jimmy, sipping coffee in a breakroom that could've been anywhere, smiled a little. "Death row's calm. Inmates respect the schedule. The staff respects the process. Nobody's talked to the press in months. If there's a last-minute legal or medical issue, I handle it before the warden even wakes up."

There was a pause, not quite awkward but dense with the knowledge of what they'd just recited. Mathew let it linger, then said, "You realize that's the whole thing. Start to finish. There's not a single part of the system we don't control."

No one argued. They didn't need to.

William raised his mug. "To the machine."

Jimmy rolled his eyes, but lifted his own. "Icebox approves."

Josie snorted. "Don't get sentimental, guys. We're not the Avengers. This is just business."

But Mark, never the sentimental type, leaned in. "It's more than business. This is a lock. The city, the state, the whole process. If there's a monster out there, we don't have to wait for the world to fix it."

Robert added, "Or break it by accident."

They sat with that for a moment, the echo of what they'd built hanging between them.

Mathew said, "No speeches, but… this is what we swore to do. What light cannot reach—"

"—shadow must cleanse," the rest finished, almost as a reflex.

They moved on to the business of the night—case numbers, transfers, who was moving where, who needed a heads-up. The language was technical, cold, but under it ran the knowledge that every action now rippled from them, through the system, into the world.

Before they signed off, Josie said, "If anyone gets cold feet, speak now."

Nobody did.

Jimmy winked at the camera. "See you on the other side."

Mathew killed the call, sat in the dark, and listened to the silence.

It sounded a lot like destiny.

***

Mark found the file by accident. He was doing a routine case review—just housekeeping, nothing special—when he saw the pattern: a string of cold-case hits on a new DNA run, names and dates that lined up with a handful of unsolved cases from a decade prior. The suspect's name at the bottom of the report was highlighted in yellow, flagged for "Special Processing." He felt his stomach twist the way it used to before a fight.

The name was Calvin Bass.

He remembered it from the old days, from the late-night crime shows and the whispered rumors in the station. Bass was a drifter, a predator, a black hole that had devoured entire families up and down the Southeast. His MO was always the same: young girls, always taken in the night, always left somewhere nobody wanted to look. The papers called him the

Creekside Killer, but the department called him "the one that got away." The Oath called him something else, though none of them said it out loud: the reason.

Mark didn't send an email, didn't pick up the phone. He flagged the file, encrypted it, and waited for the Lantern Meeting that month.

When the call started, nobody wasted time on small talk. Mark shared his screen, pulled up the file, and watched the faces change one by one as the name came into focus.

Josie went pale, all the color draining from her face. "Is that—" she started, then stopped.

William just stared, jaw clenched so hard the muscles jumped.

Jimmy whispered, "No way." He'd heard the old stories, too.

Robert's hand trembled. He reached for his coffee, but set it back down without drinking. "How many cases?"

"Dozens," Mark said. "Maybe more. The new DNA hits tie him to three in Georgia, five in Alabama, and two in Florida. All the victims match the old profile. All of them match—" He stopped, let the silence fill in the rest.

Samantha. And others like her.

Mathew spoke last, voice colder than usual. "Is it real? Is it enough to move?"

Mark nodded. "He's in custody. Waiting for extradition. But the state wants to trade him for info on other cases. They'll plead it down, give him life instead of the needle."

Nobody said a word for a long time.

Finally, Josie said, "Not this time."

Mathew glanced at her, then at the rest. "We bring him here. We run it through. Clean. No mistakes."

William said, "I can move him to Ironwood without anyone noticing.
"

Robert said, "I'll make sure the protocol is airtight. No repeats of Oklahoma."

Jimmy: "I'll keep the staff solid. No leaks."

Josie stared at the screen, then said, "We do this by the book. Nothing off script. We want it to stick; we want it to hold up on every appeal. If there's a single loose end, we cut it ourselves."

Mark just nodded.

They ran the rest of the meeting in a haze, the usual business feeling hollow compared to what they'd just decided.

When the call ended, Mathew sat in the dark for a long time, remembering the old pain and the old promise.

They'd built the machine for this.

It was time to see if it could work.

***

It started with the warrant. Mark walked it through himself, ignoring the scuffed linoleum and the stares from the night desk. The paperwork was immaculate, every date and time cross-checked, every witness statement triple-verified. Bass was in a holding cell in Alabama, but the extradition was completed in less than 48 hours. William had a van waiting at the state line, driven by an off-duty CO who owed him two favors. Jimmy ran the intake at Ironwood, made sure Bass was processed quietly, no photos, no interviews, no risk.

The evidence was a mountain. Mark worked with forensics for two weeks straight, combing every inch of the old cases. Hair, fiber, blood, even a single scrap of skin from under a victim's fingernail. He brought in the mothers of the victims, sat with them through the agony, and promised them—without saying it—that this time, the system wouldn't fail. When it was all cataloged, he sent the box to Josie, hand-delivered to her private office.

Josie built the case with surgical precision. She didn't play for the cameras, didn't call a press conference. She let the story build until every paper in the state was running it above the fold. "Alleged Serial Killer Faces Justice," the headlines screamed. She let the victims' stories come out first, not the man's. She spent nights prepping the witnesses, walking them through the questions, inoculating them against every trick the defense could try.

When the trial date hit, the courthouse was a fortress. Mark was there, posted at the door, making sure every juror was safe, every reporter kept at bay. William had already rerouted the visiting judge to Mathew's division, a maneuver so subtle no one noticed the switch. Mathew recused himself from the press, citing "personal history," but presided with the same cold clarity that had earned him his own nickname in the legal blogs: "the Guillotine."

The defense tried for insanity, tried for childhood trauma, tried to get evidence thrown out. Mathew denied the motions one by one, always with a page of citations and a signature so sharp it cut the air. Josie's team landed the blows in cross, but she took the lead on the final witness, walking Bass through his own confessions, never letting him squirm or dodge. She asked, "Did you do it?" and Bass looked up for the first time and said, "I did."

Nobody cried in the courtroom. Not the families, not the jurors, not even Josie. Mathew read the verdict in monotone: "Guilty on all counts." Sentencing took less than an hour. The judge set the date.

Bass didn't flinch when they cuffed him. He didn't beg, didn't threaten, didn't smile. He just walked out, and that was the last anyone saw of him outside Ironwood.

The Oath tracked the rest as a matter of process. William kept Bass in isolation, watching every meal and movement. Robert triple-checked the medical file, ran the bloodwork, and reviewed every protocol. Jimmy kept the block running, handled the guards, shut down every whisper of a story before it reached the outside.

Josie sent the notice of appeal, but the defense barely tried. The evidence was too tight, the confessions too detailed. It was over before it began.

CHAPTER 8

The last Lantern Oath meeting before the execution took place two weeks before Bass's anticipated execution date in the secluded cabin over a weekend. It was late, but no one looked tired; the tension in the cabin had the quality of anesthesia—muted, but absolute.

They didn't begin with the ritual. There was no lighting of the lantern, no invocation of old promises. Instead, the file sat at the center of the table: a brown folder, thick enough to bulge, with Bass's name stenciled in block letters across the top. The air above it seemed denser, as if the world itself wanted to keep its contents contained.

Mark had come straight from the precinct, his hands still stained with the ink of his own notes. He didn't look at anyone as he opened the file, spreading the contents like a dealer preparing a final hand. He didn't speak, but the way he arranged the sheets—photos, transcripts, police reports—told the story with more clarity than any oral argument.

Josie watched the papers with a surgeon's detachment, eyes flicking to the crime scene photos only once, then never again. She had already internalized every detail: the sequence of abductions, the escalation of violence, the gap years where Bass had disappeared, but the world hadn't improved for it. Her hands remained flat on the table, fingers curled inwards, as if daring the evidence to challenge her resolve.

William said, "You're sure about the time?" His voice had an almost chemical steadiness.

"Down to the minute," Mathew replied, and the matter was closed.

Jimmy tapped his pen on the table, counting off the possible points of failure. He didn't speak, and didn't need to. His job wasn't the planning, it was the doing—the control of small variables that, in lesser hands, would become catastrophic.

Robert arrived for the protocol briefing carrying a white plastic crate. He unpacked the vials first—clear, amber, and a faint blue that looked like windshield fluid—and lined them in a precise row on the table. The rest watched, silent, as he set down syringes, alcohol wipes, and a laminated flowchart. The only superfluous item was a small glass bottle of hand sanitizer, but Robert set it in the exact center of the table, as if it were a relic of faith.

"There are three phases," he said, unscrewing the cap on the first vial. "Phase one: induction. Two milligrams per kilo, IV push. Within eight seconds, the subject will be unresponsive to all external stimuli. They won't even blink."

He looked up, eyes flat behind his wire glasses. "This is the point of no return."

Nobody interrupted. He tapped the amber vial with his pen. "Phase two: respiratory suppression. Less than a cc per kilo. This one is tricky—if you overdo it, you get true asphyxia. If you underdose, the breathing stays visible." He hesitated, then said, "We need to hit the margin exactly. If the muscle relaxant takes too soon, it ruins the illusion. Too late, and you risk awareness. There's no safety net."

Josie leaned in. "What about the monitors?"

"There are no monitors in the chamber anymore, not for the subject. Just an EKG strip and a visual check. We can flatline the pulse with the paralytic. Breathing will look absent unless they use a stethoscope, which isn't protocol."

William nodded, satisfied. "Witnesses won't be able to tell?"

"Not even if they're looking for it," Robert said. "He'll look dead. He'll feel dead. Even on a close examination, the capillary response will be gone. It's enough to fool an expert."

"Any long-term effects?" Mark asked. He always wanted to know the mess left behind.

Robert shrugged. "If we wake him within two hours, probably nothing. If we screw up, he never wakes up at all. But that's better than the alternative."

Mathew didn't speak, but his hand drifted to the edge of the flowchart, tracing the bullet points. "This is what we're doing," he said finally.

Robert capped the vials and repacked them in the crate. He didn't make eye contact. "Once we start, there's no reversing it. You want to blink, this is the moment."

Nobody blinked.

Jimmy said, "You got a plan for the handoff?"

"I do," Robert said, "but it only works if we follow the sequence to the letter. No freelancing."

The Oath absorbed this, the unspoken promise in the air: the plan was both sword and shield, and there was nothing left but to trust the hand holding the blade.

Robert leaned forward, folding his arms. "Margin is less than a percent," he said. "If he's metabolically atypical, we'll know within five seconds."

"You can live with that?" Josie asked. It wasn't a challenge; she already knew the answer.

Robert shrugged, a dry gesture. "I've lived with worse."

There was silence, then Mark said, "You want a vote?"

Mathew shook his head. "There's no vote. We all know why he's here."

Nobody disagreed. The folder was a relic; the actual crime was older, elemental, the thing that had started this group in the first place. The other names on the table—victims, witnesses, the living debris of Bass's work—each one was a knot in the rope they'd built over two decades.

They walked through the plan once, then again, each time stripping out more language until all that remained was schedule and execution.

"We're not just shepherding this one through," Josie said, voice flat as a blade. "We're the system now."

"First time for everything," William said.

Mathew looked at the group, cataloging each face. He saw in their eyes the old grief, the patient fury. None of them wanted glory. None of them wanted mercy.

This was justice, as clean as they could make it.

"Are we clear?" he asked.

Jimmy nodded. Robert did too. Mark and William exchanged a glance that ended with the smallest of shrugs—acceptance, or something near enough.

Josie looked at the folder, then up at Mathew. "Let's not rehearse it again," she said. "Let's just do it."

No one disagreed.

They stood, one by one, filing out of the cabin in silence. The lantern, left on the table, cast a pale circle of light across Bass's name. For a moment, it looked almost sacred.

In the end, it was just a file.

But it weighed enough to change the world.

***

Mathew spent the night before the execution in his chambers, door locked, desk littered with printouts and single-serving aspirin packs. He was not a man who believed in luck, but he triple-checked the calendar anyway, then called the clerk's cell phone to verify every date on the docket. The city outside was sleeping off its Friday, but inside the courthouse, the lights never went dark.

The appeals were already dead in the water. Bass's last shot—a stay petition based on unsubstantiated mental incompetence—had been denied by the appellate panel before the ink was dry. Mathew had written the ruling himself, underlining every finding in language so tight it could have doubled as a tourniquet.

But the real work was in the margins: making sure no enterprising junior lawyer or outside activist slipped something onto the record in the final twelve hours. He set up a staggered rotation with the overnight staff, each one instructed to page him if any new motion hit the file, no matter how trivial. Every legal access point was covered—no filings allowed by email, fax, or even courier unless it passed through Mathew's hands.

He timed the signing of the death warrant for 04:55, a window that left no daylight for administrative error. The judge's signature was already on the line; all that remained was to transmit the order, clear the necessary notifications, and watch the clock as it ran out on Calvin Bass.

At 03:17, a call came from the Governor's office: a low-level aide trying to confirm a detail for the morning briefing. Mathew supplied the line, then politely asked if the Governor had any intention of intervening. "Not this one," the aide said, and that was the end of it.

At 04:41, a public defender left a voicemail referencing a rumor of new DNA evidence. Mathew had anticipated this; he'd arranged for a sealed affidavit from the lab director attesting that all evidence had been reviewed and cross-checked six months prior. He sent the PDF to the public defender's office and blind-copied the DA, just to kill any talk before it started.

By 05:10, the system had gone silent.

He kept refreshing the court database, just in case, but nothing changed. The window for action was closed. Even a Supreme Court intervention would arrive too late; the train was already barreling down the track.

He texted Josie: "Clear to proceed. No residuals." She responded with a single period—a punctuation mark as final as any gavel strike.

At 06:00, he closed his laptop, opened the window, and let the air hit his face. The night was thin and cold, full of the promise of new machinery. Bass's fate was out of Mathew's hands, but only because he had engineered it that way.

He watched the sunrise scrape the buildings orange, then checked the time again. No alarms, no last-minute reprieves.

The path was clear, and there was nothing in the world left to stop them.

***

Josie ran the DA's media response from her private office, two phones in front of her and a legal pad so full of cross-outs it looked like a map of old wounds. She watched the local news cycle as it advanced by the minute, each network using the same mugshot of Bass, the same recycled footage from his trial.

She had prewritten the official statement a week prior: "Today, the families of the victims saw justice delivered." She made sure every reporter got it, no room for improvisation. If they called her for comment, she had an answer ready: "We trust the process. We are confident in the outcome."

She never mentioned the protocol, never referred to the method, only to the necessity of closure.

She worked her contacts in the press, feeding them just enough detail to keep the spotlight pointed at the right place. Every story led with the list of names, not the details of the execution. She asked the local editorial board to run an op-ed on community healing, knowing they'd jump at the chance to look magnanimous. When a cable news anchor floated the idea that "Georgia's protocol may be under review," she called the producer directly and pointed them to the AG's office for a denial.

She flagged one reporter—a stringer for a left-leaning blog—who requested the witness list and chamber procedures. Josie replied with boilerplate and then had the DA's comms team send over a timeline of events, heavy on legal milestones and light on anything that could be spun as "inhumane."

She checked social media every hour, monitoring the hashtags and comment threads. There were a few voices of dissent, but waves of anger and relief drowned them out. In her world, the public wanted the case closed, not a new debate on morality.

In the afternoon, she met with the victim advocates in a closed session, made sure every family got a direct call, and offered to have a staffer accompany them if they needed to speak to the press. She knew the optics were as important as the verdict. Any display of compassion had to be visible, but not performative. She walked that line with a lawyer's grace, never overstepping, never letting a single comment slip out of her control.

Before she left the office, she called Mark to check in on the situation outside the prison. "Anything I need to know?" she asked.

"All quiet," he said. "Not a single camera van in sight. You did your job."

She closed her laptop, tidied her desk, and stared out the window at the city. The stories would be in print by morning, the cycle set and self-sustaining. The world would see the death of a monster, nothing more.

Josie poured herself a drink, sipped it slowly, and allowed herself a small, hard smile.

The only narrative left was the one she wrote herself.

***

Mark preferred the perimeter. He trusted nothing that happened inside until he'd mapped every variable out here, where chaos wore a human face. On the night of the execution, he arrived three hours early and made his first sweep in a borrowed patrol car, lights off, hands steady on the wheel.

He checked the media staging area: empty, save for a single TV crew half-asleep in their van, no sign of satellite uplinks or protestors. At the south entrance, he spotted a pair of activists setting up cardboard signs, but their social media was already saturated with unrelated outrage. He logged their license plate, took a photo, and texted it to a friend at the city desk. By the time the execution began, the activists would be at the wrong gate, yelling at the wrong guards.

He did a slow walk of the staff parking lot, looking for unfamiliar faces or the telltale glow of a cell phone aimed at the prison windows. There were none. Mark knew which reporters liked to bend the rules and which ones liked to watch from a distance. He found their emails in advance and fed them a story about "enhanced security," which usually meant a longer lens and a cold night, nothing more.

In the hour before zero, he staged a pair of cars near the back fence, one unmarked, one looking like it belonged in a retired detective's driveway. The message was clear: the place was being watched, and not just by the state.

He took a walk down the maintenance corridor, cut through a service door, and made a brief circuit of the utility basement. In the generator room, he found what he was looking for: a locked box, the kind used for evidence or property holds. He checked the tag and found it matched the chain of custody for Bass's case. Inside were three items: a length of braided cord, a cracked wristwatch, and a single Polaroid of an unknown house, its address scratched out with a ballpoint pen.

Mark lifted the watch, turned it over in his hand, and then placed it in his jacket pocket. The cord and the photo he left untouched. He signed the log, used a glove to wipe the pen, and closed the box again.

On his way out, he passed a janitor mopping the hallway. Mark stopped, flashed his badge, and asked if anyone had been through in the last two hours. The janitor shrugged, said nothing, and Mark nodded. That was the best kind of answer.

He exited through the north gate, did another drive around the campus, and then parked on a hill above the lights of the compound. He sipped from a thermos and watched the time tick down.

At 06:59, he texted Josie: "No movement. Clean perimeter." She replied instantly: "Stay hot."

Mark thought about the watch in his pocket, the heavy symbolism of the old case detritus. He knew it would matter later, in the woods, when the time came to let Bass see what justice really looked like.

He sat in the quiet, watching the world for any sign of interruption. There were none.

The system was locked, the perimeter dead silent.

Just the way he liked it.

***

William's command center was a narrow office just off the central corridor, lined with three monitors and a whiteboard filled with names, numbers, and angry red Xs. He'd rewritten the staff schedule for the night three times, always finding new ways to pare down the list until only the essential, the loyal, the incurious remained.

He started with the floor supervisors. The usual watch commander was conveniently on medical leave, replaced by a temp promoted from the records office. William knew this one—never asked questions, never lingered on a shift past his posted time. Perfect. The main control room was set to run on skeleton crew, with all eyes focused on public areas and none on the internal movement between D-Block and the infirmary.

He inserted a last-minute maintenance ticket for a glitching camera feed in the corridor nearest the execution chamber. The IT response was scheduled for 08:00—two hours after the event. Until then, the feed would "intermittently drop," a phrase that in practice meant one could move a body down the hall and no one would be able to prove it.

Next, William pulled the medical records for every inmate in the hospital ward. He transferred the two most volatile cases to a secondary facility, citing "infection risk." The med techs who might have recognized a deviation in the protocol were sent home early, replaced by a float nurse who'd worked only one previous death watch.

He drafted a memo for the internal affairs officer scheduled to monitor the chamber, citing a "procedural training audit" that would keep the conference room tied up until noon. William sent a backup auditor in his place, a retiree brought in for a single shift. The man had trouble seeing even with his glasses on, but his report would be as compliant as a blank sheet.

Every access log, every badge swipe, every digital fingerprint was accounted for. William left just enough gaps that if an auditor came looking, they'd find a system running slightly below efficiency but nowhere near suspicious. He backed up the official records every hour, then wiped the live logs of any discrepancies. By the time the Oath made their move, the only people left in the execution wing were either on his list or too oblivious to notice a change.

He sent a final check-in to Mathew: "Ironwood secured. All variables in range." The reply came back in seconds: "Proceed."

William watched the cameras, saw the pattern of movement—slow, clockwork, nothing erratic. He tracked the guard rotations, watched the kitchen deliveries, and even counted the vehicles in the parking lot. He knew the prison's rhythms better than his own pulse.

At 06:30, he sat back in his chair and watched the timer on his phone count down to zero.

Nothing left to chance. Nothing left to fate. Ironwood was a circuit, closed and flawless. For the first time in weeks, William let himself relax. It was going to work.

***

Jimmy showed up for the morning shift an hour early, uniform crisp, hair still damp from the locker room shower. He found the three guards on his team already waiting in the briefing room, their faces closed and expressionless, the way corrections officers learned to be by their second week.

"Let's run it," he said—no small talk.

He walked them through the chamber protocol from start to finish. Every step was a beat in a song: chain, secure, confirm ID, escort to gurney, fix restraints. He had each officer run through the process three times, then had them switch roles and do it again. If anyone fumbled, he stopped them, reset the clock, and made them start over.

Jimmy was not a shouter, but he had a way of making silence feel heavier than a fist. By the third drill, the guards moved in perfect rhythm, each anticipating the next gesture, each knowing exactly when to step forward and when to fade to the edge.

He assigned the two steadiest guards to the chamber itself, the third to the corridor as a spotter. The float nurse from William's list joined them at the last rehearsal, and Jimmy walked her through the steps: check IV, check restraints, step back, and do not interfere unless called.

He reviewed the protocol with the assistant warden, a by-the-book man who respected punctuality above all else. "Everything tight?" the AW asked.

Jimmy nodded. "Down to the second."

The AW looked over the checklist, found no errors, and signed off. "Let's make it smooth."

In the holding cell, Bass was already prepped. Jimmy read the file, confirmed the chain of custody, then sat outside the door for the last thirty minutes, watching the clock and listening to the shuffling inside. He told himself this was just another job, another day, but the air around the chamber had a charge to it—like a thunderstorm building somewhere out of sight.

At 07:00, he gave the signal. The guards entered the cell, did the chain and escort with absolute precision. Bass did not resist. His face was the color of printer paper, eyes flat and unreadable.

They strapped him to the gurney with the quiet dignity of men who knew this was their only job. Jimmy checked every restraint personally, then nodded to the nurse, who ran a final check of the IV.

The witnesses were behind the glass, silent as stones. Jimmy didn't look at them. He kept his eyes on the clock and his hands behind his back, waiting for the cue from the control room.

When it came, he gave a single nod, and the chamber fell perfectly still.

This was the only part he could control—the choreography of death.

He watched the team, saw that none of them shook, and let himself breathe.

They were ready.

***

Robert entered the chamber with his kit cradled like an organ donor cooler. He wore hospital blues, no name badge, and clear glasses that caught the overhead glare in hard, flat rectangles. The walls hummed with air conditioning, and the only movement came from the IV line, already threaded into Bass's left arm.

He did not acknowledge the witnesses. They were there for optics; he was there for the outcome.

He checked the IV site, confirmed the saline flow, then uncapped the first syringe: clear, viscous, a calculated burn. He pushed the plunger slowly, eyes on the stopwatch in his other hand. Eight seconds in, the first phase hit—Bass's face lost all tension, jaw slackening, eyelids sliding down like a curtain drawn against the world.

Robert waited another twelve seconds, then started the second syringe, the amber one. This was the crucial phase: a cocktail refined by years of private research and field-tested on exactly no one. The moment the amber touched the bloodstream, Robert saw the carotid pulse stall, then nearly vanish.

He leaned in, listening with his own ears, and caught the faintest hitch of breath. Good—just enough residual function to keep the subject viable.

The third syringe went in last, a blue so pale it looked like water. The paralytic. This would erase any twitches, any final protests the body might try to make. Within ten seconds, Bass was inert, the only movement the soft rise and fall of the chest, slow enough to evade the eye.

He capped the IV line, cleared the air bubble, and stepped back.

On the monitor in the control room, the EKG showed a flatline. Robert had built a lag into the feed—what the witnesses saw was the end of the curve, nothing more.

He waited another minute, then signaled to the nurse to begin the observation period.

The silence in the chamber was total.

Bass did not move, did not breathe visibly, did not even twitch under the glare of the lights.

Robert documented the times, signed the form, and waited for the final check.

Everything about the moment said closure, even as he knew the opposite was true.

The body on the table looked dead, but in the space between seconds, Robert measured the margin and found it perfect.

He let the silence linger, then nodded to Jimmy, who would handle the rest.

***

Robert entered the chamber with a clipboard in hand, eyes scanning the tableau with an artist's critical remove. Bass lay still as sculpture, skin blanched to a shade found only in morgues and unfinished basements.

He checked the pupils first: no response. He pressed two fingers to the carotid, counted to twenty, and felt nothing—no twitch, no echo, just the stillness of a plan executed with exacting force. He placed a hand on the sternum, measured the micro-movements of the chest, and found the rise so shallow it might as well not exist.

Robert recorded each step in ink, no smudges or corrections. He repeated the checks for the benefit of the nurse and the two witnesses behind the glass, making a small show of procedure but never risking an extra second of scrutiny.

He confirmed the EKG flatline, then waited the full two minutes as required by statute. The nurse signed off with a trembling hand; the guards present stared at the floor, eager for the moment to pass.

When the timer hit zero, Robert removed his gloves and wrote the time of death in block numbers: 07:03. He signed the certificate, first and last name, and handed the form to Jimmy, who stood just outside the door.

He allowed himself a single, silent moment of pride. It worked. There was no room for error, no residue of life that might bring the world crashing down on their heads. He glanced at Bass, then at the thin line of sweat condensing on the body's brow, and knew that somewhere, deep inside, the man was still there—locked in darkness, waiting for the second act.

Robert turned, left the chamber, and made a note to himself: This is the new standard.

He felt the edges of relief begin to bleed into his thinking, but tamped it down. There was still the handoff, the transport, the resurrection.

But for now, the world believed in the permanence of the moment.

That, he thought, was all anyone ever really wanted from death.

***

Jimmy waited in the corridor while the witnesses filed out. He watched them through the half-mirrored glass: some teary, some stone-faced, one or two with the flat satisfaction of people who've watched a news cycle come to life. Nobody looked at the body. Nobody looked at Jimmy.

He directed the guards to open the viewing room door, then walked the lead witness—the mother of one of the girls—back to the public exit. She didn't say a word, just clutched her purse so tight the handles dug into the soft part of her palm.

The DA's office sent a liaison to collect statements. Jimmy listened to the standard script, every phrase designed to convert horror into closure. He nodded at the right times, signed off on the incident report, and made sure the staff did the same.

The float nurse cleared the table, removed the IV, and double-bagged the used syringes. She worked fast, her eyes fixed on the floor. When she finished, Jimmy thanked her—he always did, even when it was pointless—and signed her out of the log.

Inside the chamber, nothing moved but the fluorescent lights overhead, their hum the only reminder of life in the building. The guards checked the restraints one final time, then stepped back, as if afraid the dead could reach up and grab them.

Jimmy lingered a moment, watching the shadow Bass cast on the wall. There was nothing dramatic about it, nothing to suggest a presence. But Jimmy had seen enough executions to know that the real violence was always what came after.

He closed the chamber, keyed in the code for the next phase, and prepared to move the body.

History would record this as a clean kill—one more box checked on the long spreadsheet of justice.

The room emptied, the evidence of the day's work already fading.

Jimmy set his jaw, glanced at the clock, and waited for the next signal.

***

Jimmy received the handoff from Robert in the corridor. The body was zipped and tagged, just like any other post-mortem, but the weight in the bag was unmistakably alive. Jimmy rolled the gurney with practiced indifference, eyes scanning the empty hallway for stray personnel.

William met him at the service elevator, clipboard in hand. They exchanged a single glance, then moved the gurney into the lift, closed the doors, and descended to the sub-basement. No cameras. No witnesses. William had made sure of it.

They transferred the body to a plastic coffin—standard issue, no alarms, nothing but an RFID chip glued to the lid. Jimmy locked the clasps while William ran the checklist, his hands steady even as his pulse quickened.

"Time?" Jimmy asked, not looking up.

William checked his watch. "Eight minutes to the window. Cart's in position."

They wheeled the container down the maintenance corridor, past racks of old HVAC equipment and obsolete files. William scanned his badge at the exit, then keyed in a six-digit override to bypass the security alarm. Outside, the loading bay was empty, save for a battered utility van with city decals on the door.

They slid the coffin into the back of the van, buckled it down, and closed the doors. William took the driver's seat, Jimmy the passenger. They said nothing for the first mile, listening only to the rumble of the road beneath them.

In the side mirror, the prison receded into the gray morning. Jimmy exhaled, slow and even. "No one's following."

"It wouldn't matter if they did," William said. "We're invisible."

They hit the city limits in under fifteen minutes, weaving through side streets and feeder roads mapped out the night before. The GPS tracker on the coffin pinged once every five seconds, but William had rerouted the signals to a dead mailbox somewhere in Decatur.

Jimmy rested his hand on the container, feeling the faintest warmth through the plastic. "How long before he wakes up?"

"Not before we get there," William said. "That's the plan."

They drove on in silence, the world none the wiser.

The switch was done.

No one had noticed a thing.

***

The van rolled through the rear gate without even a cursory inspection; William had submitted the maintenance work order at 05:00, and the badge logs showed a routine run. The guards on duty saw only a battered city vehicle, and if any recognized Jimmy or William, they didn't mention it.

They followed the pre-cleared route, a string of left turns and alleys that avoided every camera and bypassed the public streets. Even if someone did flag the van, the logs would show it on official business, nothing out of the ordinary.

Jimmy drove the first leg, hands tight on the wheel. William watched the clock, counting down the seconds to the next handoff. At a stop sign on an empty road, Mark's sedan slid up alongside them. He flashed his lights twice—a signal that the secondary perimeter was clear.

Jimmy and William swapped seats in the dark, with Mark taking the van and Jimmy melting into the back of the sedan. William remained at the wheel, his face a blank mask in the dawn light.

They drove the van to a storage unit on the far edge of the city, where the coffin could wait in climate-controlled silence for as long as necessary. Mark texted Josie: "All clear. Dead to the world."

Jimmy double-checked the restraints on the coffin, then stood in the shadow of the unit, scanning for any sign of surveillance. There was none. Mark waited until the GPS showed a solid hour of inactivity before locking up and walking away.

The world was already moving on. News alerts buzzed with headlines, but none mentioned anything unusual about the execution or the aftermath.

By the time the sun set, Bass was off the grid.

Invisible.

Just as planned.

***

Robert spent the morning in the records office, surrounded by the low static of printers and the sterile smell of hospital air. He logged into the medical terminal and worked through the death reporting protocol with the grace of someone who understood both the process and the audit.

He cross-checked the time of death, confirmed that the EKG log matched the chart, and deleted the backup notes from his own encrypted drive. He adjusted the timestamp on the post-mortem to account for the nurse's shift change, erasing the gap that might have raised questions.

On the state reporting portal, he filled out the transfer documentation, marking the remains for "immediate cremation, per protocol." There would be no autopsy, no outside review; the paperwork was airtight, the cause of death obvious and uncontested.

He merged the digital files, destroyed the paper duplicates, and locked the original certificate in the hospital safe. If anyone requested a copy, they would find only the official record, stamped and initialed, with nothing out of place.

He even wiped the security footage of the medical office for the four-hour window around the execution, just to be sure. The system would register a glitch, but nothing more.

When he was finished, he sat back in his chair, eyes closed, and listened to the silence.

It was over. The trail was gone. The world would see nothing but what they'd designed it to see.

Robert exhaled, slow and careful, then left the office.

His work was finished.

***

The van left the storage unit at dusk, headlights off, taillights blacked with tape. Mark drove, hands steady even as the road grew narrow and the city shrank in the mirrors. He kept the van under the speed limit, obeyed every traffic law, never once drew a second glance.

In the cargo bay, the coffin rattled with every turn, but the latches held. Mark checked the temperature readout—sixty-two degrees, right on target. He tapped the sensor pad and watched the LED flash green, indicating a slow but steady return of respiratory function.

Inside the plastic, Bass's body twitched once, then twice, as the drug's hold slipped away molecule by molecule. The first shudder was involuntary; the second, a faint gasp, so soft it was lost in the insulation.

Mark listened for the sound, heard nothing, and kept driving.

They left the highway an hour north of the city, taking a service road that wound through state forest and old farmland. The woods here were dense, the canopy high enough to hide even the moon. Mark parked the van beside a forgotten logging trail and killed the engine.

He waited five minutes, then opened the rear doors. The air was cold and clean, and the world around him was silent.

He unlocked the coffin, cracked the lid, and checked for signs of life. The chest rose and fell, shallow but regular. Mark nodded, satisfied, and closed the lid again.

The drive had done its work. Bass was alive, though still locked in a darkness deeper than sleep.

Mark set his watch, then began to unload the cargo.

It was time.

***

The woods were the same as always—dense, old, indifferent—but the clearing was transformed. In childhood, the place had seemed endless, a safe pocket in the wild. Now, under the hard edge of adulthood, it felt exposed, the dark pressing in from all sides.

Mark dragged the coffin to the center of the space, leaving a furrow in the dead leaves. He opened the lid and checked the vitals again—pulse, shallow but real; skin, warm to the touch. Bass's eyelids fluttered but did not open.

He set the watch and cord from evidence at the foot of the coffin, then walked the perimeter, scouting for any sign of light or movement. There was nothing. He texted Josie: "Staged." The reply came in seconds: "On our way."

They arrived one by one. Jimmy first, his breath steaming in the cold, a pack slung over one shoulder. He nodded to Mark, then crouched beside the coffin and checked the restraints.

William came next, carrying a lantern that cast long, oval shadows across the brush. He set it down at the edge of the circle, the flame muted but insistent.

Robert emerged from the trees with a small cooler, the vials inside clinking softly as he walked. He knelt by Bass, checked the pupils, and administered a measured dose of something clear and fast-acting.

Josie was last. She wore gloves and a scarf, her hair tied back, eyes scanning the scene like she was already cross-examining it. She brought nothing—her job was to witness, to speak the words and make them matter.

Mathew arrived behind her, as always, silent until he was needed. He carried the folder from the first meeting, now battered and creased at the corners.

They stood in a ring around the coffin, each holding to their own patch of darkness.

No one spoke. The ritual required silence.

The lantern light warped the world, throwing its shadows in overlapping bands that reached all the way to the edge of the woods.

Jimmy and Mark lifted Bass from the coffin and set him upright against the trunk of the old oak. They bound him with the cord, arms tight to his sides, ankles crossed, and lashed him to the roots. The work was clinical, not cruel.

Robert adjusted the angle of Bass's head, making sure the airway was open, then stepped back. He timed the next dose, the one that would ease the return to consciousness.

William checked the perimeter one last time, then returned to the circle, hands in his pockets, face unreadable.

Mathew opened the folder, pulled out a single sheet, and held it in both hands.

They waited.

The woods did not care what happened here, but the Oath did.

***

Jimmy and Mark worked in unison, the way experienced hands always do. They looped the cord twice around Bass's chest, then double-knotted it behind the tree, anchoring him so his head tilted slightly forward. His legs were crossed at the ankles, each foot positioned flat against the root's bulge.

Bass's body sagged, dead weight in every muscle, but the bindings held him upright. The only movement was a faint quiver at the corner of his mouth, the echo of a system rebooting after total shutdown.

They checked the knots, then stepped back, inspecting their work without pride or hesitation.

Robert took a stethoscope from his bag, pressed it to Bass's chest, and listened for a full minute. He nodded once, then wiped the stethoscope on his sleeve and put it away.

William adjusted the lantern, shifting the light so it fell across Bass's face in a perfect oval. The effect was clinical, the kind of illumination found in operating rooms or interrogation chambers.

Josie circled the perimeter, boots crunching softly in the frost. She picked up the Polaroid, studied it for a moment, then set it at Bass's feet like an offering.

Mathew reread the single sheet from the folder, lips moving silently, then folded it in half and slid it into his coat.

The circle closed in, each member of the Oath finding their mark in the choreography.

Bass's breathing, once absent, now rasped in slow, even waves. The drugs would wear off soon. Robert had calculated the moment to the second.

No one spoke. There was no need.

The preparation was perfect.

***

They waited.

The cold seeped into everything, deadening the edges of sensation. Robert knelt by Bass every ten minutes, checked the pulse, and counted respirations. He whispered the numbers to himself, then checked the timer on his watch, recalibrating the expected window by tiny increments.

The others circled the clearing, sometimes in pairs, sometimes alone. Josie walked a slow orbit, never stepping in the same place twice. Mark leaned against a tree, arms crossed, scanning the distance for threats that couldn't reach them here.

Mathew stood just outside the lantern's halo, the folder pressed to his chest, his breathing shallow and measured.

William paced the perimeter, adjusting the angle of the lantern every so often, as if a small shift in light might change the outcome.

Jimmy watched Bass's face, looking for the first flicker of consciousness.

Nothing happened for a long time. The only sound was the wind, threading through the branches above.

Then, at the forty-two-minute mark, Robert saw a tremor in the carotid. The skin above the cord twitched, then settled. Bass's eyes rolled under the lids, tracking some private geometry.

Robert called out, "Here it comes."

The others drew closer, the circle tightening.

Bass's jaw clenched. His fingers curled against the bark, then relaxed.

He made a low, animal sound—a grunt, then a ragged gasp.

He was coming back.

***

The world returned to Bass in static: light fracturing behind his eyelids, the drum of blood in his ears. His chest felt caved in, his tongue a dry scab in his mouth. He tried to move, but nothing answered except for a slow, seizing shiver.

The first thing he sensed was the cold—a raw, gnawing cold that dug straight into the nerves along his spine. He tried to swallow, but couldn't. Every part of him felt wrong, limbs pressed at unfamiliar angles, head anchored by something hard and rough.

For a long time, he heard only the wind. Then, faintly, the noise of breathing—not his own, but patterned, disciplined, the kind of breathing he remembered from the guards outside his cell.

A sour panic welled in his gut. He pried his eyelids apart, but the world was a smear: shadows over white, a fog of shapes in the edges. As sensation crept back, the pain came with it—first as an ache in his wrists, then as a throb behind the temples, then as the slow fire of his heart kicking into gear.

The world settled into place, inch by inch.

He was upright. He was outside. His hands were bound, arms lashed to a column of wood so old it flaked under his skin. The ground below him was dirt, cold as grave-soil, and he was sure—absolutely sure—that he had been dead just seconds before.

The panic grew teeth. He tried to scream, but the sound came out thin, swallowed by the night air.

He blinked, hard, and the clearing resolved: a lantern on the ground, pooling gold on a circle of faces.

There were six. All adults. All were watching him.

None of them moved, not at first. The eyes were the only sign of life—watchful, measuring, waiting.

Bass tried again to pull at the bonds. The effort made his vision spark, black spots eating the edges.

One of the figures stepped forward. The man was tall, with dark hair and eyes, the kind that never looked away from a car crash.

The man knelt in front of Bass, holding something in his hands. He waited until the world had steadied, then said, softly, "Welcome back."

The others closed in, silent as the grave.

Bass tried to speak, to beg, to curse, but his voice was a rattle in the hollow of his chest.

He could see the lantern's light flicker in their eyes. The faces didn't look angry. They looked practiced, like surgeons.

He understood, then.

This was not an execution. This was something else.

He remembered the last words from the chamber: a cold, dry certainty.

"You already had your last words."

The man in front of him smiled, just a crack at the edge of the mouth.

Then the circle closed.

***

He saw it in their eyes before they moved: the unanimity, the unyielding certainty, the conviction that this—right here, right now—was what the world owed him.

The lantern sputtered, casting the circle in strobing gold. No one in the group spoke. The ritual was beyond words.

Josie's face was hard-edged in the firelight. William's hands, the ones that once built escape for so many, now curled tight and white at his sides. Jimmy knelt to check the cords again, not with violence, but with care, as if Bass were a specimen to be preserved for study.

Mark stood just inside the circle, badge glinting at his hip. He watched Bass with the implacable calm of someone who has already rehearsed every possible ending.

Robert timed the intervals between each of Bass's breaths, counting them down in silence.

Mathew stepped forward last. He didn't bring the file; he didn't need it. He looked at Bass—really looked, until the panic gave way to raw, animal comprehension.

There was nothing to be said.

There was only the moment—the precipice of fear, the irreversible knowledge that the world's machinery had not failed this time.

Bass's mouth worked, jaw trying to shape words that would never be heard.

The circle of the Oath watched, and waited, and made no promises.

For the first time since childhood, the six felt the peace that comes before finality.

In the last second, before the sky inhaled and the forest closed around them, Mathew said, not a whisper but a verdict:

"You already had your last words."

CHAPTER 9

They made it a habit to arrive before dawn, when the fog still rolled over the razor wire, and the sodium lamps burned the world to gray. Ironwood ran at half-staff on execution days, the air stilled by a kind of collective holding of breath. On mornings like these, Jimmy could walk the cell block and hear nothing but the scuff of rubber on linoleum, every sound trapped and magnified by concrete and steel.

Today's man, Rogers, was already up—he hadn't slept, judging by the sour chemical burn in the air and the clarity of his eyes when Jimmy entered the holding cell. The procedure had changed since the old days: no clergy, no last meal, not even a window for visitors. They kept him on suicide watch until twenty minutes before curtain, then unchained him with the slow, deliberate dignity of a man untangling Christmas lights.

Jimmy kept the rhythm calm. "You ready?"

Rogers nodded once, lips chalk white, the rest of him a study in inertia.

"Stand here." Jimmy pointed to the yellow line and waited while the guards finished their half-hearted search. The new protocol—his invention—meant the condemned walked under his own power, with only two corrections officers as escort. No dragging, no theatrics. Just the steady shuffle, the click of boots, and the hum of the LED panel above the entrance to the chamber.

They moved down the hall, the doors opening in sequence like a railroad switching yard. No one watched from the cells. That, too, was by design. The other inmates had been cycled out, "for routine maintenance," but the real reason was simpler: minimize variables, minimize risk.

In the chamber, Jimmy took over. "I'm going to walk you through the steps," he said. "It'll be fast, but it'll be real." He guided Rogers onto the gurney, hands behind the back, feet side by side. The man's chest heaved once, a raw flinch, but then he went slack again, the pulse in his neck ticking like a metronome.

Jimmy nodded to the nurse—Robert's pick, and one who knew not to speak unless spoken to—and waited as she prepped the arm. It was always left, always in the crook of the elbow, because right meant the heart had to work too hard. Jimmy had timed it in the first year: the margin was three seconds. In the process, three seconds were everything.

The rest of the team worked the perimeter. William stood in the corridor, clipboard in hand, his thumb pressing the pen's clicker with the calm of a blackjack dealer. Two units down, another pair of guards rotated in, swapped keys, and logged the transition on an iPad. Up in the glass booth, the warden's eyes flicked from screen to screen, looking for anything out of range.

Through the viewing window, the only observers were a blank-faced chaplain and a lawyer with a stack of manila folders. The legal rep wore glasses thick as the old Coke bottles, and his mouth stayed open the entire time, as if trying to taste the moment in case it turned on a word.

The curtain lifted. Jimmy glanced once to his left—Robert behind the panel, gloved and gowned and already filling the first syringe. He'd taken to prepping the compounds himself, no longer trusting the pharmacy to get the weights exact. In the earliest tests, they'd learned: too much phenobarbital, and you got convulsions. Too little, and the witnesses left the room thinking the condemned had faked it. Now, with a new ratio—his own—the onset was soft, the end irreversible.

Jimmy met Rogers' eyes one more time. "Anything to say?"

Rogers shook his head. The mouth started to open, but whatever final words he'd rehearsed were gone in the grind of the moment.

Jimmy said, "Ready."

The nurse taped the line. Robert pressed the plunger slowly, eyes on the sweep hand of the clock. Ten seconds. Rogers' head rolled back, the muscles loosening with mechanical grace.

The paralytic followed. The EKG screen above the gurney dipped once, then again, and then flatlined, the beep going silent. The third drug went in without announcement. It was almost theatrical, but only if you knew how to read the silence.

The witness lawyer stood, scribbled something, then folded the file and left. The chaplain prayed in whispers, not even pausing as the curtain dropped again.

Jimmy waited until the count hit ninety seconds, then checked the pupils. Nothing. He looked at Robert, who nodded, already logging the time of death on the clipboard.

"Done," said Robert. Not a question.

They wheeled the body out on the same gurney, no need for theatrics or bagging. The nurse stripped the line, wiped the arm, and reset the room in under three minutes.

William handled the exit protocol, logging the time, the badge numbers, and the security handoff. He tapped a text to Mathew: "No issues. Clean." The phone didn't buzz—Mathew was probably at his desk already, reading the first draft of the press release.

In the parking lot outside, the sunrise hadn't touched the tops of the pines yet. The team scattered: Robert to his office, William to the admin suite, Jimmy to the block for the next round of checks.

The system worked. It worked because they made it so.

At the end, nobody celebrated. They just reset the chamber and waited for the next call.

The next one came four weeks later.

This time, Jimmy didn't bother with the pep talk. The condemned—Reynolds, petty kingpin from Savannah, never denied what he'd done—walked the hall with no resistance, hands open at his sides like a man arriving at the DMV. Jimmy fast-tracked him through the last meal, skipped the formal recitation of rights, and signed the transfer sheet in a nearly illegible scrawl.

In the chamber, Robert prepped the line with one gloved hand while answering a text with the other. The nurse needed no instructions; she'd memorized the sequence. The guards posted at the door didn't even look up from their phones, which wasn't a violation anymore, just policy.

The viewing room was empty—no family, no media, no clerics. Josie had managed the media leak so effectively that even the activist blogs missed the window.

William had adjusted the shift schedule so the control room ran on half staff, all of them pulled from a list he'd built over three years of careful observation. No one on this rotation cared about anything but the paycheck.

The process, now refined, shaved another 30 seconds off the intake-to-injection time. Jimmy double-checked the gurney straps, but the man had already gone limp. Robert watched the line for the exact moment the color went out of Reynolds' face, then stepped back, signaling to Jimmy without looking up.

The nurse announced the time of death, exactly on the minute.

No one lingered. No one spoke.

The cleanup was completed in under four minutes, the gurney reset, the body tagged and sent to the loading dock for transport.

William updated the log, then set a reminder to purge the digital file at the end of the shift.

Jimmy left the chamber and went straight to the staff break room, where he drank a cup of bad coffee, checked the basketball score, and sent a one-word text to the Oath: "Done."

Not a single question came back.

This was the new normal, and it fit like a glove.

When they woke this one, it was barely midnight. Jimmy and Mark handled the transfer: down the back ramp, through two layers of locked fencing, and into the city van that William had "borrowed" from fleet services. The new model had no cages, no security cameras. It was the perfect vessel for crossing state lines without leaving a trace.

The drive to the drop site was wordless, the kind of silence that meant there was nothing left to say. The woods north of town had changed in the years since Bass, but the path was always the same. Mark used an old hunting GPS, but he could have done it by smell alone.

In the clearing, the Oath's routine played out with less emotion than an oil change. Josie and Mathew were already there, the lantern casting its ring on the root-blown ground. Josie's face was more shadow than skin, but her hands worked the knots with deft precision, as if cinching a tie on a courtroom day.

Mark and Jimmy unbuckled the body, then hauled the man to the tree with a practiced, two-person carry. The condemned was still unconscious, body folded in on itself like a discarded puppet. Josie wrapped the cord twice around the chest and once around the ankles. Robert checked the pulse, then tapped the side of the neck with a gentle, almost affectionate gesture.

"He'll wake soon," said Robert, his voice a whisper even in the open air.

William placed the evidence bag—a length of bloody duct tape, a yellowed page torn from a Bible—at the base of the tree. He checked the site for footprints, then swept the area with a compact blacklight, which he'd programmed to the same frequency used in forensic labs.

Mathew stood at the edge of the circle, arms crossed. He didn't speak, didn't approach. The lantern's light barely reached him. He watched the man in the cord, eyes fixed and unblinking.

They waited. The silence was vast and not entirely empty; it held a pressure, a collective breath, like the last second before a race gun.

The man's eyelids fluttered, mouth moving in mute protest. When he surfaced, the panic came quick—saw the faces, the lantern, the knots at his chest. He screamed, but the sound was too small to escape the trees.

Jimmy put a hand on the man's forehead, just to steady him. The condemned thrashed, but the cords held. His eyes darted from face to face. No recognition, only the blind, animal knowledge that he was entirely out of moves.

"Let's finish," Josie said.

It was not the first time, nor would it be the last. Mark stepped forward and ended it, fast and precise.

Instead of recklessly disposing of the body in the quarry as they had earlier in the process, they now left a notification for the authorities. Mark was confident in his ability to hide the evidence that would tie the secondary executions back to the group. They were also counting on the fact that little attention would be paid to the murder of criminals who were sentenced to death.

They left the body for the rangers, just as before. William scattered the evidence, set up a call for an anonymous tip, and logged the GPS coordinates in a file that would be destroyed by morning.

They packed up the lantern, the rope, and the gloves. No ceremony, no talk of what they'd done.

The van rolled back to the city, empty but for the faint stink of cordite and fear.

In the group text, no one sent a message.

After the fourth, the Oath barely needed to coordinate. The system ran itself.

At Ironwood, the files arrived pre-sorted: a slim folder, a stack of scanned motions, a digital signature from the Governor's liaison. William signed the order with a click and sent it to the admin's "high-priority" queue, where it would be rubber-stamped and forgotten within the hour.

In the records office, a woman in tortoiseshell glasses filed the death certificate, her eyes never straying past the signature line. She liked the way the new forms were formatted—no more questions about method or sequence, just the simple, clean box for "COD: State Execution."

In the DA's office, Josie ran a presser for the local media. Her statement was a twenty-two-second soundbite, heavy on closure and light on detail. The reporter from Channel 6 didn't bother with follow-ups, just copied the quote and filed it before lunch. The paper ran the story beneath the fold.

The chaplain didn't show; the man in the cell was a registered atheist, and nobody lobbied for a substitute. The only "witness" was a paralegal from the public defender's office, who watched from the gallery with a bored, slightly queasy expression. Afterward, she went to the staff lounge and texted her boyfriend: "Just another one, nothing weird."

In the chamber, the new nurse handled the IV with smooth, robotic efficiency. Robert had eliminated the pinch point at step six—now the setup took exactly seventy seconds, never more, never less. The condemned didn't fight; he just stared at the ceiling, lips moving in silent arithmetic.

Afterward, Jimmy swept the room, made sure the straps were clean, checked the EKG printout, and reset the gurney for the next round. The janitor on duty swapped out the trash, wiped down the stainless fixtures, and left the place gleaming. He thought about how easy it was now, compared to the old chaos.

On social media, the hashtags flared and faded. Some called it justice, some called it murder, but nobody cared past the news cycle. By the second day, the trending topic was a viral video of a cat.

In the city, the only people who marked the time were the Oath.

They never met to celebrate. They never spoke about it, except in numbers.

The system was seamless, self-sustaining, and invisible.

The world saw nothing but the clean, final output.

And already, the next folder was in the queue.

They met at the cabin twice a year. At first, it was for security, a place where no one could overhear or stumble onto their business. But over time, the meetings became a ritual, stripped of all nostalgia. The chairs ringed the old kitchen table, mismatched but always set in the same order.

Jimmy was first through the door, bringing in a rush of cold air and the sharp scent of gasoline from the drive. He dropped a six-pack of cheap beer on the counter but didn't crack one. Instead, he took the seat closest to the window and began scrolling through his phone, thumb moving with metronomic certainty.

Mark arrived next, two steps behind Josie, who had a new haircut and a look that said she'd won her most recent argument before even walking in. Mark gave a curt nod to Jimmy, then took his usual post at the head of the table. He didn't look tired, just depleted, the way all men get when they've finished a big job and know another is coming.

Robert and William came together, each carrying a thin sheaf of papers. Robert wore the same battered hospital windbreaker he'd owned for a decade; William had upgraded to something from a hiking catalog, the kind with a million secret pockets. They laid their packets side by side in the center of the table.

Mathew was last, as always. He stood in the doorway for a moment, taking in the group, the chairs, the lantern on the mantel. He had not changed since the first Oath—face still sharp, hair still parted with military precision, eyes that didn't need caffeine to stay open.

The only thing out of place was the lantern. It had been polished, the glass wiped free of dust, but when Josie lit it, the flame barely touched the wick. Nobody watched the light, not even as it flickered over their faces.

"Time," said Mathew. It was not a question.

William began. "We're at critical mass on staff. Two-thirds of the current rotation are vetted. The remaining third are either retiring soon or under performance review."

"Any risk?" Mathew asked.

William shook his head. "The new intake is cleaner. Nobody's asking questions. The only one who flagged was the chaplain, and he's leaving in a month."

Robert followed. "The protocol held. No anomalies in either case. I've calibrated the dosage to a tolerance of ±0.5 seconds. The only flaw is the new nurse—she hesitated at step three, but the subject was under before it mattered."

"We can fix that," said Josie, flipping open her notepad. "Swap her for someone from the trauma team, or rotate a veteran in on double shifts. We don't want a variable at the point of contact."

"Agreed," said Mathew. "Jimmy?"

"Intake is clockwork. The men know their jobs. Only potential break is in the transfer, but the last two times it was seamless. I watched the tapes—no sign of hesitation, no panic. We could cut another thirty seconds if we streamline the walk."

Josie added, "The media's asleep. No interest, no leaks. Even the protestors have stopped showing. We're past the peak now; the city's numb."

Mark cleared his throat. "We still need to vet the disposal phase. Last time, the tip came too early. Rangers almost arrived before we could clear the site."

William frowned. "Who sent the tip?"

"Burner," said Mark. "But the voice sounded automated. I'll switch to SMS next round, using a different tower. Or better—set a timer for sunrise, when no one's patrolling."

Robert looked up from his papers. "Does it matter? Even if they catch us in the act, the subject is still dead. No one's going to check the margin on the drugs. They'll just see a body."

"Everything matters," said Mathew, voice flat.

The group lapsed into silence, each member cycling through their internal checklist. Jimmy cracked a beer and slid it to the far end of the table, where no one reached for it.

Josie relit the lantern, this time with a kitchen match, and watched the flame for exactly three seconds before letting it gutter.

When they were finished, William gathered the notes and set them on fire, one page at a time, in the cast-iron sink. The ashes flushed with a single push of the tap.

Nobody lingered after the meeting. They left in the order they arrived, each one vanishing into the woods without a backward glance.

The cabin was cold and dark when the last car pulled away, the only evidence of their presence a faint ring of burnt dust in the sink.

The Oath had become a routine. The lantern's light was just another switch, on or off.

And somewhere, the next subject was already being processed.

It was Mark who spotted it first. The new intake at Ironwood came in with the usual flurry of transfer paperwork, half the names already flagged for psych holds or administrative segregation. But one file, bottom of the stack, was thick with supplemental reports: disciplinary notes, transcripts, even a glossy eight-by-ten of a kid's bike, rusted and half-buried in red Georgia clay.

He read the name three times:

Pearson, Daniel.

He closed the folder, checked the intake log, then pulled up the old cold-case database from his first detective job. It was the same Pearson, the man who'd ripped open the Oath's world and bled it dry. No mention of parole, no chance of release. But he was here—alive, older, his face now a slab of prison meat.

Mark set the file aside and stared out his office window, watching the lights in the staff parking lot. He didn't feel rage or even satisfaction—just a slow, settling weight, like an anchor finally reaching the bottom.

He considered bringing it to Mathew first, but something about the timing made him hesitate. Instead, he sent a message to the group: "Urgent. Next candidate: Pearson. Confirm ID."

The reply came faster than he expected. From Josie: "Is it him?"

Mark sent the mugshot. Seconds later, Mathew called.

"Where is he?" Mathew's voice was barely above a whisper.

"Medical wing. He's got cirrhosis, might not make the year."

Silence on the line, then: "You want to run it like the others?"

"No," Mark said, before he could think. "We should do it ourselves."

Another pause. "Agreed. Tell the rest."

Mark didn't sleep that night. He walked the perimeter of the block, once at midnight and again just before dawn, watching the windows for any sign of movement. He rehearsed the plan, step by step, until every detail was locked in.

He met with Josie at a diner the next day, just after court. She was already there, laptop open, legal pad covered in arrows and underlines. She didn't look up when Mark slid into the booth.

"He's under full medical," she said. "If he dies, it's natural causes. No one questions it."

Mark nodded, fingers tapping the edge of his coffee mug.

She looked up at him, eyes hard. "Are you sure you want this?"

He shrugged. "Not a question."

"Alright," Josie said. "I'll handle the record."

They met with the others at the cabin, this time under the cover of a sudden January rainstorm. The chairs were closer together, the lantern unlit.

Mathew broke the silence. "This is different. It's not for the system. It's for us."

No one argued. The air was thick with the knowledge of what they were about to do.

Jimmy said, "How do we want to play it?"

"Quiet," Mark replied. "No witnesses, no evidence. In and out."

William ran the logistics. "Medical's on graveyard shift tonight. I can spoof the cameras and log us in as maintenance. We have a forty-minute window, tops."

Robert, for once, didn't argue. "I'll prepare a dose. It'll look like a heart attack."

No one said the words justice or revenge. They didn't need to.

They set the plan in motion, each member moving to their task with a focus that bordered on the sacred.

That night, as the rain lashed the roof of the cabin, Mathew lit the lantern for the first time in months. He set it at the center of the table, watched the flame flicker, and said, "For her."

It was the only time they broke protocol.

No one spoke again until the lantern burned out.

Getting Pearson alone was easier than Jimmy expected.

A week before, he'd seeded the idea with Medical: Pearson was jaundiced, listless, eating less than the DOC minimum. He flagged the file for "urgent observation," then moved Pearson off the main block into an isolation room, citing infection risk. The guards on shift didn't question it—if anything, they were relieved to have one less volatile lifer in circulation.

Jimmy rewrote the duty log so that, for four consecutive hours, no one would be assigned to monitor Pearson's cell. The shift captain signed off with a yawn, then called in sick the day of, leaving the entire wing under the control of a single float supervisor.

The paperwork for "routine transfer" was a boilerplate form, easy to copy and easier to bury. William made sure the digital trail pointed back to the warden's office, where forms went to die.

When the night arrived, Jimmy walked the block himself. He paused at the glass, watched Pearson sleep, then tapped on the frame to wake him.

"The doctor's coming," Jimmy said.

Pearson didn't reply. He looked at Jimmy with the bland hatred reserved for people who outlived their purpose. But he followed orders, moved to the edge of the cot, and sat in the posture of a man who knew nothing could get worse.

Jimmy nodded, then left. He texted Robert: "Clear."

In the hall, the only sound was the buzz of overhead lights and the distant echo of someone watching TV in the staff lounge. Jimmy checked his watch. Three minutes until showtime.

He stood by the exit and waited, the same way he always had in the cabin woods, when the rest of the Oath set the ritual in motion.

This time, the ritual was silent, invisible, as if the system itself were swallowing Pearson whole.

Jimmy felt the faintest flicker of memory—an old, sharp ache—and then let it go.

The rest would happen without him.

Robert always worked alone. It was cleaner that way—fewer distractions, fewer opportunities for anyone to observe what was actually happening. He arrived at the staff entrance with his kit in a cheap gym bag, the badge ID on his lapel reading "Consultant: Medical Review."

He found the isolation room exactly as Jimmy promised. No guards, no cameras. Pearson sat on the cot, hands slack between his knees, face drawn and pale. He looked smaller in person, the weight of the years compressing him into a coil of muscle and gristle—but the eyes—Robert noticed—still burned, unblinking.

"Evening," said Robert. His voice was soft, just above a whisper. He set the kit on the rolling table, then took out the pre-loaded syringe, the capped butterfly needle, and a small, yellow sharps bin.

Pearson watched him. "New doc?" he said, the voice dry as parchment.

"Just here for observation," Robert replied.

He prepped the line, swabbed the skin, and inserted the needle. Pearson didn't flinch. In another life, the man could have been a phlebotomist—he had the deadness in the eyes, the tolerance for pain.

Robert started the injection slowly, counting in his head. The compound was a blend he'd refined for this exact scenario: a touch of succinylcholine to paralyze, a spike of potassium chloride to arrest the heart, and a trace of lidocaine to keep the dying brain calm. The effect was perfect. Within thirty seconds, Pearson slumped backward, jaw slack, eyes staring at the ceiling.

"Easy," Robert said, more to himself than the subject.

He counted off the seconds. At one minute, he checked the pulse—gone. At two, he pressed a stethoscope to the chest, waited for the heart to go from drumbeat to silence.

He withdrew the needle, capped it, and cleaned the site with a sterile wipe. No marks, no blood. He wrote the time of death on the chart, then moved to the door.

He paused on the threshold, looking back at the body.

There was no pleasure in it. No rush, no regret. The man who had shattered their childhoods was just another patient now, as still and irrelevant as a cadaver on a stainless slab.

Robert took the chart and signed the last line in perfect, blocky letters.

He left the room, wiping his hands on a paper towel, and dropped the gym bag in the disposal chute on the way out.

In the lot, the rain had stopped. The world was scrubbed clean, no residue.

For the first time in months, Robert exhaled, slow and careful.

This time, the machine had run with absolute precision.

Pearson died in the same silence he'd carried with him his entire sentence.

He never saw the second needle, never felt the slow chill that crept up his arm. For a moment, as the room swam out of focus, he remembered a different light: a naked bulb in a basement, the hum of insects outside a cracked window. He tried to bring up a name—someone he'd hated, or feared, or perhaps loved—but the synapses refused.

The world thinned to a single point of light, then nothing.

No last words, no gasps or convulsions. Just the gentle exhale, the body collapsing on itself, the final beat of a ruined heart.

No one wept. No one marked the time, except for the entry in the log.

In the cabin, the Oath sat in their circle, the lantern wick burning down to a stub. Nobody spoke. Nobody toasted the end.

Jimmy stared at the floor, hands flat on the table. Mark's face was blank, drained of its usual tension. William cleaned his glasses and watched the fire, as if expecting it to flicker out at any moment.

Mathew broke the stillness with a single nod. Josie closed her notepad and pushed it aside.

Robert's phone buzzed once in his pocket. He checked the screen and then turned it face down on the table.

The wind rattled the windowpane, a sound so old and familiar it barely registered.

Pearson was gone. The circle was closed.

Outside, the woods waited for the new season.

Inside, the Oath waited for whatever might come next.

The next morning, Robert logged into the medical system from his home office, a mug of black coffee steaming by the keyboard. The interface hadn't changed in years—same blue-and-gray menus, same clunky font.

He searched the hospital census for "Pearson, Daniel," and found the record already flagged for discharge. He opened the event log and scrolled to the last entry: "2:03 a.m. — Code blue, unsuccessful resuscitation, time of death certified."

He clicked through the prompts, populating the cause of death with "acute myocardial infarction secondary to hepatic failure." He attached the ECG strip—flatline, exactly as the protocol dictated. In the "Notes" field, he wrote three sentences, then deleted two of them and left the last: "Patient was comfortable at time of death."

He signed the form with his digital credential. The screen flashed "Submission Successful." The record locked in, and with it, the official story.

No one called with questions. No autopsy was ordered. The coroner's office stamped the death certificate and sent it to the county archive, where it would vanish into a million other files.

Robert sat back in his chair, letting the weight of the night settle over him. The sense of closure was real, but so was the emptiness that followed it.

He refreshed his email, half-expecting a glitch in the process, a red flag, or an urgent request for clarification.

There was nothing.

Pearson's body was scheduled for state cremation. No next of kin had claimed him.

The system worked because the world wanted it to.

Robert finished his coffee, closed the laptop, and stared at the faint trace of his own reflection in the blackened screen.

One more entry. One more notch in the machine.

He felt nothing. Or perhaps everything, all at once.

But the work was perfect.

And it would hold.

There were no woods for Pearson.

No lantern, no cord, no clearing. His body left Ironwood on a Tuesday morning, zipped into a state-issued vinyl bag, and was loaded onto a medical transport van with three other unclaimed cadavers. The driver didn't bother with the names; he just signed the manifest, checked the straps, and drove north on the highway to the state crematory.

The process there was automated: the bodies were weighed, scanned, and queued in stainless-steel drawers. An attendant in blue coveralls—who'd never once heard of Pearson, or what he'd done—slid the gurney into the chamber, punched a code into the control panel, and walked away.

The fire did its work, and what remained was swept into a cardboard urn. The ashes joined a row of identical boxes on a shelf in the county morgue, labeled only with a date and a case number.

The state had no budget for ceremonies, so there was no one to mark the end, no scattering, no silent prayer.

The absence of ritual was the ritual.

At the same hour, Mark sat at his kitchen table, the police radio humming static in the background. He felt no urge to drive to the woods, no compulsion to recite old vows. He just sipped his coffee and stared at the window, waiting for the sun to finally break through the gray.

Josie read the news on her phone, scrolled past Pearson's name without slowing down. She made a note to delete the case folder at the end of the fiscal year.

Jimmy ran his block as if nothing had changed.

William logged the death in his master spreadsheet, colored the cell a soft, forgettable gray.

Mathew checked the Lantern Oath inbox one final time. There were no new messages.

Robert deleted the last entry from his encrypted file, then wiped the drive.

There was no justice in this. Not in any grand or cleansing sense.

But there was, at last, an end.

And it was enough.

They didn't plan to meet, but they all showed up.

The roads to the cabin were slick with spring thaw, the ditches brimming with runoff. Josie's car was first in the drive, windows fogged from the inside. Jimmy's truck was parked with mechanical precision, nose perfectly aligned with the split-rail fence. Robert arrived just after dark, headlights flicking through the trees before he cut the engine and walked up the gravel in silence.

Mark came late, as was his habit, and William brought the last six-pack, already one can short.

Mathew arrived to find the table already set: the lantern at the center, unlit. The chairs pulled close, the air dense with the aftertaste of unfinished sentences.

No one spoke at first. Josie traced her finger around the lip of a glass, eyes down. Robert sat with his hands folded, gaze fixed on the lantern. Jimmy stared at the knots in the wood, jaw clenched. William counted out the beers and set one in front of each seat. Mark poured his into a coffee mug and drank half in one go.

Mathew broke the silence, his voice soft. "It's done."

Nobody argued. Nobody toasted.

For a long minute, they sat with the weight of it—the decades since that first promise in the woods, the hundreds of hours spent building and perfecting the machine, the memory of a girl lost and found only in the empty spaces between their words.

Jimmy finally lit the lantern, the match hissing loudly in the stillness. The light flickered, reflected in every face.

No one said Samantha's name, but it pressed in on all sides, as present as the circle itself.

"We keep going?" Josie asked, voice barely above the flame.

"We do," said Mathew. "We do it right."

Mark nodded. William set his can down, untouched.

Robert leaned in, light pooling in the hollows of his cheeks. "For her," he said. "For all of them."

Jimmy blew out the match and set the box aside.

They didn't linger. When the beer was gone, they left in the same order they'd arrived, each into the night, headlights winking out one by one.

The lantern burned until sunrise, then guttered out in the new light.

The cabin held the silence.

The machine was changed, but it was still running.

And the world, for once, was quiet.

The first shovel hit bone just after noon.

The quarry crew had been clearing brush near the southern rim—a job nobody liked, too many snakes, and the sun always on your neck—when the blade struck something that wasn't stone or root. At first, they thought it was a deer, maybe a stray dog left by hunters. But then the foreman saw the shape: a spine, long and curled, and a hand balled into a perfect, permanent fist.

The county sheriff was there within the hour, yellow tape and squad cars turning the dust to a soup. The body lay at the base of an old erosion cut, feet tangled in wire and arms crossed like the dead were supposed to rest. The clothing was mostly gone, but the shoes had survived—a pair of canvas high-tops, the kind you couldn't buy anymore.

The bones had held together—some trick of the soil, or maybe the wire. The skull had a clean hole above the right ear, neat as a punch-out. Whoever put the body here hadn't bothered to dig deep; the earth had done the rest, grinding the man down to memory.

The coroner's van parked under a line of dying pines. The techs worked fast, snapping gloves and sliding the remains into a black bag.

By evening, the news had spread to every office and patrol car in the county: someone had turned up, long after the world forgot him.

And somewhere, the Oath's machine shivered—just for a second—before resuming its quiet, perfect hum.

The body went to the state lab, where a pathologist in blue nitrile gloves reassembled the skeleton on a metal table. She counted the ribs, checked the dental records, and confirmed the cause of death before the first pot of coffee was gone.

The man's jaw was cracked, but the teeth were pristine—good enough to pull a match from the archives before sunset. She ran the printouts against the state's database, the computer humming with the patience of a saint.

The name in the file: Thomas Lee Oglethorpe. Convicted in 2008. Executed at Ironwood Correctional in 2011.

The tech frowned, double-checking the screen. She dug deeper, found the autopsy summary, the press release, and the court filings.

She printed out the records, highlighted the date of death, and pinned it to the whiteboard above her desk.

Then she stared at the body on the table, and the date on the file, and tried to reconcile how a dead man ended up buried in a quarry more than a decade and a half after his execution.

The more she read, the less sense it made.

She made a call to the sheriff and a second to the DA's office. The first call ended with a curse. The second, with a promise to review the files.

When her shift ended, she left the printouts on her desk, knowing someone would see them by morning.

It was just an anomaly, a glitch in the system.

But as she walked to her car, the pathologist couldn't shake the feeling that the real story was hiding in plain sight.

Nathan Pike, longtime agent with the Georgia Bureau of Investigation, read the report twice before picking up the phone.

He was three months out from retirement, but a body in a quarry was still a body, and the law didn't care about your pension. Pike had done this work long enough to know that paperwork, like bones, never told the full story.

He scanned the autopsy findings, the state execution record, and the old mugshot. The face was unmistakable, even under the sunken features and time-worn skin.

Executed in 2011, and here he was, dead again in 2025.

Pike leaned back in his chair, letting the office chair creak beneath his weight. He pulled out a legal pad and started a list: dates, discrepancies, and names of anyone who might have touched the file. He drew a line between the execution at Ironwood and the shallow grave outside the quarry.

He made a note to call the medical examiner in the morning to ask for a copy of the full toxicology and a run-down of any anomalies.

Something in the back of his mind buzzed—an old intuition, the same itch that had driven him to solve cold cases long after other detectives lost interest.

Pike found the number for the Ironwood Correctional records office and dialed, listening to the static on the line as he waited.

"Records," said a clipped voice on the other end.

"This is Agent Pike from GBI, investigating the Oglethorpe case. Can you send over everything you've got from his last twenty-four?"

There was a pause, a rustle of paper. "He was executed. Everything matches the procedure."

"Send it anyway," Pike said, and hung up.

He stared at the ceiling for a long minute, then scribbled a question on the pad:

Who kills a dead man?

Pike closed the file, but left it on the corner of his desk. He'd seen stranger things in his career, but none that felt quite like this.

He switched off the desk lamp, knowing he'd be back before sunrise.

Somewhere, someone had made a mistake.

And Pike was going to find it.

Pike couldn't sleep. He woke at 3:12 a.m. and went straight to his basement office, the coffee maker hissing in the background. He dug through the old files, the ones he'd boxed and labeled by year, and found the Oglethorpe case right where he'd left it.

He remembered the arrest—how the man had run, barefoot, through two miles of swamp, and how Pike had tackled him in the muck and dragged him back to the cruiser. He remembered the trial, the press, the way the whole town treated the conviction as a kind of exorcism.

He pulled out the mugshot and set it beside the pathologist's photos. Same jaw, same scar above the eyebrow. No question.

He checked the records from Ironwood, looking for anything out of place. The paperwork was perfect—too perfect. Not a single notation out of line, no mention of delays, no witness complaints. The death certificate listed the correct drugs, and the signature matched the warden's handwriting.

But the execution file had a weird gap. The day after, the logs went silent for twelve hours—nothing entered, no logins, no call-outs. Pike circled it in red.

He read the transcripts again, noting the staff who'd been present: a nurse, a doctor, a correctional officer. Two of them still worked at Ironwood. Also, the warden, William Lee, was still there.

Pike made a list of their names, then pulled up the most recent news: nothing. Not even a mention in the archives.

He called the pathologist at the lab. She answered on the second ring, voice thick with sleep.

"This is Pike," he said. "Tell me again about the remains."

She yawned. "It's him. No question. The dental and the DNA both match. The only weird part is the internment—He was supposed to be cremated, but the bones on my table tell me he was severely undercooked."

Pike wrote that down. "Anything else?"

She paused. "Yeah, actually. There was a break in one of the bones. Not unusual for a prisoner in maximum security, but the weird thing is that it happened immediately before his death."

Pike hung up and stared at the legal pad.

Executed in 2011.

Dead in a quarry, 2025.

He knew the case. He knew the man.

And he knew, with the certainty of a dying sun, that somebody had pulled a trick.

Pike poured another coffee, set the pad on the table, and began to work the phone.

This time, he was going to chase it all the way down.

Pike spent the week running the angles.

He called every name on his list. He sent FOIA requests to the Department of Corrections, the state medical examiner, and the Governor's office. Every reply came back the same: the records were perfect, the signatures authentic, the chain of custody unbroken.

He pulled up the execution transcript and read it line by line: no last-minute appeals, no protests, no drama. The condemned said nothing. The doctor pronounced the time of death, the warden signed off, and the witnesses filed out. Every step was clockwork.

He checked the visitor logs for the weeks before and after—no one out of place, no strange sign-ins. The staff on duty rotated exactly as scheduled. The nurse listed had retired and moved to Florida.

Pike ran the death certificate against the county's vital records—same result: no errors, no amendments, no delay. The cremation order was filed within forty-eight hours, the ashes supposedly sent to a next of kin who never responded.

He called the original prosecutor, now the Atlanta District Attorney. She remembered the case, remembered Pike. "He was dead," she said. "I saw it with my own eyes."

But Pike had seen the man, too. Alive, then, and now dead a second time, dumped in a quarry like yesterday's trash.

He filled a wall in his basement with copies of every page, every photo, every timestamp. He drew lines, circled dates, and made a map of the impossible.

There was no leak, no visible break in the system.

But there was a ghost, walking years after his own execution.

The more Pike looked, the more he felt the world was laughing at him.

He stared at the wall and whispered, "How did you do it?"

Then he poured another cup of coffee and started over.

He wouldn't stop until the story made sense.

Even if it meant tearing down the whole machine.

"How does a man get executed and end up buried in a quarry?"

Pike said it out loud, pacing his basement in bare feet, legal pad in hand. The walls were covered now—court records, autopsy photos, timelines, a web of string connecting every piece of the puzzle.

He'd called old friends in the Bureau, in the state police, even a journalist he trusted. Nobody had an answer. Most laughed or told him he was seeing ghosts. One offered to buy him a drink and hear the "conspiracy theory" in person.

But the question stuck in his mind, growing louder every day.

He ran simulations on his computer, built timelines of the death and supposed afterlife of Thomas Lee Oglethorpe. He cold-called the Ironwood warden, who answered with a grunt and a list of rules. He posed as a relative, tried to get details on the cremation, but hit a wall—records lost, urn destroyed, no trace.

He reached out to the pathologist, who offered a single word: "Impossible." But she sent the DNA results anyway, and they matched the man he'd collared all those years ago.

Pike drove out to the quarry, stood at the rim, and stared at the earth where they'd found the bones. He imagined the body lying in the dark, the slow crush of dirt and time, the secret of its second death.

He spoke the question again, this time to the empty air.

"How?"

The word echoed off the rocks, unanswered.

He left the quarry with a plan—if the machine wouldn't give him the truth, he'd go inside it himself. Ironwood was a fortress, but every fortress had a way in.

He started making calls, lining up interviews, and prepping for a trip upstate.

Somewhere in the corridors of Ironwood, in the bowels of the state's bureaucracy, someone had pulled off the perfect magic trick.

And Pike was going to walk the path, step by step, until he found the ghost in the gears.

He closed his eyes and imagined the system, cold and smooth and all-consuming.

He smiled, thin as a scalpel.

Then he hit the road, the question burning in his chest.

Ironwood's morning shift changed over at 6:01 a.m., exactly as scheduled. Jimmy walked the rows, key ring heavy on his belt, nodding to each guard in turn. He checked every cell, signed the logs, and made his way to the infirmary, where Robert was already hunched over a clipboard, reading the overnight reports.

No incidents. No deviations.

In the admin wing, William sipped instant coffee and checked the staffing board. He clicked through the system, approving leave requests and rebalancing the next week's schedule. He flagged one new hire for extra screening, then deleted the note as soon as the box was checked.

Josie, downtown, met with a pair of junior prosecutors and walked them through the day's docket. She held the meeting with her back to the window, never glancing at the TV in the waiting room, where the morning news ran silent captions over a video of the quarry dig.

Mark pulled into the staff lot, took the steps two at a time, and let himself into the unmarked office at the end of D-block. He logged in, checked the tip line, and marked every message as reviewed. He noticed a brief uptick in calls about the recent execution cycle, but nothing new—no whistleblowers, no press inquiries worth mentioning.

The machine ran with the same flawless rhythm it always had. No one saw the gears turning. No one heard the grinding in the pipes, or the faint, impossible echo of footsteps in the maintenance tunnels.

But outside, on the long flat road leading to the prison, Nathan Pike was closing the gap. He'd spent the night in a motel, surrounded by photocopied files and post-its. He drove slowly, counting the mile markers, letting his mind run through the sequence of events again and again.

He called ahead and got himself added to the visitor list as a state investigator. The voice on the other end barely paused, then gave him a two-hour window.

The sun rose at his back, the prison glinting like a slab of wet concrete in the new light.

At Ironwood, the guard at the gate checked Pike's badge, nodded, and let him through.

The warden's assistant led him to a small conference room, handed him a stack of forms, and left him alone. The walls were painted oatmeal, the air thick with the scent of old cigarettes and disinfectant.

Pike took out his pen and started to write.

He asked for visitor logs, staff schedules, and records from the day of Oglethorpe's execution. He requested interviews with any staff who'd been present, even if they'd left the state.

Each request triggered a new alert, a ripple through the system, noticed first by William, then by Robert, then—through a backchannel—by Mathew, who read the email in his office and set it aside with a trembling hand.

Josie got a ping from the DA's office, an innocuous-sounding request for confirmation on a six-year-old execution.

She froze, eyes locked on the screen.

Jimmy, on his rounds, felt a twist in his gut when he saw a stranger on the security feed, a man with a detective's walk and a face set in stone.

At the cabin, the lantern sat dark and cold, waiting for the next call.

For the first time, the machine hesitated.

Somewhere in the files, in the walls, in the hush between breaths, there was a crack.

It was small. Barely visible.

But Pike saw it.

He finished his notes, closed the folder, and leaned back in the chair. He smiled, slow and honest.

He could hear the gears now, straining under the weight of their own perfection.

The Oath had built the perfect machine.

But nothing perfect lasted forever.

CHAPTER 10

The quarry was an old one, retired by the county years before Pike ever set foot in Georgia. All that remained was a bowl of red clay, scalloped by decades of cheap labor and rain. Even the fence posts looked haunted—weathered cedar crossbeams twisted into a slow collapse. But on days like this, when the sheriff's men buzzed around in high-viz and the air thrummed with radios and backhoes, the place felt alive—less graveyard, more surgery theater.

Pike arrived before sunrise, as requested. The wind at the rim of the pit chewed right through his jacket, smelling of rust and something sharper: the stench of fresh excavation. He crunched down the access road, hands buried in his pockets, letting the day's first light show him the game board. Cops moved with the directionless urgency of men ordered to look busy in front of a superior. The only real action was happening at the west end of the cut, where the earth sloped down to a tangle of brambles and deadfall. That's where they'd found the first body—what, last week?—and now they were at three, with talk of a fourth if the K9s had their scent right.

A deputy flagged Pike from the crime tape. She was young, wearing her nerves as a sheen on her skin. "You're the one the M.E. called for?" she asked.

"Yeah," said Pike. "Let's get on with it."

They ducked the tape, skirted the ruts left by the Bobcat, and slid into the shade where the crime scene techs worked the new hole. The clay had given way to something like peat, black and damp and almost springy underfoot. In the pit, two men in coveralls had unearthed a shape wrapped in what looked like green painter's tarp. One of them was dusting the edges of the wrap with a paintbrush, as if prepping a rare fossil for display.

"Don't step on the cast-off," called one. "There's a ton of fiber in this one."

Pike crouched at the edge, knees popping. He studied the tarp. The bundle was too long for a kid, too straight for an animal. At the open end, he saw a foot—bare, toenails long and caked with earth. Not recent, then. The techs peeled the tarp in slow, reverent folds, exposing a leg, a pelvic girdle, and a ribcage collapsed like a broken kite.

He had seen hundreds of remains. What caught him wasn't the violence, or the tableau, but the specifics. The careful wrap job. The perfect absence of anything that would degrade a fingerprint. The way the body had been laid in the ground—arms folded, head tilted toward the rise of the hill, as if watching for someone to come back.

He didn't need to say it, but the deputy did. "That's three," she whispered.

"Any ID?"

The tech shook his head. "We're running dental, but there's nothing on the guy. No wallet, no tags. Even the teeth look bleached."

Pike nodded, then walked a slow perimeter of the scene, keeping his eyes low. The details built up like grime: the way the hole was dug—shovel, not machine—the methodical spacing of the graves, the lack of animal disturbance. Whoever put them here knew what they were doing and had all the time in the world to do it right.

He let his gaze travel up to the ridge, where a single squad car idled with its dome light off. From up there, you'd have a clean sightline to the whole pit. He wondered how many times the killer had stood in that spot, watching the workers clear the brush, waiting for the right moment to slip in the next bundle.

Back at the grave, the forensics tech was inventorying the wrapping. He flicked at a strip of duct tape, then held it out for Pike to see. "There are letters under the adhesive," he said. "See? Like someone wrote on the tape before using it."

Pike squinted. It was faint, but there—a couple of digits, maybe a date, maybe a code.

He took a picture with his phone, then motioned for the deputy. "Where's the other two?"

"They're at the coroner's, but we've got a tent for the first one if you want a look."

He did. Inside the tent, the smell was brutal—sweet rot, the kind that gets behind your eyes and stays there. The body was a man, mid-forties, heavyset. The skin had gone leather, and the facial features were mostly gone, but the hair was surprisingly intact. Pike took in the hands: large, blunt fingers, one pinky twisted at the first joint. Familiar, though he couldn't place it.

He checked the toe tag: "John Doe 02." The label on the cooler said "Oglethorpe."

He almost laughed. The universe had a sick sense of humor. But he'd seen the file—this was supposed to be an executed man, dust in an urn by now.

He stepped back out, blinking in the flat, gray daylight. Three bodies, all from death row. All found in the same patch of ground. All supposed to be dead by the hand of the state, not buried like trash in an abandoned pit.

The pattern was forming, even if the lines were still faint. Pike felt the first ripple of it—a tug in the ribs, the thrill and terror of chasing something bigger than any one man.

He looked down at the pit, where the techs were readying to lift the new body. He thought of the other bodies that might be waiting, not just here but in every half-forgotten corner of the world.

It was no longer a single anomaly. It was a game.

And Pike was starting to see the shape of the board.

He told the deputy to call him when they pulled the next body.

He had work to do.

***

Pike's office was half-basement, half-archive. The walls bore the evidence of three separate renovations: wood paneling over crumbling plaster, dropped ceiling cut by fluorescent rectangles that never hummed in sync. The only concession to modernity was the desk, a metal beast scavenged from county surplus, drawers sticky from years of spilled coffee and sweat.

He worked with the lights off, preferred the cold glow of his monitor, and the flicker from his desk lamp. He'd learned long ago that the mind ran cleaner at night, when the world's noise dropped below the hum of his own bloodstream.

On the desk, he laid out the files. He was old-school that way: printed reports, crime scene photos, legal printouts, and a battered legal pad with the day's findings in a looping, upside-down script. He used colored pencils to connect details, not for prettiness but for the tactile jolt of making the connections physical.

Three bodies. Three names. He started with the first: Oglethorpe. Executed in 2011, the records said. Body found intact, cause of death a single cranial wound, not the cardiac arrest listed on the certificate. Pike flipped through the attached execution transcript. No deviations. Standard protocol, no witness statements to suggest a problem.

The second body—name not yet confirmed—matched a man executed in 2014. Third, even fresher: a man who should have been cremated just last year, according to the Department of Corrections.

Pike took a red pencil and circled the execution dates. All at Ironwood. All signed off by the same warden, a William Lee. All with medical certification by the same doctor, a Robert Dean.

He leaned back, cracked his knuckles. Coincidences happened, especially in a state with so few death chambers still in use. But something about the repetition—the same names, the same signatures, the same neat closure on each file—made his teeth hurt.

He cross-referenced the execution logs with the missing persons database. Several of the men supposedly had next of kin, but the relatives never claimed the bodies. He marked the addresses with a blue pencil, then drew a line from the prison to the quarry.

It didn't take long for the web to start resembling a noose.

He was still scribbling connections when the phone buzzed, just past midnight. He expected it to be the night clerk or maybe the coroner's office with a routine update. But the display showed a local number, no name.

"Pike," he answered.

A tired voice on the other end. "You're the investigator on the quarry?"

He recognized the coroner's assistant—she'd handled the Oglethorpe body. "What's up?"

"The third body just got a dental match," she said. "You're not going to believe it."

Pike waited.

"It's a guy who was supposed to be executed last December. Official time of death, 6:04 a.m., Ironwood. But the femur shows a break—fresh, just before death, his second death."

Pike sat up straighter. "So he was alive after the execution?"

"Long enough to have his leg broken, along with other injuries. It's almost like he was tortured and then killed…again."

He jotted it down, stared at the page. "Keep the details quiet for now," he said. "I need to dig."

He hung up, exhaled through his teeth. The pattern was undeniable now. Somebody was running a relay race with the bodies, and the state's own paperwork was the handoff.

He looked at the names again: Lee. Dean.

Pike circled them both, then underlined the phrase "Ironwood control." He stared at the web, feeling the story strain to break the surface.

He got up, stretched, and went to the fridge for a can of cold coffee. On the way back to the desk, he paused at the window, looking out at the parking lot. Nothing but shadows and a flicker from the only working streetlight. But he got the feeling, for the first time, that maybe he wasn't the only one awake.

He sat and started composing the request: all execution records, Ironwood, the last twenty years. If they tried to stonewall, he'd find another way.

He sipped the coffee and waited for the next shoe to drop.

***

By the time Pike finished the records request, his hand cramped and his eyes ached. The state's open records portal was a swamp—every query slowed by bureaucratic molasses, every form requiring three signatures and a notary just to reach the inbox. Pike circumvented the online forms. He preferred the direct route: old friends in the AG's office, a couple of holdovers from the last administration who owed him for cases long buried.

He started by requesting the master list: all executions performed at Ironwood in the last twenty years, including failed or postponed attempts. He knew the warden would try to redact the staff rosters—standard procedure—, but Pike added a line about "pattern-of-practice review" to the subject. That usually sets off the right alarms.

While the requests pinged their way through state servers, Pike dug up everything publicly available about Ironwood. It was built at the peak of the tough-on-crime era, a monument to brutal efficiency: two blocks for the general population, one for death row, and a surgical suite that doubled as an execution chamber. The state rotated staff every three years, except for a handful of specialists. That was the first crack.

He cross-referenced the names from his earlier notes: William Lee, warden for eight years running. Robert Dean, medical director for ten years. A few others popped up, but never for more than a year or two. Pike drew a circle around the two names, then underlined them twice.

He reached for his phone, thumbed a text to a retired corrections officer he trusted. "Ever heard of Wm Lee or Rob Dean at Ironwood? Any stories?" He fired it off, then set the phone down and started in on the execution logs he'd already received.

The logs were dense, bureaucratic poetry: date, time, inmate name, witnesses, chemicals used, and—always—the same sign-off at the bottom: "Procedure completed per protocol. No incident."

He scanned through a decade's worth, looking for deviations. There were none. Every kill was clean; every death confirmed by Robert Dean. Pike found it almost insulting—the absence of error, the mechanical neatness.

His phone buzzed. The retired guard's reply: "Lee's a ghost. Keeps his office locked, never eats in the staff hall. Dean's a true believer. Heard he did private research on 'humane' methods. Why?"

Pike grunted. He liked men with quirks; they made mistakes. These two sounded like they lived for the machine.

He composed another request, this time for staff schedules and surveillance logs for the execution wing. It would take days to come in, but he flagged it as high priority and set a reminder to call the records custodian at dawn.

Pike felt the case closing in, the possible shrinking to a single, suffocating point.

He sat back, let the darkness settle, and mapped the next move: face to face, in the lion's den. Ironwood.

He started rehearsing the interview in his head, making notes on the margin for questions no one ever wanted to answer.

***

Ironwood, in the daylight, looked even less human than Pike expected. The walls were poured concrete, streaked with minerals and graffiti too ancient to scrub clean. The approach from the parking lot funneled you straight through a checkpoint—no ornament, just a bulletproof glass booth and a sign reading, "All Visitors Must Be Escorted At All Times."

The inside wasn't better. The floors were epoxy, the air a perpetual fifty-nine degrees, scented with antiseptic and despair. Pike signed the log, surrendered his wallet and phone, then let a rookie guard badge him through three sets of heavy doors. Every door closed with a slow, hydraulic shudder, as if the building didn't want to let go.

They led him to Administration—an old classroom repurposed into a warren of offices. The receptionist gave Pike a flat smile and tapped a number into the phone. Less than a minute later, William Lee appeared in the doorway.

He was taller than Pike imagined, built like an offensive lineman left to seed in a cubicle farm. His hair was buzzed so close it might as well have been inked on. He wore a navy windbreaker over a white shirt, both unbranded and perfectly lint-free. His handshake was quick, dry, and utterly without pretense.

"Mr. Pike. Thanks for coming out," said William, leading the way to his office. "You're looking at old cases?"

"That's right," said Pike. "I've got some questions about the Oglethorpe execution, and a couple more that happened on your watch."

William nodded, shut the door, and gestured to a plastic guest chair. He sat behind the desk—metal, with zero personal decoration except for a calculator and a single, green-shaded lamp.

"I've reviewed the records," William said. "We followed protocol. The incident report is on file, if you want a copy."

"I'll take it," said Pike, "but I'm more interested in details that don't show up in the reports. Anything unusual that day? Staff sick, equipment glitches, power failures?"

William didn't blink. "Nothing out of the ordinary. The process is standardized. The only variance was a brief delay in the witnesses' arrival—one got stuck in traffic. The timelines are in the log."

Pike took out his notebook, letting the silence draw out. "You've been at Ironwood a long time, Mr. Lee."

"I have," said William. "Eighteen years."

"That's rare," said Pike. "Most wardens rotate out."

William's lips twitched—a nearly invisible smile. "My family's here. I like to keep things stable."

"Your brother's on staff, too?" Pike asked, feigning a glance at his notes. "Jimmy Lee?"

"Yes. He's the head of Corrections. Different chain of command, but we overlap sometimes."

Pike wrote it down, not missing the glance William threw at the door. "How's that work, having two Lees running the house?"

William considered. "We're professionals first. Brothers second."

Pike let the pause stretch, then pressed: "Any tension between departments?"

"Not worth noting," William said. "We're both here to make sure the place runs smoothly."

Pike thumbed through his folder. "Something is bothering me about the Oglethorpe case," he said. "The medical notes don't line up. Time of death is a minute off from the EKG strip, and the post-mortem says Dean didn't sign off until the body was already moved. Is that standard?"

William's jaw set. "I can't speak to medical protocol. But Dean is—let's say, methodical. He wouldn't skip a step."

Pike nodded, letting it hang there. "Do you mind if I talk to him?"

"I'll arrange it," William said. "Anything else?"

"Security tapes," said Pike. "From the chamber and the transport bay. Can I get a copy?"

William raised his chin, not in challenge, but as if already calculating the hassle. "You can, but there's a retention limit. Only thirty days on video. For Oglethorpe, it'll be gone."

Pike made a show of writing it down, even though he knew. "Do you ever have any issues with tampering? Lost tapes, erased drives?"

William's eyes didn't leave Pike's face. "No."

The word landed like a brick.

Pike tried a softer angle. "You said you like stability. What about staff turnover? Any pattern to who stays and who goes?"

William actually smiled this time, a real one. "People who fit, stay. People who don't find a way out."

Pike closed his notebook. "That's all for now."

William stood, came around the desk, and opened the door for Pike. "Let me know if you need anything else."

On the way out, Pike watched the way William's hands hung at his sides—loose, but not relaxed. He filed the whole interview under "Fortress." No errors. No emotion. No way in.

But then, as the door swung closed, Pike heard William's phone buzz. A low, terse conversation—just fragments. "Yes…No, nothing out of range. He's fine."

Pike smiled to himself. Nobody got spooked over a dead man. Not unless they had reason to fear the living.

He thanked the guard on the way out and started prepping for the next interview.

He wanted to see if the brother was as perfect as the warden.

***

Pike spent the next hour in the prison's public records alcove, a cinderblock cell decorated with a single ficus and an old Ironwood championship banner. He used the house computer, a slab of government-issue plastic sticky with hand sanitizer residue.

He dug into the personnel logs, searching for overlap between the warden and the staff. The Lee name jumped out immediately: William as warden, Jimmy as Corrections chief. Their personnel files were pristine—no write-ups, no transfer drama, just year after year of steady promotions and glowing performance reviews.

He scanned the files for anomalies, looking for the weird, the human. There was nothing. The most "personal" note was an unsigned Christmas card stuck in William's folder for reasons no one could remember.

Pike cross-checked the training schedules, shift logs, and incident reports. The brothers rarely shared a shift, but their actions dovetailed perfectly—if William initiated a protocol change, Jimmy implemented it without friction. The staff under them either lasted forever or washed out in under a month.

The synergy was… unsettling.

He scrawled a note: "Lee & Lee—closed circuit?"

The crack, if there was one, had to be in the handoff between them. He played back the interview with William in his head, the way he said, "Professionals first. Brothers second." But Pike had learned long ago that the family was never really separate from the work, not in this world.

He highlighted the note and circled it twice.

Then he closed the files, shut off the monitor, and asked the guard to escort him to the execution wing.

He wanted to see the younger Lee up close.

***

The execution wing of Ironwood was its own world—sterile, overlit, humming with an energy that had nothing to do with life. They met in a side corridor lined with locked doors and plexiglass windows. Pike found Jimmy Lee waiting just outside the chamber, clipboard balanced on his forearm, eyes fixed on a digital clock counting down to the next shift change.

"Mr. Pike?" said Jimmy, shaking his hand with a squeeze that was all business.

They walked a short stretch of hall, Pike keeping pace as Jimmy led the way, narrating as if giving a tour to a dignitary.

"Everything here is by the numbers," Jimmy said. "The room is prepped the night before. Drugs delivered in a sealed kit, chain of custody logged every hour. Staff rotates in three-person crews. No solo operators."

Pike nodded, scanning the blank walls. "I'd like to talk about the Oglethorpe execution."

Jimmy's jaw set, but his voice stayed even. "Not much to say. The man went in, followed orders, and took the needle. No commotion, no last words. We checked the gurney after—still had the factory tag on it."

"You did the prep yourself?" Pike asked.

"I always do," Jimmy replied. "Too many variables if you delegate. My brother says, 'Trust the process.' I say, 'Trust the hands.'"

The honesty was almost unnerving. Pike tried a new angle. "Have you ever seen anything odd in the chamber? Cold feet, staged drama, medical complications?"

Jimmy laughed, a dry sound with no mirth. "Men get nervous, sure. They wet themselves or spit. Sometimes they try for a scene—cry for mama, that kind of thing. But the protocol covers all of it."

Pike tried to catch him off-balance. "What about mistakes?"

Jimmy cocked his head. "We don't make them. If we did, you'd have heard."

Pike changed tack. "How's it working, having your brother as boss?"

Jimmy shrugged, like he'd been asked a hundred times. "He's the suit, I'm the hands. That's how it's always been. We don't hang out after hours."

Pike watched him. The guy didn't fidget, didn't break eye contact. He radiated the same sense of inevitability as a slow, heavy piston.

He walked Jimmy through a series of hypotheticals: what if a man fought the line, what if a witness passed out, what if a body went missing. Jimmy handled each question with the same steady rhythm—facts, protocol, dry humor. But when Pike mentioned "missing," Jimmy's eyes narrowed for a split second before snapping back to neutral.

"Never lost a body," he said. "Never lost a staff member, either. Ironwood runs tight."

They ended up at the threshold of the execution chamber. It was cleaner than a hospital: stainless steel everything, straps laid out in a neat grid, nothing out of place.

Jimmy rested a hand on the gurney. "Have you ever seen one?" he asked.

Pike shook his head.

Jimmy ran through the process, step by step, using the same words as the transcript Pike had read. It felt rehearsed, but not dishonest.

At the end, Jimmy said, "Nobody likes it, but everybody does it right."

Pike nodded. He tried one last shot. "What do you do after a shift like this?"

Jimmy grinned, a little too wide. "I go home, make a sandwich, and watch TV. Or I drive out to the woods and run until I can't think straight."

"You run together, you and your brother?" Pike asked, casually.

"Not for years," said Jimmy. "He's got a bad knee."

They stood in silence, the hum of the air handler filling the void.

Pike thanked Jimmy and walked back down the hall alone to the exit. He felt the weight of the place, the total control, the absence of anything accidental.

He made a note: "Final step: always Jimmy."

Whatever was happening here, it started and ended in this corridor.

He left Ironwood with more questions than answers, but one certainty: nothing left this place unless the Lee brothers allowed it.

He just had to figure out why.

***

Pike ran the whole drive back, replaying the Lee brothers' voices—how alike they sounded, how easily they ran the script, how little space there was for anything unexpected to grow between their words. By the time he reached his office, the sky had gone sullen, rain thudding on the old pane glass in irregular Morse.

He made a new chart on his whiteboard, using bold lines to track a prisoner's flow through Ironwood: Intake. Segregation. Execution prep. Medical signoff. Each arrow led to a box, and every box—no matter how he mapped it—looped back to a Lee.

He added a timeline for each execution: date, time, names of staff on duty, and chain of custody for the body. Every legible record for a decade pointed to the same closed circle. In thirty executions, not once had an outsider controlled a critical step.

Pike chewed on the cap of his marker, feeling the ache of questions stacking up in his jaw. He tried to picture how a deviation might work: could a body be swapped? Could a death be faked? The machinery was too tight, too disciplined, to allow an outsider to even see a mistake, let alone create one.

He pulled up the transport logs, looking for holes. None. He tried to catch William in a slip—maybe a day he was off the property, or a shift he'd skipped. Nothing.

He cross-referenced every blue slip, every transfer, every single moment a body was unaccounted for. It never happened.

The system was perfect.

And it had been built to be that way. Not a byproduct of bureaucracy, not a fluke. This was by design; every lever and catch was precisely engineered.

He set the marker down, stared at the loops and arrows until the lines vibrated. For a second, he wondered if he was chasing a ghost, a mirage conjured by his own bias.

But the bodies in the quarry were real, and so was the web on his wall.

Pike knew the answer wouldn't come from the prison itself. The next loop was outside the walls—medical, legal, or both.

He poured a mug of coffee, opened the file on Robert Dean, and read the first line: "Medical Director, Ironwood State, 2002-present. Specialization: anesthesiology, trauma."

Pike smiled, just barely.

He was ready to meet the surgeon who made the kills look perfect.

***

The medical annex at Ironwood was nothing like the prison proper. The cinderblock walls gave way to drywall, the lights buzzed at a human volume, and the smell was faintly chemical—like a dentist's office, minus the antiseptic cheer. Pike waited in a reception area furnished with magazines older than some of the guards, reading a pamphlet about "Compassionate End-of-Life Care" until Robert Dean emerged from behind a frosted door.

Dean was lean, mid-fifties, face shaved so clean it almost shone. He wore a blue scrub shirt and ironed slacks, no coat, no badge. His handshake was precise—two pumps, then gone.

"Agent Pike?" he said, already ushering him into the exam room.

The room was an immaculate box: vinyl floors, counters with nothing left out, not even a stray pen. The only personal item was a black digital clock, seconds ticking away in perfect silence.

Dean motioned for Pike to sit, then perched on a rolling stool, hands folded over his knees.

"You're looking at the Oglethorpe case?" Dean asked, voice not unfriendly, just preemptively neutral.

"Among others," said Pike. "I'm trying to understand your process."

Dean nodded. "It's straightforward. We use a three-stage protocol: barbiturate, paralytic, and potassium. The doses are set by weight, calculated day-of. No substitutions. I administer the IV, the nurse witnesses and logs the time. There's a double-check on every step."

Pike made a show of consulting his notes. "Is it possible for a body to show a different cause of death than what's on the paperwork? Say, cranial trauma instead of cardiac arrest?"

Dean's eyes didn't even flinch. "Not unless someone hits the head after the fact. The drugs act fast—the heart stops in seconds. Any trauma is post-mortem."

"What about the timing?" said Pike. "Can the drugs be slowed down, delayed, or…"

Dean shook his head. "Not unless you use the wrong catheter, or the line infiltrates. I inspect every vein myself. If there were a delay, I'd know."

Pike tried a different angle. "You've never had a failure? A body that didn't take?"

Dean smiled, polite but thin. "Never. We calibrate for margin. There's no pain, no struggle. That's why they brought me in."

Pike studied Dean's hands: the knuckles were faintly callused, nails trimmed with surgeon's precision. He couldn't see a single tremor.

"Have you ever had a witness question the process?" Pike asked.

"Once or twice," Dean allowed. "Usually, it's a lawyer who thinks they've spotted a twitch. But I invite them to see the EKG afterward, and that's the end of it."

Pike leaned forward. "What if someone wanted to make it look real, but leave the body alive?"

Dean cocked his head, genuinely curious. "You can't fake this. The potassium shuts down every cell. Even if you skipped the drugs, the paralytic would drop the breathing in under a minute. There's no trick."

Pike nodded, even as his gut told him otherwise. "Could someone swap a body?"

Dean smiled wider. "Not here. Too many checks. I sign off on every transport, and Jimmy Lee logs every handoff. If a body left this place alive, we'd have a riot."

Pike let the silence stretch. Dean seemed perfectly comfortable in it, like a lizard on a warm rock.

"Anything else?" Dean said, folding his hands tighter.

Pike shook his head. "Not today."

Dean walked him to the door, offered a handshake again, and watched him leave with the same polite emptiness.

Pike made it ten steps before he exhaled. He'd met a hundred liars, but Dean was the kind who could say anything—even the worst truth—without letting it get near his heartbeat.

He jotted a note: "If you want a perfect death, call Dean."

He didn't like the way it sounded.

***

Back in his office, Pike couldn't let go of the interaction with Dean. There was no tension in the man, no flicker of guilt or evasion—just a relentless confidence in the finality of his own work.

Pike dug through medical journals, case studies, and even the footnotes of the state's own execution protocols. He called two county coroners and floated a scenario—could a body be rendered apparently dead, but recover later? Both said no, not with the drugs in use. One asked if Pike was writing a novel.

He shot an email to Dean, subject line "Protocol Follow-up." He kept it casual, but loaded the questions for any sign of a slip.

Dean's reply arrived in under three minutes:

"All IVs are checked for patency prior to induction. Two staff members verify the drug order, and then it is witnessed by a correctional officer. No error is possible without detection. All bodies are subject to confirmatory EKG and external examination. Any deviation would be noted. Happy to clarify further if needed."

No warmth. No opening. Pike replied with a thank-you and left it at that.

He tried one last angle: the case of an inmate whose execution had allegedly failed years back. He requested the incident report and found—unsurprisingly—that Dean had signed off on the final death determination, correcting a "line infiltration" before the second dose.

Even when things went wrong, Dean made them right.

Pike closed the file and sat in the dark for a long time, letting the implications turn over in his head. The more he dug, the more perfect the system looked.

It didn't feel like bureaucracy. It felt like engineering—deliberate, unbreakable.

He made a note in red:

If you want to fake a death, trust the man who's never failed.

Then he started reading up on the other side of the pipeline—the prosecutors who got the bodies to Ironwood in the first place.

He suspected they'd be just as careful as the people at the end.

***

The District Attorney's building was all glass and brushed steel, a palace of transparency that made Pike smile for reasons he couldn't put into words. He was shown to a conference room with a twelve-foot table, where every seat but one was empty. At the far end, Josie Hamilton reviewed a case file, her hair a copper wire in the cold sunlight.

She didn't look up when Pike sat. When she did, the glance was calibrated—one quick sweep, then right to the heart of the matter.

"I know why you're here," she said, closing the folder. "You want to know how these men ended up at Ironwood."

"That's part of it," Pike said.

She sighed, not exasperated, just time-conscious. "Every capital case that comes through here gets a six-point review. I don't pursue unless the evidence is bombproof. You're welcome to audit the files."

Pike smiled. "That's generous."

"Not really," she replied. "It's all public record. But nobody reads the whole thing. They want a soundbite, not the work."

He pushed a little. "Have you ever had a case that went sideways? Witness recants, DNA reversal, last-minute confession?"

Josie shook her head. "Not since I took this office. If I'm not sure, I plead it down. The only men who get the needle are the ones who earned it."

Pike drummed a finger on the table. "You sign off on all of them?"

"Every last one," she said, her eyes flat and bright. "I write the memo to the Governor myself. It's the only way I sleep at night."

He let that sit, then tried a new angle. "Do you ever get pressure from outside—victims' families, politicians?"

"All the time," she said. "But the system doesn't run on emotions. I follow the process. Every box checked, every date hit. There's no margin for error."

Pike considered. "You know the Lee brothers?"

She smiled for real this time. "Everyone knows them. They're efficient. Some of the guards call them 'the twins,' but I've never seen them in the same room. I think they plan it that way."

"And Dean?"

She shrugged. "The doctor? He's a ghost. I get his reports, that's all."

Pike pulled a page from his folder and slid it across the table. "Have you ever seen an execution get reversed? Posthumous exoneration?"

Josie scanned the list, then set it aside. "Once, maybe. But never on my watch. Every case I've touched, the evidence has stuck."

Pike leaned in. "You think it's possible for a man to survive the process?"

Now she did look at him, eyebrows drawn together in a not-quite-frown. "Not unless someone wanted him to."

Pike watched her reaction: not fear, not confusion. Just a brief recalculation.

She tapped the file on the table. "Are you chasing a ghost, or a real man?"

"Right now, I'm not sure," Pike said.

Josie smiled, stood, and offered her hand. "Let me know when you figure it out."

Pike took the handshake, noting the grip—firm, over quick. As he left, she was already dialing a number on her phone.

He stepped into the sunlight, running the conversation over in his mind.

Whatever the game was, Josie played it as well as the Lees.

He had a new note to add to his chart: "Front end: airtight. DA sets the stage."

The next stop would be the judge—the last hand on the lever before the state signed off on murder.

He was almost looking forward to it.

***

After the DA's office, Pike sat at a nearby diner, nursing a coffee and a plate of fries gone cold. He flipped his notebook to a fresh page and diagrammed the process, this time from the top down.

Josie was the lock on the front door: nothing got into the system unless she said yes, and once she did, the case was built to withstand an earthquake. The chain of evidence was unbreakable. The timelines never slipped. Pike could imagine her as a conductor, each note perfectly played, every section in tune.

He made a list of all the executed men connected to Josie's office. Every case, every conviction, every press release. The language was always the same: "Closure for the families." "Finality for the state." The words felt scripted, but the results were absolute.

He remembered Josie's parting shot: "Not unless someone wanted him to."

Pike sipped his coffee and watched the people at the counter, their lives ticking by in little routines—cream, sugar, phone, repeat. He wondered if any of them had ever seen a system so perfect, so immune to the ordinary rot of human error.

He set up a call to the judge's office, asked for an appointment, and was surprised when they offered him a slot the same afternoon.

He finished the coffee, left a tip, and stepped outside, feeling the gears of the city turning just as tightly as the ones in his case file.

Josie had made the pipeline airtight. But it was the judge who hit the final switch.

Pike wanted to see the man who finished the work.

***

The judge's chambers were on the top floor of the courthouse, at the end of a hallway polished so hard Pike could see the ghosts of a hundred lawyers in the reflection. He was shown in by a bailiff who barely spoke, just nodded, and held the door.

Inside, the room was a study in order: shelves of legal volumes, old black-and-white photographs in perfect grids, a desk empty but for a single, open file. Judge Mathew Walton stood by the window, arms crossed behind his back, posture stiff enough to have survived three wars.

"Agent. Pike," he said. "Please. Sit."

Pike did, noting how Walton let the silence swell for a moment before approaching the desk.

"You're investigating the Ironwood executions," Mathew said. It wasn't a question.

"That's right," said Pike. "I'm trying to understand the review process. How does a case make it to your docket, and what do you look for?"

Mathew took his chair, folding himself into it with mechanical precision. "We are the court of last resort," he said. "By the time a case reaches me, every appeal has been exhausted. My role is to verify the record, confirm that due process was observed, and issue the final ruling."

Pike nodded. "Is there ever a case where you feel—personally—that an error was made?"

Mathew's lips pressed into a line. "The law does not ask for our feelings, Agent Pike. It asks for fidelity to procedure. I do not insert myself into the facts of the case."

Pike let that hang, then tried another approach. "Do you ever revisit old warrants? Look for patterns in how they come to you?"

Mathew shook his head once. "The system is not perfect. But it is rigorous. The only pattern is that the worst crimes get the harshest outcome. If you are looking for human failure, you will not find it here."

"Do you ever meet the defendants?" Pike asked.

"Never," said Mathew. "My contact is with the record. Nothing more."

Pike felt the chill in the room—a low-frequency hum of discipline, decades in the making. He tried to picture Mathew as a young man, but the image wouldn't come. The judge seemed constructed, not born.

"Do you remember Oglethorpe?" Pike said, almost as an afterthought.

Mathew's eyes flicked up. "Yes. I reviewed the case. I issued the order."

"Anything unusual?"

"Not at all. The documentation was immaculate. The process was executed to the letter."

Pike watched the man's hands—folded, never fidgeting, the fingers long and pale as piano keys.

He closed his notebook. "Thank you, Your Honor."

Mathew inclined his head, then turned back to the window.

Pike left the chambers with a crawling sense that he'd just visited a mausoleum—one where every mistake was buried deep, neat, and impossible to exhume.

He wrote a note as soon as he hit the street:

"Mathew Walton: nothing leaves his desk unless it's perfect. The system closes here."

It was time to map the whole thing and see if the loop really was unbreakable.

***

Pike spent the evening building his map, block by block. At first, it looked like a typical flowchart: a sequence of boxes with arrows, each representing a phase in the justice process. But as he cross-referenced names and dates, something unsettling happened.

Every link in the chain had a single, dominant name.

Mark Hughes, lead investigator on most of the cases—his signoff started the pipeline. Josie Hamilton, DA, oversaw prosecution and plea decisions. Mathew Walton issued every death warrant in the last fifteen years. At Ironwood, William Lee ran the prison, and his brother, Jimmy, ran the executions. At the end, Robert Dean certified every death and completed the final paperwork.

No substitutions. No outside influence. Not once, not ever.

It wasn't a bureaucracy. It was a circuit, closed and perfect.

Pike let the markers tumble from his hand, watched the red and black lines intersect and loop.

This was not a product of chance or even convenience. This was a machine, designed and operated by six hands, every part controlled and every motion deliberate.

He felt the cold certainty of it settle over him, a second skin.

Pike made one final note, at the bottom of the board:

Six operators. No redundancy. No oversight. No escape.

He stared at it until the numbers blurred.

If there were a crack, it would show in the results—the bodies, the burials, the post-mortem chaos.

He turned to the stack of quarry files, ready to see how many ghosts the machine had made.

***

Pike spent three days working on the quarry remains

With each new body, the scale of the thing snapped into sharper, colder focus. By the end of the week, the coroner's team had pulled six more remains from the quarry—some so old the bones had leached the color of coffee grounds, others with traces of skin and cartilage clinging in ghostly outlines.

Pike set up a second whiteboard for the dead alone. Every victim got a color-coded entry: official name, execution date, Ironwood case number, and the projected postmortem interval from the autopsy. He strung up the timelines, pinning the executions in black and the forensic death estimates in red.

They didn't line up. Not even close.

Some of the oldest bodies were men who were tortured after they were supposedly executed. One skeleton—a man named Burroughs, killed by the state in 2007—had a fresh femur fracture just prior to the moment of death. Burroughs was supposed to have been cremated and sent to a widow in Macon.

Pike picked through the photos for each one, looking for patterns in the trauma. All had the telltale signs of lethal injection—but there were no chemical burns and no signs of chronic organ shutdown. Instead, there were blunt-force injuries, stabbings, and a few skull fractures. The cause of death was violence, plain and unvarnished.

The only thread that held was the burial site: every man ended up here, in this dead pit, no matter when they died.

He called the pathologist for clarification, asked her if there was any way the drugs could have "failed" and left a man alive.

"No chance," she said, almost offended. "With the dosages in the protocol, you could kill a horse. If these men walked out of Ironwood, they were never executed to begin with."

Pike thanked her and stared at the board. He redrew the timeline, this time charting the years after each supposed death—the gap where the state thought a man was dust and where the quarry kept him waiting.

He felt sick, but also something darker—a kind of awe at the precision of the lie.

This was not a glitch. It was a system designed to make men disappear on paper, and then kill them later at the state's discretion.

He wondered if there was anyone on the outside who'd ever noticed, anyone who tried to file a complaint or raise a hand.

He started a new list for next of kin, wondering if any had asked too many questions.

He already knew the answer.

He circled the word "Gap" on the whiteboard, then wrote underneath: "Where do they go before the hole?"

He'd need to find that out next.

***

The pattern pressed at Pike's mind all night, refusing to let go. He woke just before dawn, sat in the half-dark of his office, and stared at the whiteboards until the logic clicked into place.

It was the gap. The impossible space between a man's official death and the time his body ended up in the ground. There were no official records for what happened in between. No autopsy, no news, no funeral. Just a hole in the story, stitched together with legal signatures and a few lines of bureaucratic poetry.

The only way it worked was if the death at Ironwood was a performance, a piece of theater staged for the state and then reversed as soon as the curtain dropped.

The Lees, Dean, even the judge—they weren't just running the machine. They were running an alternate circuit, one that took a man off the books, kept him alive, and then finished him on their own terms.

Pike thought about the quarry, about the bones with new injuries, about the families who never got an answer.

He wondered if the men knew they were being resurrected for a second, slower death.

He wondered who was picking the timing, and why.

He realized it didn't matter.

They weren't dying in the chamber. They were dying in the gap.

Pike made a fresh pot of coffee and started a new list:

"Who ran the transfer? Who signed the body out? Who handled the paperwork?"

He already knew where to start.

He circled the Lee brothers' names, then underlined them twice.

He was ready to dig into the records for the handoff—the moment the state looked away.

He had a hunch it wouldn't be written down anywhere.

But he'd been in this game long enough to know: people never hid the crime, only the steps that made it possible.

He sharpened a pencil and went to work.

***

Pike traced every Ironwood execution through the transfer logs, looking for a mistake, a gap, a single deviation from perfection. He built a spreadsheet with a column for every phase: chamber, medical signoff, temporary morgue, transport, and final destination.

It took only an hour to spot the trick.

After the death certificate was signed, the body should have gone to the coroner or a funeral home. But in every case that ended up in the quarry, the final transfer was handled by an "internal courier"—never an outside agency, never a family rep. The logs were always initialed by one of three names: William Lee, Jimmy Lee, or a third, always-changing alias that never matched the official roster.

For the men who were actually buried by the state—those with family, or who made the news—the handoff happened in the open. For the ghosts, it was a black box.

Pike cross-checked the van manifests, looking for a VIN or plate number. Most were state vehicles, but the ones on the ghost transfers were always marked "maintenance run," no further detail.

There were no GPS logs, no security camera footage, no sign that the body had ever left the property.

Pike shivered, even though the office was warm.

He wrote on his whiteboard:

Handoff = end of record. Real death = somewhere else.

He drew a circle around the word "somewhere."

This was the machine's genius: it didn't just hide the crime. It erased the possibility of even asking the question.

He stared at the final column in his spreadsheet, blank for every single ghost.

He wrote a single word in red:

Destination?

He knew it wouldn't be in the paperwork. He'd have to go back to the quarry, or maybe the woods, and look for the real transfer point.

He felt the first edge of fear in his gut, a deep animal knowledge that the men who built this circuit would not appreciate a stranger trying to break it.

He closed the spreadsheet, deleted his search history, and went to pack his kit for fieldwork.

He had a feeling the next steps would not be safe.

***

Pike started with the Pearson file, the one case he couldn't shake from his memory. It was the first time he'd seen true evil—Pearson had been careful, methodical, a predator who left no survivors and almost no trace. Pike had spent two years hunting him, and even when he caught the bastard, it felt like the man had wanted to be caught.

He reopened the case from the first evidence locker: arrest warrant, mug shots, every scrap of interview transcript. On a hunch, Pike started scanning the signatures and footnotes—the deputies who'd logged the evidence, the court clerks, the intake staff at the jail.

He saw the names at first as a coincidence. A Hughes here, a Hamilton there, a Lee on the transport roster. He shrugged it off. These were old Savannah names, the kind that ran through every layer of state and city.

But the pattern held. Every step in the pipeline—from arrest to prosecution to execution—had a supporting cast that never changed. Pike double-checked the DA on all of the executions. It was Josie Hamilton. The judge was Matthew Walton.

He switched to another file, same result—the same players in every case.

Pike went cold. It was like seeing the same ghost in a hundred photographs.

He mapped it on the board: generation to generation, the same six names, always circling the worst crimes, always present when the case finally closed. He checked the bar associations, the old fraternity rosters, the news clippings from the year of his own first big collar.

They were all there. At every crime scene, in every courtroom, at every last-minute appeal.

He stared at his evidence board, feeling the weight of it settle into his bones.

Pike realized he was not just chasing a criminal conspiracy. He was chasing a bloodline, a clan, a secret society engineered to self-perpetuate.

The horror and admiration warred in his chest.

He wondered if any of them even remembered the original trauma, or if they just kept the machine running because it was all they knew.

He wrote a question on the edge of the board:

"When did it start?"

He knew the answer would be in the oldest case of all—the one that made them.

Pike felt a sudden urge to check his locks, to call someone, anyone, and tell them what he'd found.

But he knew he wouldn't.

While researching the origins of Judge Matthew Walton, a case jumped out at him — and hit him hard—the case of Samantha Walton, his younger sister.

***

The first thing that hit Pike in the Samantha Walton file was how ordinary the people looked in the photographs. The victim, a girl of fourteen, all braces and blue eyes. Her brother, Mathew, in the background of a summer cookout, arm slung over the shoulder of a freckled kid who had to be Mark Hughes. On the edge, a redheaded girl—Josie, unmistakable even as a teen.

Pike paged through the file, finding the cast of characters repeating: in witness statements, as volunteers at the search parties, as the first to call in the tip line. He traced the school records and saw that every person in power he interviewed was on the same honor roll, took the same field trips, and had the same photos from the town's Fourth of July parade.

He followed the path forward in time, watching the kids turn into the state's legal backbone. Hughes went to the police academy, then homicide. Josie did law school, clerked for a circuit judge, then ran for DA. Walton did in law school, a prestigious Atlanta firm, and then became a judge before forty. Even the odd ones out—Jimmy and Robert—never left the circle, working corrections and medical, both at Ironwood.

He checked the property records, saw that their families' homes were clustered within three blocks of each other in old Savannah. Pike could picture them as children, riding bikes, learning the city's geography by running from yard to yard.

He looked back at the victim timeline and felt a sudden, bracing clarity.

The system wasn't closed for efficiency. It was closed for revenge.

Pike flipped to the transcript of the original investigation. The suspect—Pearson, a ghost now—never confessed, never left evidence, never paid for what he did. The case went cold, and the town folded up the trauma, leaving the kids to grow around it like a broken limb healing crookedly. But one detail jumped out at him. Pearson died in the medical wing of Ironwood. The attending physician at the time of his death was Robert Dean.

They'd built the machine not just to fix the system, but to erase the possibility of ever being hurt that way again.

Pike sat back, letting the story fill him. He saw the faces of adults, gathered around the table at a reunion, each one holding the line for the others.

He wondered if they remembered the moment they made the promise, or if it was just baked into their bones.

He wrote a note on his pad:

It's not justice. It's revenge.

He stared at the words, thinking about the men in the quarry, about the perfect execution of each step.

He almost felt sorry for them.

He closed the folder, knowing that he'd never look at a case file the same way again.

He wondered if there was any way to stop a machine like this, or if the best he could do was make sure the world knew the truth.

He started drafting his report, careful to list every detail, every name, every date.

He owed it to the justice system and to all the others who would never get a file of their own.

***

Pike spent the next night lining up the dominoes. He found the earliest reference to the group in the summer of 1994, a Savannah news clipping about a missing girl and the "neighborhood search party" that swept the woods for weeks. He saw their names—Walton, Hughes, Hamilton, Lee, Dean—even then, always clustered together.

He mapped their college years. Each one took a different discipline: law, medicine, police, corrections, and even the sciences. Pike watched as they spread out across the state, taking up posts that seemed unremarkable, except for the way they all steered toward the pipeline of death row.

By the early 2000s, they'd consolidated. Hughes was in homicide, Walton was a rising star in the courts, Hamilton was prosecuting capital cases, the Lees had locked down the prison, and Dean had drifted to medicine, but always in the service of state processes.

Pike built a timeline and drew a line at Samantha's death.

He started looking at the cases from before the Oath took full control. There were appeals, botched executions, and even an accidental release that made the news for a month. After the Oath closed the circuit, nothing ever went wrong. Not a single headline. Not one reversal.

He checked the death of Pearson, the old predator who started it all. The official story was "natural causes." But the intake file for his last days at Ironwood was scrubbed—no witnesses, no autopsy, just a note from Dean and a signature from William Lee.

Pike pictured the six of them, grown now, coming together in secret to finish the job the law never could.

He wondered if they considered themselves heroes or just the only ones willing to do what had to be done.

He understood, then, that this wasn't about revenge or even about justice. It was about control. About never letting the world betray them again.

Pike stared at the evidence, the names and the lines and the dates. He saw a system that could not be hacked or evaded. The Oath would live on from generation to generation because the machine was perfect.

He wrote a last note on his board:

This is not a conspiracy. It's an ecosystem.

He sat in silence, listening to the night, and felt the weight of what he'd found settle onto his shoulders.

He thought about calling the feds, or the state AG, or even the press.

But he knew that nobody would believe him.

He wondered if the Oath would find him before he found the answer to the next question:

What happened to the men who tried to break the circuit?

He closed the blinds, checked the locks, and waited for dawn.

***

He spent the next forty-eight hours running down every loose thread he could think of: old cellmates, families of the executed, even retired guards from Ironwood. Most were dead, disappeared, or in jail. The few who answered his calls remembered nothing unusual about the men on death row—no last-minute visitors, no strange handoffs.

Pike pressed harder, posing as a journalist, a distant relative, a PI looking for a payday. It didn't matter. Nobody wanted to talk, or maybe nobody could. He felt the Oath's presence everywhere, a quiet pressure that had trained the world not to notice.

He tried to get a line on Mark Hughes, the homicide detective. Most would have "retired early," after his long career, but Pike found him. He lived in a modest apartment but also had a listing in a remote county— a cabin, no neighbors, cash sale. He added it to his file and moved on.

He called the DA's office, fishing for any odd transfers or hush-hush settlements. The staffer who answered sounded almost bored. "All our cases are public, sir. Check the website." Click.

He drove out to the old Savannah neighborhood, walked the block where the Oath had grown up. The houses were different now, painted and flipped for the Airbnb crowd, but the air still tasted of wet grass and smoke.

He asked at a coffee shop about the families—Walton, Lee, Hamilton. The barista looked at him blankly. "Those are old money names," she said. "Don't see them much now. Maybe check the historical society?"

Pike did, and found a wall of plaques with the names engraved in gold.

He walked the park where Samantha's vigil had once been held. There was no plaque for her, but the old bandstand still stood. Pike imagined the Oath as kids, swearing in the dark, trying to conjure a magic big enough to fix the world.

He felt, for the first time, the futility of his own search. They weren't hiding. They were just finished.

He went back to his office, deleted his notes, and started over.

He called the warden's office at Ironwood, left a message: "Pike. Let's meet."

He called the DA and asked for Josie Hamilton. She took the call, voice dry as salt. "What's this about, Detective?"

"I need a meeting," he said.

She sighed. "Of course. Name the time."

He hung up and checked the mirror, looking for signs that the Oath was already closing the net.

He found nothing.

He packed his bag and set a route to the cabin, convinced it was the only place left where the story still lived.

He wrote a single line in his notebook before he left:

The machine runs until it's seen.

He got in the car, closed the door, and listened to the tick of his watch as he pulled out of the city.

If they were waiting, he'd know soon enough.

***

The cabin wasn't listed on any map. Pike had to piece together the coordinates from a trail of real estate transfers: a shell company in Delaware, a PO box in Macon, a string of year-end travel receipts that always overlapped in December. The final owner of record was a name he'd never seen before, but the signature was a near match for the judge's, only sloppier, more rushed.

He parked at the edge of the woods and hiked in, boots sucking at the frozen mud, breath hanging like a banner in the cold. The path was old, maybe a deer trail, but it had been cleared with the kind of efficiency Pike now recognized as the Oath's signature.

He felt the cabin before he saw it. The air changed—less wild, more expectant. The woods drew closer, pine trunks pressing in as if to block escape. The windows were dark, but Pike could see tire tracks in the slush, leading right up to a battered shed out back.

He circled the perimeter, every nerve awake, looking for a tripwire or a posted guard. There was nothing. The front door was unlocked.

He stepped inside and was hit by the smell of old wood, dust, and a faint trace of bleach. The main room was bare except for a table, six folding chairs, and an ancient lantern set at the center. The air was colder inside than out.

He paced the room, searching for clues. The only decorations were the scars in the floor—old drag marks, a ring of char, and a faint scrawl of initials under one chair leg: MW, JH, WL, JL, RD, MH.

He checked the kitchen, found a stock of bottled water and protein bars, all with expiration dates in the same year.

Upstairs, a single bedroom held a cot and a locked footlocker. Pike didn't bother with the lock—he pried it open with his multitool.

Inside, he found six black notebooks, each one labeled by a set of initials and a year. He took the top one and paged through.

It was a ledger. Every entry had a name, a case number, a date, and a column for "Final Disposition." The handwriting was neat, clinical. The last page was marked for the current month, with two names he recognized from the recent quarry finds.

If his instincts were correct, he had twenty minutes, maybe less. Pike used the time to scan the ledgers, photographing every page with his burner phone. He hid the notebooks in a loose panel under the cot, pocketed the water and a couple of bars, and slipped the multitool into his boot.

He closed the book and sat on the cot, the weight of it all settling on him.

He heard a car engine, distant but getting closer, then the crunch of tires on gravel. Just as he suspected, they must have known he was getting close and tracked him here.

Pike put the ledger in his jacket and waited.

If they were coming to the cabin, he wanted to see their faces, just once, without the masks.

He turned on the lantern, sat, waited, and listened to the world close in.

***

He debated running. The woods were dense, the trail back unmarked, but they would be expecting that. And if the machine were as perfect as he suspected, they'd have mapped the woods, every step.

So he stayed.

He watched through the window as the car rolled up. Four men got out, bundled against the cold. Pike recognized two of them instantly—William Lee, all broad shoulders and calm, and Mark Hughes, stiffer, eyes everywhere. The others hung back, faces hidden by hoods.

They didn't talk. They walked straight to the door, entered without knocking, and moved to the main room. Pike moved up the stairs to the makeshift bedroom. From above, Pike heard the chairs creak and the lantern's flint spark. They set the ritual before anything else.

He counted the steps to the stairs. Six. He had the drop if he needed it. He waited until they were seated, then walked down, hands empty and slow.

The room was the same as before: cold, sparse, the only warmth from the light of the lantern.

William looked up first. He didn't flinch, didn't move. "Agent Pike," he said. "You made it."

Mark smirked. "Told you someone would get curious."

The other two—Jimmy Lee and Robert Dean, by the build and the way they sat—watched Pike with the same studied neutrality as the others.

Pike took the empty chair, the sixth. He looked at them, one by one.

"You knew I was coming," he said.

William smiled, almost kindly. "We know how the system works. And who watches it."

Pike nodded. "You going to tell me why?"

Jimmy shrugged. "Some things don't get better on their own."

Dean said nothing, but his eyes never left Pike's hands.

"Did you ever think about quitting?" Pike said.

Mark leaned forward. "Did you?"

The silence after was as absolute as a grave.

Pike looked at the lantern, at the faces, at the ledgers he'd read upstairs.

He realized the truth: the machine could never be broken from the outside.

He'd already made his choice just by sitting down.

As if on cue, Josie and Matthew entered the room and stood at the head of the table behind William Lee. Mark Hughes nodded to them.

The Oath waited, patient, as if they had all the time in the world.

Pike felt the smallest, strangest sense of relief.

He leaned back in the chair, let his breath out slowly, and met William's gaze.

"Okay," Pike said. "Let's talk."

***

No one moved for a long time.

The lantern's flame stretched shadows across the table, breaking the men into halves: one side in light, the other in dark. Pike met each gaze in turn, feeling the weight and the weird intimacy of the moment.

"You came all this way," William said. "Ask your questions."

Pike nodded. "Why do it? Why run the machine?"

Mark chuckled, not unkindly. "Why do you chase men across half a state for a murder nobody remembers?"

"Because if you don't," Pike said, "the world just turns into them."

Robert Dean cleared his throat, the first sound he'd made. "We remember all of them."

Jimmy said, "We don't do it for glory. You know that by now."

Pike leaned forward. "So what do you call it? Justice? Vengeance?"

Josie Hamilton stepped out from the dark in the kitchen, voice like a knife. "Survival."

She poured a glass for each man, the bottle old and half-empty. She set one in front of Pike.

He let it sit.

"You know what you're doing is wrong," he said, but the words tasted hollow even as he said them.

William shrugged. "You can arrest us if you want. Take the ledgers, take the story, run it up the line."

Jimmy finished for him: "But you know it won't change a thing, not in this state. It will result in hundreds of cases that we've been involved in reopening. Those brought to justice will have a chance to reenter society on a technicality."

There was no arrogance to it, just the cold finality of fact.

Pike tried another tack. "Do you ever worry the machine will turn on you?"

Josie smiled, not angry. "That's the point. If it ever does, it means we deserve it."

Mark lifted his glass. "To the circle," he said. The rest echoed, softly: "To the circle."

Pike didn't drink. He watched their faces and realized they weren't expecting him to.

William set down his glass. "We're not the problem, Detective. We're the firewall."

Pike thought of the quarry, the holes in the ground, the bones that would never get a name.

He thought of the faces at the table, so young in the old photographs, and how nothing in their eyes had changed.

The ritual wound down. The Oath went quiet.

Josie put a hand on his shoulder as she left. "You do what you have to," she said. "So will we."

Pike watched the lantern burn lower, the smell of smoke and old bourbon filling the air.

He realized that this was not the end of the story.

It was just the latest cycle.

He stayed until the lantern guttered out, then left the ledgers where he'd hidden them.

He walked into the woods, letting the cold air clear his head, and wondered if he'd ever tell anyone what he'd seen.

The circle would keep turning, with or without him.

***

The drive back was the hardest part.

Pike let the road unspool beneath him, headlights carving a tunnel through the dark. The woods were gone after a mile, but the silence lingered, riding shotgun all the way into the city.

He replayed every second of the meeting. The way the Oath sat together, the way they answered in sequence, as if each had memorized a different line of the same script—the drink, the ritual, the sense that nothing mattered except the circle. Pike tried to catalog the tells, the moments where he could have turned the conversation, forcing an error. There were none.

The world outside the car was a ghost: empty gas stations, dead neon, a billboard advertising hope for $79.99 an hour. Pike realized that whatever the Oath was protecting, it wasn't themselves. It was the brittle continuity of the state, the belief that things could be fixed if someone just cared enough to do the work.

He got back to the office, parked in the same slot as always, and sat for a long time before going in. The night clerk was asleep at the counter, a paperback folded on her chest.

Pike went to his desk and opened the hidden ledger. He paged through the names, the dates, the neat columns. The handwriting didn't change, even over decades.

He dialed the state AG's number, let it ring twice, then hung up. He started a new email, then deleted it.

He wanted to believe that exposing the Oath would break the circuit, but he already knew better. They were not the problem. They were the firewall.

Pike poured himself a cup of burnt coffee, sat back, and watched the sun rise through the haze. He made a list of everything he still didn't know, every detail he'd missed.

He tried to imagine what Samantha would have thought, seeing the world she left behind.

The city woke slowly, street by street, as if nothing had happened at all.

He felt the urge to drive out again, to watch the woods and the cabin until the story made sense.

But he stayed where he was.

He wrote a single line in his notebook:

Some cycles can't be broken. Only witnessed.

He tore the page out, folded it, and left it on his desk.

It was enough for now.

He would wait, and watch, and keep the ledger safe.

The next time the circle closed, he'd be ready.

***

The next time, he didn't wait for night to fall.

Pike drove out in the blue hour, the sky bruised and heavy with the threat of rain. The road was empty, save for a lone pickup that passed him in the other direction, headlights down, no hurry.

He reached the cabin as the first drops hit the windshield. This time, the path was easier—his boots knew every rut, every slant of the land. He could see the lantern burning through the window before he reached the porch.

He knocked once, out of habit, then opened the door.

They were all there: William, Mark, Jimmy, Robert, Josie, and the judge. No one looked surprised. The table was set for seven, the lantern at the center, a single glass in front of Pike's chair.

William gestured to him to come in. "We were just about to begin."

Pike took his seat, feeling the familiarity settle over him like a warm coat. He didn't flinch when the ritual started, didn't blink when the words were spoken. He let the moment fill him, let the story come full circle.

The judge raised his glass. "To the witness," he said.

The others echoed it, voices steady, unified.

Pike raised his glass and met each of their eyes in turn.

He didn't know if this was the end of the story or just the next cycle. It didn't matter.

He was part of the circle now. He was wondering how he would spend his impending retirement. Now he knew.

The lantern burned bright, shadows alive on every wall.

Outside, the rain came down harder, erasing every trace of what had been.

Inside, the Oath waited, patient as stone, ready for whatever came next.

The flame held steady, and for once, so did Pike.

Acknowledgments

I'd like to thank Greg Holycross, a retired law enforcement professional, for generously sharing his time and expertise.

His insight was invaluable in shaping the realism behind some of the most critical moments in this story.

Thank you for reading The Lantern Oath.

If you enjoyed this story, the best way you can support it is by leaving a review on Amazon. Even a short review helps other readers discover the book.

Thank you for being part of this journey.

—Don Massenzio

Get a Free Frank Rozzani Story

Join my reader list and receive a free Frank Rozzani short story—plus updates on new releases, special offers, and exclusive content.

Sign up here:
https://donmassenzio.com

Also by Don Massenzio

The Frank Rozzani Series
Frankly Speaking
Let Me Be Frank
Frank Incensed
Frankly My Dear
Frank Immersed (with Kent Arceneaux)
Furlong Frank
Frank Abroad

The Brad Rafferty Series
Blood Orange
Blood Match

Other Works
Extra Innings
kongo.com
Random Tales
Ebenezer

About the Author

Don Massenzio is the author of multiple crime thrillers, short story collections, and suspense novels, including the Frank Rozzani detective series and the Brad Rafferty series.

With a passion for crafting tightly woven mysteries and complex characters, his stories blend psychological tension with real-world grit.

Learn more at:
https://donmassenzio.com

Stay Connected

Follow Don Massenzio for updates on upcoming releases, behind-the-scenes content, and exclusive previews.

https://donmassenzio.com

www.ingramcontent.com/pod-product-compliance
Lightning Source LLC
LaVergne TN
LVHW091249110826
845146LV00002BA/708

* 9 7 9 8 9 9 5 7 9 4 0 0 4 *